THIS DREAM WAS DIFFERENT. . . .

He was alone in the darkness until it opened up to reveal a distorted desembodied face hovering over him. Slowly, it became the face of a beautiful woman; then the features transformed, the flesh melting until there was a new, terrible visage there. It was a demonlike thing, with terrible black eyes and yellow fangs tipped with venom. Its breath was the stench of the millions of carcasses it had consumed. It belched fire that singed his hair and burned his skin. He screamed as bits of his cooked flesh flaked off.

The head of the demon grew a body, a huge obese mound of stinking flesh, arms and legs with claws. It swiped at Roger, taking his head off at the shoulders. Roger tried to reclaim his head, but the demon had already devoured it. As it rolled down the gullet of the beast, still capable of sight, it noticed a woman standing waist-deep in the pit of the creature's stomach, her hands outstretched—waiting to catch the head. But she missed and the head plunged into the foul pool of acid swirling in the pit, and Roger felt the flesh boil off his skull. . . .

Roger awoke and searched frantically for the light switch, forcing the terrible vision to seep back into his unconscious, where it couldn't hurt him.

Vision? That's what the psychic people called such experiences . . . and here he was, using their terminology. What was happening to him?

THRILLERS BY WILLIAM W. JOHNSTONE

THE DEVIL'S CAT (2091, $3.95)
The town was alive with all kinds of cats. Black, white, fat, scrawny. They lived in the streets, in backyards, in the swamps of Becancour. Sam, Nydia, and Little Sam had never seen so many cats. The cats' eyes were glowing slits as they watched the newcomers. The town was ripe with evil. It seemed to waft in from the swamps with the hot, fetid breeze and breed in the minds of Becancour's citizens. Soon Sam, Nydia, and Little Sam would battle the forces of darkness. Standing alone against the ultimate predator—The Devil's Cat.

THE DEVIL'S HEART (2110, $3.95)
Now it was summer again in Whitfield. The town was peaceful, quiet, and unprepared for the atrocities to come. Eternal life, everlasting youth, an orgy that would span time—that was what the Lord of Darkness was promising the coven members in return for their pledge of love. The few who had fought against his hideous powers before, believed it could never happen again. Then the hot wind began to blow—as black as evil as The Devil's Heart.

THE DEVIL'S TOUCH (2111, $3.95)
Once the carnage begins, there's no time for anything but terror. Hollow-eyed, hungry corpses rise from unearthly tombs to gorge themselves on living flesh and spawn a new generation of restless Undead. The demons of Hell cavort with Satan's unholy disciples in blood-soaked rituals and fevered orgies. The Balons have faced the red, glowing eyes of the Master before, and they know what must be done. But there can be no salvation for those marked by The Devil's Touch.

POISON PEN

JAMES KISNER

ZEBRA BOOKS
KENSINGTON PUBLISHING CORP.

ZEBRA BOOKS

are published by

Kensington Publishing Corp.
475 Park Avenue South
New York, NY 10016

First printing: August, 1990

Printed in the United States of America

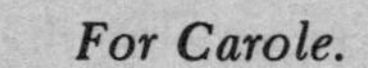

For Carole.

"We are no other than a moving row
Of Magic Shadow-shapes that come and go."

—*Rubaiyat of Omar Khayyam*
(trans. Edward FitzGerald)

"The people never give up their liberties but under some delusion."

—Edmund Burke

Prologue: Making His Mark

They had come for the magic.

They sat in a circle in the dim room, waiting. Their faces looked almost alike in the flickering candlelight, each etched in deep shadows, each reflecting anticipatory awe, each expecting to be mystified and amazed. It was late evening on an October night, an ideal time for believing in the unbelievable.

The woman sitting in the center trembled and let out a low moan. She was a small woman, perched on an ordinary wooden chair, who might be telling stories to children if it weren't for the series of pained expressions contorting her fragile features. She wore a flowing magenta robe and a long white scarf around her neck. Her wavy blond hair reached to the middle of her back. She seemed an unlikely source of magic, but no one questioned that now. She was already in a trance, and soon she would provide answers to all their questions.

There were six people watching her, four women and two men. They had paid well for the privilege of witnessing Tricia Mumford's particular magic. Her channelling sessions had made her well known among the right people in San Francisco, so she could set high fees. No one had ever asked for a refund after seeing her. No one ever left disappointed.

Tricia's face was blank a few seconds, her dark eyes staring at nothing before slowly closing. Her lips parted, and instead of words a kind of stifled roar came forth, as if there were an animal inside her trying to escape.

One of the women gasped. Another covered her mouth and bit back a scream.

Suddenly, Tricia arched her back and moaned again, much louder than before. Bones could be heard cracking in her spine. A man reached out to catch her, but he was restrained by Tricia's assistant, the thin woman sitting closest to her. Her eyes told him not to interfere. The pain Tricia was enduring was a necessary part of the process.

The man settled back in his chair as Tricia went limp and slumped in the chair. She was still a few moments, during which the quiet in the room was broken only by the occasional sputtering of a candle, or the catching of a spectator's breath. The passage of time was punctuated by the clicking pendulum in a grandfather's clock behind them.

Then everyone felt the temperature drop in the small room. Something had arrived.

Tricia's form shook violently as if she had been jolted by electricity, and she sat up straight, assuming a posture that somehow made her seem much larger. Her eyelids fluttered briefly, then her eyes opened wide. The others could see there was something different behind those dark orbs now, a different personality, a different entity, perhaps, but it was no longer Tricia Mumford; that was certain.

She started by mumbling in a voice that was barely audible. As she continued, her voice changed timbre and tone, vacillating between high and low as if it were being fine-tuned. Gradually it was transformed into a very deep, masculine voice that couldn't possibly be coming from such a diminutive person. So far, the bits of sound she uttered were nonsense, not recognizable words, as if the intelligence behind them was also fine-tuning itself.

"Is it . . . ?" a woman whispered.

The thin woman hushed her with a harsh glance.

Tricia gripped the arms of the chair and leaned forward in a posture that was almost menacing.

"I am Saul," she said in a voice so full—so com manding—that it startled them all.

The waiting was over; the magic had come at last.

"I am Saul," she repeated, the voice of the entity now consistent and sure of itself. "I dwell in another dimension, another place beyond this realm, where pure consciousness abides. I am in that place where our souls go when we pass on. This is the dimension where there is no time, where there is no past or future, where there is only being and essence. . . ."

"Oh, my God," someone said, "it *is* Saul. I know it."

"I can see *your* past, *your* future, because all earthly time is as a vast—" Tricia, now Saul, faltered, apparently searching for the right word—"a vast bowl into which I can peer and know all that has been, all that is, and all that ever will be in your realm."

"Then there *is* an afterlife," a woman mumbled.

"You," Tricia-Saul said, "the one whispering. Your name is Deborah, is it not?" The dark eyes fell on a thirtyish woman with short red hair.

"Yes," Debbie Rider replied. "Please speak to me."

"I see a person about you whose name begins with a G."

"Yes."

"A person who will bring you much sorrow unless you act now. Don't let your heart guide you in this relationship. Use your head; be sensible. There is much time left in your life for satisfying relationships."

"Oh, that's so right. . . ."

"A dark man with a crooked finger will be a benefactor soon."

"My God, that's Uncle Roy!"

Tricia waved her hand at the woman, dismissing her. "I have nothing more for you now." As Tricia-Saul continued to gather strength, her eyes began to sparkle, shining with deep wisdom. She turned her head to gaze at the woman sitting next to Debbie. The wisdom was abruptly gone; in its place was something that might be mischief.

"You there, the lady with the curled hair, Saul would

speak to you next."

The woman jerked back in her chair, momentarily struck dumb. She was about forty and appeared well-to-do. She touched her dark hair; she had recently had a bad permanent that made her self-conscious.

"You must speak to me, so I may touch with your vibrations."

"Yes?" she managed timidly.

"Your name is Frances."

"Yes."

"Frances, I see a problem with your diet. You are not consuming enough citrus. Your love life is in turmoil now, but it will settle out by the end of the Capricorn period. I see conflicting forces around you, a family affair, a doomed man with brown whiskers, an animal . . ."

"Yes?"

". . . you keep an animal, a dog, a small dog. Watch him carefully the next two weeks."

Frances seemed horrified. "Is something going to happen to Scottie?"

"I see—I see nothing else for you. Be wary, but not overly concerned. It will all be for the good, but that is beyond your understanding at this moment."

Tricia-Saul closed her eyes and took a deep breath. "The man next to you," she said, the voice achieving an even more resolute tone. "The young man with the moustache. . . ."

"Speak to me, Saul."

"Your name begins with an R. It's Randal, Robert—no, it's Roger—"

The man she addressed shifted in his heat. "Roger Kant," he finished for her.

Everyone turned to gaze on Roger, expecting to see him properly awed, but his expression was whimsical, almost disrespectful. He was young, but his hair was already thinning. There were things about his appearance that disturbed the others, the more they examined him; it was obvious after a second glance that he was really out of place in this gathering. Maybe it was the ragged suit he wore.

But Tricia-Saul didn't seem to mind. She had messages for people in all walks of life.

"Roger—Kant. Yes, you're the one. You are not yet a man of means, though an unexpected inheritance may change your life. Perhaps in the spring." Her eyes flickered open, and she stared at Roger with an expression bordering on distaste. "I sense an uneasiness about you. There are many things swirling around in your head, plaguing your mind. There are dark images, twisted thoughts, aborted schemes, considered alternatives—a lurking dread. I can't quite make it out." She hesitated, her brow wrinkling with the effort of concentration. "Now—now I see it. An evil influence trying to intrude, one of the inferior entities, a mischievous essence attempting to break through."

"You mean like from an Ouija Board?" The attitude in Roger's voice lacked the proper solemnity.

The others exchanged glances of doubt and apprehension. Had a skeptic come among them to disrupt the magic?

If Tricia-Saul was disturbed, she didn't show it. "Yes," she continued, "that sort of entity—only more powerful, much more powerful." She grimaced in apparent discomfort, her eyes glazing over as she apparently probed deeper into the otherworldly realm for answers. "I see you in an odd uniform, a livery—is that the correct term? You are serving wine. Perhaps this is an aspect of a former life."

"Have I lived before?" His tone became brasher.

"All of us have lived many times before. We all shall live many times again. You are—"

Roger stood up abruptly, almost knocking over his chair, and pointed at the medium.

"And you, Tricia Mumford, are an absolute fraud!"

The others let out cries of protest and dismay—except for the young, barely noticed woman who had been sitting on the other side of Roger. She suddenly produced a small camera from her handbag.

"Be sure you get all this, Wanda," Roger told her. Then,

before he could be stopped, he sprang on Tricia and ripped the scarf from her neck.

Wanda started taking pictures. She was a young woman, with blond hair and a pleasant-looking face. She was dressed in a navy-blue suit with a white blouse. She seemed an unlikely accomplice to the rude man now attacking Tricia.

"Stop it!" Tricia screamed, her voice caught between male and female tones. "Leave me alone!"

"Fake!" Roger persisted. He clawed at her throat and ripped something loose. It was a small boxlike apparatus; and as he jerked it free, wires trailed after it, and a battery case dropped from the folds of Tricia's robe. The case popped open as it hit the floor, and a battery rolled across the carpet to land at the feet of Frances, who regarded it as she might a small rodent that had gotten loose. She shrieked timidly, then jumped up from her chair.

Tricia rose from the chair and tried to take the box back, but Roger held her at arm's length. "Do something, Nancy!" Tricia shouted at the thin woman. Her voice was now very high-pitched and feminine.

Roger held the apparatus aloft for all to see. It seemed obscene displayed this way, almost like an organ that he had torn from her body. "This, ladies and gentlemen, is how Saul speaks—through the miracle of transistors—not spiritual essence or whatever she calls it."

Wanda continued to snap picture after picture.

Nancy, who had been immobilized by the speed with which Roger had acted, now seemed to understand. "You bastard!" She threw herself between Tricia and Roger, forcing him down on the floor. Her long nails were going for his face. Roger grabbed her wrists and just managed to keep her from actually making contact.

"Will somebody get this bitch off me? Wanda!"

Wanda took a picture of Nancy as she wrestled with Roger. Wanda knew only one purpose.

The other man in the room, a stout, balding fellow in his forties, pulled Nancy away from Roger—but not quite in time. As he wrenched her away, she reached out and raked the left side of Roger's face, cutting deep into the flesh of his cheek and drawing blood. She moaned frustration at not being able to inflict more damage and went to comfort Tricia, who was now in tears.

Wanda started to take a picture of the two women, then decided not to and put her camera away. She sat down and assumed a demure posture as if nothing had happened, while she waited for Roger's next order.

"Thanks," Roger said, getting to his knees and dabbing at his wound with a handkerchief.

"I don't want your thanks. I just want this to end," said the other man.

Roger pulled himself up. "Aren't you even a little upset that your so-called trance medium is a fake?" He glanced around the room. The faces that glared back at him told him the medium was not the person they were upset with. "I guess there are people who like to be conned. . . ."

"Tricia is no con artist," Debbie said.

"Damn it, I just showed you the proof. And that stilted language she used—didn't you think that was a bit much?"

"So, she augmented her voice," the man said reasonably. "Maybe that was a bit theatrical of her, but it doesn't mean her messages were invalid."

"You can't face the truth of it, can you? You can't admit that you've been duped."

The man turned away from Roger.

"Debbie, Frances, wasn't everything she said to you true?" Both women nodded assent. "See? I've been to her before," the man continued. "Saul has always told me the truth."

"She made vague predictions that were probably based on a little research. It would be easy to find out this woman had a dog, or that one a dying uncle. Her assistant could pose in any number of guises and ask questions of neighbors and friends."

"Maybe there's something in what he says, Tom," Debbie offered. "If she were genuine, why would she have to fake the voice?"

"There's a woman with some sense," Roger agreed.

"Her own voice was not a powerful enough instrument to express the great presence of Saul in all its glory," Nancy said defensively. "The amp was necessary to bring the truth to people—the truth that Saul offers us all. It was not intended to deceive anyone. And Saul just happens to speak that way. You call it 'stilted,' but to the rest of us, it is majestic."

"That's lame and you know it," Roger said.

"What about the truth she spoke to you?" Tom asked.

"That proves my point," Roger said triumphantly. "I made sure she would find out some things about me—things that were just as fake as she is—so that I could prove beyond doubt how phony she really is—just as all the other practicing psychics are."

"I told you the truth," a small voice said behind him.

Roger turned to see Tricia suddenly coming to life again. She broke free of Nancy's comforting embrace and approached him.

"You don't give up, do you?"

"I—that is, Saul—looked into you and saw what was really there. The turmoil. The torment. That's a truth about yourself you fail to recognize."

"Say what you like," Roger said, unimpressed. "There is no Saul, and you are no medium."

"So what do you intend to do?" Tom said, his fists clenched at his sides in outrage.

"I intend to publish these pictures and describe everything that transpired here. I have it all on tape." He patted his chest. There was a small bulge behind his breast pocket that had to be a microcassette recorder.

"So you're another sensation-seeking newsman—a reporter." He said "reporter" as if it were the most obscene term imaginable.

"For now, at least. This story will turn the right heads in my direction."

"What if we stop you?"

"You can't."

"I can try."

Roger's face registered doubt for the first time that evening. It was unlikely he could best the other man in a physical contest. But he hadn't anticipated there would be one.

"Forget about it, Thomas," Tricia said. "This is part of Mr. Kant's destiny. It will also be part of his doom."

Roger laughed nervously. "What now? A gypsy curse?"

She ignored his remark. "I don't care what happens to me, personally. The truth seeks its place, no matter what scoffers and skeptics do. I will trust others to believe in—in Saul, as they have before. Have your fun. Humiliate me all you want. You will suffer from it more than I. Saul will continue to bring messages through me."

"He may ruin you," Tom said. "Let me—"

"No."

"Why don't you and your friend just leave—now," Nancy said acidly. "We don't need any more of your interference."

"No," Tricia said again. "No, no, *no!*"

Everyone turned in Tricia's direction. She was trembling violently. Her eyes rolled up in her head, and she frothed at the mouth.

"What's this, more theatrics?" Roger asked.

"Leave, Mr. Kant," Nancy said. "Leave now!"

Tricia raised her right hand and pointed at Roger. She opened her mouth, and the sound of a fierce animal came out—roaring with displeasure at Roger's presence.

"Come on, Wanda," Roger said, moving toward the door. "This is where we came in."

His assistant followed, her eyes sheepishly averted.

As Roger opened the door, a wind blew through the room, extinguishing all the candles but the one closest to Tricia. Her face was screwed up in a tormented mask that would horrify anyone—except a skeptic who knew it was a put-on.

"Nice act," Roger declared as he and Wanda left. He dashed down the steps with joy. He had succeeded in exposing one of the most famous mediums on the West Coast. He had shown her to be a fraud. He had made his mark.

But more important than any of those things—Roger Kant had begun his career.

Later that evening, after the others had left, Tricia Mumford sat before the mirror at her dressing table, staring into her own glassy eyes. What she saw reflected there was not a familiar presence. It was not Saul, nor was it any other entity with whom she had ever made contact. And it frightened her, because she sensed it was not anything she could control or reason with.

This thing behind her own eyes was a vindictive presence, an entity that was offended by the outcome of the evening.

Tricia shuddered as she recognized the dreadful emotions lurking in this presence—emotions that indeed animated it, giving it life. She closed her eyes and murmured an incantation, a kind of twisted prayer, that she hoped would make it go away. As she finished saying the words, she swooned, almost falling over as she felt something drain from her. She caught herself, then opened her eyes and saw only her own persona looking back at her.

The presence was gone from her, but she knew it was still out there in the world, a festering thing that could sustain itself virtually forever until it achieved its goal. The emotions—especially the hatred—that drove it would maintain their existence for years to come, until it accomplished what it desired—which it had communicated to her in its brief tenanting of her own soul. It chilled her to contemplate the awesome possibilities of its revenge.

She couldn't help but feel sorry for Roger Kant.

PART ONE

DELUSIONS OF GRANDEUR

1. Descent

Mount Rainier suddenly jutted into view as if it had somehow sprung up from the earth at that exact moment. Seconds later, the Space Needle identified the Seattle skyline. Then the passengers on the plane could see both together, the ancient mountain and the modern man-made spire, marking the city below them. From the passengers' perspective, the Space Needle seemed taller than the mountain, but that was an illusion, a trick of the human vision's inability to determine distances or mass with any great accuracy, especially when such a panorama was compressed in the space of a jetliner's window.

Some passengers reacted with awe at the view, murmuring in unsubdued wonder. Parents could be heard exhorting their children to look. A baby gurgled in delight.

Roger Kant yawned and glanced away. He had been to Seattle before. Right now, he felt as if he had been everywhere in the country before—and the only difference between one place and another was a few vaguely remembered landmarks: the Space Needle here, the Arch in St. Louis, the Sears Tower in Chicago. Each city seemed to have only one mark of distinction; otherwise, they were all a blur in Roger's memory, all cut of the same dull cloth. When he was down in the streets, moving among the people, the sameness was even more pronounced, because he knew only about three percent of the population had any mind at all; the rest were ciphers with little function or purpose, random souls whose primary *raison d'être* was to occupy space on the planet.

Roger was forty-five, but was often mistaken for much older. His head was already half-bald, and his remaining brown hair was beginning to turn gray. He had tried for years to control his weight, but despite his efforts, he still retained a small paunch he considered rather unsightly; he tried to hide it by wearing loose-fitting jackets.

His left cheek bore the trace of a scar which was accentuated in harsh light. His eyes were bright blue under shaggy eyebrows, and his nose was broad. His lips were full and topped by a thick moustache which he had originally grown to appear older. He kept it now to look younger. The only other concession he made to the illusion of youth was a deep tan he maintained throughout the year. People meeting him for the first time usually regarded him as the stereotype of the middle-aged professor.

Roger was well-aware of his professorial appearance, and over the years he had learned how to use it as an asset when talking to people. It lent a certain validity to the things he had to tell them, no matter now outrageous they might be. He was able to impress; his presence commanded attention.

But not today. He felt grungy and gross. His suit, though expensive and well-tailored, was wrinkled. He wore no tie, and his shirt was the wrong color for the suit.

He rubbed his chin and felt stubble. He should have shaved before he left Chicago, but there hadn't been time. He had even forgotten to pack his electric shaver.

He listened halfheartedly to the pilot's voice on the intercom, delivering local weather conditions, then welcoming the passengers to Seattle. Then a stewardess came on, reminding them to remain seated and keep their seat belts on until the plane had landed in the Seattle-Tacoma International Airport.

The plane turned in a large arc and headed south toward the airport. Then it began its descent.

Roger glanced out the window again as the metropolitan area below seemed to swallow the plane up, its buildings, streets and highways growing larger as the jet descended. Usually, he was fascinated by how things seemed to grow as a plane neared the ground, but today he was too agitated to let himself enjoy the small amusement it normally provided. His mind was too preoccupied with details. After all, this was not a pleasure trip; it was the first of many trips he would have to make over the next few weeks and as such was the beginning of a period of constant jet lag, nausea and, often, depression.

He reached in his jacket pocket and took out the schedule his secretary, Edith Wilkins, had prepared for him. He grimaced at how much he had to do during his four-day stay in Seattle: talk show appearances on both radio and TV, autograph sessions at several bookstores, and a two-hour seminar to conduct. It was a crowded schedule to be sure, but one he had grown accustomed to in the ten years since his career had really taken off. There was a part of him that really enjoyed the hectic pace, especially when he had a new book to promote, but this time out, he wasn't looking forward to it as much. A promotional tour no longer provided the excitement it once had. This one would be especially difficult to endure without Edith at his side, constantly reminding him what was next on the schedule. She also took care of the little details for him: helping him select his clothes, reminding him to eat, and getting him out of parties and other gatherings when he was too tired to mix anymore.

He really missed her presence and her prim efficiency. Edith would have made sure he remembered his shaver. But Edith couldn't accompany him on this trip. She had come down with the flu two days before he was to leave. She was "sick at both ends," as she put it, and could hardly get out of bed.

So he was on his own this time. He noted there was nothing really to do until early evening—an autograph session at a local bookstore—and tucked the schedule back in his pocket. He checked his watch to see if he had set it to Pacific time, then leaned back in the seat and braced himself for the landing.

This pilot was good. He set the plane down without jarring anyone's teeth loose. Roger was glad of that. He hated it when planes landed like bricks dropped on pavement.

The stewardess's voice came over the intercom instructing the passengers to remain seated as the plane taxied down the runway.

Roger closed his eyes. He was very tired, already weary from anticipating the hustle required to get from the airport to his hotel. He had slept very little the night before. After packing and all the other preparations, he had been exhausted, but when his head finally hit the pillow and he fretted himself to sleep, the dream came—one of those dreaded nightmares about crippled people that made no sense whatever to him. There was nothing really terrifying in the dream—not when he examined its weird contents the next morning—nevertheless, it always left him with an eerie feeling of unresolved terror, and he feared its constant recurrence would make a total insomniac of him. If it didn't let up soon, he might have to see a doctor to get some really strong sleeping pills.

The plane came abruptly to a stop, and the seat belt sign went off. The passengers all stood up. Roger reached into the compartment above his seat and pulled down a large leather tote bag stuffed with books, papers and notes, and his microcassette recorder. He shuffled out with the other passengers, nodding at the stewardess at the door, returning her smile and bidding her *adieu* with a mumbled "nice landing."

On his way down to pick up his luggage, Roger stopped briefly in the airport gift shop to see if the latest issue of *New Age* was available. The May issue was supposed to be carrying an interview with him in which he'd had a chance to air his views on the New Age phenomenon. His remarks had been mostly negative, and he was anxious to see if the editors had tampered with any of them, though, with his reputation, he didn't think they'd dare.

The gift shop didn't carry the magazine, but he was pleased to see the third edition of his book *Optical Delusions* in the paperback rack. It had been a steady seller for years. He winced at the garish cover the publishers had chosen for this reprint, but he still couldn't resist picking it up and holding it for a few seconds. Out of habit, he read the blurb on the back, though he had seen it many times before:

> "Roger Kant . . . The Astounding One . . . destroys all the phony façades in the psychic world . . . where deception and fraud go hand in hand to bilk an unsuspecting public of billions of dollars a year. . . ."

Roger frowned at the blurb copy. It did tell what the book was about, but he hated The Astounding One title the publishers had given him. Over the years, it had become his second name, but it was an alias that made him uncomfortable. He supposed it might sell books by giving him an aura of mystery—but that was almost contrary to his intentions. In his mind, it made him sound like someone akin to the very psychics he was exposing. He had managed to get the epithet removed from the jacket of his new book, but he suspected it would be associated with him throughout his career.

He replaced the book in the rack, gave it one last longing look, then realized he had better get down to the lower level to claim his luggage.

Roger reached the conveyor just in time to grab his two Samsonite bags and suit bag before they went back inside for another trip through the system.

He started for the exit then halted abruptly. He felt as if someone was staring at him. He turned to see a young, dark-skinned woman with long black hair gazing at him. She smiled with apparent embarrassment at having been caught, then quickly looked away.

She was probably someone who recognized him and was thinking of accosting him, asking for an autograph or making some kind of stupid inquiry regarding his work.

He stopped and thought about it a second, then chided himself for being so negative. Why did he always assume such encounters would be bothersome? Maybe she was attracted to him for some strange reason. Maybe she even admired him. Had he become so jaded he couldn't enjoy brief eye contact with a pretty woman?

He sighed and continued to the exit doors, which parted with a *whoosh* to let him through to a bright day with a clear sky overhead. He set his luggage down and searched for his sunglasses in his pockets, realized he had forgotten them too, and shaded his eyes with his hand to squint at the row of cabs parked at the curb. He waved until he caught the attention of one of the drivers, who waved back and came over to greet him.

As he went to meet the cab driver, Roger stumbled over the edge of his suit bag and dropped on one knee, hitting the concrete walk with most of his weight. He yelped and cursed.

The cab driver rushed forward to help. He took Roger's arm and pulled him to his feet.

"You okay, sir?"

"I think so. I've been accident-prone lately." He massaged his wound; his knee stung, but it was essentially intact as far as he could tell. "It just hurts like hell."

"I'll help you to the cab."

"I can walk. I'm not a goddamn—cripple!" Saying the last word made a chill run through him.

"Just trying to help, sir. No offense meant."

"All right. All right. Take my luggage."

As Roger stood by the cab and the driver piled the luggage in the trunk, he felt someone tug at his sleeve.

"Mr. Kant?"

Roger turned to see a well-dressed, middle-aged woman smiling at him.

"What?" he said with annoyance.

"I didn't mean to startle you," she said. "I'm Karen Wright—from the Northwest League for Higher Consciousness. Didn't your secretary tell you I'd be meeting you here?"

Roger paused and took a breath. "Wright?" He shook his head.

"We're sponsoring the seminar on Thursday night."

"Oh, yes. I remember now. Sorry I snapped at you. I just hurt my knee."

"I saw that. I hope it's okay."

"It's fine now." He felt uncomfortable with his unshaven chin and wrinkled suit; he hated to be unprepared—not that he felt any particular need to impress this woman. He offered his hand and forced a smile. "Well, it's a pleasure to meet you, even under these trying circumstances, Karen. Now, if you'll excuse me, I have to get to my hotel. We'll have time to talk later, I'm sure."

She took his hand and beamed at him. Then she gestured at the waiting cab driver. "Why, you're not taking a smelly old cab, are you?"

"Why not?"

"We have a limo for you. We wanted your stay in Seattle to be as comfortable as possible."

"A limo? You didn't have to—"

"Oh, but we did. We don't often get a speaker of your stature at our seminars."

"All right. You talked me into it. I'll take the limo." It was difficult for him to resist flattery. He told the cab driver to unload his luggage, gave him a generous tip for his trouble, hefted his bags and followed Karen Wright to the Lincoln stretch limo parked a few feet away.

The limo driver reloaded the luggage, and Roger and the woman got in the car. There was a TV inside, as well as a VCR, wet bar, and a cellular telephone. Roger allowed himself to enjoy the luxury of it; it took the edge off his sour mood. Even his knee felt better.

As the car pulled into traffic, Karen Wright asked about his secretary, and Roger told her of the sudden illness.

This news seemed to cheer Karen, though she did her best to hide it. "If you need anything at all while you're in Seattle," she said, "don't hesitate to call on me."

"I'll keep that in mind," he said, though he didn't think

she could take Edith's place.

The ride to the hotel was uneventful, and it would have been a chance for Roger to lie back and rest a bit, but Karen kept talking about New Age issues while trying to pry opinions from him which he was not in the mood to give her. He kept her at bay with vague replies and hints, but by the time they reached the Sheraton Hotel and Towers where he was staying, his exhaustion was returning, and he was beginning to wish he never had to see this woman again.

Despite that, he had actually agreed to have dinner with her after he returned from his autograph session.

Roger could afford a suite, but he had decided on more modest accommodations. The room, on the fourteenth floor, was not palatial, but more than comfortable. The view of Puget Sound calmed him somewhat.

He sighed, realizing it was time to get down to business. The autograph session was only a couple of hours away now, and he wanted to get cleaned up and maybe grab a sandwich before he went to it. He flipped on the TV and watched a basketball game while he unpacked. Then he undressed, hung up his clothes and went into the bathroom to shower.

He had bought a can of shaving cream and a pack of disposable razors in the hotel's gift shop. He washed and lathered his face, then fumbled with the plastic razor. It had been so long since he had used a real razor with a blade in it he had almost forgotten the proper angle at which to hold it.

He shaved his cheeks, being careful not to nick a mole on the right one, then started on his throat. As he pulled the razor toward his chin, he stopped abruptly as the mirror fogged over from the hot water running in the basin. He grabbed a towel and wiped the vapor from the glass, then drew back, startled.

He shook his head and blinked. For a brief second, it appeared there was a woman's face staring back from the mirror—with eyes that were somehow very familiar. The mirror fogged over again.

"Jet lag," he told himself, "playing tricks on my mind." He wiped the mirror once more. This time his own countenance was reflected there. It might not be a pretty face, but it was reassuring to see it where it was supposed to be.

He wondered briefly whose eyes he imagined he had seen, then continued shaving, barely noticing his hands were trembling.

He cut himself twice.

The autograph session went smoothly. It was at a bookstore in a mall on the east side of the city, and the turnout was not too bad, considering he had not been on television or radio yet to promote the book. He expected the sessions scheduled later to be mobbed; they usually were after the public had seen his face on the tube or heard him talk on the radio.

It was just as well there weren't too many autograph seekers this evening. It gave him an opportunity to rest as he watched people walk by in the mall. There was also comfort to be derived from sitting behind a little table surrounded by stacks of his new hardcover book, *The New Age Con Game.* The book store had put out copies of his earlier books as well, including *Psychic Trickery, Memoirs of a Skeptic, The Subliminal Swindle,* and, of course, *Optical Delusions.* He signed as many copies of some of his previous books as he did the new one, and that gratified him. And not one person who approached him was a whack-o or New Age philosophy nut.

By the time Roger returned to his hotel, he was feeling almost mellow.

Karen Wright met him in the lobby. He insisted they have dinner in one of the hotel restaurants, because he was weary of traveling. The restaurant was crowded, but they didn't have to wait long. After they were seated, they ordered drinks, studied their menus briefly, and ordered simple meals—she a chef's salad, he a cut of prime rib with baked potato. He felt a need for extra protein to restore some of the physical resources already depleted by this trip.

The interior of the restaurant was intimate and warm. Candles sat on each table, providing most of the light. There was a buffet at one end of the room at which many diners filled plates with food.

Karen and Roger talked about the seminar on Thursday, and she gave him an expanded agenda of the evening's activities. He noticed there was a cocktail party afterward at which he was to be available to sign books and talk. He regarded that prospect with dread, but he accepted it as part of the promotional package. After all, he was the star, a reluctant one, but the star nonetheless.

As they sipped after-dinner drinks, Karen opened her briefcase and brought out a handful of Roger's books.

"Would you mind terribly signing these for me?" she asked.

"Of course not," Roger answered as graciously as he could. He opened the first book and began to ponder. He disliked being put on the spot like this; she would expect him to inscribe something "personal" for her, even though he barely knew her. But his brain was foggy at the moment—too foggy to create a false sentiment or something witty for a stranger. His exhaustion was catching up with him again, and that third Scotch and water was beginning to numb his senses. He sat and thought, his pen poised over the title page of the book.

To Karen, for all the good times . . .? came into his mind. But there hadn't been any good times. No, that was too patently phony. *To Karen, Who showed me a side of Seattle I never saw before. . . .*

Christ, that was terrible!

He looked up, pretending to concentrate, and his eyes scanned the room, noting the character of the various patrons. There was nothing unusual about any of them, really. Businessmen, tourists, people out for a good time.

Then he saw the woman.

She was sitting alone at a table across the room, sipping a glass of wine. She affected an insouciant air, but she was clearly looking at him, her eyes burning into his with an intensity and unmistakable sensuality Roger had never felt directed at him before. As his eyes met hers, it seemed for an instant there was a spotlight on her, and he could make out every microscopic detail of her appearance as if he were sitting across the table from her, not across a vast room full of strangers. Her long blond hair glistened with streaks of silver light; her eyes were dark and highlighted by magenta eye shadow that seemed to glow in the flickering of the candle on her table; rose blush shone on her high cheekbones. There was an umber cast to her skin, not quite olive, which rendered it an intriguing shade that seemed to demand a gentle touch; she wore a daring white blouse under the sheer fabric of which there was obviously nothing but skin; her hands were delicate and small; her torso, what he could see of it, tapered to a small waist set off by small, but what he would consider efficient, breasts.

But there was much more to her than that. Beyond her physical allure there was an emotionalism that called to him, a brooding ambience of character, a suggestion of consuming fires, a forthrightness of sexuality, and a sense of total abandon coupled with a lack of guile. This was a totally open woman who was inviting him to merge with her in a dance of unbridled passion.

Who was she? Or, more to the point, what was she: a fan of his, a lady of the evening, or merely a woman who had seen what she desired and made no pretense of hiding it? Somehow, none of that seemed to categorize her; she was nothing so common. Yet she was a total stranger to him, though he seemed to recall an ancient bond with her, something that existed only in her eyes, as if she were a siren from his past who had returned to claim something that had never been consummated between them.

He felt his own flesh respond to the mystery of her. His flesh didn't care who or what she was, might be, or could be. His flesh wanted to complete the bond in the most urgent way.

Was he really seeing all that in her? Was it possible a man his age, who had never really been a ladies' man, could be so easily aroused?

Or was he letting his imagination run rampant—fueled by his general tiredness and a liberal dose of alcohol?

"Mr. Kant?"

She was a shimmering presence in the room, almost an essence, he romanticized. If only she were at the table with him, instead of—

"Mr. *Kant!*"

"What . . . ?" He pulled himself away from those distant eyes and shifted his focus to the middle-aged, carefully made-up face of the woman sitting next to him. "I'm sorry, Karen. I must have been daydreaming. Did you say something?" He realized he was blushing; perhaps it wasn't noticeable in the red glow cast by the candlelight.

"No, but you seemed—well, Mr. Kant, you seemed lost for a moment."

He looked down at the books in front of him. He had signed all but one of them without thinking about it, and the last lay open ready for his next inspiration. He scribbled something silly and emotional and handed all the books back to her.

"I guess I'm awfully tired," he told her.

She glanced at his inscriptions and smiled. Evidently, even when lost in his reverie, he had come up with the properly clever sentiments. "I shall treasure these, Mr. Kant."

"I was happy to sign them, Karen. And call me Roger. After all, you are my guide here."

"Oh, thank you."

"Did we get our check yet?"

"I'll take care of it."

He didn't bother to argue with her; he was used to having the tab picked up for him; it made people like Karen Wright feel good to say they had bought dinner for Roger Kant.

"Then, if you don't mind, I'll return to my room. I have to get up early in the morning, and jet lag has given me a headache." He stood up abruptly.

"I do hope you feel better tomorrow," she said. "Remember to call me if you need anything."

"I'll remember. A good night's sleep will fix me up just fine," he said and turned to leave. He took two steps and glanced back across the room, hoping to make a sign to the woman that he was free.

But she was no longer there.

After Roger returned to his room, he stood at the window looking out over the nighttime skyline of Seattle, fretting over the missed opportunity of the evening. If only he hadn't been with that Wright woman, he might have been able to do something about the beautiful stranger. But, as often happened nowadays, romantic encounters rarely came to a satisfying conclusion—especially when they promised to be with someone he might really like.

It wasn't just sex. He could have that fairly readily if he wanted to. There was always a woman around who wanted to sleep with even a moderately famous person. He had more offers, both covert and overt, than any man could reasonably handle.

But sex wasn't the answer to loneliness. Sex was only an answer to biological imperatives, which were already beginning to wane for him.

"If you don't use it, you lose it," he said to himself. He smiled wanly in the darkness and went to lie down on the bed.

He realized he was on the verge of despair, and if he got the cycle of depression going, he might be up all night, his mind racing with all the things that were wrong in his life.

Everything was a sham; he didn't just think that—he knew it absolutely. He had devoted a quarter of his life to proving it—in his books, his lectures, his appearances on television—even in his everyday speech. Nothing was genuine. His personal work focused on the mendacity of the New Age and the psychic community, but his contact with people in other fields—the businessmen who took him into their confidence at parties, the women who told him about their love affairs while their husbands were out of town, the countless masses who led double and triple lives—showed how no one was stable; everyone was caught up in falsehood, cheating and situational ethics and flexible morality.

He often felt he was the only true, honest and right person in the world.

Maybe he was the *only* person in the world. Period. Maybe the world itself was a sham, a papier-mâché prop on which Roger Kant was destined to act out a drama of loneliness and despair. And his hell was knowing it was all fake but not being able to do anything about it but to point and scream and hope someone would listen and come to his rescue.

He chuckled to himself. "Yeah, Mr. Right himself, Roger B. Kant. That's me. No fucking flies on me."

Maybe if he quit the grind for a while, he wouldn't be forced to wallow so much in the sham of the world. But without the work, he had nothing at all.

It was impossible to think clearly about anything now. He needed a good night's rest, if he could get it. The Scotch had worn off now, though, and he'd have to rely on his own weariness to get to sleep. Surely he was tired enough to sleep through the night.

He pulled the blankets over his body and rolled on his side, his eyes shut. He tried to remember the face of the woman in the restaurant, but the face of the woman at the airport kept coming back instead.

Grumbling at his inability to control his own mental images, he drifted into an unstable state of sleep.

He was alone in the darkness. He expected to see or sense the presence of crippled people, but this dream was different because there was no light at all, as if he were trapped in a vast void somewhere beyond the edge of time.

The darkness opened up to reveal a distorted, disembodied face hovering over him. Slowly it became the face of a beautiful woman, then the features transformed, the flesh melting until there was a new, terrible visage floating above him. It was a demonlike thing, with terrible black eyes and yellow fangs tipped with venom. Its breath was the stench of the millions of carcasses it had consumed. It belched fire that singed Roger's hair and burned his skin. He screamed as bits of his cooked flesh flaked off. The head of the demon grew a body, a huge obese mound of stinking flesh, and it sprouted legs and arms with claws. It swiped at Roger, taking his head off at the shoulders. Roger tried to reclaim his head, but the demon had already eaten it. As it rolled down the gullet of the beast, still capable of sight, it noticed a woman standing waist-deep in the pit of the creature's stomach, her hands outstretched—waiting to catch his head. But she missed, and the head plunged into the foul pool of acid swirling in the pit. Roger felt the flesh boil off his skull.

Roger awoke.

He searched frantically for the light switch, realized he was in a strange room and almost went berserk before he found it.

Sitting on the edge of the bed and letting the light from the lamp pull him back into reality, he forced the terrible vision of the dream to seep back to where it belonged—in his subconscious, where it couldn't hurt him.

After his eyes adjusted to the light, he stared at his hands, almost expecting them to be fleshless. He felt his face and head. Everything was fine. It was only a particularly vicious dream—that was all.

He reclined again and took several deep breaths, until he finally calmed down.

The dream about cripples was bad enough, but this dream—so real he was tempted to call it a vision—was the worst he had ever experienced.

He left the light on and tried to get back to sleep. He was used to waking up in strange rooms, and he was used to bad dreams; but he wasn't used to visions.

Visions? That's what the psychic people called such experiences, and here he was using their terminology.

He was sure one of those phony psychics could explain it all to him.

2. The Voice

The next morning Roger crawled out of bed at six to answer the telephone. It was the hotel desk with his wake-up call. He mumbled a "thanks" to the operator and hung up.

His head ached, a sure sign of not having slept well or enough. He had no memory of falling asleep again and only a vague, uneasy recollection of the vision—no, nightmare—that had awakened him in the middle of the night. All he could recall was that it was something about a monster of some kind.

He yawned and scratched himself, then stood and stretched. He went over to the window and opened the drapes. The sun was not yet making a real impression on the day; it was still gray outside. He could see a few boats moving out on the water, but they looked like toys to him. Maybe they weren't moving at all. He looked down on the street below and saw very little traffic. Then the street lights blinked out as the sun finally made its presence known. That was as good a sign as any to get a move on. If a street light knew it was daytime, then a man should take the hint.

On his way across the room, he stopped and flipped on the television. He watched a few seconds of weather reports through bleary eyes. This certainly wasn't going to wake him up. Why didn't they have chainsaw movies on in the morning—something that would truly rouse a man from his stupor? In a civilized nation, the morning fare on TV would consist of loud, blood-stirring movies, not pap about weather and farm reports. The monster from his dream would wake people up—he could testify to that. He frowned at the notion. He was trying to forget the monster, not let it loose on the world.

He left the TV on and stumbled into the bathroom, where he dropped his pajamas on the floor and studied his body in the mirror. He sucked in the offending paunch and puffed up his chest by holding his breath. He couldn't hold it very long, however, and the parts he was forcing into the semblance of a firmer physique quickly slumped to their former, basically inert state.

"I'm a thinker," he told the image in the mirror, "not a he-man. I don't need a good body." He did need to get some rays, though. His tan wasn't as deep as he liked it, and he wondered if the hotel had a tanning booth in the health club facilities it offered.

He checked the knee he had fallen on the day before. There was a bruise there and a small abrasion. It should heal quickly enough.

He laid his watch on the edge of the sink and stepped into the shower. Starting with the water steaming hot, he gradually changed it to icy cold, then back to hot. This was his primary means of waking his body. By the time he stepped out, his blood was circulating, and he felt nominally alive.

He brushed his teeth, rinsed with mouthwash and approached the task he had saved for last: shaving. He wiped the fog from the mirror quickly—no strange eyes staring at him this morning—and applied a thick layer of lather to his face. Then he reached for the plastic razor.

"Now, you rascal, I want a clean shave with none of that biting me. Understand? When I spent eighty-nine cents for razors, I expect full cooperation."

He wondered how many men talked to their razors and started scraping his cheeks. So far, so good. The shower had softened his beard considerably, so the razor seemed to glide along his skin just as it was supposed to. Then he cut himself right over his Adam's apple.

"Jesus H. Christ!" He threw the razor in the plastic trash can, wiped the rest of the lather from his face and examined his wound. It was only a nick, but it was bleeding steadily. He dabbed at it with a tissue, then stuck a wad of toilet paper on it.

Oh, he looked really great now, half-shaven with a piece of toilet paper on his neck. That would really impress people. Maybe he ought to spray paint his bald plate with something suitably obscene and join a punk band. Or better yet, he ought to have his picture taken this way for the jacket of his next book.

Disgusted, he grabbed the pack of disposable razors, which held two more of the dangerous things, and threw them away also. He'd just have to buy an electric shaver somewhere. He couldn't take his life in his hands every time he had to shave.

He glanced at his watch and put it back on his wrist. He returned to the bedroom and dressed quickly, pulling on one of his turtlenecks, the wine-red one he liked so much. He put on navy slacks and argyle socks, slipped into his cordovan shoes, then shrugged into a gray tweed jacket. He made sure he had his schedule in his pocket, grabbed his tote bag, and took the elevator down to the restaurant.

He ordered scrambled eggs, hash browns and sausage, milk and coffee, which set him back only eight bucks. He was surprised at how many people were in the restaurant at this early hour and how good most of them looked. They seemed fresh and ready for the day's challenges, while he was all strung out and not ready at all. He wondered if the other people in the restaurant could tell how unready he really was—if his condition of uncertainty was conspicuous to them.

Roger realized he was just being paranoid, and he shouldn't be paranoid at this stage in his career—not when being in the public eye had always been one of his goals. Paranoia led to agoraphobia, and that led to the funny farm and padded rooms.

His breakfast arrived. He ate it methodically, forcing

himself to be aware of each morsel, to distract himself from the obsessive thoughts hovering at the edge of his awareness.

Eat. *Be.* That's enough for this hour of the morning.

But he couldn't help thinking about his picture on a book jacket—the one he had fantasized about in the bathroom. And that naturally led to thoughts of what the next book should be. Even though there was a book out right now, he knew it was already time to start considering a new project. The public forgot quickly, especially when a writer's subject matter was based on a trend. If the New Age suddenly dropped out of the group consciousness, then there might be no market for his books.

Well, damn it, he could create the market. There were all sorts of cons being operated in the world, of which the New Age philosophy was only a small fraction. He'd sniff out something before long. An idea for a new book could present itself at any moment.

As he continued to eat, Roger thought lovingly of his books. The creation of them was something real, something important. He had helped many people with his writings; he was certain of that. He had saved them from the charlatans and con artists in the world and ultimately from themselves. That was what really gave validity to his work; it helped people.

There might be people sitting here in this restaurant whose lives he had touched. Perhaps that attractive redhead sitting in the corner—the one carrying on an animated conversation with a young businessman in a gray suit—maybe she had been helped by Roger Kant.

Her eyes fixed on him momentarily, then she looked away, leaving behind a chill.

No. Roger couldn't have helped her. Besides, she resembled his last wife too much, and a woman who looked like her was beyond the help of anyone.

Roger winced as a memory of Sandra flashed into his mind. He tried to obliterate it by thinking of the mystery woman he had spied at dinner the night before. Maybe she was sitting in this restaurant right now, watching him. He quickly surveyed the other patrons and saw no one who even reminded him of the woman. It was probably stupid to look for her anyhow; she didn't seem the type to be up at this awful hour.

He finished his breakfast and darted out of the restaurant. In the lobby, he stopped and bought a newspaper, stuffed it in his jacket pocket and headed for the door, as prepared for an early-morning radio show as anyone could be.

On his way out, he saw a young man in a wheelchair being pushed along by an elderly woman. He immediately felt queasy and disgusted. Trying to avoid looking at the man, he stumbled and banged his knee against a large potted plant. Of course it was the same knee he had injured the day before—it had to be—and he stifled his urge to scream.

A hotel employee—a young woman in a navy-blue blazer—rushed over to him.

That's right, Roger thought, *get over here before I start talking about suing the hotel.*

"Are you all right, sir?"

"Yes. Don't worry, I'm not going to sue you. I did this to myself."

"I was only concerned for your safety, sir."

"I'm fine."

"Well, let me know if I can be of help."

Roger flexed his injured leg. Luckily, the damage was again minimal, but he didn't think he could take much more of this. He simply had to be more careful.

He tried to maintain a modicum of dignity as he strode out the door. He hopped in a cab and gave the name of the radio station, then sat back to rest.

As the cab pulled away from the curb, he realized he had forgotten to get a receipt for his morning meal.

Edith would have remembered.

Then he started thinking about her and wondered how she was doing.

* * *

Edith Wilkins lay in her bed in her apartment in Evanston, Illinois, watching the dust sparkles in the sunlight streaming in through the window. She was still racked with the flu.

She shook her head in disgust. "Leave it to Edith to get the flu in the springtime."

Edith was nearly fifty, but she could pass for ten years younger when she took the time to fuss with herself. She usually did take the time; but the last few days of nausea and diarrhea had rendered her virtually helpless, and she dreaded seeing herself in the mirror, knowing the face that looked back at her would show every bit of its age, and then some.

Still, she ought to get out of bed. Maybe if she took a hot bath and popped a few more aspirin, she could take the edge off her illness. The prescription the doctor had written for her only numbed her senses. It was obviously loaded with codeine or something equally vile, and it made her head ache. It did little to control her other symptoms: the alternating chills and hot spells she was experiencing, the difficulty with breathing, and the overall malaise that made every waking moment a study in misery.

She wished she could talk to somebody—anybody. She missed Roger. Well, maybe not Roger himself, she had to admit. He had been aloof and cold lately, even more so than usual, because he was almost always distant. He was acting the way he always did before he started a new book. Something was probably percolating in that superior mind he possessed.

No, she didn't miss Roger per se, but she did miss being needed by him. Being needed was important. It was the only thing that gave purpose to her life. Now that her children were grown, her husband dead, and her own parents gone, Roger was the only person in her life who needed her.

She made a mental calculation. In Seattle it would be—what—seven in the morning? Roger should be gone by now—off to a radio talk show, if she remembered correctly, promoting the new book. He said he hated those promotional tours, but she knew better. Roger loved being in the spotlight of fame, and he loved for people to believe in him.

Maybe that was the only thing he loved.

She felt an odd empathy for him. She had always believed that to be loved a person had to give love. And in her three years as Roger's private secretary, she had come to believe that Roger was incapable of giving love—at least to other people. So hardly anyone truly loved him. Certainly not those bitchy ex-wives of his—especially the latest, that Sandra, who called to complain if his alimony payment was even a day late. And certainly not his two children, whose primary contact with their father consisted of requests for money. The boy, who was in his last year at Northwestern, was the worst of the two; he didn't even say thank you when Roger coughed up more money. His daughter was only slightly more appreciative, but she was basically an overachiever who had bought her way into a job at a local advertising agency.

But who was she to judge? Roger had made his own decisions in life. A person had to decide to love others. Love didn't just drop out of the blue.

Edith rolled out of bed and walked wearily to the bathroom, not sure what she would do when she got there. She held her stomach as she moved. It felt marginally better; but then she hadn't eaten anything since yesterday afternoon, so there was nothing left to throw up. Her stomach muscles still ached from the last bout with nausea, though.

She turned the water on in the tub and removed her robe—the only garment she had worn the last two days—and looked down at herself. It wasn't that bad a body. Things didn't sag as much as they were supposed to for a woman her age. At one time she had even hoped to attract Roger with this body. But it was no longer even a dream. She had offered love—in her own subtle way—but Roger had not recognized it.

Roger had his work to keep him going. If he noticed

Edith at all, it was for her efficiency, not for any physical attraction she might still possess. If she had met him earlier in life, before his first marriage, before he became so sour about women, maybe she could have made a difference. Now the whole question of Roger's happiness was totally out of her hands. She could offer only emotional support and soothe him during his troubled moods—as a mother or sister would, not as a wife or a woman he could love.

Sighing, she slid into the tub, making a mental note to call her boss later in the day.

Roger could barely focus on the microphone. His eyes stung from the cigarette smoke being produced by the morning talk show host, and part of his breakfast threatened to come up. On top of that, the headphones pinched his ears. Despite it all, he somehow found the strength to stay awake. It was showtime, and he had to be lucid and alert.

"Mr. Kant, I understand you're in Seattle to tell us about your new book."

"That's right, Jay. It's called *The New Age Con Game."*

"Could you tell our listeners a little bit about it?"

"It's a study of the various ways leading figures in the so-called New Age movement are fooling the public."

"Then it's an exposé?"

"You could call it that. It reveals a lot of tricks of the trade—the way phony psychic readings are made, how channelling is faked—and what the average person can do to avoid being taken by one of these psychic quacks—all of whom command big money for their performances, by the way."

"Sounds very interesting. I'll be sure to put it on my reading list. Okay, Seattle, stand by your phones. After these messages, you can call in and talk to Mr. Kant, sometimes known as The Astounding One by his fans."

Roger cringed at the use of The Astounding One, but he said nothing to Jay.

Jay cued a commercial tape and turned to Roger. "Want some coffee?"

"Yeah. Black."

"I'll have Rita bring some in. You ready for this?"

"As ready as I ever am."

"I guess you've done this many times before, then?"

"Too many."

"Well, my listeners are pretty conservative. Not too many looney-tunes—you get those on the dead-of-night talk shows, like Larry King and Snyder. You ever do a gig with them?"

"I was on King's show once."

"Ever do Carson?"

"A couple of times."

"What's he really—? Hold on. I see the phones lighting up. Larry and his team are screening the calls now." He pointed to a group of people behind a glass partition who were taking the actual calls. "Commercial's about over. Here we go . . . okay, Seattle, you're on the air. Who's our first caller?"

"This is Mary . . ."

"Speak up, Mary."

"THIS IS MARY!"

"Not that loud. Somewhere in the middle. Do you have a question or comment for our guest, Mr. Kant?"

"Yes, I do. I was wondering if you ever met a person you considered a real psychic."

"No, Mary, I never have."

"You mean they're *all* fakes?"

"I haven't met them all. But the psychics I've encountered so far have been fakes in one way or another."

"Well, my sister went to a man for a palm reading, and everything he said came true."

"I don't know the man, of course, but it's possible to make a person think he or she's being told the truth. All the psychic has to do is learn a little beforehand and make some educated guesses. That's the way most of them do it. But, usually, they make vague statements that could be interpreted a number of ways. If you choose to believe one of those ways, then you'll be convinced it's the truth. I also think some of these psychics may be deluded themselves. They really believe they have strange powers. People with delusions need professional help."

"That's all we have time for, Mary," Jay interrupted. "Strong words from Mr. Kant this morning. He's really telling it like it is. Next caller, please. Who are we talking to?"

"Dwayne."

"Dwayne, do you have a question for Mr. Kant?"

"Yeah. You ever been in one of those seances?"

"Many times, Dwayne."

"You ever meet a ghost at one?"

"I don't believe in ghosts. The only ghosts I've seen at seances were faked."

"How'd they do it?"

"There are a number of ways: mirrors, hidden projectors, invisible wires. That's why so many seances are held in dark rooms—to hide the trickery. That's all explained in detail in my first book, *Optical Delusions.*"

"Next caller, please. Your name?"

"Patty."

"Patty, what's your question?"

"I'd like to know what it hurts to believe in the supernatural? There has to be more to existence than what we see and feel with our five senses. Wouldn't you agree?"

"Maybe, Patty," Roger replied thoughtfully. "Let me put it this way: I'd *like* to believe in the supernatural, just like I'd like to see a genuine U.F.O., but I'm afraid all these things are so much fantasy."

"Then, why do so many people believe in the occult and UFOs? There has to be something to it."

"At one time, people believed the earth was flat, but it wasn't. I've examined the evidence in all kinds of cases, and I have yet to find an example of an occult or supernatural occurence that was documented extensively enough to be validated."

"But—"

"Next caller, please."

"This is George."

"Go ahead, George."

"Don't you feel bad about all the lives you've ruined?"

"What do you mean, sir?"

"All the legitimate psychics you've hurt with your ravings. Aren't you responsible for putting them out of business?"

"When you consider all the money they've bilked out of innocent people, I think they deserved what they got. Don't you?"

"No, I don't. I think you're a—" The time delay prevented the caller from blurting the obscenity on the air.

Jay sighed and shook his head, then continued, undaunted. "Next caller, please."

So it went for the next forty minutes, the only respite being commercial breaks. Roger was doing an admirable job of handling the calls, both pro and con.

Then, at five minutes to nine, all the lines became silent for a few seconds, as if all the callers had decided to hang up.

Roger looked at his host, who was obviously nonplussed. "Seattle, keep those calls coming in. Mr. Roger Kant is still with us. He'll be hosting a seminar on Thursday evening, and . . . wait, here's another call. Who's this I'm talking to?"

"Call me Alex," a deep voice replied. One of the level meters on the control board hit the red end of the scale in response to the voice.

"Okay, Alex. Keep it down, though. You don't have to be that loud."

"I have a very interesting question for Mr. Kant." The level meter still showed too much volume.

"Go ahead," Roger said. He glanced at the radio host, who made a gesture indicating the caller had a screw loose.

"What is it, Mr. Kant, that makes you so *fucking* superior to everyone else?"

"I . . ."

The host signaled the people behind the glass to cut the caller off. Roger could see them pushing buttons, but nothing was happening.

"Answer me, please."

"I'm not superior. I just try to help people avoid being swindled by people who pose as psychics."

"So you don't believe in anything—do you?"

Roger held his hands up helplessly. Jay and the technicians were trying to control the volume of the caller's voice—and stop it, if possible—but their efforts were useless. The host whispered, "Keep talking to him." To the people behind the glass, he said, "What happened to the time delay? Why can't you cut this guy off?"

They were scrambling, pulling switches, turning dials, but the voice was unaffected. It was bypassing all their control mechanisms somehow.

"Well, I believe in God, of course . . ." Roger began.

The caller laughed, and the sound of it boomed through the studio. The tinkle of glass breaking somewhere could be heard under the rumble. "God! That's nothing to believe in. There are many other things to believe in—just as powerful as any god. You will learn to believe in them too, Mr. Kant. You will learn."

"I try to keep an open mind, but the fact remains I have yet to encounter any genuine phenomena."

"How about *this?*" A roar came through the speakers. The membranes in Roger's headphones burst as every meter on the control board went haywire. The building shook as if a tornado were passing by. The glass partition started to crack, and everyone ducked as it shattered, spraying shards of glass in every direction. Something popped and crackled, and wisps of smoke curled up from the control board. Then the voice was gone.

"Jesus!" Jay moaned, holding his ears.

Roger climbed up from the floor, brushing debris and glass from his clothing. His face was white. His eardrums felt as if they had popped—as if he were in a plane that had hit an air pocket and dropped several thousand feet. "What was that?" he shouted. "A sonic boom?"

Somebody ran into the room with a fire extinguisher and sprayed the smoking control panel.

"What was it?" Roger repeated.

The host stepped back, surveyed the damage, then shook his head. "Whoever it was, he has access to some pretty goddamn powerful equipment. He jammed all the phone lines and our time delay—shit, the FCC is going to be on our asses over this one."

"So there is—is a rational explanation?" Roger asked.

"Of course. Some dickhead out there—"

"Jay!"

"What?"

"Your mike's still open! You're going out on the air."

"Now my ass *is* grass." He sat down, looking totally defeated. He shot an accusatory glance at Roger, then bent over the mike to apologize to the city of Seattle as the stench of burnt wire and the odd smell of fire extinguisher foam filled the room.

Roger started to say something, but then he looked up and saw a woman standing on the other side of the studio, huddled in the corner, out of sight of everyone else. She seemed to be just like the woman in the restaurant—only there was something a little different about her. It was her hair. It was black now, not blond or streaked.

Without bidding his host *adieu,* Roger rushed out to meet her before she got away. But by the time he went through the door and made his way around to the other side, she was gone.

Nobody else had seen her.

3. ASTOUNDING FEATS

"Ladies—and I do see a few gentlemen out there—I want to show you that despite everything I have written, I have psychic abilities myself."

Roger paused to let the full impact of that statement sink in. He looked out over the audience filling the hotel's meeting room. There were easily four hundred people. He could sense their anticipation, their desire to be entertained, and their willingness to be surprised and astounded. Their faces were all turned eagerly toward him now. It was moments like these, when he had the full attention of an audience, that made the years of struggle worth all the effort.

He felt calm tonight. Yesterday's fiasco at the radio station was far from his mind. Since then, he'd been on TV, signed more books, and had even allowed himself to be accompanied by Karen Wright to Pioneer Square, where he purchased a souvenir to take back to Edith.

Despite all this activity, he had found time to buy a new electric shaver, so he felt more confident about his appearance and no longer worried about cutting his own throat. And Wednesday night he had slept soundly without interruption. He was primed and ready for tonight's show, all his mental and physical faculties intact and operating at full power.

He glanced over his shoulder at Karen, who sat in a folding chair behind him with other members of the

Northwest League for Higher Consciousness. He smiled and winked at her; she returned his smile because she understood what was going to happen. Roger had chosen her as his co-conspirator.

"Yes," he continued, turning back to the audience, "I can do anything a psychic can do. And I'm going to prove it to you. As you came into the room tonight, some of you were asked to write something on a little piece of paper and sign it with your name. Then you put the paper in an envelope and sealed it."

He indicated Karen. "Mrs. Wright has selected a number of those envelopes and kept them in a safe place until this moment. Mrs. Wright, will you bring me the box?"

Karen had a small, clear plastic box full of small envelopes in her lap. She rose and brought it over to Roger, who set it on top of the lectern. "Thank you, Karen. Now, you can attest to the fact that you and only you have had possession of these envelopes since they were given to you by the members of the audience. Correct?"

"Yes, Mr. Kant."

"I have not seen them?"

"No. They've never been out of my sight."

"They haven't been tampered with in any way?"

"No."

"You will also confirm that these are special, opaque envelopes that I can't possibly see through?"

"Yes."

"Thank you, Karen. You may return to your seat now."

Karen sat down, beaming. She was enjoying sharing the spotlight with the star of the show.

"Now, ladies and gentlemen, I will do a reading of the contents of each envelope and tell you what the paper inside says—merely by touching the envelope to my head. In short, I will demonstrate what the psychics call psychometry. By the way, they call these pieces of paper 'billets.'"

He glanced up at the audience and caught the eye of a young woman sitting in the first row. She blushed. "You, there, miss . . ."

"Barbara," the woman replied.

"Barbara, do you think I can do it?"

"If you say you can, you can."

"Thank you for your confidence, Barbara." He addressed himself to the audience again. "Now, I don't have a turban like the Amazing Carnac . . ." The audience laughed appreciatively. ". . . but the psychics are fond of saying everyone has psychic ability, so here goes."

He picked an envelope from the box and held it to his forehead. "This is from a man named Bill. Bill has asked a question? 'Can you predict the future?' The answer is no, Bill, I can't." He tore the envelope open and looked at the paper. "Bill, that's right isn't it? Bill?"

Roger pretended to be slightly embarrassed. "Bill must have skipped out on me. But give me another chance, folks. This is only my first envelope. I'm just getting warmed up." He wadded up the first note and took another envelope. He pressed it briefly to his head, then said, "This is from Mary Scott, who asks if I remember talking to her on the radio yesterday morning. Right?"

A portly woman stood up in the middle of the audience. "That's right. I wrote that!"

The audience started to applaud. "Save your applause, ladies and gentlemen. This is only the beginning. I feel my psychic powers getting stronger and stronger. I'm really tuning in to the vibrations now. And, by the way, Mary, I do remember talking to you."

Roger then proceeded to "read" a dozen more envelopes—all correctly. By the fourteenth reading he had most of the audience mystified. No one seemed to know how he was doing it. Roger was enjoying every moment of this demonstration. He had done it many times before, and it always impressed the crowds—because it was so simple.

"I feel my powers fading now," he said at last. "Now, is there anyone out there who doesn't realize I'm a genuine psychic? Let's see those hands. I see some hesitation. Are you saying you doubt my powers?"

There was confused murmuring among the audience.

They were uncertain how to respond now.

"I know—you saw it with your own eyes—yet you remain skeptical. Well, I'm glad to see that Seattle is a town that thinks for itself. As most of you probably suspect, this whole reading was a trick—a very simple bit of theatrics designed to impress the gullible. In fact, any one of you could read billets if you know the secret.

"Does anyone want to know it?"

The audience responded with loud assent.

"So you want to impress your friends and be the life of the party—or are you all thinking of opening up fortune telling businesses?"

The crowd laughed. Roger had every one of them in the palm of his hand now. He could ask them all to plunge into the ocean, and they would probably do it, without asking questions.

It gave him a feeling of power, but it also scared him. He didn't have that much charisma, he wasn't a handsome man who could sway people with his good looks, nor was he a particularly brilliant speaker. Yet he had manipulated this whole room of people with a simple parlor trick. That's why, he realized once again, his books were so vital—to show people how easily they could be fooled.

He looked out over them. There were so many women out there. Could the mystery woman he kept seeing be among them? Would he be able to pick her out among so many people?

As he strained to see individual faces, his vision blurred, and the people in the audience changed. It seemed for an instant they were a herd of skeletons—animated skeletons about to rise and attack him.

He blanched and gulped, then shut his eyes against the vision. When he opened them again, everything was normal. What the hell was happening now? He thought all this was behind him; he'd kept himself too busy the last day and a half for any strange occurences to happen. Yet his mind was still capable of playing tricks on him.

He gripped the edges of the lectern to steady himself, then took a drink of cool water from the glass in front of him and pretended to be clearing his throat. That made him feel a bit better, though he was still a little shaken. He continued with his presentation, hoping that would blot the awful vision—that word again—from his mind.

"Well," he said, forcing himself to sound as confident as ever, "I'm sure some of you may have guessed how this was done, but I won't keep you in suspense any longer. It's very simple. My first response was fake. There was no Bill. I read the contents of the first envelope and pretended it was the contents of the second envelope, and so on. Did you notice how hastily I disposed of the billets after I read them? That's part of the trick too—so it would be a little more difficult for them to be checked. So the fourteenth billet, the one lying on the lectern at this moment, actually says what I would have told you the fifteenth contained—if I had continued.

"I deliberately made this presentation simple. There are variations on billets—in which I could have offered answers to your various personal questions. The most impressive part, of course, is that I can 'read' the contents of the envelope before opening it. Consider this: If I had charged you a nominal fee for this psychic demonstration—say, twenty-five dollars per billet—think of how much money I could've made off a crowd like this. And, once I impressed you with billets, I might go on to offer to do a personal, private reading for a higher fee—a hundred, two hundred or even more. Does anyone want a private reading now?"

After the applause and laughter died down, Roger proceeded to duplicate other psychic feats, including bending spoons, mind reading, and a variety of other stunts. By the end of the three-hour seminar, he had convinced most of those present that all psychic powers were easily reproduced by trickery, legerdemain, or other parlor magic.

"And in conclusion," he said, "just remember to ask the hard questions and demand precise answers. These tricks have been around for centuries. Every so many years, there's a resurgence of interest in the occult. This time out, they're calling it the New Age, but there's really nothing new about it. Everything I've shown you here tonight and much more is detailed in my new book, *The New Age Con Game*. Before you see any psychic, before you get a Tarot reading, or a palm reading, before you go to a channelling session, I urge you to read what I have to say. I thank you for your attention and your kind indulgence."

There was a standing ovation. As the applause died down, Karen Wright went up to the mike.

"People! Mr. Kant's new book is available for sale on tables just outside the north exit doors. Mr. Kant himself will be available to sign copies for you for a brief period. There's also a posting of the Northwest League's calendar of events, and . . ."

Roger ducked down behind the stage and managed to slip out a side door to hit the men's room before the crowd descended on him. He hid in a stall momentarily to catch his breath. The vision of the crowd as skeletons still disturbed him; then that nasty business at the radio station yesterday morning—and his bad dreams the first nights—all came rushing back in his mind. What did it all mean? Was he going crazy? Was he working himself too hard? And this was only the beginning of the tour. By its end he might be seeing pink elephants, pixies and phantoms.

If only Edith were here! She would provide a stabilizing influence. She would keep these things from happening to him. It was obvious he just shouldn't go on any of these promotional trips alone—not in his present state of mind. If Edith wasn't well when he returned to Chicago, he would cancel the rest of the tour and not go out again until she could be with him—no matter how many lost book sales it meant.

There were more important things than selling books, after all. There was the matter of maintaining one's sanity, for example.

But this evening's activities weren't over; there were books to sign and a party to attend. He couldn't really bow out now. He had to steel himself to get through the rest of the evening and the night. At least he'd be on his way home in the morning.

He hoped they had a good brand of Scotch at the party.

He took care of nature's call, splashed cold water on his face and went out to meet his admirers.

It was an hour and a half before he could get to the Scotch.

Roger sat on a couch in the hotel suite where the party was being held in his honor. The last hour had passed slowly as he talked to members of the League and did his best to be gracious. Time's passage was somewhat enhanced by the application of Scotch and water, but it wasn't quite enough to abolish the dullness of it all. The only other women Karen Wright seemed to know all resembled her in body and mind: middle-aged and rather banal.

Roger was about to make up a phony excuse to leave, when Karen redeemed herself by bringing someone over to meet Roger who didn't resemble her at all. His pulse began to throb as he saw the two of them approaching.

The woman accompanying Karen was everything Karen was not: tall, young and fair, with natural strawberry blond hair. As she came closer, Roger's heart raced as he stared at her face in amazement. It it were not for the hair, he could swear this was the woman he had seen the other night in the restaurant. But that was impossible. It was like déjà vu—which he didn't believe in. Yet there she was—the face, the shape, the eyes.

"Mr. Kant," Karen said, "I have a young lady here who is just dying to meet you."

Roger stood up so quickly he almost stumbled over his own feet.

"Melissa Lewis, meet Roger Kant. Roger . . ."

Roger grasped the young woman's hand firmly and shook it. Her flesh was warm, the touch of her skin electrifying. "It's a pleasure, Miss Lewis."

"The pleasure's all mine," Melissa replied. "And you will call me Melissa, or I shall run away." Her voice matched her beauty; it was a melody of cultured tones that he was certain was not at all affected. She had class, reminding him of Katharine Hepburn when she was young.

"We can't have that." Roger grinned at her. He felt like a schoolboy. "Okay, Melissa, and call me Roger or I'll run away. Why don't you sit down?"

"I'll be glad to, Mr. Kant. I have so many questions for you."

The two of them sat down in unison.

Karen seemed a bit flustered. "I'll go circulate while you two get acquainted," she said. "Let me know if you need anything."

"I don't need anything at all," Roger said.

After Karen was gone, Melissa edged closer to him and peered into his eyes. Her gaze seemed to penetrate his whole being, as if she could see into his soul through the windows of his eyes. Roger was unsure how to act. No woman had ever looked at him that way before—not even the most fervid of his fans—not even any of his three ex-wives in the days before things turned sour.

She smelled of an exotic perfume, something obviously very expensive; her makeup was perfectly applied. She wore a dress of deep purple satin, with a daring neckline that begged him to look. She also wore earrings, bracelets and a large necklace—all gold. She could be a fashion model or a movie star, yet she was sitting here next to him as an ordinary woman might.

Roger was momentarily unable to speak. He just sat back and enjoyed the radiance of this extraordinarily beautiful woman, waiting for her to do whatever she wished with him.

She laid her hand on his and leaned closer. "Your demonstration tonight was quite impressive," she said, lingering on the last syllable in a way that made a chill crawl up Roger's spine.

The chill was quickly replaced by a warm glow. "Thank you," he replied, finding his voice at last. "It was not much."

"But it was. I'm sure you impressed all those people. I could see it in their faces."

"Were you out there?"

"Of course. I was in the back row."

"I wish you'd been closer."

"So do I."

Melissa squeezed his hand; he felt blood rush to his head—and to other parts as well.

"Well, as long as I get to some of them—as long as only a few of them listen to what I say—I'm happy. I feel then that I've helped someone at least—and that's what it's all about."

"Oh, I'm sure you've helped millions of people by now."

"Well, perhaps. . . ."

She withdrew her hand. Roger regarded her with an unspoken question.

"Mr. Kant, I have a small confession to make." She turned her eyes away from him temporarily. "I'm a fan of yours—a big fan—but I want something from you."

"What might that be?" He could only hope it was something he was capable of supplying.

"I'm a kind of writer myself. Trying to be. I want to be an important writer—as you are."

Roger grimaced inwardly. Could it be this lovely woman was just another failed writer wanting advice on how to succeed? That would be a cruel joke on him, indeed.

"Yes?" he said, hesitantly, already bracing himself for possible disappointment.

"I want to write a book—about *you*"

Roger was taken aback. "Are you serious?"

"Of course I'm serious. Mr.—I mean, Roger, you don't know what a true phenomenon you are. People out there would like to know more about you—about what makes you tick. You know, how you got started, how you came to realize the psychic world was a world of sham and avarice."

"But I told my life story in *Memoirs of a Skeptic*—which

didn't sell that well."

"Oh, I know. I read it twice. But it was written five years ago. I'm certain much has happened to you, and frankly, Roger, I think I could present a different perspective—the woman's point of view. I'm sure you're aware that the major percentage of your readers are women."

"Well, yes, but—"

"I could show the inner you, the vulnerable, perhaps even tender side of your nature—the side you never show to the public."

Roger's expression showed doubt.

Melissa turned to face him and took his hand again, squeezing more earnestly now. "It wouldn't be a hatchet job—or an exposé—if that's what worries you. It would be objective, analytical. And, if I do say so myself, I'm a good writer. I'd love to show you some of my work."

"I don't know, Melissa." His brow furrowed in disappointment.

"Oh, not for you to critique. I'm not one of those little dilettantes who dabbles in writing. I've been a journalist, a reporter—just as you were when you started out."

Roger rubbed his chin and thought. Maybe she was genuine; maybe she did want to write a book about him. It was flattering, but it also worried him for some reason he couldn't quite put his finger on. Was it because she was too attractive? Was he letting his male prejudice cause him to automatically assume any pretty woman was an airhead? But she sounded intelligent.

"How would you go about doing this book?" he asked.

"Well, obviously I would have to spend a lot of time with you. For example, I'd accompany you on the rest of your tour—to get a perspective on that aspect of your work. Then there'd be hours of interviews. And I'm sure I'd have no trouble finding a publisher for the finished work. The world wants to know more about Roger Kant. You're a true celebrity, Roger, even if you don't know it."

"But that could be very expensive and time-consuming for you," he said.

"I'd take care of my own expenses. I have my resources. I

wouldn't need a penny from you or anyone."

Roger glanced at the gold she wore. She could finance a world tour with that alone.

"Well, when you put it that way—but, I don't know." He couldn't help but tremble at the prospect of spending more time with this woman. If he were inclined to take advantage of people, he'd say yes right on the spot, but that would be as good as saying he had only a sexual interest in her. A book about him wasn't a bad idea, though. He had to control his urges—take some time and think about it. Approach the whole idea rationally.

"I'll tell you what," he said, almost mournfully. "Tomorrow's my last day in Seattle, and I'm returning to Chicago for a couple of days before I continue the tour. Let me think it over, and I'll give you a call in a week or so."

"Oh, Roger, is this a brush-off? Did I say something to make a wrong impression on you?"

"No, not at all. Here," he said, taking a card from his billfold, "this is my card, with my personal phone number. *You* call me in a couple of days. I promise I'll give your proposal very serious consideration."

She leaned against him and kissed him quickly on the cheek. "That's all I ask, Roger. I hope you decide to let me—well, share some of your life for a while."

"Maybe it will work out."

She stood up abruptly. "I'm sure it will."

As Roger watched her stride across the room, he ached. He wondered if he had played this scene right. Shouldn't they be sneaking off to his room together? He shuddered. He wasn't sure he could handle a woman like that.

But, God, he'd like to try.

Sweat poured down Edith's face. It stung her eyes, and as she wiped at them, they hurt even more.

It was awfully dark in her room—darker than it should be. She reached over to switch on the bedside lamp, but it wouldn't come on.

"Damn," she muttered and slid out of the bed. She

fumbled in the darkness for her robe.

The she heard a noise. Something moving—and breathing—in her room!

"Who's there?" she said hoarsely. She was too weak to shout. "I've got a gun here. I know how to use it too!" That was true. She did have a pistol in her apartment; however, she was nowhere close to it, and it was unloaded.

The breathing seemed closer now. It was more of a rasping, actually, like the labored breath of a huge animal. The air smelled of its sweat and something else—decay. Edith shook uncontrollably.

"I don't have any money in the place," she said. "And if you want to rape me, you won't get much cooperation. I'm sick."

Why didn't the prowler answer or do something—anything—so she could figure out where he was? Then maybe she could defend herself somehow—throw something at it or run in the opposite direction.

Whatever it was, it kept advancing. She sensed it moving toward her, even in the darkness.

"All right. Take the TV. Take my purse. My credit cards—everything—just leave me alone. Don't hurt me. Okay? I won't even call the police."

The breathing became more controlled. Then there was silence. Edith couldn't move.

Then a spot lit up in the darkness, and she briefly saw the face of the thing that awaited her.

Before she could scream, it was on her. With one quick movement, it slit her throat.

4. SURPRISES

Roger stood in O'Hare Airport, searching the crowd for the familiar face of his secretary. Edith *always* came to pick him up when he returned from a trip, always at the right gate, ready to tell him who had called when he was gone, if any significant mail had come, and if anything important had happened. She had been late only once, and that was when there was a major pile-up on the toll road. Why wasn't she here today? He desperately needed to see her, because it was only then that he felt he was truly in friendly territory.

Then he remembered. Edith was ill. She had the flu and was probably still bedridden. He grimaced at his forgetfulness. Was he getting senile? No, he realized, it wasn't senility; it was because he was so exhausted he couldn't think straight. His experiences in Seattle had drained him emotionally, and his brain was in a fog. He'd been nervous all the way back, his mind obsessed with the idea of something going wrong with the plane.

Without Edith, however, he'd have to find his own cab or bus into the city, and that was a pain in the ass. He stopped and chastised himself.

All that time he was in Seattle, he hadn't once called Edith! She was not only his secretary, she was also his closest friend in many ways—and he hadn't had the decency to call her up to see how she was doing. It would have taken only a couple of minutes, but he had been too caught up in his own trivial concerns and neurotic obsessions. Edith must think him an ogre—and he wouldn't blame her a bit.

Well, he'd have to make it up to her somehow. Did she like flowers? Candy? As he walked toward the exit doors, carrying his luggage clumsily, his feelings of shame increased with every step. Poor Edith, lying in bed, puking, racked with diarrhea, alternately feverish and chilled—and probably wondering why her thoughtless boss hadn't bothered to inquire about her health even once.

But then she hadn't called him, either, which was unusual for her. Maybe her illness was more serious than a mere flu bug. Maybe she was in the hospital, tubes stuck up her nose and needles in her arms, suffering. But, damn it, why did she have to get sick at a time like this?

Roger quickened his pace.

Outside, he took a cab instead of a bus. He wanted to ride into the city alone, so that he could contemplate various matters on the way. The things that had happened in Seattle still clouded his mind. It had been a strange few days. He didn't know what to make of it all—that incident in the radio station, his weird dreams, and finally, meeting that beautiful young woman, Melissa Lewis, who said she wanted to write his life story. No one had ever approached him that way before. Melissa had been the one bright spot during his visit, even though he had spent only a few moments with her.

He was at an age where he was not quite jaded with the idea of women; they still fascinated him, sometimes almost in an adolescent way, but he knew they often made demands. They weren't toys; they weren't merely sexual objects, though they could be; they weren't romanticized ideals. They were persons with whom one had to interact, which often meant compromising a part of oneself, and Roger didn't particularly care for that. Three marriages had taught him a lot about women.

But Melissa seemed to possess a quality of ingenuousness that could make him forget what women truly were.

Would he ever see her again? She might be a dilettante with no intentions of pursuing the matter beyond the conversation stage. So many people said they wanted to write a book about something. Maybe she sought out every celebrity, minor or otherwise, who visited Seattle and told him she wanted to write a book on his life. Maybe her posturing as a would-be biographer was an elaborate come-on, the actual purpose of which he had failed to understand.

As the cab approached the Chicago skyline, Roger began to feel better. This was familiar; this city was his adopted home. Here were the things that mattered to him—his apartment and his study, where he could immerse himself in work. Here he could be himself without having to bother with fawning elderly ladies or groupies or fanatics who wanted to sway him to their way of thinking.

Here he was free.

The first thing Roger did when he entered his apartment was rush over to the big picture window and pull the drapes open. The view from here—the twenty-second floor of the building—always inspired him. He could gaze out across the vast blue-gray expanse of Lake Michigan, which seemed to stretch on forever beyond the horizon, and observe a large portion of the world. Today, he could see tiny boats, mere specks of color riding on the sun-reflecting waves, fighting the wind. And many times he had watched in awe as storms rolled across the surface of the water. At times like that he felt he was viewing the world through the eyes of God.

His apartment was in one of the most expensive high-rises on Lake Shore Drive. A lesser man might be humbled by this view; Roger knew that only a powerful, potent, *right* man deserved to live in such an eyrie, where he could look down on the masses and, if the mood struck him, laugh at them and their puny enterprises. Sometimes he needed to see people from that perspective, especially when he was dealing with the foolishness of the general populace who were so willing to follow fake messiahs or embrace ridiculous tenets in the name of New Age sensibilities.

A scornful expression wrinkled his brow. The New Age was the same old whore in a new skirt—the whore of flim-flam, bunko and delusion.

Roger took in the view a few seconds more, then turned away reluctantly, his eyes automatically scanning his apartment to see if anything was out of place. It was a large apartment, designed especially for him, with three bedrooms, his study, a small office for Edith, a fully equipped and stocked kitchen, a dining area with a highly polished oak table, and a combination living room/entertainment area with a stereo, TV and Hi-Fi VCR, and a wet bar. The carpet was thick and plush, the furniture massive and comfortable, and the colors muted, dominated by the current craze for mauve and almond with touches of bright color in just the right places. Roger had paid a decorator a great deal of money to make this part of his home look like a page from *Architectural Digest.* He entertained important people here occasionally, and he wanted to impress upon them that the nature of his work allowed him all the luxuries a man might want and that Roger Kant was not a man to be trifled with.

His study, however, was another matter. It was not meant to impress anyone, because he actually worked there. The study, where he now headed, had never been touched by the hand of a decorator. It was pure Roger Kant: disheveled, sometimes dirty, almost always a shambles. He opened its door, snapped on the light and surveyed the disorderly landscape of papers, stacks of books, boxes full of clippings, piles of correspondence, and the many memorabilia and souvenirs of his career, including a wall of framed photos showing him with many famous people. A person who had never seen the room before might think an earthquake had just taken place. To Roger, it was the final assurance he was home. The only other person allowed in this room was Edith.

Edith! He had forgotten about her again. It was almost four o'clock and he should give her a call. She might be worried about him.

He made his way across the room, stepping expertly over the debris of his profession, and sat down in the leather-upholstered swivel chair behind the wide walnut desk. He reached for the phone to dial his secretary, but was distracted by the flashing light on the answering machine.

He grabbed a pad and pen in case he needed to jot down any phone numbers and punched the answering machine's playback button. The tape rewound slowly, whirring with mechanical distress, reminding Roger he needed to get a new machine. He fiddled with his pen as he waited, doodling on the pad, drawing pictures of little demons and hearts with arrows through them. Then there was a *click*, and the machine started playing back the messages. There were two from his son, requesting immediate money for college expenses—which meant he had probably spent all his money on beer—one from his literary agent, who just wanted to chat; one from an insurance company wanting to insure his life; a nasty message from his devious ex-wife Sandra, who had once again discovered his unlisted number and wanted an explanation for his being a day late on his alimony; and the final one—from the police:

"Mr. Kant? Sergeant Rollins with Chicago Police Department, Homicide. It's 11:30 AM, Friday. Please call me as soon as possible at 555-1233. That's Sergeant Rollins." The voice repeated the phone number and added, "It's urgent, Mr. Kant."

Roger replayed the last message. Sweat broke out on his forehead. His first thought was that his son was in trouble, but the word "homicide" changed his mind. Certainly his son wouldn't be involved in anything like that.

His hands trembling, he reached for the phone and dialed Sergent Rollins' number.

* * *

Sergeant Rollins was a large, tidy man, about thirty-five with short, sandy hair and dark blue eyes. He wore a wispy moustache over a mouth set in a grim expression. His jaw was square. He looked determined.

His desk was worn and old, like everything else in the room full of policemen and people who either had broken the law or were victims of lawbreakers. The noise level in the room was subdued, considering the number of people talking.

Roger sat across from Rollins, studying the surface of the desk. It bore many scars, but it was just as tidy as the sergeant. Papers were neatly stacked. There was a magnetic paperclip holder next to them and a stapler that was placed carefully perpendicular to the front edge of the desk. The phone was isolated in a corner where it was convenient but still out of the way. Pens and pencils were arranged in rows on either side of a calendar desk pad on which were written many notations.

Roger felt very guilty, not because he had anything to do with Edith's death, but because he had been unable to cry about it yet. He was still too stunned by the information, delivered to him in typical, deadpan police officialese: "Mr. Kant, I have bad news. Your secretary, Edith Wilkins, was found dead in her apartment early this morning, by the building superintendent."

Rollins had a blank legal pad in front of him. He wrote a couple of lines on it, then leaned back slightly in his chair, clasped his meaty hands together and stared directly into Roger's eyes.

Roger could read nothing in the man's expression: no accusation, no inquiry. It was the face of a man doing his job as efficiently as possible. Under other circumstances, Roger might have admired him. But he was also the bearer of bad news, and it was obvious he had more of it to unburden.

"Now, Mr. Kant," Rollins began, "we called you because, as Miss Wilkins' employer, you were the closest friend or acquaintance we could reach immediately. We're still trying to contact her children and other surviving relatives. I have some routine questions that might help us find her killers."

"Killer? She only had the flu—she couldn't have been killed." Roger suddenly realized that sounded ridiculous. If it had been only the flu, the police wouldn't be involved.

"I'm afraid there's no mistake, Mr. Kant. The details of how she died leave no doubt that she was murdered. Our speculation at this point is that maybe she surprised a burglar or a rapist, though there was no evidence of sexual assault. . . ."

"Please," Roger said. "I don't want all the grisly details."

"Sorry, Mr. Kant." Rollins said, seeming earnest. "You evidently had some personal feelings for the victim."

"She was my private secretary. We were friends, too. She's been with me for three years."

"You may know as much about her as her relatives, then."

"I suppose so."

"The apartment was a wreck, Mr. Kant. Like a tornado had been through it. We're not sure what is missing. Do you know if she had any valuables that would have attracted a thief?"

"Nothing worth her life."

"Life is cheap sometimes. A crackhead will kill for a radio."

"She had a few gold earrings, a gold chain necklace, maybe a diamond ring. She lived modestly."

"She didn't spend all her money, then."

"She put a lot in the bank. She was security-conscious."

"She had a pistol too."

"I know. I used to tell her it wouldn't do her any good. And I was right—unfortunately."

Rollins scribbled something on his pad, then looked up at Roger again.

"Okay, Mr. Kant. If our speculations are wrong—and this is probably just for the record—do you know of anyone who might have had a grudge against Ms. Wilkins? Any enemies?"

"No. Edith was on good terms with everyone, as far as I know. It's just senseless."

"These things happen, Mr. Kant. This is a big city. There are lots of nuts out there. . . ."

Roger didn't pay attention to the rest of Rollins' spiel. It was the same tired old crap about violence in the city—the violence that always happened to someone else. Except sometimes it happened to someone close to you, and then it was real.

And nobody had to tell Roger Kant there were nuts loose in the world.

He'd met more than his share of them.

After Roger returned to his apartment, the full meaning of what had happened finally hit him, and he was overcome with depression.

Edith was dead—just like that—senselessly murdered by an unknown nut-case.

And Roger Kant couldn't do a thing about it. Except feel guilty. He allowed himself to cry.

He hadn't been very helpful to the police. Although Edith had been his right arm, a better helpmate than any wife, he had known very little about her. He had remained aloof, steadfastly only her employer, a stranger who paid her for services rendered. She had always done his bidding without question, ever efficient, ever vigilant, always looking out for him, while he had barely acknowledged her existence.

She would be difficult to replace; perhaps impossible.

As the sun went down, Roger sat in the growing gloom, not bothering to turn on any lights. He kept asking himself the same stupid question: What kind of world allowed such terrible things to happen to good, innocent people like Edith? Only a world in which goodness and innocence had no meaning anymore, only a world in which life had no substance or significance, only a world in which, as he always had known, everything was a sham.

Only death was not a sham. It was real because it

displaced life with inexorable finality—which meant life itself was a fraud, an illusion of sorts. He felt his own life was now meaningless as well. It too had become a sham. This realization was too difficult to bear. He had to blot it out somehow.

Overcoming his inertia, he rose and stumbled across the darkened room to the wet bar, banging his knee—the one he had injured in Seattle—on his way. A sharp pain shot up his thigh, but he ignored it as he found the bottle of Scotch and an empty glass in the dark. He filled the glass, deliberately not diluting it, and returned to the chair.

He switched on a lamp and from his jacket pocket took the tour schedule Edith had prepared for him. Continuing the tour was out of the question now. With Edith gone, it would be a violation of her memory. He wadded up the schedule and threw it across the room. To hell with promotion. To hell with books and all the rest of his life. Roger Kant, The Astounding One, wasn't so astounding after all.

He took a big gulp of Scotch.

Pursuing numbness seemed the only sensible answer.

By midnight, Roger was struggling with demons—not demons actually, but the ghosts of his past: the many people whose lives he had touched or changed, his parents, especially his father, and now the new ghost—Edith. He begged forgiveness from her in his mind, but her lifeless lips formed words he could not hear.

"Damn it!" he mumbled in his drunken stupor. "Forgive me!"

He sat up. His head was throbbing with the effects of too much Scotch on an empty stomach, but not enough Scotch apparently to benumb him totally. He had been dreaming. That was one of the worst signs of sobriety.

He reached for the glass on the table and swallowed the last quarter ounce of lukewarm Scotch left in the bottom. It tasted bitter. Why did he have to wake up? Why did he have to be snatched from comforting oblivion and thrust into the cold light of reality?

Because there was a relentless pounding in his head, something grating on his ragged nerve endings. He placed his hands over his ears, trying to blot out the pounding. It stopped abruptly. He took down his hands and it began anew.

It wasn't pounding, after all. It was ringing, or more precisely, "bleeping," because his phones didn't ring; they made otherworldly electronic sounds he called "bleeping." Edith used to call them "tinkling," and that always made him smile.

Edith *used* to. Edith *was*. Edith *had*. Edith in the past tense—from now on.

The phone kept bleeping and tinkling insistently. Roger rose unsteadily, walked across the room and grabbed the sleek, black high-tech phone near the bar.

"What?" he said.

"Roger?" a woman's voice said. There was a buzzing in the line and the sound of voices at a subliminal level, as if a radio station were interfering with the connection. Roger thought it was a religious station.

"Yes. What is it?"

"Oh, damn, I forgot about the time difference. I woke you up, didn't I?"

"Who is this?"

"Melissa Lewis. We met at Karen Wright's party in Seattle. Have you forgotten me already?"

A blur of women's faces rushed through Roger's mind, all of them dark and featureless, with different smears of color for hair. He remembered Melissa, yet he didn't.

Melissa.

The parade of faces stopped, and he fine-tuned one of them, adjusted the color of the hair, the sharpness of the features: the strawberry blond, Melissa. He'd just been thinking of her that afternoon, and yet he had difficulty recalling her face. Had the Scotch already obliterated that many brain cells?

"Of course," he said, suddenly aware he was mush-mouthed. He reached for a glass and managed to fill it with water from the bar sink. "The biographer." He swallowed a big gulp of water, then rinsed more around in his mouth.

"I'm sorry about calling at this late hour. I really didn't want to disturb you, but you said I could call."

"I know. You didn't disturb me. It's been a very disturbing day, however, for reasons you could never guess."

"Is something the matter?" Her voice was edged with what seemed to be genuine concern.

Roger told her about Edith.

"That's terrible," she said when he was finished. "Horrible. I don't know what to say. Is there anything I can do?"

"Nothing," Roger said. "Just like I can do nothing but sit here and—well, I tried to get drunk, but I didn't quite make it."

"What are you going to do?"

"I'm going to try to get drunk again, then hopefully I'll pass out for a couple of days. Of course, I'm cancelling the rest of my promotional tour. My work seems so stupid in the light of something like this. . . ."

"Don't judge yourself," Melissa said. "After all, it wasn't your fault."

"I feel like it was."

"That's just survivor's guilt. You'll see it differently in the morning."

"Maybe."

"Well, I won't keep you. This is a bad time—and bad timing for me. I'll—"

The phone suddenly went dead.

Roger shook his head sadly. Here he had needed human contact, and the telephone company couldn't keep a simple connection going for just a few seconds more. The subliminal radio voices persisted though, buzzing on the line with barely heard words about "sin and redemption" and "send your donation to. . . ."

He replaced the phone in its cradle and waited a few seconds for her to call back. He didn't know her number, and even if he did, he didn't think he could dial it without screwing it up.

The phone remained silent. No bleeping or tinkling. He reached for the bottle of Scotch. This time, he wouldn't stop until he was good and drunk and safely unconscious.

This time, he was successful.

At eleven the next morning, Roger rolled off the couch and landed on the floor. A pandemonium of noises was bouncing around the inside of his skull.

The phone was bleeping.

The doorbell was ringing.

The TV set was on.

Roger felt as if pieces of rock had been stuffed in his head. Each noise reverberated through his head, ricocheting off the rock, threatening to set off a major quake. He climbed up from the floor and picked up the phone. "Just a damn minute!" he screamed into it and set it down. He turned the TV off, wondering briefly when he had turned it on.

He went to the door, where he fumbled with the doorknob and deadbolt for several seconds before realizing he had blacked out without locking it at all, leaving himself vulnerable to the world. He pulled the door open at last and blinked several times at the person standing in the hall.

Melissa Lewis had arrived.

"Hi," she said cheerily. She was wearing a red blouse and white skirt. A large white leather handbag hung from her shoulder.

Roger just stared at her as if she weren't real, or perhaps too real. Somehow her bright outfit didn't seem quite right. Shouldn't she be dressed for a funeral? He now vaguely recalled their telephone conversation of the night before.

She smiled broadly. "You look like hell," she said. "Aren't you going to invite me in?"

Roger opened the door wider. "This is a surprise," he

said, watching her from behind as she walked across the parquet floor, her red satin high heels clicking briefly until she hit the carpet. "A real surprise." He rubbed his chin, felt two days' growth of beard and jerked his hand back, realizing he probably looked worse than hell—whatever that might be. "Have a seat," he said, hastily tucking in his shirt.

Melissa sat on the couch, crossed her legs and watched him with bright eyes. "Nice apartment."

"Thank you," he managed.

"May I say something?"

"I guess so," he said, closing the door and walking slowly over to the chair across from her, where he plopped down.

"You look like a real person today."

"What does that mean?" he asked, startled.

"I mean, the last time I saw you it was under strained conditions. You were 'on,' being a celebrity. Now you look like a grizzly bear who needs a shave and a bath and probably a tooth brush. You seem human."

"I've usually counted myself in the same species as the rest of mankind," he said, barely unable to keep from smiling. "Do you always evaluate people this way?"

"No." She seemed a little embarrassed. "But I feel I know you. After all, I *have* read every word you've ever written. I think if you had opened that door dressed in a suit and tie as if you were on your way to an afternoon tea, I would've turned and run."

"That would be a shame," he said, "but I'm sure I look more frightening this way."

She leaned back and tucked her hands over the back of the couch, causing her breasts to jut forward just enough to make Roger temporarily forget that he was depressed and make him wonder if the color of her hair was natural. Once again, he was struck by how much Melissa resembled the dream woman he had seen in the restaurant in Seattle.

"Did you know your phone's off the hook?"

"Damn," he said, pulling his eyes away from her

breasts. "The phone was bleeping when you rang the door bell. Let me see who it is."

"Bleeping?"

"I'll explain sometime."

He got up and picked up the phone. Whoever had been calling him had hung up. At least the line was clear this morning and no subliminal voices exhorted him to be saved.

"They couldn't wait, I guess." He returned to the chair. "So what are you doing here?" he asked.

"I took the first available flight."

"Why?"

"I knew this would be a hard time for you," she said. "I couldn't bear the idea of you suffering through this alone."

"What do you mean?"

"You know, because of Edith."

"Oh," he said guiltily. "Edith."

"She must have meant a lot to you. How long was she with you—three years?"

"Going on four." Did this woman know everything about him?

"I bet you feel all alone now."

"I guess I do."

He avoided her gaze and studied his hands, noticing there was a fresh cut on one of his fingers. It was still bleeding.

"How do you feel now?" she asked.

"My head feels about six sizes too big. The rest of me feels like I look."

"That's bad, indeed." She stood up abruptly. "What you need," she said, surprisingly Edith-like, "is a good breakfast and some aspirin. Why don't you go clean yourself up and I'll see what I can fix for you."

"You cook?"

"Of course." She headed for the kitchen without asking where it was, as if by instinct, or as if she had been there before. "I'm a damn good cook too."

Roger started to remark that he didn't expect such a

beautiful woman to need cooking skills, but it didn't seem appropriate at the moment and was probably sexist. Maybe later, when he knew her better.

He made his way back to the bathroom and began the arduous process of transforming himself from a wretch to a human being.

It didn't occur to him until he was shaving to wonder how Melissa had gotten past the building security system.

But then there were probably few barriers she couldn't pass. He could tell she was the type of woman who didn't take no for an answer.

He hoped she was the type who sometimes said yes. A pang of guilt assailed him briefly; then he realized Edith would forgive him his thoughts.

Good women understood things like that.

5. Funeral Attendance

The sun was shining, and a cool spring wind was blowing in from the lake, giving the air a crisp edge that was exhilarating, making people feel glad to be alive.

It was a fine Tuesday for a funeral.

In the small chapel at Stanton's Funeral Home in the northwest quadrant of the city, a skinny, gray man with deep-set dark brown eyes and a very wrinkled face conducted the service for Edith Wilkins. He was a minister-for-hire provided by the Stanton brothers. It was obvious that he had never known the deceased and that he was delivering a standard sermon, one that would serve for just about anyone with few changes, and those mostly in the pronouns. The man's voice, which was flat and monotone except when he pronounced the word "Jesus," was grating on the nerves. He had delivered this particular text perhaps one time too many, and it was evident that he was bored with it. He probably lacked the gumption to turn to a different page in his prayer manual.

Roger sat on the left side of the chapel with Melissa, shuddering; he could barely stand to look at the minister. He was such a thin, wasted-looking man that it seemed to him he should be the one in that closed coffin, not Edith.

Edith had been such a vital woman. It was an outrage that this moribund stranger should be talking about her at all. But Edith had not attended church regularly, never professed to believe in much of anything, so there was no minister who knew her. This rent-a-reverend was provided at the insistence of the immediate family—Edith's children and her brother—who didn't think a funeral was proper unless a man of the cloth was present to mumble pious words over the departed.

That was the main reason Roger had decided finally not to deliver a eulogy: He was being treated as an outcast by Edith's family, because, he realized scornfully, he was a somebody, and they were nobodies. Some people were threatened by success because it reflected on their own lack of it. Some were so threatened that their feelings ultimately became hate. The Wilkins clan was like that; they were of a snobbish type that would challenge a movie star to a fight in a bar, or ask for an outrageous favor from a celebrity to show their contempt for fame. One of them, Edith's brother, even had the audacity to taunt Roger with a snide reference to The Astounding One.

Well, Roger had no use for them, either. He couldn't understand—didn't want to understand—people who remained downtrodden, poor and unsuccessful, when success was within the reach of anyone who wanted to grab it. Mediocrity was always self-imposed in Roger's opinion; opportunities abounded in America, and only those who wished to be at the bottom of the social strata stayed there.

Hadn't he himself climbed up from near-poverty to a measure of fame no one else in his family had ever aspired to? Hadn't he shown the world that being born in the wrong family couldn't stop the man who was sure of himself and his convictions?

Yes, he had. But it didn't impress the Wilkins family. They even refused his offer to pay for the funeral, acting highly insulted, which was ridiculous because he knew they couldn't afford it. Edith's older son was a sales rep of some kind, who barely made his commissions, and her younger son was an auto mechanic, while her daughter was married to a minor executive with the telephone company. None of the other relatives, a brother, an ancient aunt and a doddering great-grand-something-or-other, could probably produce a hundred dollars among them.

Edith's friends were nice, though, mostly women she had known in her neighborhood, who showed up with husbands, most of whom looked uncomfortable in suits. They kept their distance; they didn't fawn on Roger or ask embarrassing questions; they knew their place. Their behavior almost made up for the boorishness of the Wilkins.

Roger wished he could have paid for the funeral; he certainly would have given Edith a better send-off than this shabby affair. Even the flowers smelled cheap and looked tawdry, except for the ones Roger had sent. If it weren't for Melissa at his side, providing much needed moral support, he might not have come at all—not to a place like this.

It reminded him too much of his father's funeral, which was another reason he couldn't deliver the eulogy.

Roger was nineteen. His father was fifty, taken by a heart attack. The family was poor, and the funeral was a morbid testament to that. Simon Kant lay in the cheapest casket available, and a rent-a-reverend conducted the service then, a portly man whose face bore all the marks of alcoholism, including a large, red, spider-veined nose.

Roger had to come home from college in the middle of February. He hadn't been home to witness his father's final hours. But there had been no lingering illness. Simon had keeled over in the backyard while shoveling snow out of the driveway, as he had done hundreds of times over the years. He was just clearing the way to get his car out of the garage, so that he could drive through the snow-clogged streets of South Bend, Indiana to the bakery where he worked.

He was dead before the ambulance was halfway to St. Joseph's Hospital.

The casket was open at his father's funeral. Roger stared at his father's profile all through the service, waiting for him to get up and start yelling about something—as he always did. Simon had been a man with many opinions about many things; he knew what was wrong and what was right—especially what was right, because he always said there was only one right way to do anything; everything else was bullshit.

That meant, from Simon's point of view, that about ninety-nine percent of the world was bullshit.

That's why there was a hired minister. Church and religion were in the ninety-nine percent, according to Simon. All churches wanted was money. And that, Simon said, just wasn't right.

That was his ultimate answer to everything: It just wasn't right.

It just wasn't right for colored kids to go to school with white kids. It just wasn't right for women to work. It just wasn't right for Republicans to be running the country. It just wasn't right to take charity. It just wasn't right to get a girl pregnant and not marry her.

It just wasn't right, Roger had thought, for a man to die when he was only fifty.

When the service was over, Roger went up to the casket with the others for a final look at his father. He was sickened by the way his father's face had been made up by the mortician. He looked so unreal, so unnatural.

It just wasn't right.

But Roger said nothing. He was only a boy in the eyes of the rest of the family. His opinions meant nothing to them. He just gritted his teeth and hugged the lifeless form of his father, as he was supposed to.

The day of the funeral wasn't a fine day. There was fresh snow on the ground, and the temperature was below twenty. The wind bit at the skin, making the graveside service unbearable. Fortunately, the fat hired minister made it brief.

The earth was too frozen for digging, so the casket was not lowered into the ground. It was left behind to be stored somewhere until the grave could be dug.

Roger remembered looking out the back window of the old Cadillac limousine provided for the family by the funeral parlor, watching the casket recede in his vision until it was no longer visible.

Then he had turned and noticed how red-faced his mother was. She was still crying, but her tears were no longer expressions of grief; he recognized them as angry tears. She was angry with the old man for dying and leaving her alone to fend for herself. Roger felt he should reach over and lay his hands on her shoulders, but his mother wasn't an affectionate person. She didn't like to be touched, especially when she was in a high-strung emotional state. She wouldn't appreciate a clumsy gesture of sympathy, even from her son.

Later, at the wake, Roger had sat in the corner of the small living room of his grandmother's house, listening to the old relatives from both sides of the family. They talked of how nice the service was and how good Simon had looked; and then they ran out of things to say about the funeral, and the conversation became a buzz of gossip.

Roger suddenly noticed how ugly they all were, and he felt unreal. These crippled, old, smelly, gross and crude people were related to him! He didn't want to be a part of this family anymore. He wanted to stand up and shout at them that they were uncaring bitches and bastards, but instead he withdrew into himself, vowing he would some day be away from all of them.

Then he heard his mother say, quietly to her sister, "What are we going to do? There's no money. . . ."

And he knew he had to give up his scholarship at Indiana University and come home and work to keep his mother and his brothers and sisters from starving to death until things got better somehow.

That was the right thing to do.

But it seemed so wrong.

Maybe that was why Roger had been unable to cry until that moment.

"Roger!"

He was gripping Melissa's left hand tightly, squeezing

it white. He looked down and let it go reluctantly.

"Sorry," he mumbled.

"It's okay," she whispered. "You have a right to feel bad. Let your feelings go, Roger. No one will mind."

"I'll be all right."

The gray man had finished the service. People were filing by the closed casket, pausing momentarily to glance at the framed photo of Edith on an easel among the flowers.

"Come on, Roger," Melissa said. "You have to pay your final respects."

Roger started to get up, then he glanced at Melissa helplessly. His face was a portrait of panic: His eyes were glassy, and he was sweating.

"I can't," he said pitifully.

"What do you mean?"

"I can't move."

"Roger, you have to move. It's over."

Roger looked around desperately. The parade of mourners, the closed casket, the gray reverend, and the atmosphere of despair were too much for him. He felt as if the walls would close in on him any minute. "I shouldn't have come. I shouldn't have."

"Let me help you."

"I can't move, damn it."

Melissa studied his face, like a nurse evaluating an unruly patient. Did he detect criticism in that look? Or was it concern? Her expression seemed almost maternal. But he didn't need mothering.

Her face became placid, and she reached over to pat his shoulder; then she massaged his neck so gently and so smoothly that Roger was sure no one could see her doing it. The touch of her hand, even through the gloves she wore, seemed to revitalize him; he could feel warmth radiating from her hand through his body, seeking out the frozen places and thawing them.

Then, as abruptly as it had come, the panic was gone. Roger found himself standing in line behind the others, walking slowly past the casket and the picture of Edith.

Outside, Roger stood under the awning, hovering near Melissa as the rest of the funeral attendees went to their cars. He noticed one of the old relatives was on crutches, and he quickly looked away, trembling.

Melissa squeezed his hand to reassure him, and his trembling subsided. "Are you ready?" she asked.

"We're not going to the cemetery."

"Of course we are. Roger, I don't understand you. Why are you acting this way?"

"I don't know. It's overwhelming. This whole funeral business—laying the dead to rest in a stupid ceremony with no meaning, especially with Edith—with the way she died—and no one brought to justice for it. Probably never will be. I can't go any farther. Just let me stay here until they all leave."

"You have to go."

"No, I don't. I don't have to do anything at all."

Melissa put her hands on his shoulders and regarded him sternly. "Edith was important to you. It doesn't matter that the other people here are unworthy of you—that they even envy and hate you. All that matters is that you are here for Edith and her memory. You'll hate yourself later if you don't go through with this to the end. You know that. Don't you?"

Roger's eyes seemed unable to focus on anything, especially Melissa. Her face, up close, no longer seemed pretty. Her features were harshened by the shadow of the awning, and she appeared older than she had before. What was she trying to do? She didn't know him well enough to talk to him this way—to treat him as a child. She didn't know him at all; she just thought she did, because she had read "every word" he had ever written, but of course that wasn't true, because she hadn't ever read the words written in his mind that never surfaced on paper—the words that he dared not express for fear of what the world would think—the words of dread, of panic, of despair that came to him in the middle of the night. She couldn't know that side of him; yet, in her eyes, in the set of her features now, he could see that maybe she did know that side, by intuition, by instinct, by some sixth sense that only women possessed, or by a magic not even the New Age thinkers could conjure with.

He was suddenly startled by Melissa's face, because he could see that it reflected his present thoughts. She knew exactly what he was thinking, as if she could plumb the depths of his very soul as easily as she might read the newspaper. That was frightening. No one had ever had that kind of power over him before. He wasn't sure he could accept it.

Her lips moved and words formed—soft, right, reassuring, sensible words: "You don't want *them*—those moronic people, those imbeciles, those representatives of the vast unwashed public—to think Roger Kant is a weakling, do you? Do you want them laughing at you, driving home tonight saying, 'What a wimp that Roger Kant is'? Roger, you're stronger than any of them, and that's what they resent in you. That's what scares them about you, because a strong man is a right man, and that means they're wrong, because they can never be as strong or as *right* as you are."

Roger realized with even more apprehension that Melissa was making sense—his kind of sense. He sighed heavily. "You're right. I owe it to Edith to be there, if only to show them up."

"That's the Roger Kant I know," Melissa said, smiling with satisfaction. "That's the Roger Kant I knew really existed when I read all your works."

"I'm ready now," he said, pulling her after him. "I'll even drive the car."

The procession to the cemetery was almost comical, Roger observed. It consisted of several Fords, Chevies, and Plymouths, followed by his crystal-green Volvo. The only common denominator among them was the funeral flags attached to their cars. He remembered his mother used to say that if you saw a funeral procession, somebody was going to die, and even when he was a boy, he thought how stupid that was, because obviously someone had already died or there wouldn't be a funeral. His mother was full of illogical superstitions.

As he drove, Roger glanced occasionally at Melissa. Her black dress, while certainly necessary for the occasion, seemed almost too funereal, and now he realized it was because she wore it too well, as if she were accustomed to attending funerals.

That bothered him, but at least he was no longer depressed. Melissa had talked him out of it with an expertise that seemed professional. That was disturbing too. He knew so little about her—only that she thought herself a potential journalist—and she seemed to know everything about him, even things no one *could* know.

Some people would consider that psychic ability.

He also felt uncomfortable about the way she had handled him back at the funeral parlor. On reflection, Roger wasn't certain he liked the way she had manipulated him, even if she was right about his having to see the funeral through to the end. She had basically told him what to do, even though she made it seem he had made the decision on his own.

Maybe a stern hand was what he needed at this time in his life. With Edith gone, he was directionless. He had no talent for taking care of details; he could forget the simplest things if left on his own. Maybe Melissa could help.

He reached over and patted her hand.

She responded by turning toward him and smiling hopefully. "It'll be over soon," she said.

He withdrew his hand. The open gates of the cemetery were only a few yards away. He guided the car through the gate and slowed down behind the other cars, inching toward the gravesite.

Why, he wondered, did funeral processions have to be so slow?

Hired pallbearers conveyed the box containing Edith's

remains to a platform next to the grave, which was discretely covered with a fake-grass carpet. The gray reverend spoke a few more meaningless words. Edith's relatives broke into showy tears.

Roger's own eyes were finally moist. He made sure they saw that. They needed to know he was as caring as they were.

The sun was still bright, making Roger's eyes ache. He wished he had brought his sunglasses, but he had left them on his dresser at home.

The wind picked up a little, causing the petals of the flowers to flutter.

Melissa moved closer to him, her body emanating increasing warmth.

The casket was lowered slowly into the grave.

The wind blew a little harder, chilling the skin, causing goose bumps to rise on Roger's flesh.

Melissa's hand brushed against his. It was a gesture of support, telling him there were only seconds of the ordeal left.

A soft chuffing noise was heard as the casket hit bottom. Then the mourners started to turn away, heading toward their cars.

Roger remained. He wanted a few seconds alone with Edith before the dirt was filled in. He wished he could talk to her.

Now the wind was downright cold. Lake Michigan was making itself felt.

A wreath of flowers fell over.

The wind grew colder still and blew harder as more flowers tumbled over and trailed across the expanse of unnaturally green turf.

Roger squirmed, yet Melissa seemed oblivious to the sudden temperature drop. She just waited patiently for him to decide to leave.

He started to turn, but he couldn't.

There was something hovering over Edith's grave.

At first, he thought it was only an effect of the wind, a swirl of leaves and flowers caught in a strange formation that just seemed to resemble the face of . . .

Ice was forming in Roger's veins.

. . . the face of the demon he had seen in his dream in Seattle.

It was imagination of course. It had to be! But then the demon's face gathered more substance and it spoke, and the words resounded in Roger's head, clearly enunciated:

"I did this to your Edith!"

The demon's maw opened, and blood seemed to ooze down its fangs. Its eyes were black orbs with tiny yellow slits that bore into Roger's own eyes, piercing him to the core.

"Melissa!"

"What?"

"Melissa, look!" He could barely raise his hand to point. "Melissa—"

He collapsed, falling to the ground at the edge of the grave. His head seemed to be pressed against the earth by a tremendous force. He struggled to lift his face, and when he did, he was peering into the grave—into endless darkness, for there was no coffin there, only blackness as if the grave penetrated the depths of the earth. It threatened to swallow him. He clawed at the earth around the grave, trying to push himself away, but the force held him down. He looked up and saw the demon's hovering face once more. Then he smelled its breath.

"Roger!" Melissa screamed.

Roger couldn't hear her. He had passed out.

A cool compress rested on Roger's forehead. He blinked and finally focused on Melissa's kind face.

"I see you're back among the living," she said. "You had me so worried."

He glanced around warily, checking his surroundings. Somehow he was in his apartment where he belonged, lying safely on his own bed with Melissa sitting on the edge tending to him. He noticed she had changed clothes and was wearing an ivory skirt and mauve blouse.

"How did I get here?"

"I brought you."

"What happened?"

"You don't remember?"

"No," he said, even though he recalled every detail of his experience very clearly. He wanted to hear what she would say.

"You swooned. Yes, that's the right word. You swooned, and I thought maybe it was the heat. One of the men helped me get you to the car. I knew you'd be okay once you were back home."

"The heat?"

"It was rather uncomfortable today, don't you think? I thought Chicago was cooler this time of year."

He frowned, hardly believing what she was saying. That didn't gibe with what he had observed. Had she really not noticed the wind? Or was the wind another product of his imagination—like the demon?

The demon—she certainly hadn't seen that. If she had, he would doubt her sanity too. Only he had seen the awful apparition—because his mind was deteriorating.

But Melissa was supposed to be level-headed. Why hadn't she called a doctor or taken him to an emergency room? Either course of action would seem more logical than dragging him back here. How had she managed to get him up to his bedroom?

She removed the compress from his forehead and patted his skin dry with another cloth. Then she reached out and traced the scar on his left cheek with her finger. Her touch was light, but it gave him the shivers. He had never let anyone touch the scar before.

"You'll have to tell me how you got this someday. It's very distinguished looking—like the dueling scars the Germans used to boast about."

"I don't want to talk about it," he said sullenly.

"Okay." She removed her hand slowly. "Someday will be fine."

Suddenly he was irritated by Melissa's presence. She was acting cute, and he hated that in a woman. He wanted straight answers. He was going to ask the questions; but when he tried to sit up in the bed, dull, immobilizing pain cramped every muscle in his body, and his head seemed about to explode.

"Don't try to get up," Melissa said. "You hurt yourself when you fell, but it's minor. You rest for a while. I'll get you some food."

"I'm not hungry." He fell back against his pillow. The pain in his body lessened somewhat, but his head still ached.

"Well, you will be later. It's been hard on you these last few days. You pushed yourself to your limit. That's all. I'll fix you a Scotch and water, for now, if you like—a weak one."

"That might take the edge off," he said grudgingly. He looked down at himself and realized he was in pajamas. "Did you undress me too?"

She smiled by way of answering. "Don't fuss so much."

"But I—" He looked at his watch and saw it was nearly eight o'clock. He had been out for several hours. What had happened during all that time? His eyes sought hers, but the questions still wouldn't come to his lips. Maybe he didn't want to know the answers—just yet. Maybe she was right. He needed a little Scotch, some rest and some pampering.

Melissa arose and started out of the room. "I'll get you the Scotch, but you must promise to eat something substantial later. Okay?"

He nodded and almost said, "Yes, Mother."

She paused at the door and turned back, looking at him with concern, then said matter-of-factly, "Maybe it would be better if I stayed here for a couple of days." She waited two beats, then added, "Yes, I think that would work out just fine."

Before Roger could reply, she had gone into the other room. It occurred to him she hadn't asked him if she could stay.

She had told him.

6. RESOLVE

Roger pulled himself out of bed slowly, testing and flexing his body, expecting pain but feeling none. A good night's rest had restored him almost to full vitality.

He yawned. His mouth tasted like stale Scotch and even staler food, though he couldn't remember when he had eaten last. He didn't remember much of anything about the day before, except for the funeral and the bad feelings and experiences connected with it. Those he was suppressing—with some effort.

His pajamas stank of sweat. He needed a shower and shave and a strong cup of coffee. Disoriented, he stumbled out into the hall and started for the bathroom, but halted abruptly as he heard the sound of papers rustling. It was a faint sound, but he was sure that's what it was.

He turned and walked slowly toward his study. He pushed the door open and stepped in, then glanced to his right. The door to Edith's office, the small room adjacent to his study, was ajar, and a light was on in there.

He hadn't been in his study or near Edith's office since he had learned of her death. Now he heard the sounds of movement—and the source of the paper rustling—coming from there. He approached slowly, his heart beating rapidly, as if he expected to see a ghost in her office.

That was absurd because he had spent a lifetime not believing in ghosts.

"Bullshit," he muttered, and kicked the door open all

the way, then stared speechlessly at what he saw.

Melissa was sitting at Edith's desk. She was wearing a lavender robe, barely closed in front, and Roger couldn't decide whether that or the fact she was in Edith's place was more disturbing.

Perhaps "disrupting" was more apt, because Melissa wasn't just sitting there. She had changed things around. A lot. The mementos that had made the office Edith's—framed photos of her children, little stuffed animals, potted plants, and other personal memorabilia—had all been removed. They rested in a box in the corner, apparently designated as discards by the young woman who turned her face up now to Roger and smiled broadly.

"Good morning," she said brightly.

Now he recalled that she had told him she was going to move in. She hadn't meant it, had she? Women didn't just come and stay without an invitation. Did they? Were younger women really that much bolder than women of his own generation?

Apparently so. Her smile was as open and ingenuous as that of a little girl, but the fact remained she was in Edith's place. That was a violation of the way things were supposed to be; it was going too far.

"What are you doing in—here?" he said with barely disguised anger.

"Don't be mad at me, Roger. I'm just trying to help. There are letters to answer, calls to return, things to explain. I've been busy since seven o'clock this morning trying to get things in order."

"But this is—was—Edith's office." There was a tremor in his voice.

"I know that. But Edith certainly wouldn't want things to go to hell like they've been the last few days. I could tell by the way she had things organized that she was a very efficient person who took care of all the details for you."

"What could you tell by removing her things?"

"I was afraid they would be painful reminders of her—for you. I was going to store them somewhere. Her family will probably want them anyhow. I didn't mean to upset you."

"But it's too soon."

"Roger, the world hasn't stopped. You have things to do. This may sound cruel, but we can't make Edith come back by letting your work slide. Your work is important. Very important."

"I don't give a damn about my work right now."

"No, but in a couple of days, you'll begin to miss it, and I want to be ready for that."

She reached across the desk for an appointment book, her action causing the robe to gape open just enough for Roger to see half of her left breast. He tried not to look, but there it was.

Melissa apparently didn't care. The robe fell closed as she placed the appointment book before her and scanned a few pages. "Your promotional tour is pretty tight, I'm afraid. But if you cancel one date—in Cleveland—you can catch up. Then maybe you can reschedule Cleveland at a later date."

"What the hell are you talking about? I told you I'm cancelling the whole thing."

"You didn't mean that, and you know it."

"I know what I mean."

"Roger, do you really want to jeopardize the success of your new book? Edith would want you to go on with your career." She took a pen and made a check mark in the book. "I feel that."

"Goddamn it, I don't care what you 'feel.' I've made up my mind."

Melissa pushed herself away from the desk, came over and stood in front of him. He was distracted by her approach, unable to sustain his anger because of the way she moved, the way the satiny fabric of the robe seemed to flow with her body's curves, and the way this possibly choreographed walk seemed to hint at fathomless sensuality.

"Please, Roger," she said firmly, "I don't want any unpleasantness between us. I just want to take care of you. If you really want to cancel the tour, then of course I'll abide by your wishes. But I think you're making a mistake. Won't you at least say you'll think it over?"

Her closeness, the morning scent of her, the sparkle of youth in her eyes, all conspired to make him light-headed. He was fiercely aware of the thinness of cloth separating her flesh from his. A quick movement and his hand could be inside the folds of lavender, touching the satin skin beneath, fondling what he had barely glimpsed. Surely she must know what effect she was having on him. Was she using it deliberately to manipulate him, or, even worse, to intimidate him? Either way, he disliked being told what to do.

She touched his cheek coyly. "Will you think it over?"

"No."

"That's not much to ask."

He had to yield a little, if only to escape the implicit danger, the unspoken seduction, in her nearness.

"All right," he said gruffly, trying to show he was in charge, though it was obvious he wasn't. "I'll think it over."

"That's all I need to know," she said. "Now go clean up and I'll fix you a man-sized breakfast."

He started to say he didn't want her to fix him breakfast, that he wanted her out of his life, that he was his own man, and Edith had never manipulated him with her sex, never even tried, and that he hadn't agreed to let her stay, but he could voice none of these things. All he could do was break away from her as quickly as possible, before he acted in a way that was certain to render him totally powerless in her presence—forever.

He rushed through the study and down the hall to the bathroom.

For once in his life, he truly needed a cold shower.

After he was dressed, Roger poked his head out of the bedroom door. He didn't hear any sounds nearby, so he peeked into the room Melissa had taken, the guest room across from his bedroom.

She wasn't there. He saw two rather large suitcases on the floor, and a briefcase and a tape recorder on top of the dresser. A slip and bra lay on the edge of the bed, which was otherwise neatly made-up. He was tempted to go through her belongings, to search for something that would verify her identity—something that would indicate she was what she said she was and nothing else. He had seen no credentials she was genuine; no proof had been offered. All he knew was her face and the shape of her body. Though there were indications she was highly intelligent, she was otherwise a stranger to him.

All he had to do was open the briefcase. It probably wasn't even locked, because Melissa was so open and trusting. She would never think he would go through her personal belongings.

But he couldn't bring himself to do it. It was risky, and he simply wasn't that kind of sneak. He blushed as he backed out of the room, suddenly feeling like a retreating voyeur.

He closed the door softly and made his way to the kitchen, drawn there by the aroma of freshly brewed coffee.

Melissa was at the stove turning sausage links with a pair of tongs. She gestured to the breakfast nook, where a plate of steaming scrambled eggs and two hot English muffins smeared with butter and grape jam awaited him. "Sausage coming up," she said. "Have a seat, monsieur, and I'll serve *le petit dejeuner.*"

Roger crossed the room without a word and sat down. "Smells good," he admitted. Edith had never cooked for him. That wasn't part of her job description. She had only made coffee. Having food prepared for him by a woman was an experience he hadn't had since his last marriage. Of course, Sandra was a terrible cook.

"Monsieur is too kind," Melissa said, placing the sausages on a small dish and setting it before him. Then she poured two cups of coffee and sat down across from him. "Well, have at it, monsieur, before it gets cold."

Roger picked up a fork and stabbed a wad of eggs. He was all ready to say something negative, but as he chewed, he realized she had spiced the eggs exactly the way he liked them—with only a little salt and a sprinkle of pepper.

How could she know how he liked his eggs?

"It's good," he said, filing the question away with all the other questions he had about this strange young woman.

"Merci." She had changed into something more modest—a plain white blouse and blue skirt. It seemed that whatever she wore, however, was imprinted with her constant sensuality; she couldn't look plain if she tried, which she probably never did.

"Aren't you going to eat?" he asked, grabbing an English muffin and biting into it.

"I had something already."

Roger finished the meal quickly. He hadn't realized how hungry he was. He pushed the empty plate away and sipped at his coffee which was the proper strength and sweetened exactly as he would have done it himself. This meal was perfect—absolutely—and that bothered him on one level, but on another level, it couldn't help but make him feel more appreciative of her presence. His mood was approaching mellow, but he couldn't resist making at least one inquiry.

"May I ask you something personal?" he said, fixing his eyes on hers.

"Go ahead."

"What is a girl with your looks and your obvious culinary talents doing in an apartment with an old fart like me?"

Melissa seemed startled by his directness, but she recovered quickly. "Why, I'm going to write your life story. Besides," she said, gathering the dirty dishes and rising, "I like old farts."

By Friday, Melissa was comfortably settled in, and Roger was adjusting. He had ceased filing questions away to ask her, had decided merely to accept her at face value. He knew it was good for him not to be alone at this strained time in his life, and while Melissa was not exactly the same as Edith, she was almost as efficient. She screened his calls, answered his correspondence, seeming to know instinctively what was important and what was not, and generally ran the business end of his career with only a modicum of direction from him.

Melissa did all the shopping and cooked all the meals. She helped Roger remember to shave, bandaged him when he cut himself, and nursed him when he bumped his knees or shins, which he did frequently. She stayed up with him while he watched the late news, and went to bed each night promptly at eleven-thirty. Then she was up promptly at seven, working away in the office. Since the other day, however, he had not seen her partially dressed. That initial sexual ploy—using the revealing robe to tantalize and control him—had not been tried again. Perhaps it had been only a test to see what he would do. Perhaps she had been testing herself as well.

She was a wonder woman in Roger's mind, always fresh and virtually indefatigable. Always ready to do anything he asked. She didn't even have any bad habits. She didn't smoke, drank only moderately, and didn't listen to the radio while she worked. There were only a couple of things about her that disturbed him. One was her appearance; but she couldn't be held accountable for her beauty, and he could learn to live with it. The other was her insistence that he resume his promotional tour.

He was remaining steadfast on that issue. He had no desire to roam among strangers right now. The condition of his mind was too unpredictable. While he hadn't had any strange dreams or "visions" the last two nights, he was still wary, and as long as he was in the comfort of his own environment, he figured he could avoid any further incidents. He'd confront the outside world when he was good and ready.

Otherwise, he was back in the flow of his work, dictating letters, talking to important people on the phone, and doing research on various matters that might collect into a book later. He kept overflowing files of clippings that related to things psychic, Fortean and merely odd—anything that might provide an opportunity for him to disprove a cherished New Age myth. The latter part of the 1980's had been a time of renewed interest in the occult: in astrology, in the Tarot, in the *I Ching*, the pendulum, and other so-called oracles; in faith-healing and herbal medicine; and in just about all things mystic, psychic and pseudo-religious. The nineties promised to be just as absurd, and that meant plenty of opportunities for him.

Perhaps, Roger often reflected, it was because the world was approaching the end of a millennium. People had gone generally crazy around the year 1000 as well, expecting the world to end, expecting the return of Christ, making fools of themselves with mysticism, magic, religion and other quackery. He wondered if those people had had their Roger Kants—their voices of reason—as well.

If so, they probably burned such people at the stake.

Saturday afternoon, Roger was alone in the apartment. Melissa had gone to a sale at Marshall Field's; she seemed to have a lot of money to spend. He was taking a break, listening to Count Basie on his stereo. Most men his age still listened to rock'n roll, especially oldies, but Roger considered wallowing in the music of one's youth a sign of retarded mental development. He had recently acquired a taste for older jazz, however, which wasn't of his youth, but of his father's generation, and therefore historical, not nostalgic. Count Basie, Duke Ellington, Ella Fitzgerald and others from that simpler time of music and life often soothed him. They might have had their superstitions but they didn't identify with satanic cults as some rock groups did, and they certainly didn't sing ideological anthems or paeans to sex. They sought to entertain people on the most basic level, for the pure joy of it.

The drapes were open on his vista of the world, generating that familiar feeling of majesty in him. He sat back in his chair, listening to "One O'Clock Jump," letting the music ripple through his body, relaxing the tense muscles, massaging his inner soul.

A small noise intruded on the music.

Roger ignored it. Probably the refrigerator humming or something equally mundane.

The next cut on the compact disc was "The Basie Boogie." Roger closed his eyes for this one, his favorite.

Again an intrusion: a crinkling sound, like tinfoil being wrinkled. Again, Roger ignored it.

The boogie kept rippling through him.

There was a crash in the kitchen.

Roger jumped up. "Melissa?"

He hadn't heard her come in. He pushed pause on the CD player and went to investigate.

The silverware drawer in the kitchen had exploded. Spoons, knives and forks had shot across the floor. They lay at his feet in a jagged jumble.

Roger cringed involuntarily. A chill bit the base of his spine. He bent down and touched the silverware. It was cool and hard to the touch.

It was real.

He turned his head from side to side, looking for something, anything, that might suggest how this had happened. He approached the place where the drawer had been and looked inside. Then, steeling himself for the touch of a rodent or something equally repulsive—yet logical—he peered into the opening and felt around. Nothing.

He picked up the empty drawer, which he found leaning against the front of the refrigerator, and started to gather up the silverware: knives, forks, spoons.

He dropped the spoons as if they were red hot. They were all bent at weird angles, as if Uri Geller had had a spoon-bending party in his kitchen.

Roger dropped everything and ran from the room, a gurgling sound of anguish caught in his throat.

As he turned the corner, he tripped over the edge of the rug and fell at Melissa's feet.

She looked down at him quizzically, then set her shopping bags aside and knelt beside him.

"What's the matter, Roger?"

"The kitchen," he whispered. "Spoons."

"I don't understand."

"Go see for yourself!"

She shook her head in dismay and strode toward the kitchen. Roger got to his feet and followed her.

Everything was in order, nothing out of place.

"I still don't understand," Melissa said.

Roger went to the drawer and pulled it out halfway. All the silverware was in place. The spoons were straight. He touched one and it felt very ordinary. There were no signs of tampering.

"Roger?"

He told her what happened.

"That's another sign," she said when he was finished speaking.

"Another sign of what?"

The two of them sat on the couch. She was holding his hand, patting it occasionally, offering comfort.

"Another sign that you should continue your tour."

"How can you possibly expect me to . . . ?"

"You're back working again—a little. I see some spark in you, but I also see bad signs: your refusal to go out, your willingness to become a recluse buried in newspaper clippings. You're like a rat in a cage, running around on a little wire wheel, going nowhere. Your mind is stagnating."

"I'm happy. . . ." he began.

"You're not happy at all. You need contact with the public. I could see that in Seattle. Whether you admit it or not, the public part of your life is as important as the writing. Maybe more so. It feeds your ego, keeps you going. Isn't that so?"

"I suppose."

"Of course it is. That's why you imagine strange things

happening to you—why you have weird dreams and have to drink yourself to sleep. Half of your life is missing. You say you're mourning over Edith, but I know that's not what's really bothering you. You're mourning over not being Roger Kant the way he's supposed to be. You're hiding out here, like a child, thinking the boogie man will go away if you just ignore him."

"I am not hiding out."

"What do you call it, then?"

"Doing research," he replied weakly.

"Very convincing, Roger."

He looked away from her, shame-faced. He was confused and felt very vulnerable. He shouldn't have told her about the vision of bent spoons because it had given her a weapon to use against him. It was a sign of weakness—of the mind's continued deterioration. But in his heart, he knew Melissa was right about his continuing on the tour. She might even be right about his present hermitlike existence aggravating his mental condition instead of helping it.

He did miss the interaction with the crazy, unwashed masses, and he especially missed demonstrating to them how they were being hoodwinked and how he was among the few that could show them the truth. He missed all of that, but how could he admit that to Melissa without seeming a complete idiot?

He turned to face her again. Her expression was a mixture of disappointment and disapproval. Her eyes were intense as she waited for an answer from him, and a great deal depended on his saying the right thing; it was ultimatum time. The wrong answer would make her leave, and he realized suddenly he didn't want her to go—just yet. He was growing accustomed to her. He feared, however, he might begin to *need* her, and that was another matter entirely. Need led to dependence, and dependence set a person up for manipulation, and worse.

But the sun was shining through the window now, bathing Melissa's wonderfully red hair in shimmering highlights. He wanted to run his fingers through those highlights and feel the energy that must be there.

Was he denying himself the presence of this woman merely so he could be always right?

That was painful to contemplate. If he were left alone again, so soon after Edith's death, so soon after all the other things that had been happening to him lately, he might lose control of himself entirely and go insane. Melissa's being gone only a few hours had brought on another attack—if that was the right word. How much would he have to endure if she were out of his life? He had no one else to turn to right now.

"All right," he said rather dismally. "I'll go. But I reserve the right to cancel at any time."

"Oh, Roger!" She hugged him impulsively. "You've made the right decision. I just know it. You'll feel so much better."

He marveled at how she made it seem he had made the decision on his own. But he didn't care. The hug made up for loss of face and not being entirely right.

"I'll be coming along, of course," she said thoughtfully. "This will be the perfect beginning of my project—my book about you. And don't you worry, I'll pay my own way."

She got up and hurried toward the study. "We have so much to do. I'll have to call the airlines and reconfirm with the hotel and—but don't you worry, Roger. I can handle it."

As she disappeared around the corner, Roger nodded affirmation to her last statement. She could handle it all right; she could handle anything. There was no doubt in his mind about that.

He was briefly puzzled by something Melissa had said—something she knew about him but shouldn't—but now he couldn't recall what it was. He sighed and turned the stereo on again.

"The Basie Boogie" filled the room, washing away his doubts and fears.

7. Rain

It was raining when the plane set down in Indianapolis International Airport. It was a dark, cold, gloomy rain, of a type that seemed to fall only on Indianapolis in the spring and early summer. It chilled the bones and set the mood for depression and general malaise.

Roger didn't need the rain to be depressed. He had felt that condition creeping up on him that morning as soon as he awakened, and no amount of cheerful cajolery on Melissa's part had been able to bring him out of it. Despite all her assurances, and despite his own mental resolve to make the best of things, Roger was dreading the prospect of facing the public again. It was as if he had been hiding away from the world for years, not just a few days.

He couldn't shake the feeling that something awful was going to happen, though there was no reason for anything to go wrong; he knew that on the rational level. Everything had been planned in great detail. Melissa had prepared a schedule that was exacting down to the minutes required for meals and rest between appearances. There could be no problems, unless they were caused by divine intervention.

That's what Roger finally determined might happen: He would be zapped by the hand of God en route to Indianapolis. Flying over a storm which caused the plane to drop abruptly and bump like an old bus going over potholes was sufficient indication that God had something up His sleeve.

Roger had decided long ago that he believed in God. It was a difficult decision for him to make, since it went against his nature to believe in anything, especially since most of the people who had taken it on themselves to be God's representatives were dullards, fools and charlatans. He had finally learned to look past these people and their posturing and contemplate the nature of the universe on his own. So he at last came to the conclusion that something must be responsible for the creation of reality and the props that made it convincing, and that something might as well be called God.

The deity Roger believed in was a God tailored especially to fit his own particular rules of rightness and rationality, a God who, if He existed, would believe in Roger and his work. It seemed only right to him that belief in deities should be reciprocal, and it made his public statements that he believed in God very sincere—perhaps more sincere than anyone could imagine.

But occasionally, the Old Testament God poked his hoary head into Roger's private concept, making him feel guilty or scared during times of stress. Roger knew the concept of a vengeful God was an idea he had acquired by osmosis—as a result of the pseudo-religious society he lived in and the constant stream of pious bromides his mother had uttered through the years—and that such a concept made no logical sense within his general belief system; but he just couldn't totally cast out the old God. One had to believe in something when riding in a metal cage through the sky—God, the devil, or at the very least, the tooth fairy.

Especially on a day like this.

But God hadn't zapped the plane. The landing was a bit jerky, but it didn't raise the hairs on the nape of Roger's neck. He felt safe. He had arrived intact.

Melissa squeezed his hand and said softly, "We made it just fine, Roger. It won't be long to showtime."

"Sure," he said, "time to entertain the heathens."

She didn't reply and retrieved her briefcase from under

the seat. Roger stood and took his leather tote bag out of the overhead compartment, and the two of them joined the line of passengers filing out of the plane.

After they claimed their luggage, Roger started toward the exit doors.

"Where are you going?" Melissa asked.

"To get a cab."

"Cab? I've got a rental car reserved."

"I don't know this town well enough to drive it," he said, struggling to keep up with her brisk pace as she headed for the Avis counter.

"I do. I've been here several times. Indianapolis is easy to drive in. Nothing like Chicago or Boston, or, God forbid, New York."

"I suppose you've driven in Boston and New York too."

"I've driven everywhere," she said simply, as if he should have known without asking. "And my sense of direction is flawless, so you don't have to worry about getting lost. A couple of lectures, an autograph or two, and you'll be your old self again. So 'Don't worry. Be happy,' as the song says."

"Sure. I'm happy, Melissa. Very happy." He forced a mock smile, all teeth, that resembled the frozen smile of Mr. Sardonicus. "See?"

"Smile like that and they'll put you in the funny farm."

They both laughed.

The rental car was a light-blue Buick that still smelled new and had only four hundred miles on the odometer. It handled well on the slick, wet streets of Indianapolis.

Melissa maneuvered the car through the rain with expertise, and she did indeed seem to know exactly how to get where they were going without consulting a map or stopping to ask directions. She took the Airport Expressway to Interstate 465, then dropped south to I-70 and followed it to the downtown area. They came to a maze of interconnecting highways and cloverleafs which Roger thought would certainly confuse his redheaded chauffeur, but Melissa proved her mettle once again, guiding the Buick from one lane to another without pausing to consider which lane was correct. She didn't glance up at the green-and-white direction signs even once.

Soon they came to the Meridian Street exit off I-65. Melissa turned north and drove straight up the street to the Sheraton Meridian. She pulled up under the carport out front and let Roger out, then waited impatiently for the bellboy to take their luggage in. Then she got back in the car and parked it in the big lot out front herself.

Roger stood inside the front entrance, waiting for her. He glanced around the lobby. This was an old building, much different from the Sheraton in Seattle. Sometimes, though, the older hotels had a certain charm that made up for the lack of modern amenities.

He watched as Melissa locked the car, then sprinted across the parking lot to the steps that led up to the front. She pushed her way in without allowing the door attendant to hold the door for her.

"Well," she said, wiping rain from her brow, "what do you think of this place?" Even soaking wet, she maintained her poise; most women would complain. But then most women Roger had known looked like drowned cats when they were wet, not like a *Playboy* model greased for action.

"Not bad, I guess. Nothing like Seattle."

"This used to be a Stouffer's Inn a few years back."

"How do you know that?"

She looked blank a few seconds. "I don't know. I have this knack for picking up trivia wherever I go. I've been here before."

"When was that?"

"I don't remember right now. It must have been for a convention or something."

Roger wasn't satisfied with that answer, but he was too depressed to pursue the matter. It took quite a bit of energy to maintain a good bout of depression, and he didn't want to waste it on trivial concerns.

She waited a beat to see if he would press the issue. When he didn't, she straightened herself up and led the way to the front desk. "Let's check in. I want to get out of these wet clothes."

Melissa handled the details of getting their keys and having the luggage conveyed to their adjoining rooms. She suggested they take no more than half an hour to freshen up.

"You have a book-signing at four o'clock," she told him. "So don't dawdle."

Roger showered and lay on the bed for a few minutes. He suddenly felt different, and when he analyzed it, he realized it was because he wasn't quite as depressed as he had been earlier. Melissa—with her youthful enthusiasm and constant surprises—had drained much of the depression off. She possessed a talent for changing his moods for him, which he had not encountered in a woman before. None of his previous wives—or lovers—had ever developed that ability. If anything they tended to aggravate his bad moods, doing exactly the wrong things at the wrong time.

Maybe Melissa's ability was due to her having a personality that was so totally different from any woman he had known. Yet she resembled each of his three wives physically in one way or another; she had Wanda's complexion, Sheila's red hair, and Sandra's body—which were the attributes that he had admired the most in each of those women but she had them all without the accompanying nastiness each of his wives eventually developed. Could it be that Melissa somehow knew that she was an amalgam of the best components of the other women in his life?

She seemed to know so many things about him. She could probably tell him his weight and height to the most exact measurement and what sign he was born under and what significance it had. (He was a Gemini, but would inevitably lie to an astrologer, just so he could scoff at the horoscopes they cast for him using the wrong information.)

Statistics were a matter of record—a peek at his driver's license would tell her a great deal—but Melissa knew intimate things about him that most of his wives had not really known, and it was beginning to bother him. He was beginning to feel figuratively naked in her presence, and vulnerable.

But vulnerable to what?

That was the ultimate question, and, he admitted ruefully, he knew the answer to that one: vulnerable to her—to Melissa. He couldn't allow that to happen.

Yet he was allowing her to lead him around like a puppy. Her manner exceeded the efficiency Edith had demonstrated. Melissa seemed to be demanding excellence of him, while Edith had just quietly expected it.

It wasn't right. . . .

He smiled to himself, realizing the true source of his feelings: his father's list of rights and wrongs. And, knowing that, his fear of being threatened revealed itself as the old-fashioned foolishness it really was and suddenly dissipated.

He sat up and viewed the skyline of Indianapolis from his tenth-floor vantage point and decided it didn't look that bad, after all. Despite the steady downpour and a dark sky that promised even more rain, there was something uplifting about the view. It didn't seem like all the other cities he had been in before. Perhaps, he reflected, it was because he wasn't alone this time. Melissa was right next door, ready to take care of him in just about any way he desired.

As if to underscore his thoughts, Melissa picked that moment to bang on the door that separated their rooms. "Hey, in there, slow poke, are you ready yet?"

"I'll be dressed in a minute," he said. Melissa hadn't allowed time for introspection in her schedule. He'd have to tell her about that.

But not now. He hurriedly put on his clothes and met her in the hall five minutes later. She looked him over, pronounced him "distinguished-looking" and started toward the elevator.

She was wearing a white blouse and flowered skirt, making her appear to be a middle-class housewife about to go out shopping. He had never seen her look so plain.

"Why the subdued clothes?" he asked.

"I don't want to draw attention to myself."

"Why?" he asked while they waited for the elevator. "Are you wanted in this state?"

"Not that I know of," she said.

He looked at her as if she might be serious. He wouldn't be surprised if she were.

"You're the star," she explained. "I'll just blend into the background and let you be yourself. But I'll be close by if you need me."

"You think of everything, don't you?"

"I try," she said as the elevator arrived. "The only thing I forgot was an umbrella."

Melissa again showed her knowledge of the city by driving to Borders Book Shop, the most upscale bookstore in Indianapolis, without once faltering. As they approached their destination, the wind blew harder and rain pounded on the car, reducing visibility to almost zero, but that slowed her down only slightly. She showed no fear of skidding or sliding, seeming to know the limits of the car by instinct. Roger was impressed. He was skittish about driving in rain or snow and usually avoided either type of travel whenever he could.

The most incredible part about Melissa's driving was that Roger wasn't frightened by it, even though he usually hated being driven anywhere by a woman—it made him nervous. But Melissa's sense of direction and control made him almost feel like relaxing.

Borders was located in a massive shopping complex in

the northeastern corner of the city, made up of Castleton Square and various smaller strip malls, all of which had "Castleton" in their name. The bookstore was on Castleton Corner Lane. Melissa drove right to it as if she had been there countless times before.

She parked as close to the door as possible, but she and Roger still were half-soaked before they reached the entrance. They stood inside a few seconds, recovering from the onslaught of Indianapolis spring.

"Amazing," he said.

"What?"

"The way you did that. I never could've gotten here that way."

"No, it wasn't amazing," she said, smiling mischievously. "It was 'astounding.'"

Roger grimaced. "Ouch."

After she caught her breath, Melissa turned her head from side to side curiously. Then she pressed her face against the glass of the inner doors and turned back to him with a frown. "This is weird."

"What?" Roger asked, still shivering.

"No sign."

"No sign of what?"

"No sign saying 'Autograph Session with the great Roger Kant' or something like that."

"They don't always put up banners, you know."

"They should have. I specifically requested a special sign last week."

Before he could ask her how far in advance she had made the request, she was through the second set of doors, striding purposefully toward the center register. Roger followed her sheepishly, fearful she would make a big scene, which might do more harm to his career than good.

As he approached the counter, he could hear Melissa speaking harshly to a young man who seemed ignorant of anything that might have happened within the last decade.

"I want to see the manager," Melissa said finally.

"All right, ma'am," the young man said. "I'll get her."

He disappeared into the back of the store.

"What's wrong?" Roger asked, coming up beside her.

"Nobody seems to know anything about your autograph session. They're not set up at all."

"Are you sure this is the right place?"

"This is the only Borders in town. The manager's coming—maybe we'll get this straightened out now."

The manager was a slender brunette woman who seemed too young to be managing anything. However, she was not intimidated by Melissa's wrath.

"The books never arrived," she said simply. "So we assumed your session was cancelled."

"What do you mean they didn't arrive?"

"We've had a case ordered for a month, but I looked in the computer on Friday, and the order had been cancelled. I'm not sure by whom, but I thought it was probably done because there wasn't going to be a signing party here."

"Damn it," Melissa said. "What are we supposed to do now?"

The manager put on a help-the-customer expression. "I could set up a table with the books we have. We did receive five copies of the new book, and we have a few of Mr. Kant's previous works. Would that be okay?"

"Only five copies! Why would you order so few in the first place?"

"We don't get much call for Mr. Kant's books in this area. Frankly—" She stopped as she seemed finally to recognize "Mr. Kant" standing right next to Melissa. "Well," she stammered at last, "no offense, Mr. Kant, but this is Indiana, not New York, and we don't sell that many of your books."

Roger gave her a withering look. "My books sell well everywhere," he said haughtily.

"Not here, I'm afraid," she replied calmly. "Maybe it's our particular clientele." She looked to Melissa. "Do you want me to set up a table?"

"Forget it," Melissa said. Her face was red and contorted with barely contained rage. Roger had never seen her so angry before, and the emotion didn't look good on her.

"Let's go," she said.

They walked out of the store into the unending rain.

"Damn it to hell," Melissa said as they drove down Allisonville Road. "I should've confirmed the session before we drove all the way up here."

"Don't blame yourself. These things happen sometimes," Roger said philosophically. His own anger had abated quickly, and he now felt somewhat relieved, as if he had gone to get his teeth worked on and been told the dentist had been called away on an emergency. "Publishers are far from infallible. It was probably a computer screw-up."

"But I wanted the first event on this tour to be perfect." She glared through the windshield. The rain was so heavy now the pavement was just a dark blur. But if Melissa's eyes could have generated heat, the rain would have evaporated in her path.

"Did you expect much of a turnout in this rain?"

"It's the principle of the thing. And I didn't like that snotty bitch's implication that your books weren't big sellers."

"Maybe they're not in that store. Bookstore managers are sometimes influenced by their own tastes. For all we know, she'd never heard of me before."

"She knew who you were, all right." She slammed her hand against the dash board. "And she'll hear of you again. I'll see to that."

Roger shuddered involuntarily. He found the prospect of experiencing Melissa's wrath very intimidating.

He felt sorry for the poor bookstore manager. Or anyone else who might be the subject of that wrath.

They had returned to the hotel, and Roger took a much-needed nap while Melissa made calls and confirmed the rest of the schedule. Happily, as she reported to him later, there would be no more foul-ups. Everyone else in the city was prepared to receive Roger and treat him with the respect he deserved.

That evening, they dined at The Ramsgate, the restaurant on the top floor of the hotel. There was a beautiful view of the nightlit city from their table, but neither Roger nor Melissa was appreciative. He was uncommunicative, brooding all through dinner, and she seemed distracted. Together they spoke fewer than a dozen words.

After dinner, they went to their respective rooms, she to work on her book project, he to go over his notes for his talk show appearance in the morning and his seminar in the evening. But Roger couldn't get interested in his work. He had done these things so many times before, he didn't really need to prepare. He was sure he could conduct a seminar in his sleep. He spent a few minutes browsing through a few supermarket tabloids he had bought for amusement—and possible book material—but he quickly grew bored and tossed them aside.

He turned the television on and numbly watched Showtime's offering for the evening. There was a comedy special, then an action movie with Mel Gibson and Danny Glover, then finally one of those R-rated sex comedies in which women undressed in the oddest places at the strangest times. All the women, of course, were amply endowed and shaped like the subjects of adolescent wet dreams. Even this mild titillation did not engage Roger's interest long. He was asleep by eleven-thirty, all the lights and the television still on.

Rain beat on the windows, providing rhythm for his fitful slumber.

It was very late. Roger was caught in a subdued alpha state, not quite awake, not quite asleep. He was just barely aware of being in a strange room somewhere. Vivid swirling objects, fragments of geometric patterns, and zigzag colors flashed on and off in his consciousness.

A scene formed in his mind. There was a large crowd of

people, and he was viewing them as if from a great height. In the center of them was a man wearing a turban. The man began to twirl around, at first dancing, then spinning faster and faster like a whirling dervish.

Then he disappeared. No fanfare; no smoke. He simply ceased to be.

Roger sat up abruptly, opening his eyes. He was scared, frightened to the marrow, by what he had seen, even though nothing really terrible had happened in the dream. He had seen people "disappear" in magic acts many times.

It wasn't a dream, he admitted to himself reluctantly, and the true nature of the experience was what terrified him.

It was a vision, a genuine glimpse of something happening somewhere—in the past, present, or future. His research into so-called psychic phenomena had described such experiences in detail, and he was certain this was the same kind of experience.

But skeptics didn't have visions, he told himself. Skeptics had dreams like normal people.

He shed his clothes, showered, then put on his pajamas. He felt better, though still a bit shaky. The bedside clock said it was past three in the morning. He had to get some rest or tomorrow would be hell to get through.

He yawned and lay on the bed, crossing his feet. He stared at the TV, hoping it would help him go to sleep. The fare had proved soporific enough earlier in the evening.

On the screen an ax murderer wearing a hockey mask chased topless teenaged girls through the woods. Roger rushed over to turn the set off before the blade connected with flesh.

As he pulled his hand from the knob, something pinched him, and he yelped. He looked down to see blood oozing from his finger. He examined the TV's control knob and found a tiny burr right on its edge. The chances of anyone touching it were minute; yet Roger had managed to cut himself by turning off a television.

He must have yelped louder than he thought he had, because he heard Melissa rapping softly on the door between their rooms. She either had very acute hearing or was a very light sleeper.

"Are you all right in there?" she whispered.

"What? Yes," he said, watching the blood flow from his finger. "I'm all right."

"Let me in."

"I don't need anything."

"Please, Roger, I want to talk to you."

"Okay." He grabbed a tissue from the box on the dresser and wrapped his bleeding finger. Then he let her in and jumped back in bed, throwing the covers over himself and hiding his hurt finger before she could see it.

Melissa was wearing a sheer, light-blue satin nightgown. She sat on the chair next to the bed.

Roger tried to focus on her eyes, but his gaze kept wandering to other places. "I didn't mean to wake you," he said.

"You didn't really. I was only half asleep, because of you."

"Why is that?"

"I'm worried about you, Roger. Today was not a good day, and I don't want it to spoil the rest of our trip."

"I'll be okay, I tell you."

"Then why did you—why did you moan?"

"Bad dream."

"Are you sure that's all it was?"

"What else would it be?"

"I don't know. Anguish?"

He laughed. "Anguish? That's rather melodramatic."

"Well, maybe it does sound a bit silly."

"Don't magnify things, Melissa. I'm just fine." He pulled his hands out and held them up to show how fine he was. "See? Just having trouble getting to sleep."

"What happened to your finger?" she asked.

"Just cut it on the—on the damn TV."

"Let me see it."

"It's okay."

"It could get infected," she scolded.

"Oh, all right." He took the bloody tissue off and presented his right hand to Melissa.

She held his hand and touched the wound. Before Roger cold react, she slipped his hurt finger in her mouth and sucked on it gently, then pulled it out and regarded it curiously. "Better?"

Roger was blushing. "Much." He was tempted to tell her he had other appendages that needed attention.

"Promise me you'll put a bandage on that. I put a supply of Band-Aids in your tote."

"I will," he said, his voice cracking.

"Would you like me to get you some Scotch and water?"

"No. I want to be fresh in the morning."

"Are you sure?"

"Yes, I'm sure."

"I don't mean to be overly solicitous," she said, sounding like the young Katharine Hepburn she resembled, "but it's so important that things go well, so you can become your old self. I wish I could have foreseen that incident at Borders today. I wouldn't have wished anything like that to happen to you for the world."

"I've forgotten all about it. You can call the publisher and scream at them if that will make you feel better."

"Okay, Roger."

She fell silent and stared at him a long time before leaning over and kissing him on the forehead. "You're such a strong man inside," she said, her warm breath burning his cheeks. "If only you'll draw on that strength. . . ."

"I'm not sick," he said. "Just tired."

"Of course," she said. She started to kiss his forehead again, hesitated an instant, then pressed her lips against his, quickly and efficiently thrusting her tongue in his mouth, then withdrawing it.

An eternity of seconds rushed by before she was finished. Roger was breathless when her lips left his.

She drew back from him, horror on her face. "I'm sorry," she said. "I'm so sorry. I didn't mean to compromise our professional relationship."

"It's—"

She ran from the room and slammed the door before Roger could complete his sentence. He heard the lock click with finality.

Roger lay stunned for several minutes. He suddenly remembered that glimpse of her breast back in Chicago, the fresh scent of her in the morning, the color of her hair when the sun shone through it. . . . Those had all been mere flirtation, accidental or otherwise. But her kiss was deliberate and potent; it could revive the dead.

It was a good thing she left. He couldn't be responsible for his actions if she had remained a second longer.

He finally broke out of his trance long enough to get up for a Band-Aid. Then he discovered he didn't need it anymore.

His finger had stopped bleeding, and it didn't hurt a bit. He climbed back into bed and shut his eyes, but it was a long time before he finally fell asleep. He had formed a new opinion of Melissa, and the possibilities kept him semi-awake for hours, fantasizing as he listened to the soft patter of rain on the windows.

The next morning, he awoke with the hardest, tautest erection he had had in years.

8. REEMERGENCE

The next day, as Melissa promised, things went more smoothly—except for breakfast in the hotel.

During the morning meal the two of them tried awkwardly to talk around the incident in Roger's bedroom the night before. Neither could look the other in the eyes without embarrassment. Melissa studiously avoided any physical contact with Roger, directing her attention and his to the schedule of the day's activities. The result was an atmosphere of tension between them, which neither would broach or acknowledge.

Roger finally determined in his own mind that her kiss was the result of an impulse, and he would have to settle for that. Which meant nothing. She had probably given in to the impulse because she was tired herself and felt overly concerned about him. It was an expression of motherly or sisterly pity, then, not lust, despite the kind of kiss it was, and Roger didn't want affection—or sex—based on pity of any kind. It was demeaning and not a very solid foundation for a relationship.

Besides, he didn't even want a relationship.

Still, the taste of her kiss, spiced by the blood she had sucked from his finger, lingered on his lips. It would be some time before he recovered from the aftershock of the physical sensations she had caused to rise in him. But, he reminded himself, he was no adolescent; he'd get over it soon enough. He'd been kissed before.

It wasn't only the kiss that had him agitated; it was Melissa herself. Again, he was beginning to pile up questions in his mind about her, because that kiss was not just wonderful; it was exactly what he needed at that moment to totally eradicate the fearsome effects of his vision. Her timing was incredible, which made him speculate that perhaps the true purpose of her kiss was simply that: to erase the vision. It also seemed more than coincidental that she should be up at that hour. Nor did he believe she could hear that small cry of pain he let out when he cut himself. The walls in the hotel were thick, and that door was solid oak. She had to have been lying about that. She knew he needed her, and she had come to him as a mother does in the middle of the night when the baby cries.

She instinctively knew things about him, without being told—anticipated his needs before he anticipated them himself.

It was absolutely uncanny—almost enough to make him think there was something to pyschic abilities after all.

Maybe Melissa was merely more clever than the average person. She didn't have to be psychic. For all he knew, she slept with her ear against the door, just in case something happened.

That was absurd. But so was being psychic.

All of these speculations led him to the same conclusions and the ultimate question: What were Melissa's true intentions?

It was still raining in Indianapolis, though the sun appeared about to break through any minute. After breakfast, Melissa drove Roger down the street to the NBC TV affiliate where he made an appearance on *A.M. Indiana,* a locally produced talk show.

The host of the show was well prepared; he had even read Roger's book and asked questions specific to the material in it. That was unusual, since most local talk show people just held his book up for the camera, then made a series of banal inquiries, such as "What's the book about?" and "How long did it take you to write it?" This guy was sharp, providing mental challenges for Roger that made him really use his brain.

Melissa stood out of camera range, at the edge of the set, encouraging him with strained smiles and nods, then coming over during commercial breaks to see if he needed anything. She still avoided being physical, touching only his tie to straighten it, or picking lint off his tweed jacket. Again, her actions could be interpreted as maternal concern, not love.

After successfully sparring with the host in the first half hour, Roger proved himself a worthy match for any stupidity the phone-in viewers or people in the audience could provide during the second half hour. The more stupid the beliefs they put forth, the bolder Roger became in putting them down. He flattened one woman who claimed blue quartz crystals had healed her of rheumatism, he heaped scorn on a young man who protested Roger's views on astral travel, and he made a complete fool of an elderly lady who said she talked to her deceased husband on a daily basis.

The best part of all was that Roger could see that the audience was with him. They understood he was right and confirmed his approach to the New Age by their continued applause. Only once, when he was talking to the elderly lady, did he hear a "boo" from the audience, and it was so meekly delivered, no one seemed to notice it.

By the end of the show, Roger's former crusty self was beginning to reemerge, and he was feeling smug. He had once again successfully demonstrated the folly of believing in supernatural events and New Age hogwash, and unless he was mistaken, he had sold a lot of books, because afterward many people came up to him and asked where they could find *The New Age Con Game*. Many others already had copies of the new book, thrusting them toward him for his signature.

Later, as they returned to the hotel, Roger had to admit to Melissa the whole experience was therapeutic.

"I feel better than I have in ages," he said.

"You really put the 'heathens' in their place," she commented, speaking for the first time since the show was over. There was a note of implied criticism in her tone.

Roger felt a need to defend himself. "You have to get tough sometimes, even cruel."

"Why, cruel?" she asked.

"Because these silly beliefs of theirs are so unredeeming that shock therapy—in the form of seeming cruelty—is all that works. Like in the old movies when a woman kept screaming until someone slapped her in the face."

"That's an odd simile to choose," she said. "You might even call it a cruel simile."

"It's just an example. I didn't mean you to take it literally."

"I'm sorry," she said. "I'm out of sorts today."

Roger knew enough about women to take the hint; she was no doubt talking about some mysterious female ailment. But he still craved company. "Well, I feel terrific. And hungry too. Where are we going for lunch?"

"I'm begging off. I have some things to go over. Why don't you get a sandwich and come to my room later—about two-thirty?"

"All right," he said, crestfallen. He really longed for her to be with him, so that he could continue his braggadocio with an appreciative audience, but he could see she was no longer in the mood to listen. That was strange, since he expected her—especially her—to share his joy at his performing as his old self, even if she weren't feeling well.

"Why don't you tell me what's the matter?" he asked.

"Nothing. Nothing at all." She paused and stared out the windshield into the gloom. "I just wish it would stop raining."

The afternoon signing party in the Glendale shopping center was a gratifying success; Roger signed about fifty copies of his new book. Many people stopped to chat and commented on seeing him on TV. The bookstore manager was helpful and provided him with coffee.

Melissa didn't stay around during this session. She wandered off into the mall, returning just before Roger was finished at six o'clock. She carried several shopping bags of clothes, shoes, and other items, including two new shirts for Roger. Apparently, as with many women, shopping was therapy for her.

They had dinner at a Steak 'N' Ale nearby, then returned to the hotel. Roger talked all through the meal, while Melissa remained taciturn, still in her semi-depressed mood. He didn't let her condition deflate his newly discovered elation however.

They returned to the hotel to prepare for the evening's seminar. The Sheraton had a large meeting hall on the first floor where get-rich-quick real estate meetings were often held. By seven-thirty, a half hour before Roger's seminar was to begin, the hall was full to capacity with many people standing up in the back.

Roger arrived sharply at eight. As he entered the hall, he was overwhelmed by the number of people who had shown up. Usually rain meant a poor turn-out, even among the most ardent of his supporters and fans.

Melissa sat on a metal chair behind the lectern. She had typed up index cards for him, made sure the pitcher was full of ice water and even had a pint of Scotch in her purse in case Roger needed it.

Roger didn't expect to need any liquor. He was high on himself tonight. He had a feeling things were turning around for him at last. A couple more days like this one, and he'd be completely rejuvenated.

He was introduced to the crowd by a woman who was the head of a local feminist organization. She was noted in the community for being anti-New Age, not for religious or rational reasons, one or the other of which was usually the case, but because she had decided the New Age was a sexist movement.

Roger didn't care what she thought. After she made her

little speech, he took his place in the spotlight. Before he could say his first word, the audience applauded long and loud, and Roger basked in their unabashed display of approval, beaming with a smile that was genuinely heartfelt.

After the applause died down, Roger proceeded to astound his audience. He didn't try anything new for this seminar, he wasn't quite that confident yet. But he was very good at doing the old routines, including his standard billet presentation, fake mind reading, and a short demonstration with Tarot cards. He ended by causing the Tarot cards to burst into flame.

The audience gasped in amazement. Roger was reminded of the time when he was twelve and had seen his first live magic act at a theater in South Bend. He had been amazed too, even though, years later, he discovered that the magician was considered mediocre at best. But as a child he was so impressed he asked for a magic kit for Christmas and even performed at one of his friends' birthday parties, causing the other children to regard him with awe. This crowd could be compared to a mob of twelve-year-olds, easily amazed, easily duped too, he suspected. If he were so inclined, he could sell them just about anything.

After doing the magic part of his seminar, Roger launched into his standard short lecture on New Age charlatanism and how easy it was to be convinced something psychic was happening when it was only trickery.

"As you can see from my simple examples," he concluded, "it's really a New Age Con Game, and nothing that can't be duplicated by anyone with only the least bit of knowledge and the cleverness—and audacity—to pull it off."

The audience responded with more applause.

"Now," Roger said, "I will take questions from the audience. You first, the lady in the front row."

A middle-aged woman stood up. She was wearing a bright red dress and a silver Egyptian ankh on a chain around her neck. "Do you mean to say, Mr. Kant, that none of the New Age philosophies have any validity?"

"Philosophy per se has validity. There's nothing wrong with studying Taoism, Plato, or other systems of philosophies, but the New Age gurus have perverted these philosophies. Don't seek wisdom from Shirley MacLaine or other New Age writers. Go directly to the source. Read the *Tao Te Ching* on your own and form your own conclusions. That's all I'm saying. Think for yourself."

"Thank you," the woman said, nodding her head, and sat down.

"Anyone else?" Many hands went up. This seminar was going well indeed. He singled out a young man in the third row. "You in the black T-shirt. What's your question?"

The young man rose. His shirt had a skull and the logo for Guns N' Roses printed on it. "Mr. Kant, it seems to me you've proven nothing here tonight—"

The crowd shouted at him to sit down.

"Let him have his say," Roger said.

"Thank you. You see, it seems to me that duplicating a psychic 'stunt,' as you call it, doesn't prove there's no such thing. I mean, movie people duplicate and fake all kinds of things that are real, but that doesn't make the real things fake."

"You have a good point, sir," Roger responded. "I never said my duplicating psychic stunts meant there was no such thing as real psychic pehnomena. So you're right about that. But my ability to fake them does show that other people can fake them as well. Unfortunately, I have yet to encounter a psychic demonstration that didn't turn out to be faked in one way or another."

"But it couldn't all be fake."

"In the middle ages, there were bazaars where indulgences for sins were sold, and hairs from the beard of Christ. There were so many bone fragments of the disciples for sale, you'd think there had been a thousand of them instead of twelve. Do you think any of that was genuine?"

"This isn't the middle ages."

"It could be a New Middle Age if we aren't careful. I'm only demonstrating how easily people are gulled into believing the most extravagant of lies. If anyone can demonstrate a psychic phenomenon to me—under the proper testing conditions with the right controls—I'll gladly admit its veracity. In fact, I'll pay any such person twenty thousand dollars. This is an offer I've made for years, and I have yet to pay the money. Does that answer your question?"

"I think so," the young man said and sat down amidst a chorus of boos.

"Who's next?" Roger scanned the audience. There were so many eager faces out there. He was about to explode with the excitement of it.

"I am!" a high-pitched masculine voice shouted from the back.

"Where are you, sir?"

"Here." A man stood in the last row and made his way to the center aisle. He was a very slender man, possibly in his mid-thirties, and he was wearing a white floor-length cassock. He also had a bandage on his head.

"Come forward, sir," Roger said, "so I can hear you better."

As the man approached, Roger began to feel apprehensive. He realized why when the man was about twenty feet from the speaker's platform—he wasn't wearing a bandage on his head at all; it was a turban.

But if it was only a turban, why was blood seeping through the front of it?

"My name is Darrell," the man said, "Darrell J. Prince." His voice was not entirely clear, due to the fact he had no teeth. He had a pointed chin and mischievous blue eyes. "I'm a psychic, a spiritualist, a metaphysician, a practicing shaman, an astrologer and a numerologist. I can heal by the placing on of hands, and levitate if I so desire. I may want to collect that twenty thousand from you."

He giggled at the last statement, sounding like a witch cackling in an old cartoon. Everyone in the audience had turned to watch the strangely attired man.

"Well, Darrell," Roger replied, "if you can demonstrate a genuine phenomenon, I have the check in my pocket." Sweat broke out on Roger's lip, stinging the skin under his moustache. There was a quality of déjà vu about this man he didn't like at all, and it made him nervous.

"It may be difficult," Darrell answered, lisping. "I think I may be dead." The audience responded with jeers, then quieted down abruptly when Darrell squinted at them and frowned. Then he faced Roger again. "Of course, you only die if you believe in death, and I don't acknowledge it. I know it's there, but I don't own it. Do you see the difference?"

"What's your point, Mr. Prince?"

"No point, just an observation. If I were so inclined, I could tell you a few things about *your* future, such as the fact that I see blood in it, and a betrayal, and a big surprise. How do you like those predictions?"

"Anyone can make vague predictions that might come true."

"You're right. You want something more tangible evidently. If you want a demonstration of real magic, I'm only too happy to provide it. What would you like to see, Mr. Astounding One?"

"Anything at all that can be verified." Roger was growing impatient with the man, but he could see the audience was interested—too interested—in his antics. Even Melissa was standing to watch. Darrell would probably perform some outlandish parlor trick and claim it was real magic.

Darrell came forward a few more steps. The blood was running down the side of his face now, and Roger's sense of déjà vu was heightened.

"All right," Darrell intoned, closing his eyes, "I'll levitate. That's easy."

Roger thought he was going to be sick as he recognized the weird man at last. Darrell was the man from his vision.

"No, Mr. Prince!" Roger shouted.

"Here I go."

"No! Somebody stop him."

Darrell began to spin, just as he had in Roger's vision. Then he stopped and leaned back slowly, until his feet lifted from the floor. He seemed to float, rising above the breathless spectators, then sailed out over them.

"How am I doing?" he shouted gleefully. After circling the audience several times, he whipped down the center aisle, hovered a few feet before the speaker's platform, then evaporated in a burst of red. On the carpet beneath his point of departure was a pool of dark blood.

Some of the audience members left their seats and put their fingers in the blood. They gasped.

"It's real!" someone shouted.

Roger was temporarily at a loss. He looked to Melissa for help. "I don't know what to do," she whispered, her face as distraught as Roger's.

Roger became frantic. He was losing control of the crowd. The faces that had seconds ago been eager to listen now registered doubt; some seemed angry.

"Ladies and gentlemen," he began, his mind racing for the right words, "this is just another cheap example of trickery. I'm sure—I'm certain—local New Age people put this man up to this—to try to sway you from the truth."

Most of the audience glared. They weren't buying his lame explanation. Their twelve-year-old group consciousness wanted to accept magic.

"This blood is real, damn it!" a man said, holding up his hand. "Real!"

"You, sir—were you in on this hoax?"

"Don't blame me, you son of a bitch!" The man was large and threatening. He wore a sleeveless shirt, and there was a snake tattoo on his left bicep. He ran toward the platform, his eyes afire with rage.

"Come ahead," Roger said. "I'm not afraid."

Before the man could get to Roger, two hotel security men grabbed him by the arms and pulled him away, kicking and thrashing. "Roger Kant is full of shit!" the man screamed.

Other obscenities issued from the crowd. People began

to leave.

"It's a trick, I tell you. A trick! Keep your seats."

"If it's a trick," someone shouted, "where's the guy now?"

"I don't know," Roger admitted. "But you can rest assured he's hiding somewhere. He was sent here to humiliate me. That should be obvious."

There were more obscenities shouted and much booing.

Melissa came to Roger's side and tugged at his arm. "This is useless," she said, tears running down her face. "You'd better leave before one of them gets past the guards."

"I can't leave. It'll show I'm wrong."

"They're a bunch of hicks. Can't you see that? This state is a haven for spiritualists and half-baked religions. Jim Jones had his church here. Remember?"

"But I have to stay to convince them I'm right."

"Look at them," she said. "Can you think of anything that would convince these yahoos?"

Roger felt the wave of anger radiating from the audience. His whole seminar had been invalidated by a magician's trick.

"No, I can't," he said. "It's pointless. They want to believe in bullshit."

"And they don't deserve any better," Melissa added. "Let's get out of here."

"Thank you for your kind attention," Roger mumbled into the microphone; then he let the security guards help him and Melissa to the side exit, where they saw people tearing up stacks of Roger's books that had been put out for sale.

"Don't look," Melissa said.

"Goddamn it," Roger said. "I had them in the palm of my hand. I had complete power over them."

"Not anymore."

The guards took Roger and Melissa to their car. The two of them drove away, Melissa taking a circuitous route through the streets of Indianapolis, making many sharp turns before she was finally convinced no nut-cases were following them. Then she headed east until they came to a Pancake House.

"Let's eat and forget it," she told Roger.

"All right," he said. "But first give me a swig of that Scotch. My nerves are in shreds."

Melissa ordered a patty melt, and Roger had ham and eggs. Then they sat and drank coffee for a couple of hours. Roger evidenced a whole range of emotions during and after the meal. He was angry, disgusted, disappointed, and finally, just plain confused.

Melissa, by contrast, seemed almost happy. She was talkative and animated and even touched him a couple of times on the shoulder while she talked. She kept emphasizing the good parts of the seminar.

Roger kept dwelling on the bad ending. They never agreed on what it would really mean to his career. There would be bad press about it, which might affect his next personal appearance, which he was determined to make despite the fiasco this evening.

"Sometimes," Melissa pointed out, "bad press is better than no press—or even good press. It might actually work out for you in the long run."

"Sure. Next time, I'll have you catch bullets in your teeth, and we'll have a shill in the audience help me with mind reading. Maybe I'll just go over to the other side and open a New Age consciousness-raising temple in New Mexico. What do you think of that?"

"I think Roger Kant is tired and full of—well, as the man said, shit."

"Maybe I am," he said, and they both laughed. They were having a good time for some reason, despite the circumstances, and Roger was more confused by that than anything that had happened earlier in the evening.

Melissa was similar to other women in one respect—she was unpredictable.

* * *

By eleven-thirty, they decided it was probably safe to return to the hotel. Before going up to their rooms, Roger insisted on inspecting the meeting hall. He had a guard let him in and went to the center aisle where Darrell J. Prince had disappeared.

He examined the spot of blood on the floor which was dried and caked now. "I'll bet you a hundred bucks this is pig's blood or something like that," he said to Melissa.

"How did it get there?"

"That's the damnedest thing about this," he said, standing. "I can think of a dozen ways to do this levitation and disappearance act, but I don't see how he did it in here with this high ceiling and apparently no wires. There must have been some kind of rig. But where did he put it? That ceiling is acoustic tile, and those light fixtures would get in the way. The only thing I can think of is some kind of holographic projection, but even that would be an elaborate set-up and virtually impossible to do under these bright lights. Whatever it was, it's probably been dismantled and carried away by now."

"There's another possibility," Melissa said, her voice trembling.

"What?"

"Maybe—just maybe—it was a real paranormal event."

"You're not serious, are you?"

She hesitated before answering. "Of course not," she said. "I was only teasing." Her expression was difficult to read.

"Okay," he said. "You had me worried there for a moment. I don't need you going over to the other side."

"I'm happy just that you need me."

Roger merely smiled to hide his discomfort. The word "need" had an ambivalent effect on him, and this was the first time he remembered Melissa using it in a context that was, at the moment, a bit presumptuous. He didn't press her to expound on her comment, however. He was exhausted by the evening's ordeal.

He took her by the arm, and they left the hall. They returned to their respective rooms, saying, "Good night" in the hall as they unlocked the doors.

Roger thought a moment, then made sure his side of the door between their rooms was locked. No matter what happened, he didn't want her coming in. He could barely concentrate as it was.

He prepared for bed quickly. He didn't read or watch TV. He just lay in the bed, thinking. Before going to sleep, Roger fretted over Melissa's paranormal remark. He wondered if she had really been teasing. Could she possibly have been convinced by Mr. Prince's demonstration?

What would Melissa say if she knew about his vision—which he now identified as what the psychics called precognition? Would she think he was teasing her?

He could never tell her about it. It would be humiliating. Besides, he still didn't believe it himself. It must have been temporary insanity.

That was the only sane explanation.

9. Innards

Since the Cleveland part of the tour had been cancelled, the next stop for Roger and Melissa was Columbus, Ohio. It was sunny the afternoon they arrived, and no rain was forecast for the next several days. It was close to the first of May, and flowers were already blooming in the plots in front of the airport.

Again Melissa rented a car, but she had to consult a map to get where they were going. Columbus was apparently one of the few large cities with which she was not very familiar, though she did profess to have been there before. She still managed to drive unerringly to their destination, the Radisson Hotel on Sinclair Road, in the northern part of the city. It was more modern than the Sheraton in Indianapolis and more plush in general.

It was Wednesday, and there was not much to do, only a book-signing session on the south side of the city, then they were pretty much on their own for the evening. They dined at a Brown Derby Restaurant, where Roger and Melissa both had thick steaks and made several trips to the salad bar.

"I don't know what it is about traveling that makes a person so hungry," Melissa commented.

"It's lack of having your own refrigerator to snack from," Roger said and got up to take his turn at the dessert bar, where he fixed himself a hot fudge sundae sprinkled with nuts.

After the two of them were thoroughly stuffed, they sipped coffee and talked over plans for the next seminar, which was to be held at the Radisson the following night.

"I hope nothing goes wrong this time," Melissa said.

"Maybe it's my fault," Roger said.

"Surely you don't mean that."

"Yeah, in a way I do. I was almost my old self yesterday, but not quite. I did the same tired old crap I've done a million times before."

"But it was new for that audience."

"Maybe. But it wasn't new for me, so I wasn't as sharp as I could have been. I need to try something different—something that will keep me alert. I might have avoided that awful incident in Indianapolis if I'd had my wits about me."

"But it was so cleverly done."

"I still should've reacted better."

"What could you do that's different?"

"I don't know. I'll have to think about it. I need to do something that will attract more attention—get the media interested."

"What do you have in mind, Roger? You have the look of a child about to do something very naughty."

He laughed. "A bald-headed child? I haven't looked like a child since I was twenty."

Melissa leaned over and touched his hand. "You know, some women think bald men are sexy."

"Are you one of them?"

She smiled coyly. "Maybe."

"You're not trying to start something with me again, are you?"

She pulled her hand away. "I'm sorry."

"Don't sweat it, Melissa. Do you think I'm so dense I don't see how you turn on and off around me?"

"What do you mean by that?"

"You know, one minute you're coming on to me, the next minute you're a shy, retiring schoolgirl. It seems to me you should make up your mind."

"Roger, I can't help it if I feel affection for you. I've

studied your work. I know you. I admire you."

"Is that all there is to it?"

"Maybe."

"That's what I like—a straightforward answer."

"I'm just confused right now. I want things to remain—you know—professional."

"Okay," he said, accepting her statement rather placidly, though inwardly he was going through sexual turmoil, which she probably knew too. "Just remember," he added, "I'm over forty, and I don't go in for teasing, flirtation or any of the 'relationship' bullshit I hear about. I'm a hard man to live with, a difficult man to endure, and I usually get what I want. Is that clear?"

"Yes, Roger."

"So don't play around with me anymore unless . . ."

"Unless what?"

". . . unless you're willing to play for keeps."

After they left the restaurant, Melissa drove back to the Radisson, taking a long route that let them see some of the city. There wasn't much to see. Columbus resembled so many other Midwestern towns on the surface and appeared to be not much different from Indianapolis. Even the skyline was about the same.

Roger said little as they rode. He had said his piece in the restaurant, and he was waiting for it to sink in with Melissa. He didn't care if she decided to treat him coldly from now on; he wanted no more coyness, no more hints at sexuality, no more kisses, unless they meant something. He didn't want to be her toy. He was attracted to her—very much so—but he couldn't allow himself to be caught in another relationship that ended with a lot of screaming and the inevitable day in court. If she wanted to be his traveling companion and his biographer for a while, that was fine. If she wanted more, then it had to be on his terms.

He was proud of himself for speaking up like that. It was another encouraging sign he was regaining the strength of character he'd had in the old days, before his life and his career had become repetitive and boring, which was due, as he told Melissa, to his doing the same tired old crap over and over. His presentation—his "act"—was stale. That was why it was so easy to disrupt, and it might explain his mental condition. The idle mind, without challenges to keep it entertained, was prone to conjure demons and other monstrosities from the subconscious and present them under the guise of visions or under seemingly extraordinary events.

But what could he do that would be different? What did the public want of him now? He'd debunked everything from UFOs to astrology. He had written thousands of words on hundreds of subjects. Yet the public was still gullible, still willing to acept parapsychology, the paranormal and other para-concepts, because they all wanted magic—maybe because their own lives lacked magic of any kind. The vast majority of people just bumped through life from day to day, achieving at best a mild level of mediocrity, because they believed the rich and successful had secrets they shared only with their own kind. That was why they were so susceptible to the bullshit artists who offered them mysticism and messages from the beyond. They thought they were gaining access to the secrets the highbrows used.

Of course, many intelligent, successful people *did* believe in the paranormal. The media was full of stories about famous personalities who consulted astrologers or psychics before they did anything. That lent even more credibility to the New Age quacks, because if astrology worked for Ronald Reagan, then surely it could work for Joe Blow, John Doe or Harriet Housewife.

Why couldn't they see that the only persons they could depend on were themselves? That success came from within the individual? Why couldn't they learn from his example?

He shook his head ruefully. If they ever learned that, then he would be out of business.

But so would all the quacks.

* * *

Back at the hotel, Roger returned to his room, while Melissa went down for a couple of drinks in the bar. She had to think things over, she said, and needed to be alone.

Roger was also relieved to be alone. He needed to concentrate on how he might impress the audience for tomorrow night's seminar. Billets, spoon bending, mind reading and his other standard fare lacked excitement. The jaded audiences of today wanted sex and violence, or the promise of wealth. That's what pulled crowds into movie theaters and to the real estate seminars.

It occurred to him that the supermarket tabloids might give him a clue. He still had those he'd bought in Indianapolis, so he sat and started flipping through them, hoping something would inspire him.

He spent two fruitless hours that way. Most of the stories were so absurd most people with any intelligence at all would recognize them either as fake or outrageously exaggerated embellishments on minor incidents.

Perhaps if he slept on it, he'd wake up with a good idea. That had worked before. He knew the subconscious mind often took over in the sleep state and solved problems that the conscious mind couldn't. There was nothing paranormal about that. It was a scientific fact, proven not only by his own experience but also documented by many case histories. Most geniuses worked through the subconscious mind—which was the ultimate source of all inspiration.

Roger prepared for bed early, drank two tall glasses of Scotch with very little water, turned out all the lights and waited.

Soon he drifted into an agitated state of sleep, one interrupted by dreams of constantly shifting objects, none of them quite identifiable. His mind struggled to make sense of the dreams—tried to make them become something definite. Subconsciously, he hoped this series of dreams was not the prelude to another terrifying vision.

Finally, the shapes came together, forming a gooey mass of purple and red, and when Roger realized what they were, he screamed—not in terror, but with joy.

He had recognized the shapes as chicken innards.

He awoke with bloody hands. He ran to the mirror and

saw blood running from his nose. But that didn't matter. He had the idea he needed.

He threw on a robe and went next door to Melissa's room. He banged on her door until she finally answered it.

"Roger?" Her eyes were still crusted with sleep. "It's six-thirty in the morning."

She was clad in a thin, white nightgown through which her pinkish nipples and reddish pubic hair were distinctly visible. Roger barely noticed this immodest display; he was too excited by what was going on in his own mind.

"I've got it," he said. "A new idea."

"What?" She rubbed her eyes, then finally focused on him. "Oh, my God, your nose is bleeding! Get in here and let me take care of it."

"I don't care. I've figured out what I want to do."

"Come in here before you wake up the whole hotel."

He almost pranced as he entered her room.

"Now calm down and sit on the bed. You can tell me all about it while I fix your nose."

"Take an inch off the end while you're at it," he said.

She clucked disapproval at him, then disappeared into the bathroom. When she returned, she held a wet washcloth and some gauze in her hands. She had also covered her semi-nakedness with a robe. "Now lean back and let me work on this." She stuffed an edge of the washcloth up one of his nostrils.

"Melissa," he said, his voice altered comically by the cloth in his nose, "I want you to get in touch with the local TV stations before noon. I'm holding a press conference. Also . . ." He paused as she swabbed his nose and stuffed gauze in it. ". . . also see if you can hire a crew to videotape tonight's seminar. I don't care what it costs. And get me a doctor. . . ."

"You may need one for this nose. Did you stuff a razor up there?" She looked at his bloody hands and wiped them with the cloth.

"Not for me. I want a doctor as a stooge—to stand by while I do my act."

"I don't understand."

"There's more. Call a local talent agency and get an actor. Somebody who looks ordinary as hell; somebody who won't be immediately recognized. The only thing is he can't have an appendix scar, and I'd like him to be about twenty pounds overweight."

"Lie down now."

He did as he was told. "Have you got all that, Melissa?"

"I think so." She grabbed a pad and pen and began scribbling. "Press conference. Stooge doctor. Video crew. Unknown actor who's pudgey and who still has his appendix. Roger, what are you up to?"

"It's going to knock their socks off. I should have done this before. I just never had the guts." He laughed until the plug in his nose almost expelled itself.

"What's the joke?"

"Later you'll understand. I just made an outrageous pun."

"Roger, are you sure this is what you want to do?"

"Yes, ma'am. Oh, one more thing—find out where the nearest grocery store is. And a drugstore."

At eleven o'clock, three representatives of the local TV news showed up for Roger's press conference. Roger had set himself up in a corner of the Grand Ballroom on the hotel's lower level where the seminar itself would be held that night. Melissa was sitting behind the media people, as curious as they were, since Roger had told her nothing. She had made all the arrangements he requested.

Roger nodded readiness to the news people and took his position behind a lectern and waited till the mini-cams and microphones were on to make his announcement.

"Tonight, I, Roger Kant, The Astounding One, will perform psychic surgery during my seminar."

"What *is* psychic surgery?" one of the reporters asked. She was typical of the breed—with the latest hairdo and a polished, carefully made-up face that hid a rather dull mentality.

"It is the performance of surgery without the benefit of

anesthetics or tools. In short, I will attempt to remove a man's appendix with my bare hands."

"Mr. Kant, can you really do this?"

"It's done all the time. Don't you read *The National Enquirer*? My demonstration will show just how easy it is."

"Mr. Kant—do you anticipate any of the uproar that broke out at your last seminar—in Indianapolis?"

"No." He paused dramatically, then added, "That was the result of too many people wanting to believe in magic."

"Isn't what you do magic?"

"Could be. Let's just say it's an illusion—or maybe it's really paranormal. The people of Columbus can judge for themselves tonight at my seminar."

"I'll certainly be there," the woman reporter said.

"That's all I have to say at the moment," Roger said. "I promise everyone will be astounded."

The cameras and microphones were off. A couple of the people paused to consult with Melissa, assuring her Roger's remarks would be featured on the six o'clock news, then they packed up their equipment and left.

Melissa went up to Roger. She looked more puzzled than the media people had. "You're looking smug," she said. "Are you serious about this psychic surgery bit?"

"Certainly."

"But it's not like what you usually do."

"I know. I'm giving the public what it wants—blood and guts."

"I sure hope you know what you're doing."

"I do. It's a cinch. Now, when is my actor coming? We'll need to rehearse before the big show tonight."

Melissa said he would be at the hotel no later than five o'clock.

"Great. Now, if you'll excuse me, dear Melissa, I have some shopping to do."

Roger took the car and drove down Sinclair Road to Morse, where he turned left. He kept going till he found a Kroger's supermarket and a SuperX drugstore. He visited both stores, coming out with a brown bag from each one.

Then he rushed back to the hotel. He didn't want anything to spoil before tonight's performance.

At eight o'clock the ballroom was full. There were video cameras and monitors set up and a stooge doctor, and representatives of the local media present. In short, it was just as Roger had planned.

Roger also planned arriving ten minutes late, knowing that would heighten the suspense and the ultimate effect.

As he entered, the audience applauded only tentatively. They weren't certain how to respond yet. By the end of this evening, Roger knew, they would change their attitudes and opinions about him.

Roger opened the program with a simple billet demonstration. As he stretched it out to twenty minutes, he could hear grunts of impatience from the crowd. Good. He wanted that too. More suspense. That would make his final act that much more exciting.

He lectured them another ten minutes until he was sure they were about to bolt from their seats from anticipation. Then he looked out over the audience and smiled slyly.

"Now, ladies and gentlemen, I will show you how easy it is to do psychic surgery. I need a volunteer—someone who is not afraid to face the unknown, someone who believes I can do this, someone who has faith."

Several hands went up.

"You, sir, the man in the red shirt in the front row."

The actor he'd hired stood up quickly before anyone else rushed forward. He was about six feet tall and weighed over two hundred pounds with long brown hair and a pudgy face. He was about thirty but looked like a boy just off the farm.

"Me?"

"Yes. You look like the adventuresome sort. Come on up here."

The actor mounted the platform. He was very good. He even acted properly sheepish when he shook

Roger's hand.

"What's your name?"

"David."

"May I call you Dave?"

"Okay."

"Dave, are you absolutely certain you're ready for this?"

"I think so."

"Good enough. All I need is a little faith. Do you have that?"

"Yes."

"Then please lie down on the table." The actor hefted himself up on a long banquet table which was covered with a white sheet. "Be sure you're comfortable."

"I'm fine, thank you, sir."

"Good. Ladies and gentlemen, I will now remove this man's appendix with my bare hands as I promised in my press conference. Cameras will be providing close-ups of my surgery which you can watch on the monitors. I have a doctor standing by, just in case, of course, but he won't be needed. Doctor Wilson, would you please take a bow?"

The doctor stood and bowed.

"Thank you." Roger went behind the table where the actor lay. He pulled up his shirt, exposing his bare abdomen. Roger glanced up at the nearest monitor to make sure the camera angle was right, then proceeded.

His hands were already prepared. He had done the procedure six times in rehearsal that afternoon and was sure he had it perfected. He shot a look at Melissa and smiled, then turned back to his patient and announced, "I need complete quiet now. Dave, I want you to concentrate. You will feel no pain. Do you understand?"

"Yes, sir."

"You can still back out now, if you wish."

"No, sir. I'm ready."

"Let's begin."

The audience complied with Roger's order to be quiet. The only sounds in the room were an occasional nervous cough and the hum of the air conditioning running.

Roger began by kneading the actor's stomach, pinching

and tugging at the flesh until it was pink.

What he was going to do was simple actually. In his left hand, he had a wad of chicken liver. On his right hand, he had fashioned a fake thumb—cut from the tip of a pair of surgical gloves—which held fake blood he had made with food coloring, ink and water. He would push two folds of flesh together, pretend to insert his thumb into the man's abdomen, then puncture the bloodfilled thumb. With his other hand, he would slide the chicken innards into the folds of flesh, pretend to be manipulating something inside the man, then pull out the bloodied chicken pieces, hold them up and claim they were the man's appendix. Even in close-up, the procedure would look very real because there would be the fake blood all over everything, blurring the details of what was actually happening. Finally, Roger would knead the man's flesh again and wipe it all clean, explaining he had psychically healed this man.

After the inevitable commotion died down, he would explain how it was done and point out how easily he had fooled an audience of hundreds with about five dollars' worth of props purchased at a drugstore and supermarket.

Roger was now forming the folds of flesh. The actor winced as Roger pinched his flesh, but he knew to expect a little discomfort. Besides, his reaction was good for the act, adding to the verisimilitude.

"I am now going to thrust my fingers into this man's abdominal cavity and pull out his appendix."

Some people looked away. Not everyone enjoyed graphic violence, Roger noted.

"First, I make the incision." Roger secretly punctured the fake thumb. On the monitors it seemed blood was flowing freely from the man's abdomen.

Many members of the audience groaned. A few of them arose and left the room, rushing for the nearest bathroom.

Roger slid the chicken livers into the fold, then kneaded the flesh back and forth as if he were tearing it. He buckled his fingers under, so that it appeared they were deep in the man's gut.

The actor grunted convincingly. This was better than rehearsal, but Roger frowned at him as a signal not to overdo it.

The actor grunted again, and his eyes sought Roger's for assurance. Roger nodded at him: Everything was okay.

The actor moaned, twisting against Roger's manipulations of his flesh.

"Lie still," Roger whispered. He beamed confidence into the video cameras as he pinched the flesh together. Blood was flowing freely.

The actor screamed from deep within his diaphragm, screaming so intensely the sound of it vibrated up Roger's arms.

What a ham, Roger thought. He certainly hadn't been this melodramatic in rehearsal. Vaguely, Roger was aware that his fingernails were caught in something mushy and warm. He glanced at the nearest monitor; if he didn't know this was a sham, he'd be losing his dinner himself right now. It was a sickening display, reminding him of a geek show he had seen as a young man. Now he wished he hadn't chosen this stunt; it was entirely too graphic, and the point he would make from it was hardly worth the effort. But he had started and was resolved to finish. The showman in him wouldn't quit in the middle of the act—not before the grand finale.

The actor groaned in excruciating agony, heaving his abdomen against Roger's hands, thrashing on the table.

Roger started to hush him because he was ready to display the chicken liver now. He didn't need any more exaggerated histrionics.

But that gooey stuff in Roger's hands was not chicken innards. It was the actor's innards. Roger glanced down and saw a gaping hole in the man's flesh, and his own hands were thrust into it up to the wrists.

Suddenly, blood gushed out of the actor's stomach, splattering Roger's face and arms. Roger jerked his hands away. "Oh, my God!" he shouted. "Doctor, come here. Quick!"

The video cameras zoomed in on the hole torn in the

man. Pulsating, sticky, red and purple, gooey things were in there, and they were about to explode out of him.

The doctor rushed to the man's side, pushing Roger out of the way roughly. "Jesus Christ, man, you've opened this man up! Somebody give me that satchel and call an ambulance. Quick!"

Roger stood back against the wall, staring at his bloody hands—bloody as they had been that morning. The blood hadn't been an inspiration then at all; it was another portent, part of another goddamn vision, a vision that he had failed to interpret properly—because he didn't believe in visions.

Stupidly, he wondered where to wipe the blood, as if that were the most important concern he had.

The doctor gave the actor an injection and started applying gauze and bandages.

Roger pressed his wet hands against his jacket. In that moment, he realized, trembling with fear, that he was truly going insane. That was the only explanation—yet, if he were insane, why was he so lucid? Why did everything seem so clearly defined in his vision? Reality wasn't eluding him; if anything, reality was asserting itself with an impact Roger had never experienced before. It was as if he were finally awake at the end of a long, involved dream.

He scanned the audience numbly. There was chaos amongst those people who had come expecting to be fooled and astounded by Roger Kant. People were getting sick on the floor. Most were trying to get out, while others stayed behind, screaming and shouting profanity. One voice rang out over the rest with amazing clarity, calling Roger "The Astounding Asshole."

But one among them, a man in the front row, whom Roger had not noticed before, was smirking. He was enjoying this spectacle very much indeed.

The face of the smirking man was quite familiar. Roger blinked several times before he focused and remembered. It was the face of Roger's own personal demon, the very same visage that had taunted him in his dreams and at Edith's grave.

Roger was no longer stunned. He became enraged. "You did this—you son of a bitch!" he screamed and jumped down from the platform into the audience, fighting his way toward the man with the demon's face, intent on stopping him from intruding in his life.

He reached out for the throat of the demon and felt the creature's cold, slimy flesh beneath his fingers. He dug in with his nails and squeezed hard.

Yes, he thought, *that's it—kill the demon!*

Dark eyes peered back at him. Dire images danced in those eyes, taunting Roger with torments of the past, of the present, and most dreadfully, of the future. The images were of disease and torture, death and putrescence, and crippled people—thousands of them—spitting on Roger's grave.

Roger squeezed the demon's flesh harder—until it emitted a choked cry. Roger grinned with satisfaction. He would keep squeezing until the demon was dead.

Then the flesh beneath his fingers became soft and supple, and the odor of expensive perfume filled his nostrils. He blinked again, and reality gave him another jolt.

The woman in his grip—who didn't resemble a demon at all except in the way she fought back—kneed him in the groin.

Roger let go of her throat and breathed out a soft whimper of pain as he tumbled to the floor. The woman called him a "butcher" and kicked him in the side.

Roger bent over from the new pain. Dazed and disoriented, he was in danger of being trampled under the heels of the audience, which had become a raging mob of people who seemed to hate him. This was much worse than the pandemonium in Indianapolis. Here people had murderous glints in their eyes; they didn't understand at all that Roger had merely made a mistake.

Perhaps he deserved their rancor, he decided, and he didn't even try to escape. Part of him didn't care what happened because he had brought it on himself.

The stench of the actor's blood was still on him.

Tucking his stained hands under his arms so that he wouldn't have to look at them, he waited to be crushed.

Then Melissa appeared out of nowhere to save him, pulling him up and guiding him out of the nearest exit, fighting mightily against the crowd herself, kicking and scratching if necessary to get through.

She took Roger up to her room and directed him to her bed. She lay next to him, just holding him for hours, while he mumbled incoherently, seeming to sob as he shook uncontrollably.

But his apparent sobbing wasn't due to anguish or to any other normal human reaction to what had happened that evening. He wasn't sobbing at all. He was hyperventilating because he was so angry he could hardly catch his breath.

10. the fix

It was almost noon when Roger awoke alone in Melissa's bed. He was still fully clothed. Nothing had happened during the night except that his paroxysms of anger had finally subsided and he had blanked into a fitful, deep sleep from which he remembered no dreams of demons.

He pulled himself up from the bed with some effort, then staggered to the bathroom to splash water on his face. He felt hung-over, though he hadn't drunk anything. His brain was bereft of any specific thoughts and was proving only moderately useful for motor control.

The cold water on his face was both harsh and stimulating, and he kept dousing himself until he was reasonably awake. Then he turned the tap off and stared at himself in the mirror. The man staring back at him resembled a demon of sorts—one in a business suit. He was a literal mess: rumpled suit, wrinkled tie, unshaven jowls, mussed hair, and bloodshot eyes accentuated by dark circles underneath them. He stuck out his tongue, and it was coated with white goo, which tasted even worse than it looked. He tried rinsing with mouthwash, but it had little effect. His mouth still had the taste of a thousand stale pizza dinners.

He stood back to study his image in more detail, as if he were not totally convinced he was viewing his own reflection. There were dark brown smudges on his jacket and something that looked like rust under his fingernails. He couldn't quite remember how he had stained his hands and jacket. Had he hurt himself again? His mind wasn't up to full speed yet, as if his entire life before this moment was a blur with no detail whatsoever.

Though most of his mental and physical facilities were operating below par, his bladder maintained full function and abruptly made its presence felt with extreme pressure.

Roger lifted the lid of the toilet with his foot—a habit he had acquired after years of being married—and unzipped his fly. He fished out his penis and was surprised to find it at least felt normal in his hands. As he began to pee, however, a sudden, dull ache in his groin recalled everything to his mind, and he shuddered.

Last night had been a nightmarish experience, culminating in his being kicked in the testicles by an irate woman who he had thought was a demon. No, *the* demon, the one that had somehow become a symbol of something in his life, at least on the subconscious level. Why, he wondered, had his mind conjured up such a fierce image? Was it because he was so opposed to the reality of such things? Maybe. The mind was a trickster; there was no doubt about that. Roger's studies had shown him the mind was capable of making its possessor believe in anything and making it somehow real. That's how the psychics, the New Age people, the faith healers and all the other nuts in the world today deluded themselves. Their minds were playing big practical jokes on them.

But his mind was basically sound. He had thought at odd moments he was going insane, but he had decided that was due to exhaustion and pushing himself too hard. He was, in reality, a rationalist, not a deluded seer.

After he finished peeing and zipped up, other details rushed into his mind; remembering these—especially the source of the stains on his suit and his hands—he felt grungy and unclean.

He grabbed the tiny bar of hotel soap on the basin and scrubbed his hands vigorously, trying to remove the dried blood stains. He succeeded except for the stuff caked under his nails, which he scraped out with his pocket knife. Then he washed again—and again—rubbing his skin until it was pink and virtually raw.

He wandered back into the bedroom and sat down on the bed. His rage was returning now too, and that somehow made him feel uncleaner than anything else, because the edge of his anger was unresolved, awaiting consummation. He satisfied it temporarily by kicking at the nearest object—the bedside table—and stubbed his toe.

"Goddamn it to hell!"

That felt better. A good "goddamn" was worth a thousand therapy sessions, and it was certainly a great deal cheaper.

But he still felt dirty. He got up and went to the closet for a fresh change of clothing. Dresses, blouses and skirts hung there, and a pink bra and a pile of panties littered the floor. He had forgotten he was in Melissa's room because he hadn't remembered yet how he had gotten there.

But where was Melissa?

Melissa had been taking care of business all morning. She had agreed to pay the stooge doctor a certain amount to keep him quiet, convinced the police no criminal act had been perpetrated, and was pretty certain she had persuaded the hotel management not to sue for the damages that had resulted during the near-riot after the seminar concluded much earlier than expected.

"They're still pretty steamed," Melissa told Roger that afternoon in his room. "If I keep working on them, maybe they'll settle out of court."

"Did you call my attorney?" Roger asked. He wore only a robe, having finally showered and shaved. He sat at the round table in the corner of the room, having deliberately put space between him and Melissa, who sat on the edge of his bed.

"Of course."

"What did he say?"

"He said he'd take care of it. All of it, one way or

another. All it takes is money."

"What about the videotapes?"

"What videotapes?" She smiled like a child keeping a secret.

"Of what happened?"

"There never were any videotapes. At least not as far as we're concerned. I bought them from the video company this morning and made them sign a paper saying there were no other copies. Then I destroyed them."

"You couldn't do that with the local media." He was amazed at her in spite of his underlying feeling of general misgiving. He was also having trouble accepting Melissa's apparent ease at covering up the whole debacle. She seemed entirely too cheerful about it, and that grated on his nerves. This was a solemn matter, not something to be brushed away like a minor annoyance.

"You're right, but I've obtained a temporary injunction prohibiting them from showing them. That part wasn't so easy. But I know a local attorney, and the judge owed him a favor; and this particular judge doesn't like TV media people. If any local station shows any portion of the tapes they made, you can sue *them.*"

"What about the newspapers?"

"I couldn't do much about that. There's a story in the Columbus paper, of course, and it'll go out on a national wire too—but, well, I think it might help us more than hurt us."

Roger noted her use of "us," and shook his head. "How in the hell can you say that?"

"Publicity."

"But it's bad publicity."

"That doesn't matter. You'll be in the public eye, and that means people will flock to see The Astounding One more than ever—if only to see if you'll screw up."

Roger was suddenly outraged. Her flippant manner had finally become too much to take, especially her calling him The Astounding One so casually. "Melissa! I can't believe you're taking this so lightly. I almost *killed* a man, for Christ's sake, and I didn't even know I was doing it.

And you say this is covered up, and that is covered up, and we pay off this guy and that son of a bitch, and everything will be hunky-dory."

Her bright blue eyes fluttered a little, but otherwise she didn't seem visibly upset by his outburst. "Roger," she said evenly, "I was just trying to do what's best for you. I had no intention of making you angry. What's done is done. You can't let it stymie you, or impede the progress of your career."

"What about that actor? How can I let that just slide by as if it never happened?"

"I think he's going to sign a release saying he won't sue you—for a slight fee, of course. I've been working on him, and I'm sure your attorney will manage to get it through his thick head that suing you isn't going to help his acting career, such as it is."

"But what about what I did to him?"

"It's between you and your conscience, Roger, of course. But you didn't mean to hurt him, did you?"

"Of course not!"

"Then let it go. Don't let it fester. The man isn't going to die. As it turns out, it was only a superficial wound, and the doctor overreacted—and the actor was over*acting*. There was so much stage blood mixed with the real blood it appeared a lot worse than it was. By the way, you'll have to show me how to make that fake blood sometime—it was really convincing."

Roger held out his palms, regarding them with horror. "But I had my whole hands inside the man. It couldn't have been a minor wound."

"Roger," Melissa said calmly, almost patronizing him. "It didn't happen that way."

"It did! My hands were covered with blood."

"Fake blood. You used too much in your prop thumb. Your hands never went into the actor's abdomen. Maybe it just seemed that way to you . . ."

"Seemed, my ass. I know what I saw—what I felt. Just get out one of those tapes . . ." But the tapes,he realized, were gone. There was no real record of what had happened, unless he approached the local media. They'd be unlikely to cooperate the way Melissa had taken care of the whole affair. She had fixed everything. It was all very tidy too, with no loose ends. Anger started to rise in him, but abruptly drained away, as if numbed by an unseen force. He was unsure whom he should be angry with—the actor? The media? Melissa?

"Then it's all taken care of, I suppose," he said with weary resignation. He knew he was supposed to be appreciative, but he felt impotent and vulnerable.

"All of it. Except for your statement to the press, which I've made a first draft of for your approval. This will be the finishing touch."

She rose from the edge of his bed, her face a mask of pure innocence as she took a sheath of papers from her purse and handed them over to Roger. He barely glanced at them. He was studying Melissa, trying once again to decide exactly who and what this woman was. She was so young—too young in his estimation—to know so much about manipulating people, and she seemed to like doing it. She was even excited about it as far as he could judge, probably even thankful for the opportunity Roger had unintentionally provided her. What did she expect in return from him?

What *could* she expect?

Suddenly, the smell of her perfume seemed to fill the room as if on cue. It was one of those musky-smelling concoctions women wore when they were truly serious about snaring a man. Its odor made Roger feel weak at the knees and blunted the already dulled edge of his awareness, while awakening a primal urge in the parts of him that didn't rationalize at all. He remembered a psychic trying to tell him once that women became "in season" just as most animals did, only the trappings of civilization had diminished man's ability to detect the mating scent. Deodorants and soap masked it; certain perfumes enhanced it. Melissa was wearing that sort of perfume, and it was causing another kind of ache altogether in his bruised groin.

He had cautioned her against teasing him. He had told her he was not a man to be trifled with. Yet, despite his ultimatum, her mere presence was a constant tease; her beauty called to any man who wasn't too old or too crippled to perform. He had been a fool to let her accompany him on this tour because of a supposed biography she was doing. It was obvious she had other things on her mind besides writing about him. She had usurped Edith's role almost totally, by becoming a part of his life—on a platonic basis, at least—but how long would such a relationship be enough for her? Or for him?

There were still so many things he didn't know about her; but every time he considered the questions, he also considered the consequences of knowing the answers, and he didn't want to face the truths Melissa might have to offer about herself. Her manipulative ability, her conveniently knowing the right people in the right places, her seemingly magical capacity for knowing what he needed—all of that bothered him. It made him angry too, he had to admit.

And ultimately it scared him. He had never met a woman *he* couldn't manipulate—or at least dismiss from his life. He had parted easily from three wives. Melissa represented the ultimate challenge to his manhood and his ego.

Melissa returned to his bed and leaned back on her elbows, lounging dreamily as if there were nothing in the world wrong with any part of Roger's life or their relationship. Her movement caused her skirt to hitch up past her knees, and from Roger's point of view, the white vee of her panties was clearly visible. Was that a deliberate signal or only the carelessness of being casual?

He didn't want to know. Not yet. He shifted his eyes to the papers in his hands and began to scan them. He was surprised and astounded by the words of the speech. It was both brilliant and meaningless, like a politician's speech.

If the press bought this—if anyone bought it—they'd have to be either gullible or damned foolish. It was all a big lie, conceived in Melissa's mind.

But, he reminded himself, big lies were the easiest to believe. If they weren't, he would have no purpose in writing books.

". . . and that, ladies and gentlemen, is what really happened. The actor simply overacted, causing me to scratch his skin superficially. The fake blood made it look worse than it was. I suppose I should get a job as a special effects man on the next *Friday the 13th.*"

The small audience of local media people—and at least one UPI correspondent—responded with appreciative laughter. Roger smiled back at them.

He could tell they had bought the whole explanation. It was an elaborate tissue of lies and bullshit, but they had fallen for it—because, he realized with chagrin, they *wanted* to believe it. Roger had established himself as the witch-hunter of the New Age, the rationalist with a cause, and the press had been with him most of the way through his career, not only because of his own journalistic origins, but also because journalists on the whole were skeptics who loved to debunk psychics and paranormal phenomena as much as he did. It made good copy and even better headlines.

"That concludes my statement," Roger said. "Any questions?"

There were a few, but they were not particularly difficult or pointed, and Roger fielded them readily. He glanced over his shoulder at Melissa a couple of times during the questioning, to see how she was reacting, and he thought she was gloating. After all, the statement he had made was her tissue of lies, not his, and he had agreed to deliver it to the press without really thinking about it.

Or perhaps he had thought about it—through the haze of her perfume and the thickening of thought processes that came from viewing the seductiveness of her pose on his bed. Under such circumstances, it would be difficult for any man to make a fully reasoned decision. But he had gone along with this duplicity—this utter fraud—without pausing even to feel guilty. There was something wrong about perpetrating lies, even when they were beneficial to one's self. It violated a personal code of his, but still it didn't bother his conscience as much as it should.

Maybe it wasn't his own code he was violating, he realized. It was his father's code, imprinted on his mind since infancy.

But in this case, even his father might go along with the plan—because the alternative to the big lie was the possibility of lawsuits and great losses of money. Roger had finally succumbed to the logic of that, though his decision was still unduly influenced by Melissa's presence—which was a motivational force in itself.

After the press conference was over, Roger joined Melissa in the hotel bar for a couple of drinks in a dark corner. A band was playing raucous rock—badly—so loudly thcy could barely talk.

Finally, the band finished its first set of the evening and went on break. The absence of their music was a cue to everyone in the room to talk freely, and the buzz of conversation began even before the band members left the bandstand.

"So, how do you think it went?" Roger asked Melissa. He stared into her eyes over the flickering red candle in the middle of the table. The flame reflected there created an illusion that her eyes contained tiny fires. She was wearing a light-blue silk blouse and navy-blue skirt. She looked both businesslike and seductive.

"It went beautifully," she said. "You are the most persuasive speaker and natural showman I've ever seen. I suspected as much when I read your books and saw you on TV a couple of times, but now that I've seen you perform in person—under the most trying of circumstances, I might add—I'm convinced you have that touch of greatness only a few men ever achieve."

Roger blushed and regarded her doubtfully. "I'm not Abraham Lincoln, for Christ's sake."

Her laugh was high-pitched and loud, almost embarrassing. "Oops! These margaritas are potent stuff. I think three must be my limit. Or was it four?"

"That's why I stick to Scotch. It's a controlled substance."

"That's funny. I think. Oops." She started giggling. "I better not laugh so much. You'll make me pee in my pants." She laughed even harder.

"What's so funny now?" Roger asked, about to break out into laughter himself.

"It's a big secret," she said.

"You can tell me."

"Okay. I can't pee in my pants."

"Why not?"

"I'm not wearing any."

He gulped Scotch, and some of it came up the back of his nose, stinging his nasal passages. "You're what?"

"Not wearing any panties. Want to see?" She started to pull her skirt up.

Roger grabbed her wrist to stop her. "Melissa! Quit carrying on. People are staring."

"No, they're not. You're just self-conscious. Here, if you don't want to see, then feel."

She gripped his hand and thrust it up under her skirt. His fingers brushed her pubic hair, and he jerked his hand away.

"Melissa," he whispered. "Why . . . ?"

"Why not?" she answered.

They waited at the elevator. Nothing had been discussed, but they both agreed with their eyes that this evening was going to end a certain way. There was also a tacit understanding that no commitment was involved; this was sex for its own sake, a spur of the moment thing decided by impulse and alcohol, merely to see what it would be like with each other. They barely touched each other now, standing together more like father and daughter than potential lovers.

"Are you sure about this?" Roger asked.

"Very sure."

The elevator arrived, and they stepped in. Roger worried that he may have had one too many Scotches and that could affect his performance. His mind had a rigid hard-on, however, and maybe that would suffice.

The elevator stopped at the second floor, and a greasy, old bum teetered in on a single crutch. One of his legs was shorter than the other and twisted at an odd angle from his hip. He wore ragged clothes and stank of cheap wine. He clearly was not a guest of the hotel, though he punched the button for the third floor with authority. Roger and Melissa pulled away from him instinctively. Roger felt cold sweat break out on his upper lip at the sight of the man's deformity.

"Fuck a duck," the old man mumbled, "screw a pigeon, go to hell and learn religion."

Melissa glanced at Roger and stifled a laugh. Roger stared straight ahead, refusing to participate.

The elevator stopped at the third floor. Instead of getting off, the old man lurched forward halfway between the door and the floor of the hall. He couldn't seem to move any farther, and the elevator door started to close on his bad leg. "Goddamn sunabitch!"

His crutch was caught in the door.

"I guess we have to help him," Melissa said, her speech only slightly less slurred than the old drunk's. "Give him a help—I mean a hand, Roger." Melissa pressed the "Door Open" button so that the door would stop bouncing back and forth on the man's leg.

Reluctantly, Roger approached the man and stooped down to get the edge of the crutch out of the rubber molding of the door. He avoided looking at the man's leg, which was making him feel queasy; no amount of Scotch could banish his phobias. He fumbled with the tip of the crutch until it was free. The old man fell backward into the hall.

"Help him up," Melissa insisted.

The smell of the man and the sight of his twisted leg were difficult to endure; Roger felt bile rising in his throat, but he forced himself to help the man to his feet and propped the crutch under his arm.

"Thanks a million, bud," the man said. Then he squinted at Roger with his glassy eyes, and his face became an ugly scowl. "So it's you, is it? Roger Kant."

"Yes, I am," Roger said, retreating to the elevator.

"I seen you on TV down at the bar," the man continued. "It's all a fucking lie! All that shit you said. A fucking—"

The elevator door slid shut.

Roger trembled next to Melissa.

"Don't let that old fart get to you," she said. "He's only trying to spoil our evening."

"He was right. It was a lie."

"So what? It's over and done with now." She reached up and touched his earlobe with her tongue as she put her hand down the front of his trousers. "We have other fish to fry tonight."

They didn't face each other as they undressed in the semi-darkness of his room. Roger was self-conscious about his paunch and didn't want to reveal its naked ugliness to her while he was standing. Lying down, he didn't think it was quite as noticeable—or repulsive.

There was an awkward moment as they slid under the covers and their bare flesh touched for the first time, but it was quickly over. Then they started exploring each other, she rubbing her hands over his hairy stomach, he playing with the tangle of hair between her legs. Soon they started kissing, and Roger discovered the Scotch had not taken the lead out of his pencil after all.

Melissa proved to be as sensual as she appeared. She did tricks with her tongue and with the muscles inside her that Roger didn't know any woman was capable of. But the months of deprivation were too much for him, and it was over much too quickly.

Roger lay spent on his back, trying to catch his breath. "I'm sorry," he muttered.

"About what?" she asked languidly. She still seemed fresh, though he was certain she'd had several orgasms.

"About it being over so soon."

"That's okay. The second time will be better—and will last longer."

"You're expecting a lot from a man my age."

"You're not old," she chastised him, "unless you think you are."

"I still don't think I can go a second time."

"What's the matter with your toe?" she asked, changing the subject. "It's all purple."

His toe was illuminated by the light from the bathroom, the door of which they had left slightly open to act as a night light. The toe was indeed a sorry sight, and now that he thought about it, it began to throb with pain.

"I stubbed it this morning," he admitted, "in a fit of anger."

"Poor Roger—always hurting himself." She crawled down to the end of the bed and examined the damaged toe closely. "Looks pretty bad."

"I'll be all right."

"No. This needs attention." Without warning, she wrapped her lips around his toe and sucked on it gently.

Roger felt a wave of warmth shoot up his leg and stop at his crotch.

She sucked it several seconds, then let go, smacking her lips. "Better?" she asked.

"Much better," he said, his voice cracking.

Melissa turned over and crawled back up beside him. "I see you're ready again. I knew you had it in you."

"And now it's going to be in you," he said, and matched his action to his words.

The demon came that night. It waited till Roger was deep in slumber, his body still aglow from three sessions of sex with Melissa, and hit him right between the eyes.

The demon was coming from between Melissa's legs. Its body was a scaly, snakelike thing that lived up there, and it threatened to attack him if he attempted to make love to her again. But Roger wanted more of her, despite the demon's having made her insides his dwelling place. If only he had a weapon, he would cut the demon's head off!

But he was naked and weaponless.

The demon grew in size until it split Melissa open and pieces of her insides pelted Roger in a rain of bloody flesh. Enraged, Roger rushed at the demon, grasping at its slimy skin, determined to twist its head off if he could.

But the demon was too quick for him. It opened its huge maw, and its fangs came down over Roger, ready to bite him in two at the waist . . .

"No!" Roger screamed.

"What—what is it?" Melissa asked, awakened immediately.

Roger sat up in the bed. His body was soaked with sweat.

"The thing," he said haltingly. "The demon. The one I saw at Edith's grave. I had a nightmare about it."

She pulled him over to her, wrapping her arms around him. "You don't have to worry about nightmares with me here. No demon can conquer the two of us."

"You don't know all about it," he said.

"Tell me," she whispered. "Tell me all about it, and then it will go away."

Roger began slowly, searching for the right words; then the more he told about his various encounters with the demon, the more easily the words flowed. He told her how he had been having visions of horror for weeks now. Sometimes they were so intense he could hardly function, and he blamed his exhaustion and his inability to cope with Edith's death for the persistence of the demon. Worst of all, he had visions that seemed to be planned by the demon to lead him astray, as his vision the night before last had done. He had seen the demon many times now.

"I saw him in the audience last night," he said, "just after the accident with the actor."

"It was your imagination, of course."

"I could've sworn I had him in my hands. I was trying to strangle him." He sighed. "So, now, I guess you don't think much of me. Seeing visions and imaginary demons is the sign of a weak or sick mind. My mind is both weak and sick at the moment, and you probably should get shut of me while you can." He felt very vulnerable and guilty at the same time. He hadn't needed to tell her everything, yet it had all come out, as if she were his psychiatrist.

"Roger, you fool, this makes no difference at all. I'm impressed that you're man enough to admit all these things to me. I understand completely. I've studied psychology and know that this demon is just something your mind is projecting—as a way of undermining your success. Because part of you doesn't believe you deserve success. It happens to many famous people. You have to fight back, Roger. Put that demon back in hell where it belongs."

"I don't know if I can."

"You can, if you'll let me help you."

She closed her eyes and snuggled against his chest. "Now let's go back to sleep. We have to get up early to go to Pittsburgh."

"May I ask you one question first?"

"What?" She yawned widely.

"Why are you so much happier when I'm failing than when I'm succeeding? It's been bothering me for days."

"Am I?"

"You know you are."

"You wouldn't understand."

"Try me."

She opened her eyes and made contact with his. "Because I was afraid you wouldn't need me anymore—that you'd grow tired of me if things were going okay."

"Did you wish for things to go wrong?"

"Of course not. It's just that—well, now it's all different. I understand about the demon and the visions, and knowing that, I realize you do need me; and that means I have a place in your life, no matter how successful you are. I don't have to wait for something bad to happen to be necessary. Okay?"

Roger mumbled assent, but he was still confused. Was it just feminine logic that he failed to understand, or was

Melissa manufacturing another elaborate lie?

Her warm body was so reassuring, it was difficult for him to confront the possibility of her lying to him. Sex brought out the truth, didn't it? How could anyone lie after such intimacy?

His wives had lied plenty after sex, he recalled. But none of them had been as innocent or truly loving as Melissa.

He liked being near her; he liked having her body respond to his. He didn't want to give up even a brief fling with her, no matter what compromises he had to make personally. She had made him feel like a man again, and certainly his renewed self could conquer any demon—any monster of the subconscious, he amended—his mind could manufacture.

At least he hoped so.

"Everything's going to be okay," Melissa said, intruding into his thoughts. "Melissa can fix anything."

Roger had no doubt about that. But before he fell asleep again, the crippled old man's words echoed in his mind:

"It's all a fucking lie!"

PART TWO:

Delusions of Love

11. Travelogue

Melissa was wrong that night in Columbus. Everything was not going to be okay. The rest of the tour continued to present problems and nightmares for Roger. If Melissa hadn't been with him, he would have cut the tour short, but she provided the support he needed to keep going while he provided the anger, which drove him almost as much as her support.

He had a great deal to be angry about. Everytime he made a public appearance, something would invariably go wrong in some totally unpredictable way despite all the paranoid precautions Roger took. None of it seemed to matter; it was as if all the machinery of the universe was set to get Roger Kant, to make him seem an utter fool, to destroy his ego, to ruin his reputation. If Roger had believed in a vengeful deity, he would certainly have thought that deity was testing him, but Roger was having difficulty believing in any deity, benevolent or malevolent.

He was, however, beginning to contemplate the possibility of the existence of demons. He would sometimes wake in the night and imagine his room was populated with hordes of demonlike creatures crawling over everything like berserk gremlins. When he saw these things, he would inevitably experience a bout of formication, followed by chills, and sometimes fever and nausea.

It made no difference if Melissa was in bed with him or not. When she was, she could only hold him and assure him this period of his life would pass, that things would change.

But Roger had little reason to accept her reassurances. There was just too much going against him.

In Pittsburgh, Roger attended a book-signing session and ended up signing only four books, one of which turned out to have been shoplifted; it was as if no one in that city had ever heard of him. Later, on a radio show, only one person called in.

The second night in Pittsburgh, Roger held a seminar that was poorly attended—the hall was only seventy-five percent full. However, it went well the first hour, which almost restored his confidence. He bent spoons and challenged the audience in a billet demonstration that duly impressed them. Then he attempted a levitation trick he had learned from a famous magician and levitated a woman halfway off the floor, when something snapped in the hidden apparatus and she fell, breaking a bone in her calf. She filed a lawsuit the next day.

Roger challenged a local astrologer on a Baltimore TV program and exposed himself to unrestrained mockery. The astrologer, to whom Roger had deliberately given false information about his birth data—as he did with all astrologers—still read Roger correctly, guessing his sun sign with no apparent effort. He then proceeded to dissect Roger's character in minute detail, all of which even Roger had to admit was true. Roger became livid, swearing on the live TV show and making himself appear even more foolish, while the astrologer sat smugly by, damning him with silence. During the commercial break, Roger was chewed out by the director of the show, and when the cameras came back on, he had to restrain himself from screaming more obscenities as the astrologer correctly read nine people chosen at random from the audience.

Roger almost had to pay the man twenty thousand dollars, except he had agreed to read ten people, and he failed on the tenth person, which made Roger feel mildly relieved. But his speech afterward, in which he tried to convince the studio audience that astrology was bunk, was lame and uncompelling, and he was shouted down by hoots and boos. It was evident the audience was on the side of the astrologer, or, for all Roger knew, in league with him.

Roger's seminar in Baltimore was also poorly attended; he barely broke even on the expense of hiring the hall. It was just as well, since the people who did attend were halfhearted in their support of him. He was so nervous, he flubbed the billet demonstration and began to mumble incoherently during his speech. Finally, Melissa had to lead him away from the stage while the audience booed.

He sold no books, signed no autographs.

He and Melissa didn't make love in Baltimore.

In Boston, Roger did a little better. His appearance on a radio talk show was moderately successful, and he had a chance to plug his book shamelessly between phone calls. The result was that a respectable number of people showed up at his autographing session in a local bookstore, though few bought books. Those who came were mainly people who had been long-time fans, and many of them asked him to sign ragged copies of his old paperbacks.

That gave Roger the confidence he needed to get through another seminar. The crowd was receptive, and Roger was encouraged when they applauded his spoon bending and fake mind reading act, and he spoke at length on the chicaneries of the New Age. He felt he persuaded many of the audience to his way of thinking.

During the question and answer period, however, Roger was challenged by a skinny young man who resembled a person he had seen at another seminar elsewhere. He stood in the center aisle of the hall and made bold, defiant eye contact with Roger.

"What is your question, sir?" Roger asked, beaming with the rapport he had established that evening and ignoring the man's challenging posture.

"Did you know that psychics *have* to be vague in their readings?"

"I don't know what you mean."

"You make a big point out of how vague readings are, but the fact of the matter, Mr. Astounding One, is that the laws in each state vary—and determine how a psychic may make his reading. Most of these laws make it impossible for a psychic to render the truth—without incurring possible legal action."

"I don't see how that applies . . ."

"Well?"

"Well, what?" Roger said, suddenly feeling nervous and breaking eye contact.

"Did you know that, Citizen Kant?"

Roger could feel the gaze of the audience pressing on him. His mind raced for an answer. He looked over to Melissa, whose expression showed ignorance as well.

"I'm a psychic and I know all the legal ways to make a reading," the young man continued. "If you knew them, then you'd understand why we must be vague in some cases. But obviously, you don't know much, because if you did—and I'm *not* being vague, so sue me—you'd know your life is going down the drain—and it's all your own doing."

"I didn't ask for a reading from you, sir!"

"It's free." The man turned around and headed for the side exit.

"That man is a fake," Roger screamed. "A posturing quack, promulgating psychic mumbo jumbo, a—" Then he lost the ability to speak as he realized his inquisitor resembled the man in a turban who had seemingly disappeared in Indianapolis . . . .

The audience was full of demons, all their faces contorted masks of malice. He stood there at the lectern a full five minutes, too stunned to speak, before Melissa realized he had blanked out. She pulled him away from the microphone and tried to encourage him, but she couldn't reach him.

It was too late anyhow; Roger had lost his audience. He found his voice long enough to apologize to them, but they were no longer listening; most of them had gone. Melissa took him back to their hotel room.

That night they attempted to make love; but Roger was clumsy and unresponsive, and Melissa gave up quickly, contenting herself with holding him until he fell asleep.

After Boston, Roger and Melissa stopped briefly in Rhode Island before going on to New York. They had no real business there, since nothing was scheduled for the tour for a couple of days, but Roger liked that part of the country and insisted on taking Melissa on a tour of the mansions in Newport. Melissa was only semi-impressed, and Roger wondered why; but he said nothing.

After Newport, they went on to Providence, where Roger visited an occult bookstore, primarily to check out what the competition was doing. He was disgusted by the artifacts for sale in the small, dark and dusty store—crystal balls, Tarot decks, pewter figures of sorcerers and enchantresses, sets of Runes, and other paraphernalia—and he was disturbed by the display of New Age magazines.

The books upset him even more. There were tomes on crystals, faith healing, herbal medicine, channelling, the Tarot, the Kaballah, the *I Ching*, the paranormal, parapsychology, the occult, the supernatural, ghosts, reincarnation, ESP, time slips, and critical studies of such figures as Aleister Crowley, Dion Fortune, Uri Geller, and Arthur Waite, as well as books by these people.

"Think of all the waste," he muttered to Melissa.

"What do you mean?" she asked.

"All the trees cut down to make all the paper this crap is printed on. Why do people keep seeking magical answers to their problems? Did you know that even seemingly intelligent people—even people in Mensa—are starting to buy this New Age baloney? It seems the more logical a person is supposed to be, the easier he or she is fooled. The only thing worse than this is organized religion, but even that's getting a run for its money from the New Agers."

"You shouldn't let it bother you," Melissa said. "There's always been madness in the world."

"But I don't like this madness. I don't like people believing in this nonsense."

"You can't control the masses."

"But I want to. I can't help myself. Where are my books in this store? Where's the voice of reason?"

Melissa scanned a row of magazines and said, "Here's your voice. Your name's on the cover of this copy of *New Age*!"

"My interview! It's finally come out! Grab a copy and let's get out of here before I go berserk."

Melissa paid for the magazine, and they left the store. Roger fumed and fretted all the way to the car they had rented for their tour of Rhode Island.

"I shouldn't go in places like that," he said. "It's not good for my blood pressure."

As Melissa drove to the airport, Roger read the interview the magazine had done of him—supposedly in the interest of presenting a balanced view on the New Age and its philosophies.

Roger was livid before he finished the second paragraph. "The bastards! They tampered with my comments. I sound like an utter asshole here—a charlatan. And look at this . . ." He pointed to a paragraph, and Melissa glanced at it warily, while trying to keep her eyes on the road. ". . . this makes me sound like an ogre. It sounds like I'm calling that channeller out in New Mexico a child molester! I never said that. I didn't say any of this."

"Maybe they misinterpreted your words, Roger."

"Bullshit. They rearranged my words so that none of their readers' cherished beliefs would be challenged. They wanted to make me seem like an idiot."

He cast a sideways glance at Melissa. He had expected more outrage on her part, but she seemed calm.

"Well?"

"What do you want me to say, Roger? It's in print. You can't change that. You have to live with it. If you want, we can sue them, but a magazine like that isn't going to have much money."

"I don't want to sue them," he ranted. "I want to put them out of business!"

"Roger," Melissa said, expertly weaving in and out of traffic on the interstate, "you can't control the world."

"I don't care," he said. "I want to put them all out of business."

Once they were on the plane to New York, Roger had more cause to rave. He found a review of his book, *The New Age Con Game*, in the back of the magazine, which called it "a diatribe of ignorance, perpetrated by a hack, semi-professional magician with no credentials other than his own deluded and jaded view of the world."

Roger was so enraged he couldn't speak.

Roger had several reasons for going to New York. He was conducting a seminar there and was scheduled to be on national TV, but he also needed to visit his publisher and agent.

The New Age Con Game was published by a subsidiary of a major conglomerate with offices on Madison Avenue. Roger called his editor there, Dan Ransom, with whom he had always maintained friendly relations, to invite him to lunch with him and Melissa. Ransom couldn't make it for lunch, but he agreed to meet with Roger at ten that morning.

Roger left Melissa at their hotel and met Ransom in his office. When he walked in, he was overwhelmed by the mess. There were unopened manuscripts piled everywhere, as well as stacks of manuscripts on Ransom's desk, some read, most evidently unread. There were contracts, mock-ups of book covers, catalog sheets and a chart on the wall showing sales figures.

"Have a seat, Roger," Ransom said, after they shook hands. "I'd say excuse the mess, but that wouldn't be honest, because there's always a mess in here."

Ransom was about forty-eight, a squat, balding man with a sparse beard who always reminded Roger of an older Richard Dreyfus.

"So how are things going?" Ransom asked, after Roger sat down. His tone was one of forced friendliness, lacking the cordiality he normally offered all authors.

"You're supposed to tell me that."

"I gather you haven't talked to Gretta, then."

"My agent?"

"It's really her place to tell you the way things are going right now."

"Come on, Dan, we've known each other too long for you to beat around the bush. Tell me what this is about."

Ransom sighed; he hated telling authors bad news, especially in person. "It's your book," he said. "It's not even a good-news-bad-news thing. It's all bad. Stores are cancelling orders. We're not going to earn back the advance."

"What about the paperback?"

"Jesus, Roger, there may not be a paperback. The publicity that's followed your tour has the paperback publishers running scared. And the reviews have been pretty bad, too. One editor told me, 'Roger Kant is poison.'" He paused and grimaced. "But don't take that personally. I probably shouldn't have said that."

"How else can I take it?"

"Look, the book business is based on trends, and the trend is *for* the New Age movement right now, not against it. That's the bottom line, and we live and die by the bottom line. Hell, from what I hear, even your previous books aren't selling the way they used to."

"But I see them everywhere I go."

"You won't for long—not at the rate you're going. The public is seeing you in a different light now—as a destroying influence—because you're fucking with their dreams. Every age has its messiahs, and there's a whole flock of them out there now, spreading the New Age gospel."

"I'm only telling the truth, but I suppose that doesn't count for anything."

"The truth is what any two people agree on at a given moment. It's not an absolute. You're a majority of one right now. You're coming on too strong."

"What do you want me to do, put on a crystal and start writing about meditation?"

Ransom looked irritated. "Hell, no, Roger. You have to be honest with yourself. But you can't buck trends. Don't let it get you down. The whole thing may change back the other way before you know it. But now—at this present moment—we're having to eat a lot of books. We did a big print run, and I'm afraid most of them are going to be remaindered. Which means we'll lose money, and the boys upstairs will get pissed off, and they won't want your next book, unless you can come up with something that won't offend people so much. Why don't you meet with Gretta and talk it out? She'll have some ideas, I'm sure."

"You're telling me I'm an anachronism? The voice of reason is an anachronism too, then." He stood up and pounded the edge of Ransom's desk. "Why do *I* have to change? Let the others change."

"Don't shoot me, man," Ransom said, holding up his palms against Roger's ranting. "I'm only a fucking editor."

Roger walked back to the hotel in a state of depression. As he moved through the mob of New Yorkers, he suddenly felt paranoid.

He found himself remembering some of the things he had done: infiltrating faith healing sessions, planting his own people in the audience when astrologers or psychics spoke—among many other acts that might be considered semi-criminal. But he had done all that in the pursuit of truth, and that used to mean it was okay. But it also meant he had made many enemies, none of them in high places, but some of them with money behind them. Perhaps some of the things he had done were coming back on him; perhaps people were out to get him. Maybe everyone was after him.

Any one of these people might recognize him and attack him. He had to watch them closely. A quick hand could reach out and stick a knife in his back. Someone could pull a gun. That old bag lady might have acid in her bag to throw in his face. That dude with the ghetto blaster might be concealing a razor in his shoe or that well-dressed woman might take off her spiked heels and use them to pummel him to death. That little kid might . . . .

Then he saw the person who would do all those things and more, without remorse or compunction: the demon.

Dressed in a black raincoat and wearing a dark gray hat, he was standing on the corner next to a news kiosk, picking his nose. He watched Roger out of the corner of his eye, affecting an insouciant air, which didn't fool Roger a bit.

Roger approached him slowly. He wasn't going to startle him into making a break for it. He was going to catch him this time and make him confess how he was responsible for all that was going wrong in Roger's life.

The demon seemed not to care. He didn't move at all.

Roger went up to the kiosk and bought a copy of the *Times*. He tucked it under his arm and started to walk past the demon, then halted abruptly and turned on him.

"You. . . ."

"Yes, Roger?"

"You son of a bitch."

"Quite true. My mother was a mongrel; there's no doubt about that."

"You bastard."

"Also true, unfortunately. I think that affected my upbringing."

"I'm going to kill you."

"No, you're not, Roger. You can't kill me."

"Why not?"

"Because, Roger, if you'd only look close enough, you'd see I *am* you. I'm the product of your diseased mind."

"That's bullshit."

"Then, what am I?"

"I—I don't know, but I'm going to rid myself of you forever. Now."

"Go ahead. It matters little to me, whether I live or die. One state of existence is as good as another."

Roger dropped his paper and reached for the demon's throat. As he gripped the scaly skin of the monster's neck, he felt something crack in his fingers.

"Hey, lookit that dumb muthafucker," an onlooker said. "Tryin' to choke a fuckin' stoplight."

Roger eventually wandered back to the hotel. Melissa was worried by his absence, but almost went into hysterics when she saw the condition of his fingers. She worried they might be broken, but they were only bruised and bloodied by his encounter with the metal post of the stoplight on Madison Avenue.

"I have to talk to Gretta," Roger said, ignoring Melissa's concern. "My career is down the drain, just like the little man in Boston said."

"It's not that bad. Things will work out."

"Stop it, Melissa. Stop being a Pollyanna. This is serious. I think the whole world is out to get me. My book isn't selling. I'm seeing the demon in broad daylight. I even talked to him."

"Roger, maybe you ought to see a doctor."

"Why a doctor? I can go buy some crystals and wear them around my neck. I can go to a faith healer. Who needs a fucking doctor when we have all this wonderful magic available to us?"

"What's really the matter?"

He told her everything Dan Ransom had said.

"No wonder you're feeling down. But he's just one man. Why don't you have a drink and eat something. Then we'll go talk to Gretta and plan our strategy. There are other publishers."

"I guess you're right," Roger said without conviction. "But let's have something sent up to the room. I can't stand to be out in public right now. Okay?"

"Sure, Roger, anything you say."

Roger sighed as he watched Melissa walk through the room to the telephone to call room service. She was his voice of reason now. She was the one who always knew what to do, while he was becoming an idiot. How fortunate he was to have her by his side in this time of adversity. At least he had that much going for him. She was like a mother, a sister, and a lover all rolled into one, and the best companion he ever had.

But why, he asked himself, did she always have to be quite so positive? Why didn't she participate in his jeremiads? After all, his troubles affected her as well.

Maybe it was because she was too sensible.

She ordered lunch, then fixed him a strong Scotch and water.

He sipped the drink, which definitely calmed his nerves. "Get Gretta on the phone for me, will you?"

"Sure." She dialed the number of Gretta Powers, his literary agent, whose office was in Manhattan.

She talked briefly, then handed the phone to Roger.

"Yes, Gretta?"

"I hate to have to do this, Roger. You've always been a good client—but I have to drop you from my client list."

"What? Why? Is it because of what Ransom said?"

"Not exactly. He's a jerk; but he knows the business, and right now, your stuff isn't selling the way it used to. I don't have the time to nurse your career back to health. I have other clients who need me full time."

"But, Gretta, I've been with you for years."

"I know. It's not personal. I value you as a friend and always will, but business is business." She made a grumbling noise. "I hate to tell you this, but having you as part of my client list is affecting my deals for my other clients. It's affecting my credibility. You've become a liability, and I'm not big enough to absorb it. You understand, don't you?"

"So I'm a liability. That's great. Just great."

"Honest-to-God, Roger, I don't mean it to sound like that, but it's just facts. I have to make a living and—"

Roger didn't wait for further explanations. He hung up without saying good-bye.

"That bitch," he said. "After all the money I've made for her."

"What's the matter?" Melissa asked.

"I'm a liability," he replied. "A big liability. If you're going to hang around me, you'd better take out extra insurance."

12. Persistence of the Demon

"You don't need her if she doesn't have any more faith than that in you," Melissa told Roger. "Why, I could be a better agent than she is."

"You probably could at that," Roger said. "But we don't have to worry about an agent at the moment. The way my books are selling, I'm not sure it makes a difference. Did you check to see if my appearance on *Later* is still on?"

"Yes. You have to be at the studio tomorrow at five-thirty in the evening for make-up. I'm not sure when the actual taping begins."

"Well, I'd better get my act together. Costas is always up on things. He may ask some tough questions."

"You can handle it, Roger. I still have faith in you."

He touched her hand, then kissed her lightly. "That's fine, Melissa. Now, if only you could convince the rest of the world I'm not a total fuck-up, things would be great."

That night, as Melissa lay next to him, Roger stared into the darkness. It was probably three in the morning, and he had yet to close his eyes, though he had drunk close to a pint of Scotch. He kept comparing the nature of his life a year ago to the way it was now, and it didn't seem possible he had fallen so far in such a short time.

He was sure it had something to do with the demon. The

demon was out to get him, to destroy his career. And since he had decided the demon was a projection of his imagination, that meant he was the one responsible for his continuing failures. If he were one of the New Age people, he would believe in the demon as an entity, but he knew enough about psychology to realize the demon was only his personal delusion.

He pondered how he had created the demon and decided his subconscious mind had produced that particular monster by putting together pictures Roger had seen in many of the occult books he had read. There were supposed to be classes of demons, all of whom answered to the devil himself. He wondered what class his demon was. He hoped he wasn't too low in the echelons of hell; that would be insulting.

As he stared and thought, a translucent silver cloud appeared to form in the middle of the room, swirling out of the darkness.

Instead of being fearful, Roger found himself fascinated as figures began to form within the cloud. The demon's face appeared first, its twisted visage five feet wide. It laughed at him soundlessly. Roger had seen the demon too many times now; its appearance no longer terrified him or even made him angry.

"You'll have to do better than that," he whispered, smiling at the pitiful effort the demon was making.

Then slowly the demon's face transformed into the harsh features of his father scolding him silently. This face was also large, the way it must have looked to Roger when he was a small boy and was being reprimanded for some infringement on Dad's Law. Perhaps he was being lectured for losing money. That always put Dad into near-hysterics. Once, Roger had lost a dollar on his way to the dry cleaners, and his father had raved about it for nearly two hours, impressing upon Roger how valuable a dollar was. In 1959, perhaps, a dollar did buy more, but even then, it wasn't the end of the world to lose one. Roger remembered that scolding in detail, because even as a boy he knew it was out of proportion—that his father was making a big thing out of something very trivial. He had hated his father that day—and many days in the years to come he would find reason to hate him again.

It stung to remember that, but Roger had learned to deal with such childhood flashbacks. He merely put them aside, in a corner dustbin within his mind, where they were out of the way.

"This is piss-poor," Roger taunted. The demon was reaching for something that would upset Roger, but he was failing. His father's stern face came close, but it fell short of terrifying him, because his father had been a real person.

So the demon brought on a dumb show representing Roger's greatest phobia: cripples.

A parade of them hobbled and skittered through the cloud. Some of them had twisted legs and arms; others, hideously disfigured faces. They paraded on crutches, in wheelchairs, or legless on wheeled platforms. Some were children; others were ancient people barely propped up by their walkers as they trudged by. Each figure would stop briefly and extend its arms or stumps in a mute plea for some reaction from Roger.

Roger had to admit the demon was trying harder. This panorama of the unfortunates whose bodies were tortured shells struck at the core of Roger's fears. He had feared cripples since he was a child, for reasons he could not recall, and this was definitely making him queasy and nauseated.

But I can avoid cripples too, he thought. *All I have to do is close my eyes.*

He closed his eyes, and for a moment, he thought he could actually feel alcohol coursing through his brain, numbing the spots that needed deadening. Scotch could be an effective tonic against demons and cripples.

He opened his eyes, and the cloud had dissipated. He yawned as if he had witnessed a particularly bad play, which he had sat through only because he had paid for it.

He was tempted to awaken Melissa and tell her about this latest vision, because now that it was over it seemed droll. She might get a laugh out of it too.

He nudged her gently. She didn't stir.

He nudged her again, harder. This time, something odd happened. His finger went through the fabric of her nightgown and into her flesh, as if he had plunged it into dough. He pulled his finger out quickly and saw it was covered with something gray and gooey, which was alive with maggots.

"Melissa!"

The woman in the bed rolled over to face him. Worms were crawling out of her nose, mouth and ears. Most of the flesh of her face was rotted away, but enough remained for him to recognize her.

It was Edith.

She sucked air through her lipless mouth, smiled and several of her teeth fell out. She reached out her bony arms to embrace him.

Before Roger could move, she was on top of him, twisting her rotted corpse against him in a gruesome parody of sex.

Roger tried to escape, but he realized he couldn't.

Because he was no longer in the bed. He was inside Edith's coffin.

"I insist," Melissa said the next morning at breakfast. "You're going to wreck your health if you don't get more sleep. You're driving me crazy too, with these awful nightmares and supposed visions."

"But I don't want to see a doctor. I have as much faith in those quacks as I do in faith healers."

"You don't have to see a psychiatrist. Get some sleeping pills. At least buy some Nytol. You look like hell."

"I can handle this," Roger said. "It's just a temporary aberration."

"You know it's worse than that. It's not going to go away if you don't do something about it."

"I'm stronger than you think."

"But you've been pushing yourself." She shifted her

eyes away from him. "Frankly, Roger, I'm really concerned. It's hard for me to sleep with you every night, never knowing when you're going to wake up screaming."

"You don't have to sleep with me. You're not chained to the bed."

"But Roger, I *want* to sleep with you."

"You just said I disturb your sleep."

"You're not understanding—are you? It's gone deeper than just sex. I'm in love with you."

Roger regarded her silently for a moment. "You can't mean that."

"But I do."

"Jesus, Melissa, I'm very flattered, but I'm twenty years older than you, I'm bald, and I have a pot belly. Not to mention I'm a psychological wreck and I look like hell. What interest could you possibly have in a man like me?"

"I like sex with you."

"Sex. That's nothing. Anybody can do it."

"You don't understand that, either. Probably never have. A woman doesn't make love to a man's body; she makes love to his mind—or his personality. Haven't you ever seen beautiful women out with ugly men? Women don't see the physical flaws—unless they are very shallow women. What I love about you is your strength, your mentality, your resolve in the face of adversity. Those aren't qualities you find in just any man."

"You could love me for my money," he ventured, half joking.

"You know that's not true. I don't need money. Have I ever asked you for any?"

"No, I guess not."

"You don't know very much about me, Roger. You've wanted to ask questions—I've seen that in your expression many times—but you were afraid, because I think deep down inside you love me as well, but you don't want to take the risk a serious relationship entails."

"Maybe. . . ."

"No 'maybe' to it. I come from a wealthy family. I've paid my way all through this trip, without asking you for a dime, because I wanted to be near you. It started out as a whimsy, I'll admit—my writing your biography—but then I realized my place in your life was much more important. You needed me, and I needed you. Neither of us realized it at first, but now it's pretty clear if you'll own up to it."

"I don't know, Melissa. I've never had good luck with women. I married three times. And I screwed up three times. And every time I've pursued a woman in between marriages, it ended up with both of us hating each other."

"It wouldn't be that way with us. I know it."

"I have to think about it, Melissa. It's been a long time since anyone said she loved me."

"And meant it?"

"I guess that's it."

"And do you love me?"

"I don't know yet. I just don't know. My life's such a mess right now I can't think straight. I don't trust my own judgment."

"Then trust mine. Get some sleeping pills, and let's kick that old demon in the ass. Okay?"

He couldn't help smiling. "You have such a way with words."

Roger and Melissa arrived at the NBC studios on the Avenue of the Americas at quarter of five and rode the elevator up to the studio where the *Later* show was to be taped.

Roger spent a half hour in makeup. Melissa hovered behind the makeup people, making suggestions. Normally such interference wouldn't be tolerated or appreciated; but Melissa seemed to know what she was doing, and when the makeup lady did what she asked, Roger looked ten years younger. Even the scar on his cheek was barely visible.

This youthful appearance made him feel better about Melissa's profession of love for him; he wasn't such a bad-looking guy after all. However, he still worried about getting her involved any deeper in his life. He feared something might happen to *her* as a result.

He had to put his worries and cares aside now, though. It was showtime. *Later* was a national broadcast, and even though it didn't air until one-thirty in the morning in most cities, it still had a wide audience that just might be impressed enough to go out and buy his new book. His appearance here might even counteract the sales slump and turn it around completely.

After makeup, Roger chatted briefly with Bob Costas about possible topics of discussion. Roger wanted to start the show with a stunt—a simulation of psychic photography—and Costas agreed that it would be a "grabber" for the opening of the program. Fortunately, a Polaroid camera was readily available, and Roger had already prepared a Ted Serios type device to make the stunt work.

Ted Serios was a figure often mentioned in paranormal texts. He claimed to have the ability to make images appear on film with the power of his mind. He had demonstrated this miraculous power on several occasions in front of many witnesses, producing "mind photos" of well-known buildings, and sometimes people. He would make a show of concentrating with great effort, then slap the camera lens as someone clicked the shutter. His performance was quite impressive.

Serios was a sensation for a while, then later, he seemed to have lost his ability—when he had to perform under very strict protocols as a test for skeptics like Roger. He failed to produce a single identifiable photograph under those conditions.

Roger and other anti-paranormal skeptics had figured out several ways to fake psychic photography, one of which they determined had to be a small tube palmed by the psychic photographer. The tube could be an inch in length with a positive lens on one end and a small transparency on the other. When this was pressed against the camera's lens—held in the hand so it could not be seen—and the shutter was clicked, a photo of the transparency would be produced. Only very elementary sleight of hand was required to pocket the device or change the transparency. In short, it was easy.

Roger had prepared his Serios-type gimmick with three transparencies, one of the Empire State Building, one of a shapely woman, and one of Johnny Carson. He rehearsed the bit with Costas a couple of times, and the resulting pictures were very good, especially the one of Carson. Even Melissa was impressed by how well the gimmick worked.

Roger went to sit in a chair until it was time to tape. Melissa sat next to him where she would watch off-camera. "You're going to be good," she said. "I can feel it."

"Well, I feel a little better myself. At least here there aren't hordes of nitwits sitting in an audience. I can go one-on-one with anybody."

A director gestured to Roger to take his place in the big easy chair on the *Later* set, and he kissed Melissa quickly, then went to his seat. He immediately tripped on a cable and fell on his face, banging his nose. Blood flowed from his nostrils in gushes, reddening his moustache.

Everything had to be delayed while Roger's nose was attended to. It stopped bleeding after a few minutes, but then his makeup had to be redone, and his blood-stained shirt changed. Fortunately, the crew on the set was prepared for any exigency that might present itself with a guest, and a new shirt and tie were made available.

Roger refused to be shaken by the incident. He was all smiles and proclaimed, "I'm not hurt; I won't sue NBC," but inside he was seething.

He knew the demon had tripped him.

Finally taping began.

"Tonight on *Later*," Costas announced, "we have world-renowned psychic debunker Roger Kant, who's just published a new book entitled *The New Age Con Game*. Roger is often known as The Astounding One because of his ability to duplicate so-called psychic feats, though he tells me he doesn't really like that title."

"That's right," Roger replied, "it's very theatrical, and early in my career it helped to have that kind of title to make my name more memorable; but now it's kind of an embarrassment, though I still do astounding things from time to time."

"I understand you're going to do something astounding tonight."

"That's right. I'm going to take pictures with my mind. It's called psychic photography, and was first performed by a man named Ted Serios."

"Exactly how does it work?"

"I will project pictures in my mind onto the film in the camera. This is a very difficult feat and requires great concentration."

"I'm ready when you are," Costas said, picking up the Polaroid camera.

Roger struck a pose of a man in deep concentration. Then he struck the camera—with the gimmick palmed in his right hand—and said, "Now!"

The camera spat out a picture. While that one was developing, Roger went through the bit again. Then one more time. He smoothly pocketed the device at the end of his demonstration; he doubted it would show up on tape.

"The first picture should be ready by now, Bob," Roger said.

Costas took the first one from the table next to him and held it up for the TV camera.

"The Empire State Building."

"Right. That's what I was thinking of."

"This is astounding, Roger. I think the next one's ready now. Let's take a look."

The monitors in the studios displayed a fuzzy, but clearly recognizable woman in a brief bathing suit.

"I could've thought of her without clothes, but I didn't think it'd get past the NBC censors." Some members of the taping crew laughed mildly.

"Now, what's the third picture."

"A man who is God on this network," Roger said, referring to Johnny Carson. "His influence is felt everywhere."

Costas picked up the third photo, and the camera zoomed in. "Here we have a picture of God, all right," he began. "It's Johnny—"

Roger was dismayed. Why did Costas stop? He looked at the nearest monitor and saw the photograph his host held. It wasn't Johnny Carson at all.

It was the face of a demon, in sharp focus, not fuzzy at all. It wasn't exactly Roger's demon; it was more human-looking than the apparition that visited him, but it was a demon nonetheless.

"Stop the tape," Costas said, nonplussed. "What the hell is this?"

"I don't know!"

"I thought it was going to be Johnny Carson."

"It was. I prepared it that way."

He fumbled in his pocket for the transparencies. He held them all up to the light.

Each one bore the image of a demon. Roger's face turned purple with rage. "Damn it to hell! Someone replaced these! Someone's out to make me look like a fool. I demand an explanation!"

Costas looked off-camera and gestured for someone. A man wearing a set of headphones came over to talk to Roger.

"Mr. Kant," he said in a conciliatory tone, "no one on this set would do a thing like this."

"It's the fucking demon," Roger said, his eyes starting to glaze over with anger. "He's everywhere. He's in this studio somewhere, hiding."

Melissa came to his side. "Maybe we ought to put this off till tomorrow."

"There is no tomorrow," the man in the headphones said. "We're taping Mike Tyson tomorrow. It's now or never."

"Give him a chance to settle down," Melissa snapped. "You can see he's upset."

"Hey, we can edit this all out. It's tape, not live. But if Mr. Kant wants to be on this show, he has to do it now."

"Roger?"

"I'm right, damn it!" he shouted. "It's the demon's fault."

"Roger, calm down. If you don't, you'll miss this opportunity. Forget the psychic photography thing. Just talk with Costas about the book. That would be okay, wouldn't it?" she asked the man.

"Sure. But we haven't got much time. We have to get the tape rolling right away."

"Roger, can you do it?"

He took a deep breath. "If I have to."

"You have to."

"All right. Get me a drink of water and I'll be fine."

The show went poorly. Roger never did settle down, and his responses to Costas' questions were poorly thought-out and vague. He made at least two outrageous statements—one about Julian Shock, the man he supposedly maligned in the *New Age* interview—which would no doubt lead to lawsuits. But he didn't care. Let them sue him. They wouldn't find much to take at the rate he was going.

He ended the show looking like an utter buffoon, and he knew it; but there was nothing he could do about it.

Later, he told Melissa he had probably discouraged people from buying his book. "In fact, they'll probably return it. Maybe I should've gone on *Pee-Wee's Playhouse*, except I don't have enough personality."

"I keep telling you—this is only temporary."

"It's the end," he said. "My career is over."

"You still have a seminar tonight. Maybe the New York crowd won't be so tough."

"It doesn't matter. Cancel the fucking thing."

"We can't cancel. You're going to get yourself together and do a good seminar tonight, even if I have to prop you up like El Cid."

Roger went up to the lectern. There were five hundred people out there. Five hundred out of a possible fifteen hundred the hall would hold.

He stared at them a long time before he opened his mouth. But his lips moved without sound.

He could think of nothing to say. Then he panicked. He felt as if the whole audience was going to rise against him. All of them were demons in his mind now.

The whole world was populated by demons.

He swooned and collapsed.

Melissa took it upon herself to get a doctor. He pumped Roger full of sedatives and remarked, "This man is suffering from severe depression and panic. He needs to see a psychiatrist."

"I know," Melissa said, "but he won't go."

"I'm right, damn it!" Roger shouted, suddenly sitting up in the bed. "I'm right." Then he lay back down and fell into a drug-induced slumber that was black and bereft of demons of any kind.

The next morning, it was almost noon before Roger awoke. Melissa had been up for hours and had most of the packing done.

"I feel like an army of elephants has been tap-dancing on my brain," he said.

"The doctor gave you a strong sedative. He also left a prescription for sleeping pills. And I'm going to get it filled."

"You're so efficient, Melissa. I'd never remember everything the way you do."

"I'm blessed with an orderly mind," she said simply.

He stood on shaky legs and wandered over to the closet. "Where's my gray suit?"

"You don't have one."

"Melissa, I may be absent-minded, but I know I have a gray suit. I wore it in Indianapolis, or Columbus."

"I sent it out to the cleaners," she called over her shoulder, "and they couldn't get the stains out, so I gave it to the Goodwill."

"Oh. You didn't tell me."

"I did, you just don't remember."

There was something wrong about his suit being missing, but he couldn't quite put his finger on it. His head ached so badly, he couldn't think straight. He'd speculate on that particular puzzle later. He selected a tan blazer and light slacks, then laid them out on the bed.

"I guess I ought to shower and shave. Where do we go from here? Philadelphia?"

Melissa faced him with a frown. "We don't go anywhere except home—for you. Philadelphia cancelled. So did Atlanta, and Charlotte. In fact, the whole rest of the tour has been cancelled. I think your performance last night had something to do with it—but it's been leading up to this for some time."

Roger sat on the bed. "I'm a jinx. That's what is it. I knew I shouldn't have gone on this tour."

"You didn't know what would happen. It's only a temporary thing. You're just going through—"

"Don't feed me any phony bullshit today, Melissa. I can't take anymore."

"All right." She came over and sat next to him, putting her arms around him and laying her head on his shoulder. "I still love you, though, if that's any consolation."

"I suppose I love you too," he said. "I don't know how I would have endured the last few weeks without you."

"If we love each other, then what are we going to do about it?"

"I have no idea," Roger said. "If either of us had any sense, we'd break it off before one of us got hurt."

"I don't have any sense," Melissa said and gave him a long kiss.

"Neither do I," Roger agreed, gasping for breath after her kiss. "Let's go home and talk this thing over."

Roger dressed and pondered what he and Melissa had just said to each other. Love was not a word that came easily to Roger's lips, yet he had just said it—as blithely as any adolescent.

He wondered how the demon would react to this new development.

13. a new life

The plane sailed over the expanse of Lake Michigan, its blue-gray water distinctive even from ten thousand feet. Then the jetliner began its gradual descent as it approached the city.

Chicago never looked better.

Roger had always liked the Windy City. It was more than home, more than the place where he could feel free. The city's rhythm drove his life, providing impetus when he was down, providing extra energy when he was up. It wasn't quite like New York; the pace wasn't that hectic. Chicago was its own entity, a place apart from all the other cities in the country. It was Roger's adopted home, and its particular essence had rubbed off the rough edges of Roger's Indiana background. It had given him a more cosmopolitan view of the world, but not with the harshness other major cities demanded.

The city was especially welcome now, after so many failures in other cities in the past few days. Chicago wouldn't let him down as those cities had. He could recharge his batteries here, perhaps think more clearly and plan strategies to turn his career around. Chicago would let him just be—without having to prove himself one way or another. He could hole up in his apartment indefinitely if he chose, and no one would bother him. He might indeed do that if it weren't for another consideration that presently preoccupied him.

It was, of course, Melissa. She had presented him with a different potential scenario for the rest of his life. She said she loved him, and he probably loved her; but did that really mean anything in today's world? Life wasn't really like the ending of *Casablanca.* Life was fraught with real problems, and romance was a challenge, requiring total commitment to another person, and commitment had become troublesome. People didn't just marry nowadays—as his father and mother had—and stick it out through all of life's adversities. When the least little thing went wrong in a relationship, it was off to court.

Roger had learned that firsthand. His three marriages had shown him the error of believing in love and romance. Of course, he was older now, and presumably more sensible. He had allowed himself to be swayed by the physical attributes of his other wives, except perhaps with Wanda. She was pretty and had fair skin, but she was no knock-out. She was a photographer who had accompanied him on many assignments during his journalistic days, and the two of them had made love—casually—a couple of times and mistaken that for love; they were both young. That marriage, fortunately, proved easy to dissolve. There were no children, and Wanda wanted the divorce; she had fallen in love with the staff artist at the newspaper, and she didn't think Roger would ever make anything of himself.

Sheila was another matter. Her thick, flowing red hair—almost exactly the color of Melissa's, perhaps redder—had drawn him to her—that and her voluptuous figure which so reminded him of a Titian nude. He met her at the party his publisher threw for his second book, *Psychic Trickery,* which was a best-seller. She was a divorcee, about thirty, with what seemed at the time to be an interesting personality, because she was a reader at the publishing house. Later, after they were married, she proved to be very shallow, and even worse, her figure advertised something she didn't really enjoy: sex. He had managed to pry her legs apart enough times for her to bear his children, but after ten years with her, he grew tired of begging and obtained a divorce.

Sandra, his last wife, was a beautifully formed woman with an appetite for sex that revitalized Roger as he approached forty. She loved to create crude fantasies for them to act out together, and the strange part was that he found himself enjoying them. Unfortunately, Sandra couldn't cook at all, she had frequent bouts with PMS, and her sexuality was not totally satisfied by her husband. In fact, she had, at one time, five other men she was seeing. Roger was devastated by this knowledge; he couldn't believe any woman could be so deceitful, but then he had never married a pathological liar before. Sandra would lie about anything at all and apparently had no conscience about it. She lied out of habit, about trivial things as well as about major things, such as where she had spent the night. The divorce from her was messy; she hired (with his money) a powerhouse attorney who all but demanded the gold from his teeth. Fortunately, his own lawyer was a tough bastard too, so Roger kept more than he expected.

He had made many mistakes with his previous wives—mistakes in judgment primarily—but the worst was that he hadn't been intimate with them before marriage in any serious way. He hadn't opened up to any of them, and they hadn't told him much either.

He glanced at Melissa, who was dreamily observing the skyline of Chicago. She knew him intimately; she had seen him at his worst and at his best, as no other woman—no other person, actually—had ever seen him.

On the other hand, he still knew so little about her. She had confessed she had money, but she never explained how she had been so many places and how she knew so many people—or how she knew anything for that matter. Yet Roger felt he knew enough about her to consider taking her profession of love for him seriously.

He gulped involuntarily. He was actually considering married life again, and that chilled him. Marriage could be a living hell. But Melissa was different from all the other women he had known. She seemed really to love him, and she appreciated his work. None of his previous wives had really understood what his work meant to him, that it was his life. That single factor made Melissa a prize beyond his wildest expectations.

He wondered how she felt about Chicago.

When Roger and Melissa finally arrived at his Lake Shore apartment, they both felt a sense of relief. Roger felt he was in sanctuary, away from the angry mobs his audiences had become. Melissa seemed at home, even though she had stayed here only a few days before. Roger stood in front of the picture window as always when he had been away for a while, and reclaimed the city spiritually by taking in the view; Melissa stood by him a few moments, then quietly reminded him there were things to do.

It was almost six o'clock, so Melissa set about scrounging a meal for them from what was in the freezer. She found some frozen trout, and a few potatoes that hadn't rotted, and balanced the meal with frozen peas. It wasn't a sumptuous feast by any means, but somehow it tasted better than any of the hotel or restaurant food they had been consuming for so many days. Roger sat in the kitchen watching her, trying to imagine what it would be like if she were there every day. He thought he could get used to the idea, but still wasn't sure how to approach her about it.

After dinner, Melissa occupied herself with unpacking, and Roger went to his study. Usually, he would spend this time after returning from a long trip going through the accumulated mail; but by the time they got out of O'Hare and rode through the rush hour traffic, the post office was closed, so he would have to pick up his mail in the morning. Therefore, he had to content himself with puttering around while he listened to the messages on his answering machine.

There were several messages from his attorney, Sid Goldstein, on the machine. These he had expected. He'd have to call Sid in the morning and go over everything.

There were also a couple of hateful messages from Sandra, which he also expected, and one from a real estate man who was trying to sell him a condo in Florida.

Roger sat back in his chair and sighed. Coming home was always bittersweet. It was his refuge, but it was also the place where he had to do his work. At the moment, he had no particular desire to work on anything. He surveyed the massive collection of papers, books, magazines and clippings and was suddenly tempted to get rid of it all and start from the beginning. He had no new ideas for books, anyhow, and even if he did, he wasn't sure who would publish them. He had become a pariah. His fame was in jeopardy. His career was in stasis.

Maybe with the right woman. . . .

Damn it, he was thinking about marriage again. Melissa had only said she loved him. That didn't necessarily mean marriage.

Still, the idea was becoming very attractive.

But Melissa wasn't a fool. She couldn't really want him, not with his life in such a shambles. He had little to offer her but continued chaos. She couldn't want to be a part of that, and he couldn't expect any sensible woman to share his personal hell.

It just wasn't right, as his father would've said.

Melissa said yes.

Roger didn't even know he was going to propose until after they made love—in his own bed for once—and the afterglow was so wonderful, he gave in to impulse and asked her to marry him. What was more surprising was that she didn't hesitate a moment.

"Are you sure?" Roger asked her, still breathless from what had turned out to be a marathon of sex. The musky scent of it still hung in the air.

"Absolutely."

'But my life is all screwed up. I don't have any idea how I'm going to turn it around. Maybe you should forget I even asked."

"Are you trying to back out of it already?" she asked, turning on her side and presenting him with a view of her twin pink nipples that was very distracting.

"No. I'm just giving you a chance to think it over."

"I don't have to think it over."

"What about the age difference?"

"I'm not that old," she said playfully. "I can keep up with you."

"This is serious, Melissa. Marriage is not a thing to take lightly. I know. I've already had three wives."

"I know all of that." She pressed herself against him, flattening her breast against his side. The warmth of her body was so reassuring. "I know things in your life are in turmoil at the moment, but the two of us can face anything together. With my love to support you, I can help you straighten out your life."

"You seem awfully sure of yourself. There are many challenges ahead, and I have no ideas at all."

"I do," she said. "And father can help as well."

"Father? I didn't know you had a father."

"Silly! Everyone has a father. He's my only living relative. Mother died some years ago."

"I mean, I don't know anything about him."

"Well, he knows all about you. He's very wealthy, and very educated. It will please father so much to meet you," she said, rolling over on her back. "He's followed your career for years."

"Really?"

"Oh, yes. Father is a Renaissance man. He's studied the occult and the paranormal, and like you, he doesn't put much faith in any of it. That's why he'll be so pleased to meet you."

"Well, of course, I'll want to meet him too."

"You don't understand. You have to meet him before we can get married. I want Father's blessing. It's only a formality. I'm an only child and spoiled, but Father is a little old-fashioned about some matters. He'll want to be consulted, and of course he'll want to give me away at the wedding."

"Darn," Roger said, "I guess that means we can't get married next Tuesday."

"No, lover, we'll have to wait, but it won't be for that long. I guess we'll have to have a July wedding instead of a June one. Or the first week of August would be nice."

"Why then?"

"The astrology's good then—for both of us."

"You know about astrology?" he asked, slightly dismayed.

"Yes." She blushed. "I mean, I don't believe in it, but it's kind of fun if you don't take it so seriously."

"Maybe that's my problem," Roger said. "I take everything too seriously."

"Then let's get serious about this." She grabbed his hand and placed it on her red pubic mound. Before he could voice any objections, all thoughts of astrology were out of his mind.

He had to concentrate on something much more substantial.

The next morning, Melissa went to the post office to pick up the mail, and Roger called his attorney.

Sid was not in a good mood. He never was particularly sanguine, but today he was spitting fire.

"Roger, I don't understand how you can fuck up so much in so little time."

"I don't need a personality analysis, Sid. I just want to know what the problem is." He imagined the chubby little man at the other end of the line, dressed in an expertly tailored suit, chewing on the end of a cigar. His face would be red, as always, because he was always angry or fed-up about something.

"You want a list. You want a fucking catalogue? How many hours you got to spend on this?"

"Sid, it can't be that bad."

"You're in the shitcan, buddy. I got to get down on my knees and fucking beg judges not to hang you."

"Cut out the theatrics, Sid. Get to the point."

"Okay. Can't a man let off some steam?"
"To the point, Sid!"
"That woman you levitated is suing you."
"I knew that."
"Well, I think I can get her to drop the suit with a settlement. Liability insurance might cover some of it, but you may have to come up with some cash. You got any?"
"Some."
"How much is some?"
"About five hundred thousand in CDs, bonds and other investments."
"How liquid?"
"Most of it. Two-thirds, at least. My stock in Trevor Consolidated—"
"You bought that fucking dog! It's dropped ten points in the last week. The feds are investigating them."
"Don't tell me that, Sid." Roger's stomach suddenly felt very hollow.
"Okay, I'm not telling you."
"Tell me something good."
"There ain't no fucking good. That actor from Columbus is holding out for more money, and frankly he's got you by the yang. I don't know how much it's going to take to buy him off."
Roger sighed. "I expected that."
"He's a scumbag. But that ain't the worst of it. You're being sued by a writer—named Arthur Cavendish—who claims you plagiarized from him in your new book."
"That's bullshit, Sid. I've never even heard of him."
"Well, you're going to hear a lot of him in the future. He's got a real cocksucker for a lawyer, fucking Joe Maronelli. I can't promise you I can win against that s.o.b."
"I know you'll do the best you can."
"That won't be good enough. It would be better to settle out of court, because Maronelli will make you look like a shitheel just for the fun of it, and you don't need that kind of circus in your life. And there's another guy suing you over your calling him a child rapist or something. Julian

something or other."

"Julian Shock?"

"Yeah. Is that name for real?"

"Probably not, but I expected that too. It's a big mistake. The magazine misquoted me."

"What a fucking mess that's going to be." He paused to cough, as he perpetually did when smoking cigars, because he often swallowed half the smoke.

"Jesus, Sid," Roger said, after his attorney's coughing fit was over, "don't you have any good news?"

"Yeah, I'm fucking my secretary."

"That's great, Sid. Is that all, or have I been accused of murder and rape too?"

"Wait a minute, pal. I just remembered. I do have some good news. Your ex is getting married to some schmuck from Milwaukee, so you don't have to pay her anymore."

"Sandra's getting married?"

"That's what I said."

Roger didn't know quite how to react. His practical side realized it meant he wouldn't have to send her alimony checks, but there was a part of him that was jealous. Even though Sandra was no longer his wife, he didn't like the idea of another man having her exclusively. He might even miss her acid voice on the answering machine.

He thanked Sid for filling him in on the parts of his life he didn't know were all screwed up and hung up, feeling worse than ever. He made a quick call to his broker, telling him to dump the Trevor stock, then sat at his desk and trembled.

Why, he asked himself, was he contemplating marriage when his life was disappearing down a black hole?

When Melissa returned, Roger told her the gist of his conversation with his attorney. She was sympathetic but could offer no ready solutions.

"Maybe Father will have some ideas," she said, sorting through the mail as they talked, making neat stacks of bills, of junk mail, and of personal correspondence.

"What could your father do?"

"I don't know, for sure. But he has lots of money—and connections. That reminds me—when is it convenient for us to visit him?"

"Any time, I guess, assuming you still want to marry me."

"Of course, I do. I told you things will change for you. Everybody's life has ups and downs."

"But I'm really down."

"Wait till you meet my father. He'll help you figure things. Daddy can fix anything."

That evening, Melissa called her father, Alexander Lewis, in California. She told him she was getting married and wanted him to meet his prospective son-in-law as soon as possible. After she hung up, she turned to Roger with a broad smile on her face.

"Father's really excited about meeting you," she said, coming to join him on the couch, where he sat sipping Scotch.

"Really? He's not going to sue me, is he?"

"No, *really*. He's impressed that I should even know you—let alone snare you as a husband. I told him we'd be there in a couple of days. We can leave Saturday, if that's okay with you."

"It's fine. I don't have anything to do. I read all my hate mail already, and my mind is totally devoid of any ideas for a new book project. Maybe if I go away a few days, people will forget about me."

"People will never forget Roger Kant."

"Melissa, you're wonderful, but you don't have to puff up my ego constantly."

"I'm sorry. But I sincerely feel that way about you. You should know that by now."

"I know. I shouldn't snap at you, but this marriage thing is making me nervous. I hope you don't think getting married will solve any of these problems for me. It's not a panacea." He set his glass down and held her hand while looking into her eyes with his most earnest expression. "You're not doing this—you're not marrying me—out of pity, are you?"

Melissa's eyes went wide. "Roger, you can't think that!"

"I sometimes feel that's the only reason any woman would want me."

"I wouldn't patronize you with pity, Roger. Not ever. I'm marrying you out of love, pure and simple, and my love will give you strength. You'll see."

"All right, Melissa. This is your last chance to back out."

"I'm not backing out, Roger. And neither are you, you foolish man!"

She threw her arms around him and gave him a deep tongue kiss, and he forgot all about pity. The kiss was the beginning of an evening of particularly exquisite love-making.

It was marred only by Roger imagining another man on top of Sandra. For some reason, that image kept tormenting him, and he couldn't let it go.

Nine-thirty the next morning, the doorbell rang. Roger was still in bed, but Melissa was up, as usual, working in the little office that used to belong to Edith. She was wearing only a robe, but she went to the door anyhow, expecting to see a delivery man, the building superintendent, or someone else equally unimportant.

When she opened the door, however, a young woman was standing there. She had short auburn hair, a slender figure and a round face with full lips. She was wearing a pair of white shorts and a halter top, and she held a large pocket book under one arm. Dark sunglasses hid her eyes.

"Who are you?" the woman asked in an acid tone of voice. Melissa could just barely see her eyes critically examining her attire.

"I'm Melissa. So who are you?"

"Cindy Kant. Is my dad home?"

"Oh, Cindy, come on in."

Cindy seemed doubtful but walked in. She looked over the apartment as if she had never been there before. It was clean and tidy, but something about it seemed out of place. She decided it was this woman who answered the door in a robe.

"Your father's asleep, but I'll go wake him up."

"Are you Dad's mistress?"

The boldness of the question threw Melissa temporarily off-guard, but she recovered quickly. "No, I'm not."

Cindy sat down on the couch and took a pack of Virginia Slims from her purse. She lit a cigarette and blew the smoke out into the room in a studied manner. She didn't remove her sunglasses. "You're sleeping with him, aren't you? A secretary doesn't answer the door in a robe."

"I'm your father's fiancée. We're getting married next month."

Cindy yawned. "Oh. I thought he'd learned his lesson about marriage."

"It's not what you think. I have money of my own."

"Okay. If you want to marry him, that's your business, I suppose. I guess he's got the middle-aged crazies or something to go for a woman like you."

Melissa grimaced. "Is there some reason you don't like me? You don't even know me."

"I know your type. I'm in advertising. I've seen a lot of ambitious women try to horn in on a man's success. You couldn't possibly love my dad. He's way too old for you."

"He's not that old."

"How can you go to bed with somebody like that? Thinking about it gives me the creeps. I mean, I've slept with men who were older—but not people old enough to be my father. Doesn't it make you sick?" She sat back and blew more smoke in Melissa's direction.

"Of course not."

"It would me. Older men smell funny."

"Cindy, you've got a lot to learn about men. And love too, for that matter."

"Skip the soap-opera crap with me. I've been around the block a couple of times."

"You look like you have at that," Melissa replied, her face reddening.

"Bitch."

"You don't have to like me. In fact, I don't even care—"

"What's all the commotion out here?" Roger said, coming into the room. He was clad in his pajamas and was rubbing sleep out of his eyes. He scanned the room and saw Cindy on the couch and Melissa towering over her. Their body language told him their meeting was not entirely pleasant. But Cindy didn't get along with anyone that well.

"Hi, Dad," Cindy said smoothly. "I was just getting acquainted with my new stepmother-to-be."

Roger eyed his daughter warily. She never visited to be sociable. It was usually due to some trouble she had gotten herself into, which required some of the old man's cash to fix.

"I want to talk to you in private," Cindy said.

"All right. Come into my study."

Cindy finally removed her sunglasses when she and her father went to the study. If she hadn't, she might have broken her neck by tripping over a pile of magazines or papers. She sat on a metal folding chair in front of the desk and started to light another cigarette, then remembered her father forbade smoking in his study and put it away.

Roger sat on the edge of the desk, bracing himself for his daughter's latest problem. "All right. What is it now?"

Cindy's cool blue eyes were dilated, as if she might be on drugs. The attitude of her body was one of harsh judgment, reminding Roger of how her mother, Sheila, had struck such a pose whenever she wished to chew him out about something.

"Where did you pick up that evil bitch?"

Roger was stunned momentarily. "Are you talking about Melissa?"

"Yes. You can't be seriously considering marrying that woman."

"Why do you call her evil?"

"I know women, and she strikes me as the evil type.

She's bad news, only you can't see it like I can. She'll turn on you the first chance she gets—like a wild animal. I've seen her type before."

Roger sighed heavily. His daughter loved to pick people apart. It was one of her more endearing qualities. "Did you two have words?"

"I just told her what I thought about her, that's all."

Roger shook his head. He could only imagine what Cindy had said, but he knew it wouldn't be flattering. Cynthia Kant viewed every other woman in the world as an adversary. She respected no other woman at all except her mother. He should have expected her to react this way; in fact, he would have been surprised if she hadn't.

"Well, that must have flattered her," he said. "And I'm serious about marrying her, if it's any of your business."

"She'll drain you of all your money, and frankly, I don't think you and she make a good couple. You look like an old man with a toy girl."

"Melissa's not that young, and I don't like being called an old man. I'm not even fifty."

"Well, I don't think it's right."

"Whatever you think doesn't matter. I'm marrying her regardless of what anyone says or thinks. Is that clear?"

"I just wanted you to know how I felt about it."

"You young people today are too free to tell others how you feel. I don't need to know how you feel about my life. Okay?"

"I guess so."

"Now, what's your real problem?"

As usual, Cindy needed money.

After Cindy left, Roger had a quiet brunch with Melissa. He apologized for his daughter's behavior, but Melissa didn't seem that disturbed.

"She's jealous, that's all."

"Jealous of what?"

"Jealous of her father getting what he wants. It makes her feel threatened, I imagine. She's uncomfortable with the changes my marrying you will bring."

"Maybe. Personally, I think she's a spoiled brat."

"She'll learn someday," Melissa said. "She's still young—a kid actually. But someday she'll understand she can't go around telling people what she thinks of them without getting into trouble."

"I hope it's soon. God knows I want to like my daughter, but I just don't. She only comes to see me when she needs money. And I think she has a coke habit, but I'm not sure. She doesn't listen to anything I say anymore."

"Maybe she'll change."

"I doubt it."

As they finished eating, Melissa started to clear the table and put dishes in the dishwasher. As she bent over to load the machine, her robe hitched up, and Roger forgot all about his daughter. He was suddenly entranced with the idea of having this beautiful woman near him every day, and that made up for a lot of the trouble he'd been experiencing lately.

Melissa turned around abruptly as she shut the door to the machine. She knew he had been looking up her robe and reached over to pat his crotch.

"Enjoy the view?"

"Yes, indeed."

She swished past him and sat down at the table again. "I've managed to get us an early flight to California. We leave tomorrow morning."

"So soon?"

"The sooner you meet Father, the sooner we can get married," she reminded him.

"But I don't know if I'm ready."

"You're ready," Melissa told him. "You just don't know it."

That night, Roger had difficulty falling asleep, even though he had taken two of the sleeping pills Melissa had the doctor prescribe for him. His mind was fighting the medicine, forcing him to remain awake by tormenting him with all the aspects of his life that were changing.

He was getting sued. His book wasn't selling. His agent had dropped him. He had lost ten thousand dollars in the stock market.

And he was getting married.

It seemed so stupid. It was as if he were getting married to solve all his problems, but the rational part of him acknowledged this simply wasn't a solution to anything. It might make matters worse.

But he wanted Melissa in his life. Everytime he looked at her, something inside him twitched. The mere sight of her—and he had seen all her guises now, from her morning face to her fully made-up, face-the-public face—comforted and boosted him at the same time.

She was the type of woman he should have met twenty years previously, when he was floundering in the early part of his career and needed unconditional support. He felt fortunate, at least, to have found her now, when he needed support again. He just hoped she would stay with him—that he would say or do nothing to drive her away.

Only one thing bothered him about Melissa, and it was his daughter calling her "an evil bitch." He couldn't imagine how anyone—even his irascible daughter—could consider Melissa evil in any way. It was so absurd.

But still it ate at him.

Evil. It was an ugly word.

Roger tried not to think about it. Abruptly, his thoughts were interrupted. He heard moaning. He edged closer to Melissa, thinking she might be moaning in her sleep. But the sound wasn't coming from her.

He heard it again, and this time he knew it was coming from another room. He rose from the bed, slipped into his robe and slippers and went out into the hall to investigate. As he approached the living room, the moaning grew louder. He was getting closer to the source.

He stepped into the room and stopped. There were candles burning everywhere. A stone altar occupied the space where the couch was supposed to be. Stretched out on the altar was his daughter, Cindy, naked and bleeding from every orifice of her body. She was moaning in absolute pain—pain so great it had gone beyond the screaming stage.

"Cindy!" He tried to move, but his feet wouldn't respond.

A figure in a black robe appeared at the head of the altar. His face was shrouded by a hood, but his teeth could be seen gleaming in a mock smile. He held a large curved knife over Cindy's heart.

"No!" Roger shouted.

The knife came down into Cindy's chest. Blood exploded from her body, spraying the dark figure.

His hood fell back, and Roger beheld the face of the demon.

No, no, no! Roger covered his face with his hands. When he pried his fingers away, after an eternity of waiting, he was sitting in the bed next to Melissa.

A bad dream.

He snuggled against Melissa, trembling. He closed his eyes and tried to blank the horrifying image of Cindy and the demon out of his mind. Maybe he should take another sleeping pill. He snuggled closer to Melissa, then reached over to caress her left breast, as he often did at night.

He pulled his hand back quickly. His fingers were covered with gore. He threw the covers back and saw the ravaged body of his daughter. Her cold dead eyes accused him.

He ran from the room, down the hall. He heard the demon's chattering laughter echoing in his head. He tripped on a seam in the carpet and fell against the wall, bruising his head, then dropped to the floor. He tried to sit up, but he couldn't quite make it and slumped over, unconscious.

That was an awful nightmare last night, he thought, lathering his face. He peered at his face in the bathroom mirror. His eyes were bloodshot and puffy. *The goddamn demon—it was his doing. Melissa's right; I need to see a doctor.*

He reached in the medicine cabinet and took out the straight razor. He tested the edge with his thumb and drew blood. It was sharp all right—too damn sharp—which meant he'd get a nice close shave this morning. He wanted to look as good as possible for his first meeting with his soon-to-be father-in-law.

He closed the medicine cabinet and held the razor poised at his throat.

Where's my electric razor? he thought, then he slashed his throat open.

The demon's face laughed at him in the mirror. Roger stood helplessly as blood flowed from the wound in his throat. He tried to scream, but a bubbly gurgle came forth from his mouth.

He threw the razor down and grasped his throat, trying to stop the gushing blood. He closed his eyes and waited to die.

Melissa, he thought, as his mind blanked out.

Melissa lay sleeping peacefully next to him. He touched his throat, and it was intact.

Am I really awake yet? He touched Melissa gingerly. She seemed real.

"Why didn't you save me?"

Roger jerked around to see his daughter standing at the foot of the bed.

"Or me?" Edith stood next to her.

"I couldn't—" he gasped. "I wanted to, but I just—"

The demon shot up between the two of them. He grew larger then opened his mouth and bit off the heads of both women. Their bodies tumbled over on the bed, and Roger covered his face against the twin gushes of blood spurting from their necks.

Stop it! Stop it!

"Melissa!"

She was slow to respond.

"Melissa, wake up!"

She turned over, her face intact, no blood on her anywhere. There were no headless bodies at the foot of the bed. There was no demon.

"What is it, Roger?" She turned on the bedside lamp and sat up.

"The grand-daddy of all nightmares," Roger said, his voice hoarse.

"Tell me about it, honey. That will make it not so bad."

He related the dream in detail. When he was finished, Melissa drew him to her. "Didn't I tell you to take the sleeping pills?"

"I did. I couldn't sleep anyhow—or I was asleep and didn't know it."

"We'll have to get you a new prescription. Something stronger. Maybe we'll have time in the morning for the doctor to call it in—before we leave for California."

"I shouldn't be meeting your father," he said. "I should be meeting a psychiatrist."

"Don't be so hard on yourself. It was only a bad dream, and it's over now. Just stay close to me and I'll protect you from the boogeyman." She yawned widely. "Everything will be better after you meet Father. I feel our lives will take a different turn very soon."

Roger didn't answer. He lay on his side, and she pressed against his back. Soon she was sleeping again, and the rise and fall of her breathing against him was very comforting.

Roger eventually fell asleep, but not for a long time. He kept closing his eyes and opening them again, over and over. He was trying to make something disappear.

But the cut on his thumb was real.

14. xanadu

Melissa and Roger arrived in San Francisco about four o'clock local time. The flight was uneventful. Melissa spent most of the time reading while Roger slept. He awoke half an hour before the plane was scheduled to land. Melissa scolded him about missing the beautiful scenery, but he replied he'd seen it all before. He knew a great deal about San Francisco, since he'd spent a few years there as a beginning reporter.

"It was in San Francisco I had the first major triumph in my career," he told her. "It involved a psychic faker named Tricia something. I can't remember her last name, but I think she was a lesbian."

"I remember now," Melissa said. "The whole incident was recounted in your *Memoirs of a Skeptic*. It was Tricia Mumford, and she was well-known in psychic circles then."

"Your memory's better than mine. I'd forgotten all about her."

"Didn't she put a curse on you, or something?"

"Yes, she did. Lots of people have put curses on me, I suppose. Somewhere there's probably an old *mambo* sticking pins in a doll of me, which might explain this crimp in my neck."

"I can fix that," Melissa said. She messaged the muscles around his neck, almost but not quite, pinching him as her fingers expertly probed his flesh.

"How's that?"

Roger rolled his head around, testing the effectiveness of Melissa's massage, then flexed his neck in every direction. "Praise the Lord," he said with mock sincerity. "I've been healed!"

Melissa nudged him to keep quiet.

Roger smiled mischievously and remained silent until the plane landed in San Francisco International Airport.

Melissa rented an orange Oldsmobile and drove from the airport north through the city along the Great Highway bordering the ocean. Roger allowed himself to enjoy the view for once, admiring the Transamerica and Bank of America buildings jutting out of the skyline. After a while, Melissa took a right and followed Geary Boulevard over to Park Presidio Boulevard, where she headed north again until she picked up Highway 101 and crossed the Golden Gate Bridge. Roger kept looking from side to side, seeing the ocean on his left and San Francisco Bay on his right. The vast expanses of water on either side had a soothing effect on his nerves. For a moment, he wished he were on a sailboat out on the Pacific, far away from his troubles, just flowing along with the breeze.

After crossing the bridge, Melissa continued on 101, which was now called the Redwood Highway, passing through the beautifully wooded countryside. Eventually, she turned off the main highway just north of Six Rivers National Forest onto an obscure state road and drove for miles until they entered a mountainous region.

They had been driving for three hours at least, and Roger was losing patience. "Where the hell does your father live—in a cave?"

"We'll be there shortly. Another hour or so."

Finally Melissa turned onto a road with no sign that wound around through heavily forested hills. There were steep grades and sharp curves, which Melissa took at sixty miles per hour without even flinching. Roger flinched considerably, though.

"Aren't you going a little fast?"

"I could drive this blindfolded. See?" She shut her eyes and maneuvered the Olds around a curve that bounded the edge of a seemingly bottomless precipice. The tires squealed.

So did Roger.

"Okay, I'm impressed," he said. "Open your eyes."

She did. "Don't you have any of the daredevil in you, Roger?"

"Maybe twenty years ago, before I knew I was going to die, but not now."

"Is that what getting older means? Knowing you're going to die? That doesn't seem very fair."

"Whether it's fair or not is immaterial. When you pass forty, you'll understand. So please slow down a bit. You may know these roads, but you don't know this car."

"Okay, spoilsport, but only to please you."

After another half hour's worth of curves and grades, Melissa came to a stop at the base of a steep hill. She turned onto another nameless road that led back half a mile to a large, wrought-iron, black gate. The gate was Victorian in style with gargoyles, griffins, and other mythical beasts stamped into its design, and it was at least twelve feet high by fifteen feet wide. It was set in stone walls ten feet high, on the top of which were spikes and barbed wire. Roger could see no end to the walls on either side of the gate.

It was near sunset, and the setting sun glinted off the spikes, some of which looked as sharp as razors. It was an imposing entrance, and Roger was glad it was still light; he didn't think he could enter through those gates at night.

Melissa stopped the car, got out, and went to a small metal box near the left side of the gate. She opened the box and pulled out a handset into which she spoke a few words. Roger could barely hear her. She replaced the handset and returned to the car.

"Daddy's waiting," she said. "He's all excited. I can tell." Suddenly the gates opened. "These can only be opened by a switch up at the house—or a remote transmitter if you have one. I don't know whatever happened to mine."

They drove along a paved road bordered by evergreens.

"Why all this security, Melissa?"

"Father values his privacy. He's somewhat of a recluse and doesn't have much use for the world. This is *his* world, and has been for thirty-odd years. It cost a fortune to have it built up here, where nobody can find it."

"How did your father make his money?"

"I'd rather not say, just yet."

"Is he a gangster?"

"Of course not. I'll tell you—or he'll tell you—when the time is right. I hate to be secretive, but when you meet Father, you'll understand."

Roger was about to press the issue, when they turned a corner and came upon a huge stone mansion—no, more like a Gothic castle—in a clearing that covered several acres. The main part of the building was three stories high, with spires at three corners and a tower at the fourth corner which was two stories higher than the rest. There were flying buttresses supporting the massive, arched, tiled roof. Carved stone gargoyles sat atop the buttresses. One of them had a huge erect penis with barbs on the end, and Roger couldn't recall ever having seen such a creature.

The multi-paned windows on the front were also huge with wrought-iron bars protecting them. The overall impression was of a building from the past dropped into the middle of California. The only modern aspect of the setting was a satellite dish mounted on the roof. Roger gaped at the imposing structure. It seemed larger than the Hearst Castle, or more aptly, it was Xanadu from *Citizen Kane* made real.

He realized fabulous wealth indeed was needed to build such a structure in this out-of-the-way place. No wonder Melissa hadn't been impressed by the mansions in Newport. They were shacks compared to this edifice.

Melissa pulled up next to the door and turned off the engine. "Here we are at last. Let's get out. The servants will take care of the car and our luggage."

The entrance was under a stone-roofed porch with a carved pediment and columns and consisted of two tall, iron-hinged oak doors, intricately carved with mythical creatures, much like the iron gate. As Roger examined them more closely, he realized the carvings depicted the Major Arcana from the Tarot. This seemed a strange way of decorating for a man who supposedly was as skeptical as Roger.

Melissa pressed the doorbell. "How do you like these doors? Father found them in Europe. He collects artifacts of all kinds."

"But isn't he anti-paranormal?"

"Yes—of course. But he also has a taste for the grotesque. These Tarot figures mean nothing to him spiritually; they're just decorative."

Roger was still uneasy. He would never decorate his home with objects that represented philosophies he opposed, not even for a joke.

One of the doors opened, and a liveried servant dressed in black stood at its edge, peeking out of them.

"Come in," he said in a flat, shrill voice.

As they passed by the servant, Roger noticed he had a slightly deformed left hand, possibly from being badly burned. He was short and had thin, silvery hair. His expression was totally blank, as if he were turned off inside. He walked slowly before them.

"Charles," Melissa said, "is Alexander—my father—ready to see us?"

"Yes, ma'am. I am taking you there now," the servant replied in a robotlike manner.

Roger's attention strayed from the servant as he took in the surroundings. They were in a vast hall at the end of which was a large spiral staircase. The ceiling was at least sixteen feet high and was decorated with a mural that extended its full length, depicting demons and angels at war with each other in a style reminiscent of Michelangelo. A gilt-edged border encircled the ceiling, carved with gaudy, grotesque faces.

Double doors were set at even intervals on either side of

them in the hall. The walls were covered with medieval tapestries, original paintings (a Rembrandt! a Van Gogh!), and ornate shelves on which stood rather hideous artifacts: ceramic figurines representing various mythologies from Roman to Old Norse, African dolls, and at least one crystal skull. There were sconces between shelves, holding unlit candles. The hall was illuminated by a series of crystal chandeliers, each one different. There was wealth here, all right, Roger reflected, but much of it had been squandered on ugliness. Only the carpet was plain, a plush wool with a muted plaid pattern that dampened their footsteps to the point of inaudibility.

The servant led them to a set of doors near the staircase on the right. He tapped on one door lightly. "They are here, sir," he squeaked.

"Bring them in," a powerful voice said.

The servant opened the doors, and Melissa and Roger followed him inside. Then he left them without bothering to announce them formally.

The room was a library. The ceiling here was twelve feet high and plain, and there were no windows. Every wall but one was lined with thick oak shelves from top to bottom, necessitating the use of a rolling ladder in order to gain access to the upper shelves. A cursory glance at the books showed many of them to be expensive folios and quartos from centuries past; but there were contemporary books as well, and they seemed to cover every subject imaginable. Roger tried to calculate how many books there might be—ten thousand? Twenty? No, he decided, it was closer to thirty thousand.

There was a small loveseat in one corner and a big, tufted leather chair; between these sat a table piled with more books. A floor lamp—at least sixty years old, judging from the style—illuminated this space. Behind this was a small cabinet, on top of which stood glasses and liquor decanters.

A small bookcase with glass doors sat against the opposite wall. Next to this was a wooden case which looked like the old-fashioned card catalogues libraries used to keep before the age of computers. Directly in front of these was a huge walnut desk, eight feet wide by three feet deep, covered with more books and stacks of paper behind which sat the master himself.

Alexander Lewis was examining an old book with a magnifying glass under the harsh glare of a brass gooseneck lamp, the only other light on in the room. Alexander also wore glasses, so his eyesight must have been very weak. He had a brooding expression on his face, which from the set of his features seemed to be the expression he wore the most. His head, set atop a thickly muscled neck, was disproportionately large, and his puffy face was dark and wide, with a Roman nose and dark gray eyes. His chin was adorned with a goatee, and a thin moustache rode his upper lip. His thick, black hair was cut short and was gray at the temples. His shoulders were broad, and even from across the room he radiated a presence of potency and aggression that was difficult to ignore. It was obvious no one would dare intrude on his personal space without good reason.

Melissa and Roger waited patiently for the man to acknowledge their presence. Minutes ticked by, marked by the ancient grandfather clock in the corner nearest Alexander.

"Ah, damn!" Alexander exclaimed suddenly and slammed the book shut. He peered over the edge of his glasses at Melissa and Roger, his eyes squinting in the dimness of the room. He smiled sheepishly and took his glasses off, laying them on the desk.

"Melissa, dear. And Mr. Kant! What a rude host I've been. Please forgive me." He stood up and walked around the desk, then across the room to greet them. He was about six-feet-four and probably weighed two-seventy-five, Roger guessed, yet he carried himself well—with the carriage of an old-fashioned gentleman. He wore a dark suit and a red turtleneck. His shoes appeared to be made of aligator hide.

He kissed Melissa on the cheek and grabbed Roger's hand and shook it firmly. "This is indeed a pleasure, Mr. Kant. A great pleasure."

Roger looked up into Alexander's face and was intimidated, not only by the man's physical presence, but also by something else—something subliminal—a hint of familiarity in the man's features, which close-up seemed almost artificial, as if he were wearing a mask of some kind. Perhaps it was the bushy eyebrows, or the goatee; whatever it was, it put Roger off-balance. He was also struck by how little Melissa resembled Alexander. They shared no features in common.

"Please call me Roger," he said, almost choking on the amenity because it didn't feel quite right—maybe because his hand ached from Alexander's grip.

"Of course. And do call me Alexander. No need for formalities here, not with my prospective son-in-law. Let's sit and get acquainted, shall we? Dinner won't be ready for another few minutes, so we'll have time to chat. Would you care for a brandy?"

Roger hated brandy, but he was too cowed to say so. "That sounds very good." He didn't like feeling timid; he had been afraid before, and unsure of himself, but he didn't like the idea that one man's mere presence could diminish his own. He sensed Alexander had an outsized ego, and that was threatening to a man whose own ego was usually rather inflated.

"Three brandies coming right up," Alexander said. "And sit down. You two look so stiff."

Roger and Melissa plopped down on the loveseat while Alexander prepared three snifters of brandy. Melissa didn't sit very close to him, and he suddenly felt like a teenaged boy out on his first date with a girl.

Alexander handed them their glasses and sat opposite them in the leather chair.

"I must explain my rudeness just now," he said. "As you can see, I am a bibliophile with very eclectic tastes. My personal library is one of the greatest joys in my life. And I hasten to add they're not just for show or for investment. I read them. Well, this very morning, I received a copy of *Cupitas Neronis* from a dealer in Italy who assured me it was a first printing of the 1747 edition in the original

Latin. There are perhaps four copies of this book extant in the world, Mr. Kant—Roger—no more. The book is one of my favorites among the scatological classics of the early Roman period. I consider it better than *The Satyricon,* and I've read it in translations and the original Latin many times. So, when this dealer told me he had found a copy of the 1747 edition, I was elated—that is, until I examined page 103 and discovered it was not the first printing at all. You see, the verb *fellare,* which means suck—from which we get the exquisite term 'fellatio'—had been amended to *felare* with one *l* which means to smell. Of course, it changes the whole meaning of the passage, but the worst of it is that this amendment was made for the second printing of the book, which is a common and trivial volume. I guess I'll have to write the dealer and demand my *lire* back, won't I?"

"I suppose so," Roger responded, his throat burning from the brandy.

"Father," Melissa said gently. "Roger came here to meet you, not to hear about your troubles with an old Latin book."

"I was just explaining, Melissa dear. You don't mind, do you, Roger?"

"No. I love books myself. I've never been a collector per se, though."

"That's because you write books. They're too close to you and therefore not as highly prized. Could that be the case?"

"Well, I'm not sure."

"Think about it. Let me know what you come up with later. And speaking of your books, you should know that you find in me one of your greatest admirers. I have every book you've written and have managed to collect most of your articles in periodicals as well. You've had quite a career, haven't you?"

Roger glanced at Melissa nervously. She kept her eyes on Alexander. "I have. It has its ups and downs, of course."

"Of course. I've heard you've had some difficulties

lately. But those things will blow over, I'm sure. You know, your latest book really intrigues me, *The New Age Con Game*. When did you realize the New Age movement was what you call a con game?"

"I don't know exactly. I suppose it was when I saw it was nothing but the old psychic con games with a new name. Then I knew I had to write about it—to warn people."

"Ah, so you see yourself as a deliverer of the people. You deliver them from evil, so to speak."

"Evil? I don't know if it's evil. That word has connotations that don't necessarily apply to the New Age. Some of these people sincerely believe in crystals, pyramids, and the like—but others are using them as a way to get rich off the gullible."

"So you *do* make distinctions. That's splendid. I was afraid you'd be a hard-headed man with no sensibilities. I am glad to discover how wrong I was. So there are true believers, and there are scoundrels, and then there are the rest of us."

"Us?" Roger was having difficulty following Alexander. His voice was loud and hard on the ears. The brandy was upsetting Roger's stomach, and he wasn't yet recovered from the awful roller-coaster ride up to the house.

"The skeptics. Isn't that what you are, a skeptic?"

"Yes. I guess that sums me up in a word."

"It's difficult being a skeptic sometimes, though, don't you agree?"

"In what way?" Roger felt like he was being backed into a corner from which there was no escape. Alexander's face seemed to loom larger before him, almost as if it had grown. He felt alone; why didn't Melissa sit closer to him? Why didn't she come to his defense?

"A skeptic has nothing to believe in, nothing to hold on to, and as a result, he can be the loneliest man in the world. Like me. I'm secluded here, away from the world, because I'm a skeptic. I don't believe I could survive in the outside world. It's too tawdry and noisome. It's gross and absurd, and the common lot of people one has to mingle with are too awful for words. Haven't you ever thought how nice it would be if we could take all the ciphers out there—the utter zeros of human beings who take up space and contribute nothing to the universe—and push them all off into the ocean and let them drown like lemmings?"

"Who would be left?" Roger asked innocently.

"Us. The intelligent few. The skeptics. The ones to whom the world truly belongs. Think how much better off we'd all be without the morons."

"Are you talking about genocide?"

"I mentioned no particular race. There are ciphers in every race and geniuses in every race. We'd weed out the ciphers."

"But who would take out the garbage?"

Alexander laughed heartily. His booming mirth echoed in the large room. "That's the catch, isn't it? When we have that solved, then we can get rid of the ciphers. Perhaps we could train monkeys, or—what do you think, Melissa dear?"

"I think Alexander Lewis is having fun at Roger's expense, but he doesn't know you as well as I do—or he's too polite to tell you your theories are half-baked, elitist, and probably fascist."

Alexander beamed. "Quite a girl, isn't she? She sees through all my poses. But I did have you going there for a minute, didn't I?"

Roger felt like he was going to sink into his seat. His ears burned with embarrassment. "Yes, you did," he admitted, feeling betrayed and angry.

"You were buying the whole argument. I didn't expect a man of your genius to be so gullible."

"But—"

"I'm sure Roger didn't expect a man of your genius to be so crude," Melissa interjected. "Really, Alexander, it was uncalled-for."

"Oh, well, just having fun. No harm done. I like to sit around and think up these theories and various scenarios for fixing the world and controlling it, but, of course, I never act on any of them. It's merely mental masturbation, of course, a way of releasing the tensions a man my age accumulates."

Roger studied Alexander's expression. He was totally confused now. He didn't know what he had expected Melissa's father to be exactly, but he certainly hadn't expected a boorish man who sat around dreaming up weird theories for the sheer fun of it. But a man who lived like a hermit in a castle in the middle of nowhere, with very little contact with the outside world, would have to have his eccentricities.

"Are you going to be good now, Alexander Lewis?" Melissa asked with undisguised ire.

"Of course, dear. Only mental masturbation, that's all. Which is better than no masturbation at all."

"You're incorrigible!"

"No, I'm just a man who likes fun." He glanced over at the grandfather's clock. "It's time to eat. Let's go see what the chef has whipped up for us tonight. He's an excellent cook. I found him in France in 1963, and he's been in my employ ever since. His name is André. He's a good person too, though he refuses to learn English and is continually making advances on the maids. But what can you expect from a Frenchman?"

Alexander heaved himself from his chair with considerable effort and led the way to the dining room.

The dining room was smaller than Roger expected, barely large enough to contain the long oak table with seats for twelve. There was one painting on the wall, a copy of one of Bosch's nightmarish canvases, but no other decoration. Alexander sat at the head of the table with Roger on his right and Melissa on his left.

"This is where we have our intimate suppers," Alexander explained as if he had read Roger's mind. "There is a banquet hall on the other side of the house, but it's so huge, I never eat there. I only maintain it for the occasional parties I throw. Unfortunately, I haven't had anything grandiose to celebrate in many years."

"What sorts of things do you celebrate?" Roger asked.

"Oh, you know, marriages, births, making a killing in the stock market."

"I dabble in the market myself."

"Do you, indeed? I just made a killing selling Trevor Consolidated short. Were you in on that?"

"I don't speculate on failure," Roger said.

"It's just a means of greasing the wheels of commerce. One stock goes up, the other goes down. It's like roulette—you can bet for or against the wheel. Is one way more moral than another?"

"I guess not, if you consider the stock market a gamble."

"Anything connected to business is a gamble, Roger." He patted Roger's hand. His flesh felt cold against Roger's skin. "Where in the hell is the wine? Gabriel! Damn, are they asleep in there? Excuse me." Alexander arose and went through the swinging doors at the end of the room. His voice could be heard yelling at the servants.

"Well, what do you think of Father?" Melissa asked.

"He's eccentric. And he seems to be making fun of me all the time—or is that my imagination?"

"That's just his way," she said. "He wants to be the king in his own castle, so he feels he can treat people any way he wishes. Don't let him get to you."

"Where *does* he get all his money?"

"Shush," she said, "he's coming back."

The swinging doors burst open as if hit by a charging rhino. Alexander's face was a scowl. "Servants!" he muttered on his way back to his seat. "They're so difficult to keep in line sometimes. In the good old days, in the antebellum South, for example, you could just beat the holy hell out of them if they sassed or peformed below one's expectations. Civilization has done away with corporal punishment—which I believe is one of the reasons the world is in such a mess."

"Alexander, you're being outrageous again."

"I know it," he said. "Of course, I wouldn't harm any of my beloved servants for the world. But I do get frustrated by them sometimes."

"What do you do besides make money in the stock market?" Roger asked idly.

"Oh, many things, Roger. Many things. Ah, here's the wine!"

The door had opened soundlessly, and an old servant awkwardly pushed a cart into the room. The man had a terrible limp, and Roger saw with horror that one of his legs was shorter than the other. He dragged the other foot behind him, and his hips moved oddly, like cog wheels out of synch, as he approached the end of the table.

"This is Gabriel. He's our wine expert. What have you selected tonight, Gabriel?"

Gabriel said nothing. He merely took the bottle from the cart and held it up to Alexander's eyes for inspection.

"Excellent, Gabriel! A fine vintage indeed and most appropriate for the occasion. Please pour it now."

Gabriel filled their glasses and waited. Alexander took a sip and seemed satisfied. "Very good. Leave the bottle and go about your business."

Gabriel nodded and left. The sound of his foot dragging behind him on the carpet gave Roger cold chills; it was worse than fingernails on a chalkboard.

"I propose a toast," Alexander said, rising. "To Roger Kant and my darling Melissa—may you both know unending happiness."

They raised their glasses and drank. The wine, a red port Roger guessed, tasted bitter. But then he was no wine expert; perhaps fine wines were supposed to taste bad.

Alexander clapped his hands and yelled, "Peter! The soup."

Another servant came in, a tall, thin man, also pushing a cart. His legs were intact, but his face was severely disfigured, covered by a jagged network of scars. The tip of his nose had been severed, so one had to look directly into his nostrils. His head was not bald, but barren, as if all his hair had been burned off. His eyes bulged slightly, so when he blinked, the lids barely met. He smelled of disinfectant as he came to the end of the table and stopped next to Melissa.

A large silver tureen was on his cart. It contained a soup that smelled much like chicken. He placed a bowl before Melissa, then ladeled soup in it.

Melissa leaned down to sniff the soup. "Polish, isn't it?"

"Correct, Melissa dear. Duck soup with raisins and all sorts of wonderful exotic vegetables. André discovered the recipe when he was in Poland last summer visiting his parents."

"I thought he was French," Roger said.

"He is French, but his parents are Polish."

"Oh," Roger said. Apparently this answer was supposed to explain everything, but upon reflection, Roger realized it made no sense at all. A lot of things he had seen and heard in the last hour didn't make sense. He was beginning to wonder if this feeling was due to his own condition of malaise or attributable to Alexander's quirky behavior. And Melissa seemed different too, very distant and aloof, as if she had no real connection to Roger. Was she also intimidated by her father?

The disfigured servant served Alexander, then came to Roger's side. Roger avoided looking at him when he placed the bowl on the table, but when he ladled the soup into it, Roger found his gaze pulled to the man's face.

Up close, it was even more hideous. It made Erik, the Phantom of the Opera, look like Robert Redford by comparison. There was no part of the man's face that was unscathed, and peering into those awful, piglike open nostrils was sickening. There were fresh scabs among the scars, and one of them was oozing puss. The man's eyes appeared dull, without gloss, as those of a dead man. He seemed to be appraising Roger as well, his eyes shifting very slightly. The corner of his mouth twitched as if he might speak, but he said nothing.

Roger looked away quickly. His stomach was rumbling, and he felt on the verge of retching. He swallowed back bile and stared at the steaming bowl of soup before him until the disfigured servant had left the room.

"Ah, dear me," Alexander said, "I'm sorry if Peter's appearance upset you. I have a soft spot in my heart for the handicapped, and these people could obtain no other employment except as my servants. Some of them are dull-witted—Peter is especially because his brain was damaged in the accident that made his appearance so wretched—but on the whole, they are very loyal servants and don't bear themselves haughtily as so many servants do."

Roger nodded in agreement, then dipped his spoon into the soup. He brought it up to his lips, but the smell of it nauseated him. He dropped the spoon on the table, where its contents spilled out, forming a dark stain across the linen tablecloth.

But it wasn't just the soup. It was everything: the long drive, the off-kilter intimidation of Alexander, the crippled servants, and at last this disfigured man—who, under all the scars and wounds, resembled a man Roger had once known.

He couldn't endure any more.

"I'm sorry," he said, almost choking, "but I've lost my appetite. I can't eat."

"Oh, I'm sorry," Alexander said with a noticeable lack of sincerity. "Is the cuisine too exotic for your tastes?"

"I'm ill," Roger said. "I have to excuse myself, or I'm afraid—"

"We could get you a dose of bicarbonate of soda or something. We have all sorts of medications here."

"No, thank you. I just need to rest."

"Say no more, Roger. I'm sure it's been a trying day for you. Melissa, why don't you take Roger up to his room? He's to be in the north bedroom, across from your room."

"Yes, Alexander," she answered, rising.

"A pity. And André had prepared such a nice capon for us." He emitted a great sigh. "Melissa, you will come back and join me, won't you?"

"I'll be back."

"Good. I hate to eat alone."

Melissa led Roger up the winding staircase to the second floor. Ascending the stairs was an experience in itself.

Roger was so dizzy, he felt like he would tumble over the side at every step. At the top, they turned right and continued down a corridor until they came to the last door at the end. "This is your room, Roger."

"I'm sorry. It's just that—"

"I should've warned you about the servants. I didn't know they would upset you. You'll get used to them in a few days."

"Days? How long do we have to stay?"

"At least a week, or Father will feel offended."

"I don't know if I can last a week here."

"You have to, Roger. I thought you were stronger. Am I seeing a side of you you've kept hidden?"

"I'll manage somehow. Maybe I'm just feeling jet lag. I'll probably be all right after a good night's sleep."

"Don't forget your sleeping pills."

"I won't." His voice dropped to a whisper. "When will you be coming up?"

"Oh, I won't be sleeping with you during our stay, Roger. Father would never stand for cohabitation right under his nose—in his own house. But I'll be right across from you, though. Maybe we can sneak a couple of tumbles in when Father's occupied." She kissed him without passion and left him at the door. "I have to go back now," she said. "Father will be getting impatient."

Roger watched her walk down the hall back to the stairs. She seemed a stranger to him now, and as she disappeared from view, he suddenly felt very lonely.

And afraid.

15. NAKED RUNNER

Roger was not pleased to have to sleep alone. He had grown used to the comfort of warm flesh pressed against him at night. He wished Melissa had at least warned him about her father's proscription against cohabitation. Then, at least, he would have been able to prepare himself mentally.

Nevertheless, he'd still be alone.

He opened the door to the bedroom. The light was on in the room, coming from a modest fixture in the ceiling—modest for this house, anyway—it was gold-plated. The room was large, thirty by thirty at least. In the center of the wall opposite him, between two barred windows, was an oversized four-poster bed with a canopy. There was a vanity, a chest of drawers, two Queen Anne chairs, and a table next to the bed on which sat a lamp in the shape of a Chinese woman. The carpet was also of Oriental design and depicted dragons on its border. The walls were papered in a nondescript design, the background of which was maroon. There were two doors in the wall against which the vanity sat. There were no artifacts in this room, except for a strange piece of pottery shaped like a flattened pregnant woman, which Roger concluded was an ashtray. Overall, it reminded Roger of a room in a French whorehouse, as Hollywood might depict it without all the frills. It needed a mirror on the ceiling, though.

Roger went to the bed and discovered all his clothing

had been unpacked and laid out for him to put away. He did this quickly, putting everything in the chest of drawers, leaving out his pajamas.

He sat on the bed and considered his physical condition. He was no longer nauseated. Indeed, despite the chill in the room, he realized he felt pretty good. Maybe being alone—away from the pressure of having to impress Alexander—was a curative.

Of course, there was still the problem of sleep. It would be difficult. Then he realized he hadn't seen his sleeping pills or shaving gear among the articles on the bed.

He tried the doors in the room. One was locked. The other was the entrance to his own private bathroom. With relief he spotted his shaving gear and the amber bottle of prescription sleeping pills he needed to insure a good night's rest on a shelf above the wash basin.

He needed a warm bath, so he turned on the taps and stripped while the large tub filled. His jowls were ragged with a day's growth of beard, but he decided to put off shaving till the morning. Since he was sleeping alone, he didn't have to be immaculate.

When the tub was full, Roger slipped in. The water was warm and relaxing, and Roger sighed with pleasure. He closed his eyes and dozed off.

The cold water lapping against his chin awoke him. He must have been out for some time for the water to have become so cold. Shivering, he climbed out of the tub and pulled the plug. He sprinted into the bedroom and hastily donned his pajamas. His teeth were chattering now; he'd forgotten how cool it could be in California at night, even in July, and especially this far north. He slipped under the blankets and waited for the chill to subside.

Then he heard a strange sound outside his door, like someone scuffling. He heard voices too.

He slid out of the bed reluctantly and walked slowly across the room. He opened the door and peeped out.

He saw a naked woman running down the hall. There was a nasty red welt on her left buttock. She disappeared around a corner at the other end of the hall.

It wasn't Melissa. Melissa's ass was not quite so plump, and her hair wasn't brown. He hesitated, then followed the path of the woman. When he reached the corner where she had disappeared, he turned into a short hallway where there were only three doors, one on each side, and a third at the end which had three steps leading up to it. Roger wasn't sure if he should investigate further. If he did find the woman, then what? She might be a maid, the wife of one of the servants, or even Alexander's mistress. The old boy certainly seemed randy enough to keep a woman.

Well, it wouldn't hurt to look around. He could always say he was lost. He walked slowly toward the doors. He put his ear to the door on his left and heard muffled snores. Nothing was happening in there. He went to the door on his right, and as he approached, he heard grunting noises. Then he noticed the door was open a crack. Swallowing his apprehension, he crept closer and peeked inside.

The room was lit only by a small lamp, but it was enough for Roger to see the woman—he recognized the welt on her left cheek—astride a man in the bed, bouncing up and down on what appeared to be a very large penis. It had to be André the womanizing chef, but when Roger's eyes adjusted to dimness, he could see the recipient of the woman's favors was Peter, the horribly disfigured servant.

He jumped back from the door, turned and ran, not caring how much noise he made and not daring to look behind him. He fell at the corner, stubbed his toe on the baseboard, and stifled a curse, but recovered quickly and kept running in a limp-step back down the hall. He reached his room without encountering anyone else. He closed the door behind him and twisted the knob to the deadbolt. Out of breath and panting, he stood pressed against the door for at least five minutes, listening for the sound of someone coming after him. When he was satisfied no one was coming, he went to the bathroom and grabbed the bottle of sleeping pills. He shook out two and swallowed them with a handful of water.

He was going to need them tonight for sure.

At three in the morning, Roger struggled to awaken. The pills were keeping him under, forcing him to have the dream.

Peter was naked, pursuing Melissa, who was also naked, down an endless corridor. Roger was running sluggishly behind him, trying to save her, but he could barely keep up with the man. Suddenly, they all stopped running. Melissa turned to face her pursuer. She had acquired a small ax from somewhere and was going to defend herself with it.

Peter laughed nastily and lunged toward her. Melissa buried the ax in Peter's skull. Peter turned around, rivulets of blood streaming down the scars on his face. He stared at Roger as he dropped to his knees, then fell over.

Melissa cackled like a witch and pulled the ax out of Peter's head and held it over her head.

"You're next!" she cried and jumped over Peter's body, and before he could act, Roger felt the blade plunging into his own skull. He stumbled around, trying to pull it out, while Melissa laughed and laughed.

Finally he stopped in front of a mirror and saw his own face was as mangled as Peter's.

Someone was knocking at the door. Roger pulled himself from the drug-induced slumber. His pajamas were plastered to his skin with sweat, and he felt feverish. He switched on the bedside lamp, arose shakily from the bed, and dragged himself across the room and opened the door.

It was Melissa, dressed in a robe. She stepped inside quickly and shut the door. He should have been glad to see her, but he was apprehensive, especially since he had just seen her put an ax in his head. Dream or no dream, he wasn't comfortable in her presence just now.

"Are you okay?" she asked.

"No. I was having another nightmare."

"Oh, that's terrible." Either her concern was not

genuine, or he was too sleepy to see it. In any case, he didn't feel comforted by her response.

"You killed me in it." How would she react to that?

"I did? Oh, God, Roger, that is dreadful. Dreams can be symbolic of things to come, you know."

He gave her a puzzled look. "You don't believe in dreams being portents, do you?"

"No, of course not. But people say those things."

"What people?"

"Lots of them. It doesn't mean anything."

He was suspicious, but decided not to pursue the subject of dreams further. "Have you come to sleep with me?"

"No. I wish I could, but Father's likely to awaken at any hour of the night and wander around. I was just checking on you. Besides, you wouldn't want me now. I just started my period."

"Oh," he said. He never knew exactly what to say when a woman told him that. Books of etiquette didn't stipulate a proper response. Should he say, "I'm sorry," "That's quite all right," or "Thanks, anyway"?

"Oh" was usually sufficient.

"Will you be up for breakfast?" she asked him, already opening the door to leave.

"If someone wakes me up. I should be pretty hungry by then."

"I'll have Charles wake you." She closed the door and was gone.

Roger frowned. She could at least have given him a kiss. She had been behaving strangely ever since they arrived; he was used to a Melissa who was forthright and not quite so mysterious. Maybe it was her father's influence, or the ambience of this house, which in itself could induce temporary insanity. He certainly didn't like it, whatever was causing it.

He also didn't like the idea that Alexander awoke and wandered about the house at all hours. He made double-sure the deadbolt was in place.

When he returned to the bed, he noticed the time on the

clock sitting on the bedside table. It was nearly three-thirty, and that generated more questions: Why in the hell would Melissa wake him up in the middle of the night to ask him if he was okay? And why was she up at that hour herself?

He slipped under the covers again and tried closing his eyes. Latent images of the disfigured servant's face shimmered behind his eyelids.

He opened his eyes wearily. If only the servant didn't resemble someone he knew, he would be easier to put out of his mind. But that resemblance was festering in his memory. The man's name was Peter, but he could remember no Peter in his past.

His stomach growled at him. He should have eaten dinner, but he didn't hink he wanted to prowl around this place at night looking for a snack. He told his stomach it would have to wait and took another sleeping pill.

He slept the balance of the night without further annoyance.

At eight the next morning, there was pounding on the door. Groggily Roger answered it, and he saw Charles standing in the hall.

"Breakfast in twenty minutes, sir."

"Thanks, Charles old boy." He watched for a hint of reaction in the man's face, but it remained blank as he turned away.

Twenty minutes wasn't much time, but Roger rushed through his bath and shaved and dressed in record time. He arrived at the bottom of the staircase with a minute to spare. Melissa and Alexander were waiting to join him.

The three of them went through a set of glass doors Roger hadn't noticed before behind the staircase. The doors opened on a flagstone terrace where a small, white, iron round table with a glass top stood waiting with three place settings and three glasses of orange juice. The view beyond the terrace was of heavily wooded hills. There was a swimming pool next to the terrace, but it was empty and apparently hadn't been used for a long time; many of the tiles lining the pool had cracked or fallen off.

"I always eat breakfast outside when the weather is good," Alexander said. "There's a bit of a chill in the air, but I find that invigorating. Don't you?"

"It's nice to be out in the open," Roger said, though he wouldn't mind having a sweater on, as both Alexander and Melissa were wearing. He had come down in lightweight slacks and a short-sleeved shirt.

"Let's sit," Alexander said.

The three of them sat around the table on iron chairs. Though the seats were upholstered, Roger found his chair impossible to get comfortable in. The back was too straight and grated against his spine. He was too hungry to complain, though, and reached for the juice and gulped it down.

"André is ill this morning," Alexander said. "So breakfast has been prepared by Suzanne. She is a good cook, but can prepare nothing fancy. I hope ham and eggs with scones is to your liking."

"It sounds great to me," Roger said. "I'm starving."

"I'm glad to hear your appetite has returned, Roger. I was worried you were puny and inclined to fall ill. One needs a sturdy constitution to survive in this world. Isn't that right, Melissa dear?"

"If you say so."

"Have I upset you? You seem rather depressed this morning."

"It's nothing. My—I didn't sleep well last night. This old place is so cold. It's like a tomb with furniture."

"Oh, I see. The accommodations were lacking. We can fix that. I'll have the furnace running tonight. Does that cheer you?"

"It will do for now."

"I want you to be pleased."

"I said it would do."

Roger sensed there was something to this interchange

he wasn't picking up on. There had been a quarrel, perhaps. In any case, he knew better than to be sucked into it.

No such luck.

"Were your accommodations up to par, Roger?" Alexander asked.

"Yes. It's a very nice room."

"But colder than hell," Melissa said.

"How would you know that, dear?" Alexander asked.

"All the rooms are cold. The whole house is like a morgue."

"Testy, aren't we? Sounds like a hormone imbalance to me. Wouldn't you agree, Roger?"

"I don't know. . . ."

"Here's our breakfast."

Suzanne, a young brunette woman wearing a maid's outfit with a very short skirt and a deep neckline, brought out a cart on which were scrambled eggs, thick slices of ham, and a basket full of scones for which there was plenty of butter and jam. She also brought over a silver coffeepot and filled each of their cups.

When she returned to the cart to bring over the eggs and ham, she bent over, and the bottom of her panties was visible under the hem of her skirt. Roger recognized the shape of her rear end and thought he could make out the welt underneath the sheer fabric of her panties as well. He quickly shifted his gaze back to the table. Alexander and Melissa were sipping their coffee and glaring at each other, so neither had apparently noticed Roger's staring at the maid's ass. He still blushed at his own voyeurism.

When Suzanne served the rest of the food, Roger watched her more closely. One of her fingers was missing on her left hand—the little finger. Roger swallowed hard. This, then, was her handicap. She saw him watching her, and caught his eye, but had apparently misunderstood his gawking. She winked at him and smiled lewdly, then deliberately leaned forward to offer Roger raspberry jam, giving him a provocative view into the depths of her cleavage; he could see the edge of one dark nipple.

Not knowing what else to do, Roger smiled back, hoping the smile was noncommital, and thanked Suzanne for the jam.

"Will there be anything else, sir?" she asked Alexander.

"No," he replied, his mouth already full of eggs and ham, "but check with us later in the event we need more coffee."

"Yes, sir."

She went back into the house.

"What a slut!" Melissa said.

Startled by the coarseness of her remark, Roger coughed on his food.

Alexander grinned. "What of it? What does it matter to you?"

"I saw her pushing her behind toward you, Alexander."

"And I'm not too old to appreciate it," he said. "Indeed, her behind is rather well formed. Don't you agree, Roger, or are you not appreciative of callipygian women?"

"I wasn't really noticing—"

"That's because she had her *tits* in your face!"

"Melissa, such crudity is unbecoming. You could have said 'breasts' or even something a little less coarse, such as 'knockers,' but for the word 'tits' to come out of your sweet mouth is quite startling. You're going to make your future husband think twice."

"Oh, I don't care." She tossed her napkin on her plate and strode back into the house.

"Don't let that outburst upset you," Alexander told Roger. "Women are often unpredictable creatures—and always jealous of their men looking at other women."

"I'm not upset," Roger said, devouring another scone. That was true; he wasn't upset at all, but he was terribly confused. Melissa seemed more jealous of her father's leering than she was of his.

He thought of his own daughter's reaction to Melissa. Had that been some kind of jealousy? Cindy didn't seem to have much affection for him anyhow, so why should she care if he fooled around or got married? Were all the men in a woman's life considered their personal property?

He realized he didn't know much about women, after all. But Melissa wasn't just any woman; he planned to share his life with her. Maybe she was so much more complex than any other woman he had known, she had to be even more unpredictable. Or was that a sexist view of womankind?

He didn't think he was sexist. But, looking at Alexander's face, his jaws busily masticating a scone smeared with jam, Roger could well imagine his prospective father-in-law was sexist.

Why else would he have the maid dressed in such a provocative outfit?

After breakfast, Alexander offered to give Roger a tour of the house and grounds. "Melissa will probably sulk the rest of the morning," he told Roger, "and we men need to get better acquainted."

"I'm up for it," Roger said. He had nothing to do anyhow. He had brought no books to read or papers to work on because he hadn't planned on an extended stay. In the back of his mind, he fretted about his various troubles, and he wondered if Sid had made any progress in settling any of the outstanding lawsuits. He would have to call in at some point and find out what was going on. For now, a tour of the estate would suffice to keep his mind off things, but at some point he would have to get serious.

He remembered Melissa had told him her father could fix anything and wondered if she had approached the old man about Roger's difficulties yet. Or did she expect him to do it? He needed desperately to get Melissa alone for a couple of hours, so that these things could be discussed.

He felt as if she had abandoned him.

Alexander and Roger strolled around the outside of the mansion, starting from the terrace. "The pool was very usable until a couple of years ago," Alexander said. "Then we had a minor earth tremor, and this awful crack developed in it. I need to have it repaired, but just haven't gotten around to it yet. Fortunately, there's a natural lake just through those woods, where one can take a dip."

"I might want to do that later," Roger said.

"Of course, it's up to you, but we always go skinny-dipping."

"You too?"

"I always swim in the nude. That's the only way you get the full benefit of the water."

Roger tried to imagine this bulk of a man naked, but his mind was not equal to the task. He wasn't sure he wanted to expose his own nakedness to the world, either.

"Now, over here," Alexander said, "is the garden." He pointed to an expanse of flowers and vegetables that covered at least two acres. In the middle of the vegetation was a large marble statue, Roman in style, of a naked woman. "There's Freddy, our gardener, attending to the marigolds. How are you today, Freddy?"

Freddy was a short little man with a very old face, squatting down in a flower bed with a garden claw, raking sprouts of weeds away from the marigolds.

"Fine, thank you, sir." Freddy had a British accent.

"How are our flowers doing?"

"There's a bunch of aphids on the loose, but I've been spraying them. The stink of the spray will linger awhile, but it's a dire necessity to get rid of aphids."

"Very good. Freddy, meet Mr. Kant, our house guest."

Freddy stood up—he was barely five feet tall—and extended his hand—or, more accurately, his claw.

Roger's eyes went wide. The man's right hand was gone, and what he had thought was a garden claw was actually a prosthesis for the missing hand.

"Excuse me, sir. Force of habit. Have to shake with me left one."

Roger awkwardly accepted the left-handed shake. His breakfast gurgled uncomfortably in his stomach.

"Pleased to meet you, Mr. Kant."

"Good to meet you, too," Roger managed to say. His throat had suddenly gone dry.

"You may return to work now," Alexander said.

"Yes, sir." Freddy happily squatted amongst the flowers and resumed clawing at the weeds.

"Poor fellow," Alexander said, continuing their walk. "Lost his hand in the war, I believe."

"Which war?"

"Oh, I'm not sure. The Crimean War, for all I know. I can't remember everything. He makes clever use of his artificial hands; he has a whole set of them, all adapted to specific purposes. I had them made up for him by a specialist in San Francisco. Freddy's a very industrious person and provides us not only with beauty, but with groceries. All our vegetables are the result of Freddy's efforts."

Alexander then took Roger to the six-car garage at the far north end of the house. Inside were a 1952 Mercedes, a 1963 Rolls Royce, a Tucker, a half-restored Duesenberg Model A Phaeton, a battered old '78 Chevy station wagon, and a fairly new Ford Bronco. All the vehicles were dirty, especially the Bronco, the wheels of which were caked with mud.

"I don't really care much about automobiles anymore," Alexander remarked. "I don't drive, and I'd just as soon ride in the Chevrolet as I would the Rolls. I tinkered with the Duesenberg for a while, but lost interest in it. Automobiles are, after all, only a means of conveyance. They're mechanical things, not true artifacts, and for that reason, I can't become very excited about them."

"What do you consider a true artifact?" Roger asked as they walked around to the front of the house. He thought about the crystal skull, the Tarot-carved door, and the squashed woman ashtray.

"A good question, Roger. A true artifact is one that when you pick it up, or touch it, or see it, brings forth an emotional response of some kind. Sometimes such artifacts are, admittedly, rather ugly, but in general there is beauty lurking within even the ugliest object."

"It sounds mystical to me," Roger commented.

"Perhaps it is. Maybe I am a psychometrist and don't even realize it. Maybe I'm reading the history of my artifacts, and that why I'm drawn to them . . ." He paused and regarded Roger's dubious expression. "Of course, I don't believe psychometry is a valid experience."

"No. It's a delusion. I've proven that on numerous occasions."

"Yes, I recall your thoughts on the subject in *Optical Delusions*. Of course, you were quite a young man when you wrote that, but your arguments were most convincing."

"Thank you," Roger said automatically, but he wondered if it was really a compliment, or a disguised criticism.

Alexander led him into the house, and they examined all the rooms on the first floor. In addition to the library, the kitchen and small dining room, there was the banquet room, a billiards room, a small room with a television in it, which Alexander said he rarely watched, a parlor, a large sitting room with a fireplace in it large enough for a man to stand in, and what Alexander called his artifacts room.

Before they entered that room, Alexander cautioned Roger: "You may see things in here that seem hideous, or contrary to my philosophies, but remember I am a collector and I buy whatever strikes me as interesting, with no interest whatsoever in its use as a talisman or any other supposed supernatural quality."

"I understand. Melissa already told me that."

"Did she? She's such a clever girl."

Alexander took a ring from his pocket on which there must have been thirty or more keys. He searched through the keys until he found the right one, inserted it in the lock and threw open the door. *"Voila!"* he said.

Roger entered a room that was twenty-five feet wide by thirty-five feet long. There was no carpet on the floor.

There was only one window. And almost every square inch of space was taken up by display cases, trunks, and boxes of every shape and size, many of them unopened.

"Consider yourself privileged," Alexander said. "Few people are ever allowed in this room—only those I know will appreciate its wonders."

Roger moved through the accumulated artifacts with a genuine sense of wonder. There were golden chalices inlaid with jewels, Samurai swords, large chunks of quartz crystal formations, sculptures, busts, chess sets, crystal balls and pyramids, ceramic figures many of which were obscene, a suit of armor, an Egyptian mummy case, paintings, and so much more it was impossible for Roger to take it all in, most of it covered in thick layers of dust. He walked through the room, his mouth open in awe like a country bumpkin in the big city, wondering what could possibly compel a man to collect so many artifacts merely to hide them in a room others rarely saw.

He stopped in front of a cherry-wood case at the end of the room which bore a brass plaque engraved with the words, "The Bizarre."

Inside the case were many things that fit that label well, among them a shrunken head; a whithered, mummified hand with a ring on it; a drinking cup fashioned from a human skull; a voodoo doll; obscene figurines of women giving birth; the claws of a bird; and on the bottom shelf a row of jars, each containing something organic floating in liquid. Roger stooped to examine the jars more closely and saw they contained human embryos, a heart, a brain, and—

Roger could no longer look.

"Quite a collection, is it not?"

Roger thought he would have a heart attack; Alexander had come up behind him without making a sound. He wa so startled he fell back against the case, almost breaking the glass. Alexander caught him by the arm.

"Sorry," Alexander said, "I didn't mean to surprise you like that. Are you recovered?"

"I'm all right," Roger said. "It's just that your collection is so overwhelming. There's too much to take in."

"Oh, you'll have opportunities to examine it again. Many of them. After all, you're going to be part of the family." He slapped Roger on the back. "And one hell of a welcome addition to my world too."

"I'm looking forward to it," Roger said, wondering if he had made a big mistake proposing to Melissa. He could not imagine being part of this crazy family.

"Oh, by the way," Alexander said, as he led Roger toward the door, "I'm told by a reliable source that the thing in that big jar *really* did belong to Dillinger."

Roger grimaced; he had no need to know where it had come from. He wanted it blanked from his mind.

Once outside, Alexander locked the door. "That's the grand tour except for the second floor, and that's all bedrooms." He looked at his watch. "Lunch is in an hour. It will be on the terrace. Perhaps you'd like to freshen up a bit before then."

Roger's ashen face gave the answer to that question. "That's a very good idea," he said, his voice quavering.

"See you then."

Roger approached the staircase. As he mounted the first step, Alexander called back to him, "Roger! Before you go. . . ."

Roger waited as the older man came over to the stairs. Roger was looking down on him for once, and seeing his face from that angle, he was disturbed once more by Alexander's resemblance to someone he knew.

"What is it?" Roger said wearily.

"Well, I just wanted to know if you might have seen Suzanne—the girl who served us breakfast—running around last night?"

Roger considered answering truthfully, but he suspected this inquiry was part of a sick mind game. Alexander's expression was too earnest.

"What do you mean?" he stalled.

"Well, I could've sworn she was running down the hall in the buff." He said this as if naked people running down the hall were an everyday occurence in the house.

"I slept all night," Roger said, straining not to show any hint he was lying.

"Be sure to tell me if you *do* see any naked women running around," Alexander replied, making a joke of it now. "At my age, I like to see such things."

"I'll keep you informed."

Alexander turned away and chuckled. Roger had the feeling there was indeed a game involved and he had lost.

But what was the prize?

He climbed the stairs slowly, gripping the bannister tightly. When he reached the second floor, he cried out in pain.

A large splinter was sticking out of the palm of his hand.

16. Deformities

"Son of a bitch!"

Roger plucked the splinter out of his palm and regarded it with distaste. It was an inch long. Blood was oozing from the wound. He wrapped his handkerchief around his hand and continued down the hall, stopping in front of Melissa's door. He knocked with his left hand, since his right was stinging from the splinter. When she didn't answer immediately, he knocked again, louder.

She came to the door, opened it, and peeked around the edge, so he could see only her head and right hand. Her face was puffy and her eyes watery. She had been crying or sleeping—or both.

"Oh, it's you," she said.

"Can we talk?"

"What about?"

"Melissa, what's the matter with you? We haven't had a decent conversation since we've been here. There are things we need to discuss."

"I don't feel good. Go away, Roger. I'm not in the mood." She slammed the door in his face.

Roger didn't know how to feel now. Melissa had never treated him this way before.

She hadn't even noticed he'd hurt himself.

Melissa didn't show up for lunch. Alexander entertained Roger with more of his half-baked theories on how to save the world from itself. Roger was beginning to think the old man was not entirely rational, despite what Melissa had told him. He also knew Alexander liked to put people on, and that irritated him because it meant one could never tell when Alexander was being serious—if he ever was.

Like that tour he had taken Roger on in the morning. He had barely shown him half the place, as if he didn't really care one way or the other if it impressed Roger. And he still refused to even hint at how he had acquired such wealth.

Roger didn't think he could endure much more of Alexander's tedious crackpot chatter, so after lunch, he asked Alexander if he might browse around in his library.

"I didn't bring anything with me to read," he said. "I promise not to destroy any valuables. With Melissa sulking, I don't have much to do, and I didn't get a good look around the library last night. Of course, if you'll be using it. . . ."

"No, I have other duties to attend to, and my library is, of course, open to a person of your stature, Roger," Alexander replied. "Look at anything you please. Perhaps you will find something that inspires you in there. Here's the key. You are one of the few people on earth I would allow in there unattended."

"Thanks," Roger said. He wished Alexander would utter at least one simple, declarative sentence without so much filligree and embellishment.

Roger left the terrace and went directly to the library's double doors. He inserted the key in the lock and stepped inside. Immediately he felt a kind of awe descend on him. Being in the room by himself was almost frightening. The thousands of books seemed to emanate a kind of aura—of history and the accumulation of centuries of human thought—that dwarfed Roger's puny intellectualizing by comparison.

He switched on the overhead light and spent nearly half an hour just walking back and forth along the shelves, sampling titles and subject matter. There were probably books here that existed nowhere else in the world, and that was spooky—because they were in the hands of an eccentric who might just let them rot, as he did the old cars in his garage.

But Roger was wrong about that, he realized. The shelves in here were dusted often; everything was clean. It wasn't like the garage or the awful artifacts room at all. Alexander truly had pride in his library.

After browsing awhile, Roger stopped at the section of books on the supernatural and the occult. There were probably two thousand such books altogether. Roger recognized the authors of many of these, because he had cited them in his own books, but many others were rather obscure. Many were also in German, Spanish, French, Latin, Ancient Greek, Russian, and Arabic. Roger wondered if Alexander was really a polyglot or if these volumes in other languages were collectibles only, or for show.

Roger picked out a French book and tried to read a few sentences. He gave it up quickly; his ability to read French had dwindled considerably since high school. He replaced the book and sorted through others, looking for something that might intrigue him. In the back of his mind he had a purpose which had not yet become clear to him; he was looking for something specific.

He scanned another shelf and came across a section of books by Tricia Mumford, the woman who had unwittingly started him on his career as a professional psychic debunker. He had never known she had written any books. He picked one at random, entitled *Trance Mediumship & Eros.* The title certainly piqued his interest. He tucked it under his arm and scanned the other titles. There were eight other books by Mumford there, all of them twenty-five years old or older, judging from the looks of them.

Roger wondered what the old fraud was doing nowadays. Was she still bilking suckers with her fake channelling routine? Was she still sleeping with her lesbian girlfriend, Nancy? He picked another title by her,

Beyond the Psychic Horizon, and laid the two Mumford books on the table in front of the leather chair.

He realized now what he was really looking for—his own books. Roger spent a frustrated forty-five minutes checking every section his books might be in, even a shelf that contained other anti-paranormal writers. He was about to give up the search altogether when he spied the bookcase behind the desk, the one with the glass doors.

He went over to the case and found it was locked. Peering through the glass, though, he saw all his books, including his latest, *The New Age Con Game*. Alexander had more than one edition of some of them. Also in the case were various scrapbooks, and a few volumes of obvious antiquity that were properly locked away.

He was relieved to find his books in the library, but he had to wonder why they were locked up. They certainly weren't valuable collector's items. One thing was evident, though. They had been read. The spines and book jackets showed a great deal of wear, more than most of the other books in the library.

Roger was impressed. So Alexander really was a fan of his; it wasn't all false flattery. He'd offer to autograph the books for Alexander later. That ought to make the old man happy.

Feeling somewhat better, Roger returned to the table, picked up the two Mumford books and started to leave. As he opened the door, he heard a commotion out in the big hall.

He looked around the edge of the doorway and saw the servants gathering together while Alexander stood before them, tapping his foot impatiently.

"Hurry up, damn it!" Alexander barked. "This is an inspection, not a party."

Roger wondered what Alexander's inspection consisted of. He had the air of an old military man; perhaps he considered the servants his troups. He went out into the hall and hid behind the staircase, where he could watch the inspection take place without much fear of being detected.

"Now get in line!" Alexander shouted. "You, Milicent, you're supposed to be next to Charles, not André. You can boff him later if you want, but I'll have no shenanigans during inspection."

After they were all lined up in the proper order, Alexander faced each of them, one by one, scrutinizing all details of their dress and appearance. "Suzanne, you have on too much eye makeup; André, you need to scrape your fingernails cleaner; Gabriel, polish your shoes; Carla, your hair is an utter mess." And on he went down the row, finding something to pick on with each servant.

Roger was amused by the spectacle to a point, but then he became bored and, ultimately, annoyed. Alexander was swaggering too much; after all, these people were merely his servants. He didn't own them.

Roger couldn't wait for the end of inspection, so he walked boldly out from his hiding place as if he were just leaving the library and started up the staircase.

"Hello, Roger," Alexander said.

Roger stopped in mid-stride. Alexander came over to the staircase and looked up at him.

"I'm just making sure the servants are in tip-top shape. After all, we have a distinguished house guest, and we don't want you to feel you're receiving less than the best service we can offer."

"Oh, I'm quite impressed," Roger said. "The service had been—" he searched for a word he thought Alexander might use—"impeccable."

"Still, I want *you* to be totally satisfied, Roger. Will you please also inspect my servants to make sure they meet your expectations?"

"I don't think that's necessary. I trust your judgment."

"But I insist, Roger." His expression showed he was quite serious and would be offended if Roger didn't comply with his wishes. "I won't rest unless I know they please you as well."

"All right," Roger said. "I'll look them over if it'll please you."

"It will, indeed."

Sighing, Roger turned and reluctantly descended the stairs. He followed Alexander over to the line-up of servants.

"Let's start at the far end with Thomas, my chauffeur."

"Whatever you say, Alexander."

The two men walked in front of the servants to the end of the line. Roger counted twenty of them. Some of their faces were familiar: Charles, Gabriel, Suzanne, Freddy, and of course, Peter, whose scarred visage seemed less harsh today, perhaps because he was standing so motionless he seemed to be a wax figure. He tried to catch the man's eye to see if there was any hint that he had seen Roger last night peeking in his door, but the man was unflinching.

"Each of you will bow or curtsey to Mr. Kant as he inspects you. Is that clear?"

A chorus of "Yes, sir" echoed in the vast hall.

"Thomas, meet Roger Kant. He is a man of genius. Do you understand that?"

Thomas nodded.

"The man is mute, Roger, but I believe that nod was sincere. Here we have Silvia, our downstairs chambermaid. Silvia, Roger Kant."

"Pleased to meet you, sir." She bowed clumsily, and Roger realized it was due to her left leg being artificial.

"Suzanne, you know, but she must curtsey anyhow. Here's Robbie, our maintenance man. He'll have the furnace going for us tonight, won't you, Robbie? Robbie, Mr. Kant."

"A pleasure, sir." Robbie had a slight speech impediment. As Roger passed him, he saw why: Half of Robbie's face was slack, as if he'd had a stroke, and that side didn't cooperate with the rest of his face. He also had a long scar along the base of his neck which hadn't healed properly.

Roger was beginning to feel the queasiness creep up on him. By the time they came to the end of the line, he was swallowing back acid that kept threatening to boil up out of his stomach. If he didn't swallow it, he might throw up on the spot, and he didn't think Alexander or the servants would appreciate that.

But he couldn't be blamed for his nausea. It was a natural reaction to what he had just seen:

All the servants were disfigured, handicapped or crippled. There was not a whole person among them.

Roger was woozy, but he managed to stand in place long enough for Alexander to finish his part of the inspection.

"You all pass, but just barely, and only if you take care of the little details I mentioned. You are lucky Mr. Kant is a kindly, tolerant man who was courteous enough not to find fault with any of you. Now, you are dismissed. Get back to your duties."

The servants scattered in every direction, some of them limping, others skittering like spiders minus a leg.

Roger was about to swoon. After the servants were gone, he was able to regain his composure to a degree. He thought he could make it up the stairs and vomit privately in his own bathroom if Alexander would only let him go.

Alexander approached him, smiling. Again, Roger felt there was a game involved, but this time he refused to play it.

"Thank you ever so much for helping with inspection, Roger."

"It was a privilege," Roger replied, burping.

"I see you found some reading matter."

Roger had forgotten about the two books under his arm. The spots before his eyes were much more important at the moment.

"Yes. Tricia Mumford," he mumbled.

"Ah, yes. You should find those amusing, I would guess."

"I'd like to go now, if you don't mind." He could feel a bilious bubble rising in his throat.

"Of course, Roger. I didn't mean to keep you. Go on up to your room and rest awhile. Dinner will be at eight. I'll busy myself in the library."

"Thank you." Roger started up the stairs.

"Oh, Roger, I need the key!" Alexander called.

Roger halted and fumbled the library key out of his

pocket. He tossed it down to Alexander.

"Thank you, Roger."

"Thank *you.*" He climbed the stairs slowly, trying not to shake the bubble loose too soon. He looked down at Alexander, who watched his every step, his head twisting with the curve of the staircase as Roger followed it.

"You should learn something from this," Alexander shouted.

"What?" Roger yelled over the bannister. When would the man let him be?

"Hire the handicapped—they're fun to watch!"

Roger was sick for half an hour. Then he cleaned himself up and went across the hall to bang on Melissa's door.

When she answered, her appearance had changed considerably since that morning. Her face was carefully made-up, and she was wearing a white blouse and white shorts, as if she were going to play tennis.

"What is it, Roger?"

"Melissa, please talk to me."

"About what?"

"I can't stay in a house full of deformed, crippled people."

"You mean the servants?"

"They unnerve me. Can't we tell Alexander I have to return for business reasons or something?"

"I didn't think you were prejudiced against the handicapped."

"It's not prejudice. It's a phobia, I guess."

"So you're not so 'astounding' around the handicapped. Is that it?"

"Melissa! How can you talk to me that way?"

"I'm sorry, Roger. It's difficult for me to sympathize with you over such a silly matter. How would you like to be one of those poor unfortunates? Alexander has given them usefulness. He lives with them all the time; you could endure them at least a few days. Maybe it would cure your phobia."

"Maybe I could—if you'd not be so distant. I feel alone—totally alone—and you're right across from me. Don't you know what torment that is?"

"Oh, Roger, you're being melodramatic. I'll tell you what. I'll come to your room tonight. I promise. Maybe about one or two. Okay? I'll take a chance on sleeping with you if it will hold you together for a few days."

"That's what I need, Melissa. Just some comfort and kindness—and a little love."

"All right. I'll see you at dinner."

She closed the door—again without so much as a kiss or a caress—and Roger didn't feel comforted at all.

He wasn't even surprised when she didn't show up for dinner.

That evening, after a lengthy, boring and ultimately meaningless after-dinner chat with Alexander, Roger excused himself and went up to his room early.

He bathed and shaved and splashed cologne on his body, but he refrained from taking any sleeping pills. He kept hoping Melissa would keep her promise to him, and he didn't want to be unconscious if she did.

He lay on the bed for a long time, just staring and thinking. He couldn't figure Alexander out at all. The man made a big show of how kindly he felt toward the handicapped, yet he made a crude joke at their expense the minute they were out of sight. His behavior reminded Roger of the many phony businessmen he had met who hired women in executive positions, then called them "cunts" behind their backs. In short, he was a phony, and much of his posturing was no doubt a sham. That was a major disappointment after the build-up Melissa had given her father.

Roger shut his eyes and let his mind drift, pushing away throught of Alexander and deformed people.

He was in a dark hall with stone walls.

Sconces holding torches lined the walls, and there was a

smell of decay and death in the air. He heard distant sounds of someone screaming. He walked down the hall until he came to a door with a barred window in it.

The screaming was very loud now.

Roger looked in through the bars and saw several people chained to the opposite wall. Flickering torches lit their naked bodies. A man in black, whose face Roger could not see, approached a woman and scraped her stomach with a jagged instrument. She screeched in pain, then fainted.

The man in black grunted and went to the next person, a middle-aged man. He put a thumbscrew on him and twisted it till the man cried out for mercy. He left the device hanging on the man's thumb and turned his attentions to the next person, another woman. He caressed her breasts with a gloved hand, then probed between her legs while she squirmed.

He chuckled.

Then he lifted a torch from one of the sconces and brought it close to the woman's pubic hair. Roger could smell it being singed. The woman bit back a scream as the man took the torch away. He patted her singed hair until he was satisfied it was not really afire. Then he put the torch to her feet.

The woman bellowed in pain.

"Stop that!" Roger shouted. "Leave those people alone."

As Roger yelled, he realized he was no longer outside the door; he was hanging on the wall, next to the woman.

The man in black carried the torch toward him. Behind the flame, Roger recognized the man, even though his face kept changing.

It was the demon; it was his father; it was the demon; it was *Alexander*.

Roger rolled out of bed and hit the floor with a thump. Momentarily disoriented, he rose on his hands and knees and climbed back on the bed.

The dream was excruciatingly real. It was no mere vision; it was as if he were witnessing something actually happening. The only surreal part of it was when his body traveled to the wall of torture. The experience seemed like one of those out-of-body experiences described by so many people.

But Roger didn't believe in O.B.E.'s. He had read about them plenty of times, though, so he could *dream* about having one. Still, this experience had no quality of a dream. His senses were not altered. Time flowed at the proper rate, and there was no distortion of his vision.

He couldn't have left his body, though, because it was impossible. Every rational cell in his being agreed with that, but there was dissension in a part of his mind—the part that was a scared little boy who lived in all men's minds. It was a little boy who would believe anything.

The vision of Alexander's face superimposed over the demon's lingered in his mind. What did that mean? Roger decided not to think about it or examine the experience any further. He had to occupy his mind until the after-effects of it wore off.

It was twelve-thirty now. Melissa ought to be arriving within the hour if she really planned to come. He longed for her embrace; but thinking of her would not cure his mental ailments, and it aggravated his sexual condition.

He remembered the two books by Tricia Mumford he had taken from Alexander's library. He hadn't really looked at them yet. He had been too distracted by the inspection of the servants and had fretted about it all afternoon, pacing in his room like a prisoner, unable to do anything or even think about reading.

He picked up the first book, *Trance Mediumship & Eros*. He opened it and turned to the copyright page; it had been printed in 1955 by a vanity press. Underneath the copyright notice was the dedication: "To Alexander Lewis, with love and affection."

He put the book down. He could hardly believe it. Writers didn't dedicate books to people who didn't believe in them.

Or maybe, to give Alexander the benefit of the doubt, he had changed his thinking since 1955.

That didn't ring true in Roger's mind, however. He sensed the makings of another game here, one in which Melissa must also be a participant.

Where was she?

Roger put on his robe and slippers and went out to find her.

Melissa wasn't in her room. The door was unlocked, and when he switched on the light, he could see her bed was made and hadn't been occupied this night at all.

Roger continued down the hall, uncertain where he was heading. He turned at the end and went back to the door that had three steps in front of it, where he had been the night before. He thought maybe this door might lead to the master bedroom where Alexander would be.

Instead, the door opened on a flight of steps leading up into the tower on his left, and a kind of half-hidden passageway on his right. Instinct told him to follow the passageway. The path was very narrow, and the floor was carpeted with very thick pile, so his movements were virtually silent. He crept along a few feet, came to a sharp turn and saw a series of small lights spotting the opposite wall. He went to the first of these and discovered it was not a light at all, but a hole in the wall, which was letting light in from one of the bedrooms.

Roger put his eye up to the hole and could clearly see into the room where three servants—two women and one man—were participating in a ménage à trois.

He pulled back from the hole. He could imagine who used these peepholes. Alexander would have great fun watching his servants copulate. He would probably encourage it. He might even take pictures.

Roger, however, was sickened. It wasn't right, a voice in his head told him, to watch people having sex. It was perverse and perverted.

Nevertheless, he continued along the passage, peeping into each hole, watching only long enough to see who was in the room. Finally he found the person he was seeking. It was at the next-to-the-last peephole. He looked through into an ornate bedroom with a mammoth bed set against the opposite wall. The room was full of Alexander's artifacts, most of them pornographic.

On the bed lay Alexander and Melissa, both nude. She was grappling with his penis, which barely extended from the folds of fat in his abdomen, trying to get it to respond.

"Gently, Melissa dear," Alexander said. "Gently."

She let go. "It's useless. You're just not good for more than once a night."

"I'm sorry, dear."

"It's all right. Maybe I can get some off Roger."

Alexander's face purpled with anger. "You wouldn't dare."

Melissa shrank away from him. "Of course not, Alexander. I was only joking."

"It wasn't a good jest, Melissa dear."

"He's a bad lay, anyhow," she said. "He doesn't know all the tricks you know."

Roger couldn't believe what he was witnessing. Was this another dream, or vision?

No. If it were, he could accept it.

"Melissa, we can't carry this on much longer," Alexander said. "You don't even remember to call me Father most of the time."

"It sounds so ridiculous. I can't bear to say it. I don't think Roger notices."

"The man isn't a complete fool, you know."

"He's close to one, though. I got him up here, didn't I?"

"Yes, and I must commend you on that devious machination."

She sighed and tucked her arms behind her head. "When will it be over, Alexander?"

"When I'm ready."

"You nasty old bastard. You're playing with him like a cat with a mouse, aren't you?"

"Just having a little fun. And why not? You had your fun with him."

"But you didn't have to screw him. . . ."

Roger could listen no more. He backed away from the peephole and floundered along the passageway till he found the entrance again. When he emerged into the hall, he allowed himself to let the reality of what he had seen and heard sink in.

He was being set up for something; that was clear. He would have to be perpetually on guard. That was bad enough; but it didn't really hurt him, and it wasn't really surprising considering the insanity of the inhabitants of this house.

What really hurt him the most was that Melissa's love for him was—as everything in his life was becoming—another sham, a delusion.

He walked back to his room, turned out the lights and curled up in the bed, cringing, even though he had no idea what was planned for him. It didn't really matter that much; his life could not be any worse.

He slept for a while, then at four o'clock in the morning, she came to him.

Melissa came—because the game evidently wasn't over yet.

Roger didn't say a word. He pulled her into the bed and screwed her out of spite.

Part Three:

Delusions of Faith

17. SCRAPBOOKS

Melissa had once told Roger a woman didn't make love to a man's body; she made love to his mind or his personality. Roger wanted to ask her if she had been making love to Alexander's mind when he saw her through the peephole. Or was she, after all, one of those shallow women who went for the body and the money? It had to be the money—because Alexander's naked body was a repulsive blob of bloated flesh.

Roger wanted to discuss those things with Melissa, but as soon as they finished their "lovemaking"—a strange phrase for a particular act in which there had been love on neither side—she had rushed out of the room.

Roger gloated a few minutes after she left. Despite what she had told Alexander, she had come to him. He knew it didn't mean anything like love this time—that perhaps she was doing it out of spite for Alexander, as much as he was doing it for spite in general. Or perhaps she wished to defy Alexander for the sake of defiance, because she was an independent woman who didn't like to be ordered around. Or maybe it was simply because Alexander had not satisfied her. It didn't matter why she had come to his bed, because Roger had triumphed in his own way. He had, at the very least, the satisfaction of knowing they had done it right under the old bastard's very nose.

Or right before his eyes!

In the passion of the moment, Roger had forgotten

about the peepholes. He hadn't followed the passageway to its end after finding Alexander and Melissa together. If he had continued, he would no doubt have found a peephole to his own room as well.

Alexander could have been watching them.

There wasn't much light in the room—only what the moon provided through the window—but Alexander wouldn't need any light to know what they were doing.

Roger pulled the covers up over his head. What if Alexander were watching him right now, plotting how he would take revenge on him for violating his Melissa—who he probably considered his property?

Roger had another thought, and he suddenly felt very dirty. Being secretly watched while he was having sex with Melissa was bad enough, but he now realized that in his haste to spite Alexander, he had taken Melissa fresh from Alexander's bed. She'd had Alexander's sweat still on her when she came to him. Her mouth had been on his. His body fluids still lingered in her.

It was sickening, and the idea of it was repugnant to Roger's sensibilities. He was the one who had been violated, and conversely, maybe Alexander was the one who was gloating; he had forced Roger to have his seconds. He may have even encouraged Melissa to come to his bed, just for jollies.

Who was spiting whom, after all?

Roger trembled under the covers. He felt victimized; he had become involved in another of Alexander's games, and this time he was definitely a loser. Even if Alexander weren't gloating, he would most certainly be angry, and Roger instinctively knew the old man's anger would compel him to extract some kind of recompense from Roger, possibly involving him in yet another sick mind game, which might have an even more revolting conclusion. The big question was, where would all the mind games lead to? Who was keeping score—and how would he know when it was over?

Roger felt something hard bump him from behind. It felt like a small animal.

"What the hell?"

He reached back and felt around. There was nothing behind him but the clammy cloth of the sheet, made damp by his bout with Melissa. He rolled over, and he felt it again, only this time, it was prodding him in the ass. Something was trying to force itself between his cheeks. Roger explored with his left hand and felt something hairy.

Roger yelped and jumped out of the bed. He switched on the lamp and jerked the covers off the bed. There was something hard in the bed, all right; it was a large disembodied penis wriggling around like a snake searching for its prey.

Then as Roger watched in disbelief, the awful thing faded away. It was another illusion, a sham.

Somewhere, behind the walls, probably in the passageway, he heard the hearty laughter of an evil man.

Roger had lost this round as well.

By taking three sleeping pills and washing them down with Scotch, Roger managed to numb himself into an unconscious state which got him through the rest of the night and part of the next morning. He didn't come to until almost noon. His ass still stung—or he imagined it did.

Remembering the awful thing made him retch, but nothing would come up, not even the bile the Scotch and drugs had become by now.

He still felt clammy and dirty and went into the bathroom to bathe and shave. As he sat in the warm water, vigorously trying to scrub away his shame along with the dirt, he wondered how he was going to face Melissa and Alexander today. The game was in full progress now, but he was the sole player who had no idea what the game was or who was to make the next move.

As he thought about the situation, he became very angry. What right did these people have to toy with him? He was better than either of them. He was equal to any of their psychotic shenanigans, and he intended to prove it. Before this particular game was over, he vowed there would be more than one loser.

Having made this vow, Roger felt more like his old self. There was a restorative quality to anger; it provoked action in the strong, *right* individual. Roger had forgotten who and what he was for a while. He was a man who had successfully outwitted dozens of wily opponents in "psychic" warfare. Melissa and Alexander had taken advantage of his current vulnerability, hitting him while he was down. But they hadn't counted on his dogged determination to rebound. They had hurt him as much as they could. From now on, he would be a more cunning adversary. He would destroy them somehow; he would emerge the victor, because he was in the right. He had only to come up with a suitable plan.

He dressed in a lightweight sweater and white slacks and went downstairs. He hoped he didn't encounter either Alexander or Melissa alone. He wasn't quite ready for that; he needed ammunition. If the two of them were together, the game would have to remain unplayed; appearances would have to be maintained, and civilized behavior would be required. But, if he had to confront either of them in a one-on-one situation, it could get quite nasty, and Roger wasn't sure he was up to any such confrontations just yet.

At the bottom of the stairs, he was met by Charles. "Is it time for lunch?" he asked the apparently benumbed servant.

"Yes, sir."

"Are Melissa and Alexander waiting for me?"

"They will not be joining you, sir. They have gone on a ride."

"When will they return?"

"I don't know, sir. Luncheon is ready on the terrace." Charles had been programmed well. He said only what he had to.

"Thank you, Charles."

"Yes, sir."

Charles led the way out. Roger sat down and ate quickly, because he had things he wanted to do before the other game players in the triangle returned, and he didn't want to get caught. As soon as he heard they were gone, he had formulated a plan that just might give him the ammunition he needed.

First, he had to break into the library.

Roger had pocketed a knife during lunch. It was an ordinary dinner knife, but it had a thick handle and a sturdy blade; it should be strong enough to do the job he had in mind.

He made sure none of the servants were around and jammed the knife between the latch of the two doors to the library. The knife bent a little, but by applying more leverage, Roger managed to pop the bolt and open the doors. He was lucky the doors had old-fashioned hardware. He examined the bolt to see if it was marred and saw no revealing nicks or scratches; then he closed the doors as softly as he could, cringing at the small click they made when the bolt slid back in place.

Now, he had to perform another break-in. He believed the answers to many of his questions—and perhaps the key to the whole game—lay in the locked bookcase behind Alexander's desk. His books were there, along with what must be other revealing things—or there would be no need for it to be locked.

He went to Alexander's desk, then turned the gooseneck lamp on and adjusted it to shine on the case. The knife proved useless on this lock. Its blade was too thick to jam between the doors without leaving a deep gouge in the wood. He searched around for another tool and found a brass letter opener on the desk. It was much sharper and thinner than the dinner knife. He worked the point of the letter opener into the lock on the case, while prying—ever so gently—with the knife between the doors. After several frustrating tries, the doors finally gave, popping open easily on the last attempt.

Roger was surprised at how easy it was. Maybe he had missed his calling in life; he should have been a burglar, although he knew a true cracksman wouldn't be shaking so much.

He was most curious about the scrapbooks, all of which were bound in leather. People kept scrapbooks for specific reasons, either as part of a hobby, or to preserve memories; these books could reveal more about Alexander and his mind than anything else. He lifted the stack of scrapbooks from the case and laid them on the desk, readjusting the lamp so that he could scrutinize the books more easily. He pulled Alexander's chair up closer and found it was very uncomfortable. It was leather and smelled old, and he could swear it retained Alexander's body heat. But as he began to flip through the books, he quickly forgot the discomfort of the chair.

The first scrapbook was a volume of Alexander's memories. It started with newspaper clippings and playbills dating from the 1930's about a magician called Artemus the Amazing. Then there was a series of old photographs of Artemus on the stage, with various women, and at parties. In many of them he was performing common illusions, such as sawing a woman in half. There was no mention in the clippings or any indication in the photos that any part of Artemus's act was original. He wasn't much more than a parlor magician.

It was obvious from the first photo Roger saw that Artemus and Alexander were the same man. He was much thinner in the pictures, but his height and the face—even then adorned with moustache and goatee—positively identified him. Even if these physical characteristics didn't give him away, there was that unmistakable glint in his eyes that betrayed the evil within.

Roger studied the old photos several minutes, fascinated by them for reasons beyond his avowed purpose. The yellowed snapshots were rousing something long-buried in his mind, stirring up ancient memories. Then it came to him.

He had seen Artemus on stage when he was a boy. He

was the magician who had so impressed him as a youth and made him want to be a magician too.

But surely that wasn't possible.

Roger flipped through more pages. Yes, he was right. Here was a clipping from an old South Bend *Tribune*. Alexander had been there, and the date could easily coincide with Roger's viewing of the performance.

He closed the scrapbook and laid it aside, stunned that there should be a link between him and Alexander. It was eerie. It was no wonder Alexander seemed familiar to him, then, but that didn't explain why Alexander also reminded him of the demon—unless his own mind had confused the two faces somehow.

He reminded himself he had little time to speculate. He would put all the pieces of the puzzle together later. He couldn't linger. He had more books to get through, and he had no idea when Alexander and Melissa would return.

The next scrapbook was about a man called Alex the Magnificent, which turned out to be another incarnation of Alexander. This book began much the same as the previous book had, with clippings about a new, but equally undistinguished, career as a magician with a different name. Then, in the middle of the book, the billing abruptly changed. Alex the Magnificent was no longer a magician. He was Alex the Seer, and he billed himself as a psychic, not as a magician. There were many photos of him attired in cornball mind-reader get-ups, such as robes with stars and crescent moons on them, and even a turban with a jewel in the middle.

Toward the end of the scrapbook, there were a few photos with a woman, who apparently assisted Alex in his mind-reading act. She was quite attractive in a skimpy outfit designed to distract audiences from the illusionist's sleight of hand. Her body was very shapely. In some photos, she had light hair; in others, dark or black hair. Her face was the same in all of them, however.

She was Melissa.

But that was impossible, Roger told himself. Melissa wasn't even born when these pictures were taken in the mid-50's. Yet here she was, a full-grown woman, standing next to Alexander over thirty years ago. Could it be Melissa's mother? No, it was Melissa herself; he was convinced of that, even if it made no sense.

Roger was becoming irritated. The scrapbooks were providing more questions than answers. He was tempted to give up on them, but then he flipped to the last page and saw nothing but a business card:

Alexander Lewis, Psychic Consultant
Private Readings
Let Me Tell You Where Your Future Lies.

There was a phone number and a pentagram, but no address. So Alex the magician had turned mind reader, then Psychic Consultant. Roger could imagine how that progression came about. There was little money in being a magician if you weren't very good, and Artemus, as Roger later learned, was mediocre at best. Failing to find fortune doing tricks, Alex the Magnificent became The Seer, and he had realized at one point that the big money was in the so-called private readings, where he could bilk superstitious, wealthy people out of thousands of dollars.

And they would be generous to him too—giving him stock tips and inside information that a smart operator could parlay into fortune.

No wonder he wouldn't tell Roger how he'd made his money.

This was becoming interesting.

He picked up the third scrapbook. Instead of being about Alexander, it was a collection of articles, photos, sketches and other memorabilia about Aleister Crowley, the infamous metaphysician who called himself The Beast. He was quite well known in the early part of the century as a member of the Golden Dawn and a contemporary of such leading occult figures as Arthur Waite and Dion Fortune. He was also a drug addict, a man of many perversions, which he indulged in with both sexes, and a man whom any person of decency—to Roger's way of thinking—should revile.

But this scrapbook demonstrated that Alexander didn't revile Crowley at all. Indeed, he seemed to revere the man. Crowley's motto had been "Do What You Will," and he had meant it literally. He had tried to do everything and anything he wanted, and had been called "the wickedest man in the world," because of his venery.

Alexander might fancy himself the same type as Crowley. A man who watched people have sex through peepholes—a man who encouraged his servants to have sex, so that he could watch them—certainly deserved to be the current title holder for the world's "wickedest," as far as Roger was concerned.

He took the next scrapbook off the pile. On the first page were the words, "Do What You Will." When Roger turned the page, he saw photos of people performing all sorts of sexual stunts. He flipped halfway through the book, seeing it was nothing but pornographic pictures, many obviously taken through one of the peepholes.

He laid that book aside without close scrutiny, his face flushing at what little he had glimpsed. He was no prude, but he was afraid he might see Melissa in there, and he didn't think he could endure that.

The next scrapbook also had a title page. It was called *Enemies of the Faith.* The first few pages were clippings about Alexander, all of them bad reviews of him in his various career guises. Beneath each of these he had written a scatological reply to the reviewer. Then there were more photos. Roger flipped through these pages idly, becoming bored, until he came to a photo of a man whose face he recognized. It was Peter, the horribly disfigured servant—before his face had been destroyed.

It was the eyes, Roger realized, gazing at the old photo, those eyes that now peered at the world through a mask of pain and perpetual suffering. This was the same man who groveled at Alexander's feet, an abject wretch who was forced to work as a servant to a madman.

Roger's stomach tightened. He had known Peter—under another name, before this awful thing had happened to him—because he was the man who had told Roger many of the secrets he later used in his books to debunk fraudulent psychics.

He shuddered as an awful thought came into his mind. Why was this man now working for Alexander? And had Alexander anything to do with his present condition? Had he been punished for revealing the secrets of the trade? If so, then Roger was responsible in a way. He had pried the secrets from the man; it wasn't right that he should suffer on Roger's account.

Do What You Will.

Did that mean torture too? Was Alexander even more wicked than his apparent idol, Aleister Crowley?

Roger flipped the page and came across clippings about his own career, dating back to the very beginning, when he was a young reporter in San Francisco.

Beside each clipping was an angry comment, scribbled by a man who obviously hated him. One said, "Arrogant Pup." Another, "Utter Asshole." Another, "Who does he think he is—God?" As Roger continued through the pages, the comments became more hateful. One of them chilled him:

"I must have him!"

The pages that followed after that contained clippings about Roger's recent failings. These bore no comments. After all, they were damning enough without further embellishment. Alexander must have had quite a few chuckles as he watched Roger's career cascade into the proverbial pits.

The rest of the pages were blank. Roger wondered how Alexander planned to fill them in.

Suddenly he had an impulse to look through the pornographic scrapbook again. He had not examined it carefully enough; it had something to tell him. He flipped past the halfway point and came across pictures of another nature—depicting torture—just as Roger had seen in his dream-vision of the night before. The pictures showed Alexander—and others—torturing and mutilating people. This brought a new aspect into the game; mental manipulations he could fight, but he had never expected true violence.

But these photos proved Alexander was capable of anything, and there was no doubt in Roger's mind now: Alexander was responsible for the deformities of his servants.

He also wondered who had taken the pictures.

Roger hurriedly put the scrapbooks away. He grabbed one of his own books and saw its margins were covered with nasty comments. Then he discovered all his books had been annotated by Alexander—with an unbounding hatred.

After returning the books, he shut the doors to the case, but he couldn't relock it. Nor could he lock the library doors as he left. Alexander would know he had been in there. He should have thought this out better. If he had known Alexander would actually use violence against him, he wouldn't have been quite so careless.

Panicking, Roger went outside to the garage. Maybe he could escape before Alexander and Melissa returned. The Ford Bronco was missing, but the Chevy station wagon seemed promising. Maybe, just maybe, the keys were in the ignition.

Of course not.

Could he talk the chauffeur into giving him a key? Probably not. He didn't even know where the chauffeur was. Besides, he was a loyal servant—any servant would be with the threat of being maimed or disfigured constantly hanging before him.

But surely a servant had attempted escape before. One of them must have made it. There had to be a way out.

Roger rushed around to the front of the mansion and looked forlornly down the winding road that led up to the place. He could get down to the gate, but what then? Even if he could manage to climb over the spiked fence without impaling himself, he wouldn't know which way to go. He could wander for miles before he reached a major highway, and that might take days. He could easily starve to death out there.

And all that time, Alexander would be looking for him.

Melissa—maybe she could be conned into taking him into the nearest town on some pretext. He needed books, or a razor, or something. No. She wouldn't cooperate, either. She would know Roger was onto them too. She would laugh in his face.

Suzanne? No. She would probably want to keep the rest of her fingers.

Peter? His face was already destroyed. What more had he to lose? His life, that's what. Unless—Roger's mind searched for persuasive arguments—unless he could be convinced to escape with him.

Roger reentered the house and ran up the staircase. He turned left and went down the hall to where it turned, where he had seen Peter having sex with Suzanne. He went up to the door and knocked loudly enough to drown out the sound of his own heart pounding.

Peter came to the door.

"I know," Roger said, involuntarily flinching at the sight of Peter's face.

Peter's dull gaze seemed uncomprehending.

"I know *everything.*"

"What do you know?" Peter said through his ravaged lips. His voice sounded like someone gargling.

"I know what happened to you, and why it happened, and unless your brain has been damaged, you remember me. Don't you?"

"No." He backed away from the door. "I don't know you."

"Damn it, I know you do. You told me all those secrets, and that's why you're here. You were lured here so Alexander could have his revenge on you—probably by Melissa. Am I guessing right?"

Recognition flickered in Peter's eyes, but not much else.

"But you weren't called Peter then."

"I was John Sellars." The way he said "was" made it sound as if that identity had been destroyed forever. "Mr. Lewis gave me the name Peter. He named us all."

"John Sellars! I knew it. I dedicated a book to you."

Peter just sighed; such recognition meant nothing to him now.

"Then I'm right about everything?"

Peter bowed his head in despair. "Yes, of course you are right, but I can't—do—anything," he said despondently.

"Yes, you can. I have to get out of here. And you do too. I'll take you with me, and once we're away from this awful place we can do something about this maniac."

Fear showed in Peter's face; at least, Roger thought it was fear. The face was too mangled to register emotions accurately enough for another man to read.

"I couldn't do that—go with you. Mr. Lewis would find us. It would mean horrible death for us both."

"What the fuck have we got to lose, then?"

Peter was persuaded.

Peter knew where the car keys were kept. They didn't have to worry about running into the chauffeur, since he was driving Alexander and Melissa around—somewhere. So it was easy to lift the keys to the Chevy from the hooks on the wall in the chauffeur's room. Roger didn't even ask about keys to the other vehicles; he doubted any of them were in running condition.

"Do you want to bring anything with you?" Roger asked Peter before they descended the stairs.

"I have nothing worth bringing."

"Then let's move out. We probably don't have much time."

Peter hesitated a moment. "I wish I could bring Suzanne," he mumbled raggedly.

"I don't blame you, but we can't make this a major prison break. If we're successful, we'll be able to get her out of here later. We'll free all the servants."

Peter fell silent. He couldn't argue with that, and there was no time to round up everybody. Some of them were so paranoid—or brainwashed—they wouldn't want to leave, or even worse, they might oppose their leaving.

"Don't lose your nerve now, Peter. All we have to do is

make it to the garage."

They slipped out the back door and walked over the terrace, past the empty swimming pool and into the garage. No one had seen them.

Peter pulled up the garage door, and Roger unlocked the Chevy. He stuck the key into the ignition and turned it.

The Chevy wouldn't start.

18. The Demon Revealed

Alexander and Melissa stepped out of the Ford Bronco in front of the house, then Thomas took the vehicle back to the garage. They had argued all through the ride—the purpose of which was to discuss their plans for Roger without any possibility of his overhearing them.

Melissa strode ahead of Alexander, let herself in the house and slammed the door. She had not been able to persuade Alexander.

Alexander just grinned. He'd known from the beginning he would get his way ultimately—no matter how much she sulked.

He planned to give Roger the full treatment.

Roger heard the Bronco coming around the driveway.

"Too late," he told Peter. "They're back."

The planned escape had proven futile. Roger had tried to start the Chevy several times, before he looked under the hood and discovered the car's distributor cap had been removed.

Peter was highly distressed now. "We can't escape," he said. "The punishment will be—"

"Just act natural, damn it," Roger said, pulling down the garage door. "Go into the house as if you'd been on a stroll in the garden or something. We'll get another opportunity later."

"I don't think—"

"Let me do the thinking. Just get out of here—now."

Peter went out the back door in a labored run. The Bronco pulled into the last bay. Roger was relieved to see Melissa and Alexander were not inside. Thomas turned the engine off and stepped out. He regarded Roger curiously.

Roger was pretending to admire the Tucker. "A hell of a car, the Tucker. Less than fifty in the world, and old Alexander has one. I have to admire his taste."

Thomas merely nodded and passed on by, leaving by the same exit Peter had taken.

Roger had forgotten he was mute, but he certainly would have a way to communicate with Alexander. What could he tell him, anyway? There was nothing wrong with Roger admiring one of his cars, was there?

He could tell him the keys to the Chevy were missing, which he would soon find out.

"Damn it to hell!" He should have given the keys to Peter to take back. There would have been time.

Roger was going to have to make his next escape plan more carefully—if he had another opportunity.

He ran after Peter and caught him out on the terrace, puttering around, pretending to clean the table. He pressed the Chevy keys into his hand.

"See if you can slip these back without being caught. Okay?"

Peter nodded.

"And, if you can, steal the keys to the Ford. If you get them, come and get me—no matter what time it is—and we'll escape. Do you think you can do that?"

"I'll do my best."

"A lot depends on it—for both of us. There isn't much time left. Alexander's bound to make his move soon, especially when he finds out what I know."

"How would he find out?" Peter asked, his voice rasping.

"I'm going to tell him."

Stealing the Ford was plan B. Plan A was much bolder. Roger had thought it over, and he had determined he might not need an escape plan. He was a well-known person. He couldn't be kept a prisoner here. All he had to do, simply, was *demand* Melissa and Alexander let him leave, and if they didn't, he would threaten to call the authorities on them.

He was *Roger Kant,* not some obscure person like John Sellars—now Peter—whose disappearance would cause little or no comment in the press. He was a somebody, a celebrity. He would brazen it out with them. He'd call their bluff.

So when dinner time was announced by the ever-present Charles, with a knock on his bedroom door, Roger felt he was ready to cast the final die in the game.

In fact, he was looking forward to it.

Dinner was especially sumptuous tonight. There was fresh lobster, Caesar salad, baby carrots, creamed asparagus, and for dessert, a multi-layered chocolate cake.

Roger ate heartily, barely looking at either Alexander or Melissa as he dined. He was no longer intimidated by them, because he had two plans. One of them had to work.

They were apparently angry with each other again, because they were barely speaking. That was good, Roger figured; he might be able to play them off against each other.

After the dessert, Alexander suggested they have coffee out on the terrace. "It's such a beautiful moonlit night, I think we'll all enjoy it outside. Won't we, Melissa dear?"

"It's okay, I guess," Melissa said.

Roger readily agreed. He liked the idea of confronting them on the terrace, outside the gloom of the house. It might give him an advantage.

Suzanne brought out the silver coffeepot and cups and

saucers for the three of them.

Alexander was right. It was a beautiful night; the moon loomed large and red just above the wooded hills behind them, creating an effect that seemed unreal. The moon also provided sufficient light for the triangle of adversaries sitting around the glass-topped table to see each other, although each person's face seemed to have a blue cast.

"It's always pleasant this time of year," Alexander said. "Cool but comfortable. How do you like the climate, Roger?"

"Oh, it's fine. But I like the different seasons we have in the Midwest. I miss Chicago. The winters are rough, but there's variety in our weather. It never gets boring."

"How did you find Chicago, Melissa dear?"

"Windy," she said curtly.

"Not very articulate tonight, are you?"

"Leave me alone."

"Roger, I must say you seemed to enjoy the meal tonight."

"It was excellent. Lobster's one of my favorites."

"You were right, Melissa, about that. She just knows everything. She has the most annoying habit of being right all the time. Wouldn't you agree, Roger?"

"Frankly, Alexander, I don't give a damn." It was time to cut out the chit-chat and get on with the final round of the game.

"Oh?" The old man didn't seem startled at all. He merely sipped his coffee and regarded Roger with detached amusement.

"I know what you two are up to."

"You do?"

"I broke into the library today."

"I know," Alexander said placidly.

"And I broke into your bookcase too."

"I know that too. I appreciate your not marring the finish."

"I looked at your scrapbooks—all of them—and I know what kind of man you are."

"Is that so? I'd be very interested in your opinion."

"You're a vile, disgusting monster. You should be in prison—or the electric chair."

"You're probably right about that," Alexander replied, the hint of a smile on his lips. "But perhaps all of us would be in prison if all our acts were known."

"That's a specious argument, and you know it."

"Perhaps, Roger. I would say, however, you have done some things you probably shouldn't have."

"That's not the point."

"What is the damn point?" Melissa said, breaking in.

"The point is, I know a lot about you two, and there are many more things I suspect. I have knowledge that could put you both away forever. But I won't use it."

"Why not? Aren't you famous for exposing people? I would think a sordid life such as mine would make for a rather fabulous book. Think of the chapter you could do on Melissa!"

"Very funny," Melissa said.

"Because I don't want to expose you." Roger stood up and leaned across the table for emphasis, looking Alexander dead in the eyes. "I'm calling an end to this sick mind game of yours right now. I demand that you let me go—and in exchange, I'll promise not to reveal what I know. Besides, you forget I'm a well-known person. If I'm missing for very long, there'll be a search."

"Maybe, but the searchers would have to know where to look, and I assure you Melissa didn't leave an easy trail to follow. It could take quite some time for anyone to trace you here."

Roger had no answer to that. "Maybe. But we don't have to worry about that if you'll agree to my terms."

"What do you think, Melissa?"

"I think Roger is lying."

"I disagree. Whatever else Roger Kant may be, he is no liar. If he promises he won't expose us, then I, for one, am willing to take his word as bond."

"Sucker," Melissa sneered.

"Then, you'll let me leave?"

"Of course, Roger. What else can I do? You have presented a forceful argument, which as a gentleman, I can't ignore. I'll have a car waiting for you first thing in the morning."

So much for Plan A, Roger thought. Now he had to see if Plan B was in progress. He went to Peter's room and knocked. Peter seemed relieved to see him.

"Did you get the keys back?"

"Yes. Thomas did not see them missing."

"What about the Ford keys?"

"I thought I'd wait till Thomas was asleep."

"Good thinking. When will that be?"

"Most likely by midnight."

"Then I'll expect you between midnight and one."

Peter nodded. "I should be able to do that."

"Look," Roger said earnestly, "if something goes wrong tonight, I want you to call this phone number." He handed Peter a slip of paper with his attorney's number on it. "Ask for Sid. Tell him where we are, and he'll do something about it. Can you do that?"

"No."

"Why not?"

"All the phones are constantly monitored—in shifts by the other servants. You can't call out without Mr. Lewis knowing."

"Damn it. That means we can't trust anyone. It's just you and me in this. Do you understand that fully?"

"Look at my face. Do you think I understand?"

Roger did look, and he knew Peter understood.

Plan B was in effect then. One of them had to work. But Roger was no fool. If Peter didn't show up by one, he was going to take his chances on foot.

It would be better to die out in the woods than to die by Alexander's hands.

* * *

They came at twelve-thirty.

They burst through the locked door, sending splinters of wood flying through the room.

There were two of them: Thomas the chauffeur, and a bigger man Roger had never seen before. He was husky and broad, with a shiny bald head; he looked like a TV wrestler. Both were wearing skin-tight black outfits.

Roger tried to resist, but he was no match for their combined physical strength. They dragged him out into the hall and down the spiral staircase. Then they took him to a small door behind the kitchen, which led to a cellar.

Sconces bearing torches lit the way down a stone flight of stairs. Roger had seen this place before; it was the dungeon of his nightmares, or rather his vision of the day before.

Melissa and Alexander waited for him at the bottom of the stairs in a small alcove just off the end of a long hallway which was also lit by torches. Alexander was dressed in a black robe, sitting in a chair that resembled a throne. Melissa stood at his right side, wearing a similar robe. Then, with a shock, Roger noticed who stood behind them.

It was a shame-faced Peter.

Roger had been betrayed.

"So you demanded we let you go," Alexander said. "That was certainly amusing." He started to chuckle. "It was very much like you, though—an egomaniac to the very end. Roger Kant is always right. All he has to do is ask, and we have to let him go." His chuckle grew to a guffaw, until he was choking on his own laughter. "Goddamn, that's funny."

Melissa pursed her lips, but didn't smile. Peter looked away.

"Some joke, you perverted son of a bitch," Roger snarled. The burly man holding his right arm gave it a muscle-wrenching twist. Roger bellowed.

Alexander stopped laughing suddenly. "Not yet, Garth, you imbecile. Just hold him. I'll tell you if I want him hurt." He looked at Roger with an expression that almost bordered on pity. "Poor, dear Roger. You spoiled the game by forcing the end so early. We had so many more things planned. It was a pleasure matching wits with you, if that's any consolation, but you should have heeded your own advice to Peter and trusted no one. Trust is what got you into this little predicament in the first place. You should never have trusted Melissa."

"I know that now," Roger said bitterly.

"Women are peculiar creatures, though. She pleaded with me not to hurt you."

Roger raised his eyebrows in surprise.

"She just wanted me to kill you and get it over with."

"Bastard!"

Alexander laughed again. "But I'm afraid Melissa was not persuasive enough. So we'll do what I like, and Melissa will just have to sulk. She can't always have her way."

"I never get my way."

"Oh, you do, but we shall come to that later. For now, we have the problem of Roger Kant. The Astounding One. The man who knows it all; the man who debunks psychics and destroys their careers—and often their lives. But that is all right with Roger Kant, because he's always right."

"You can't do this," Roger said, still hoping he could reason with them. "They'll come looking for me."

"Ah, Roger, that's the pity of it. For such an intelligent man, you are also an utter fool. Did you think—really—that you were dealing with ordinary people here? Surely, after you perused my scrapbooks, you must have gained some insight into what we are—but, then again, maybe you wouldn't. Because that would require you to believe in something more abstract than the only reality you recognize—Roger Kant. You are a stubborn man, and that is your downfall."

"What are you, then? Or what do you believe you are?"

"Still the skeptic, I see. We shall change that shortly. I am many things, Roger. You know I was a magician; but anyone can perform illusions, and I found it an unworthy calling. One night, while I was doing my act, I discovered I had true psychic abilities. I inherited them, I believe from Eliphas Levi, the man who wrote *Dogma and Ritual of High Magic*—a copy of which I have, of course. I am his second reincarnation. Aleister Crowley was the first. When Crowley died, I believe the spirit of Levi searched among mankind for a few years until he found a suitable vessel for his spirit in me."

"That's the most outrageous bullshit I've ever heard," Roger said.

"You may believe that if you wish. I know it is true. How else do you explain my sudden psychic ability, my sudden total knowledge of several languages—and how else do you explain my powers?"

"You have no powers. You're just a swaggering, insane bully with a lot of money to make people believe you have powers."

Alexander continued without bothering to acknowledge Roger's outburst. "As for Melissa, I suppose the only thing you could call her that you would understand is a witch. She's quite mortal, but her powers have enabled her to do many things no ordinary mortal could. For example, she is the same age I am. I would like to appear younger myself, but I find the rituals involved tedious and repulsive. But you know women—they'll do anything to maintain their looks."

"This is all very interesting," Roger replied, "but you don't really expect me to believe it. You know me better than that."

"That's true. Because we know you—more intimately than you imagine—we had to bring you here. We have sworn to avenge the people whose lives you have touched and often ruined, beginning with Tricia Mumford. We have had others like you here before, and I suspect there will be more. We cannot allow your kind to upset the coming of the New Age any longer—an age in which supernatural forces will rule the world. It's a pity we couldn't have caught you sooner—but we had to wait till you were vulnerable. You are—*were*—a strong man, Roger Kant. But once your defenses were down, you were no match for us."

"I don't buy it. The New Age is nothing but more psychic bullshit, and you make it sound like the coming of a new millenium."

"I'm afraid, Roger, you have been mistaken all your life. The New Age is valid, because there *are* real psychic phenomena. There are powers you never dreamed of, and we intend to show you just a small sample of a part of the world in which you refuse to believe."

"No parlor magic is going to sway me," Roger said. "I've seen it all before."

"Perhaps not *all,"* Alexander replied. "Didn't you ever wonder how Melissa knew so much about you—how she anticipated your every need? Could an ordinary person do that? Let's start with something simple. Melissa, demonstrate for Roger how you became the woman he needed."

Melissa's face became fluid and elastic. Her skin changed color, then her hair, then her features. She showed Roger many faces; she was all the strange women he had encountered in Seattle: the woman in the airport, the alluring woman in the restaurant, the briefly seen woman at the radio station. Finally, she had drawn parts from all the women she had been and created the familiar Melissa incarnation—with the red hair and all the other best features of his previous wives. She reverted to this form again after the demonstration.

"It's some kind of trick," Roger said. He tried to break free from the two men holding him. "If I could examine it closely, I'd see how it was done."

"You are difficult to convince, aren't you?"

"I told you no cheap trickery would convince me of anything."

"Ah, Roger, you are such a bull-headed man. Didn't you notice the change in your life after you met Melissa? She—and I—are the ones who ruined your career, reducing you to your present state, so that we could lure you here."

"You take credit for that?"

"Indeed, once you became vulnerable it was all very easy. You worked yourself too hard; you drained away your energies, so you began to imagine things, which we later made real."

"That's meaningless mumbo jumbo."

"Roger, we went to great lengths for you. We removed—let's use that rather polite term—your secretary Edith, so that you would need Melissa. In fact, we made Edith ill so that she could not accompany you on the trip to Seattle."

Roger's eyes started to water. Edith had been murdered so that they could get to him. He started to shout obscenities, to scream that he didn't believe they could have done such things, but he knew in his heart they were quite capable of any monstrous acts. He went limp in the arms of the men restraining him. How would he live with himself with this knowledge?

That was a droll thought—as if he could escape from here alive.

The man's smug expression was beginning to annoy Roger. Alexander knew he was getting to him, and that hurt; Roger wanted to punch the man in the face.

"We affected every aspect of your life, Roger. We even made you accident-prone as a way of constantly agitating you. We caused your dreams and visions. We expended a great deal of effort on you, sir, more than we ever had to before. You might take some pride in that."

"Fuck you."

"Crude, but well-said. But," Alexander continued, "we are tenacious, stubborn and hard-headed too. We had to use a great deal of ammunition on you. I was the one who called you on that radio station talk show. Remember? I blew up the equipment. That was fun." He leaned forward, pointing his finger at Roger's face. "From that first day in Seattle, you were totally ours!" he said triumphantly.

"You're insane," Roger said. "I don't believe any of this."

"Are you stupid? Think, man. Think of Melissa and what she did for you as soon as she usurped Edith's place in your life."

Roger lifted his head to face Melissa. Her eyes were staring past him, and her expression was blank. She was merely an observer at this point, but Roger remembered how she had been involved in every bad thing that had happened to him since Seattle. She had encouraged him to continue the tour; she had hired the actor and the doctor in Columbus; she had arranged virtually everything while Roger blithely went on, contributing to the continuing catastropes merely by being himself, never suspecting her—because his goddamn male ego had been too flattered by the presence and ultimate advances of a beautiful young woman for him to think clearly. If not for that—if not for her coming to him and forcing herself on him—maybe he would not be standing here today, facing some kind of punishment for his supposed misdeeds.

But he had been so vulnerable, any woman could have manipulated him if she knew the right things to do and say. And Melissa had always known—often before he did—what he needed. And she had used her knowledge to betray him.

But was that psychic ability? Couldn't she have researched his background—talked to his previous wives and others who knew him? Perhaps, but it didn't explain everything.

Roger was bewildered. He had never encountered frauds of such complexity. It was almost enough to make him believe in real magic.

Finally, he said, "You went to a lot of trouble to get me here too, didn't you, Alexander? That was your ultimate goal."

"Yes. We had to have you here where I am king and you are nothing. You often wondered what kind of game this was—I picked up on that rather easily—but you never really guessed the prize was you. Did you?"

"No," Roger admitted somberly.

"There were many things you didn't guess because you used only your reason. You never understood that what you put out in the universe comes back to you. You put out destruction, and now it's retribution time. First, however, there are some minor manners to attend to. Peter?"

"Yes, sir?"

"Come out here and face me."

Peter reluctantly came from behind the throne and bowed before Alexander. "It was good of you to tell us Roger planned to escape tonight. For that, I shall allow you to live. But, I do believe you would have run away from us if Roger had been able to start the other car."

"No! I wouldn't."

"Peter, you're only making it worse by lying."

Roger could see Peter's body trembling.

"Yes, sir," he admitted. "I would have gone with him."

"Thomas, take him to the chamber. Remove his left hand."

"No!" Peter screamed. "I didn't try to escape! I don't deserve this."

"I'm sorry, Peter; but if I let you go unpunished, the other servants might lose respect for me, and I must have absolute respect. A hand is not the worst thing you could lose. Think on that, and perhaps it won't be so bad. I'm sure Suzanne will still appreciate you."

Thomas let go of Roger and came forward. He took Peter's arm and began to pull him along the torchlit hallway to the right. Peter's screams echoed back to them all.

Roger jerked forward. Held only by Garth, he could just about reach Alexander. "You loathsome bastard! What kind of monster are you?"

"An interesting question, Roger. This is the kind of monster I am."

Alexander's face became a mass of puttylike flesh, then assumed a new shape. His eyes turned dark, losing their whites, and the irises became slits. He stood up, his robe dropped to the floor, and his body changed too—flesh flowing into different places, muscles taking shape where there had been none before. His teeth became yellowish fangs dripping greenish, malodorous spittle.

Alexander had become the demon—the same entity that Roger had seen so many times in his visions.

"As I told you before, Roger," Alexander's demon voice said, "we are not ordinary people."

Melissa flinched involuntarily. Garth, who apparently had not witnessed this transformation before, eased his grip on Roger's arm as he gaped at his master's different form.

Roger felt the grip relax and twisted away from him. He turned and ran back up the stone steps.

"Get him!" Alexander boomed.

Roger was much faster than the lumbering Garth. He made it to the top of the stone stairs and was through the door before his pursuer was halfway up. There was a cabinet nearby—a tall, heavy wooden cabinet for holding kitchen supplies. Roger heaved his shoulder against it, pushed mightily, and toppled it in front of the door.

He knew it wouldn't hold Garth long, but it would delay him.

Roger ran first to the kitchen door. It was deadbolted for the night. Any window he went to had bars on it. Then he remembered the terrace doors out in the big hall. They were also bolted, but they were glass.

He heard Garth roaring in the kitchen. He had gotten past Roger's obstacle. Too easily.

Roger had to risk getting cut. He propelled himself through the terrace doors, exploding onto the flagstones and rolling as he hit the ground.

A shard of glass protruded from the top of his left hand. He plucked it out and kept running. Blood streamed down his face, and he touched his forehead, feeling a ragged flap of skin where glass had ripped his flesh. It was a minor wound, though, and the least of his worries at the moment.

It was late enough that the moon had already begun to

disappear behind the hills behind the house; so it was dark, and there were many places to hide. But he couldn't hide long; he had to do something. If he headed toward the woods, he might get across the lake Alexander had told him was there. Maybe there was a way out over there.

But he would also encounter the stone wall, which must certainly circle the entire estate.

Alexander's words haunted him; he had said Melissa pleaded with him not to hurt Roger, but to just kill him and get it over with. He shuddered to think what that meant.

That demon trick was very clever too, but Roger knew it was just that, a trick, expertly executed.

He cautioned himself that he had no time to think about Melissa or Alexander. He'd puzzle their illusions out later. Now there was only time to keep moving.

He stumbled on a stone in the dark and almost pitched into the empty swimming pool. He scraped his knee, but stifled the pain. Garth would be coming through the terrace doors any second.

The garden—he could cut through there and get to the garage. Maybe he could hot-wire the Bronco.

But he didn't know how to hot-wire a car.

Damn Peter for betraying him! He was paying for his actions, but that gave Roger little comfort.

And Melissa—how could she have led him on, pretending love for so long when all the while she apparently hated him?

Damn it!

Quit thinking, Roger. Keep moving.

He felt flowers and the tops of vegetables crush under his feet. He'd go around to the front of the house, make for the road, get to the gate, and climb over the stone fence somehow. Then he'd get to the main road. If he kept heading west, he'd have to eventually encounter a thoroughfare where he could hitchhike to civilization.

He heard glass shattering. Garth was outside now too.

He kept running toward the edge of the garage. All he

had to do was get around the corner to the front of the house.

He made it.

But the front of the house was not dark. Floodlights lit the area like a ballpark at night.

Roger couldn't let that stop him. He ran toward the winding driveway. A quick sprint and he'd be out of the light and into the secure darkness of the trees.

As he passed the front doors, they burst open and two figures emerged. He didn't stop to see who they were. He just kept moving, his legs powered by the instinct to survive.

He was almost to the woods. Let them try to find him in there.

One of the figures took off from the ground and flew ahead of him. The demon—Alexander—whatever—was using his only true weapon: intimidation. But Roger knew it was a trick now, and he couldn't be slowed down by anything so obvious.

The demon disappeared, as if it also knew it was no longer effective.

The other figure tackled Roger by the legs, pulling him to the ground. Something bit into his flesh, and he moaned. He looked down and saw Freddy the gardener. His right hand was fitted with a sharp hook with a barb on it, and it was embedded in Roger's calf.

Roger kicked at Freddy's face with his uninjured leg and knocked the man unconscious. He kicked at the barb, and the apparatus came loose from Freddy's arm, revealing the ugly end of his stump.

Roger half sat up and worked the hook out of his flesh, biting back howls of pain. Then he stood up and kept moving toward the woods, dragging his damaged leg behind him.

He was only two yards from the darkness that would envelop him—the friendly darkness that could save his life.

One yard away. The pain in his leg was slowing him

down. He forced the leg to move, even as blood soaked his socks and seeped into his shoe.

A foot away. His eyes were focused on the trees.

He was going to make it.

He could hide out there for hours; they'd never find him in there. He would make them pay for what they had done to him.

A burly arm came around from behind and jerked his neck backward.

The last thing he heard was the popping of his own vertebrae.

19. the wall

Count Basie!

Roger couldn't believe it, but he was hearing an original old recording of "One O'Clock Jump" coming from somewhere. It sounded scratchy, as if it were being played on an old phonograph. The music stopped, there was a click, and "One O'Clock Jump" started over again. It was mellow music, one of his favorite songs in fact, but it was irritating to hear this beautiful piece of jazz turned into a grating cacophony, raking at his nerves.

Roger wanted to protest.

But he wasn't sure if he could, because he didn't know where he was yet. His senses registered pain in various parts of his body, particularly in the calf of his left leg. His neck ached too. His wrists felt like they were being cut in half, and his arms were stretched out, forced to hold the full weight of his body. He tasted sweat and blood running off his moustache.

He forced his swollen eyes open. Everything was a blur. There was a dark, tall, heavyset figure standing a few feet in front of him. Next to him was a shape that resembled a woman, and next to them, slightly farther away, other figures lurked.

Somebody threw ice water on his face.

The shock of the cold liquid startled him to full awareness. His eyes focused, and he recognized Alexander and Melissa, and two of the servants, Thomas and Freddy.

They were all dressed in dark robes. It was Thomas who had thrown the water on him. His skin stung where the little bits of ice had touched him.

He lurched in anger toward them, then realized his arms and legs were chained to a stone wall and restrained by heavy iron shackles. The slightest movement made the metal of the shackles slice into his flesh. He also became aware he was hanging there naked, just as he had seen those unknown people in his vision—in this very same place, a torture chamber. Being truly naked—not nude, which was polite in its own way—before people who could do anything they wanted to him, made Roger cringe. His whole body was blushing and covered with goosebumps.

"Ah," Alexander said, "at last the dead awaken."

Roger surveyed the torchlit room. There were no windows and only one door with a barred opening in it, the door behind which he had stood in his vision. The ceiling was low, less than eight feet, and the room itself small—probably no more than forty feet square. These dimensions lent a claustrophobic quality to the room, which no doubt enhanced the terror of the acts committed here.

There were enough shackles and chains hanging around the four walls to hold up to twenty people. Dark, reddish-brown stains marked the spots where other victims had been restrained. The room smelled of stale blood, urine and excrement, which the smell of the pitch-burning torches did little to hide.

There was a large, rough-hewn wooden table in the center of the room on which lay many implements of torture, some of which Roger recognized, others of which he could only shudder at, trying not to imagine what purpose they could serve.

"He's not dead," Melissa said, clearly displeased.

"No. But you almost joined the spirit world, my friend. Garth almost killed you, the stupid lummox, with that neck hold of his. I would punish him, but it's not entirely correct to punish someone for being stupid. Fortunately, I believe your neck is only sprained. I hope it is not too painful."

"As if you cared."

"Ah, but I do care. I wouldn't want anything to happen to you that would spoil all the fun that's ahead."

"I hate to think what your idea of fun is." Roger's mouth was dry, making it difficult to talk, but he felt compelled to reply, if only to annoy Alexander.

"My idea of fun is to show people the error of their ways, to teach them lessons. In order for them to learn, they must be alert and attentive. That's why I'm concerned that you're not in such pain it distracts you from your lessons. Your mouth sounds dry. Perhaps you'd like a drink of water."

Roger started to say something properly defiant, but he needed liquid. He barely nodded his head.

"Thomas, give him a drink."

Thomas carried over a small bucket with a ladle in it.

"Carefully now."

Thomas lifted the ladle to Roger's lips and let him drink. He gave him three ladles full of water. Roger lapped it eagerly, letting some linger in his moustache.

"That's enough, Thomas. That should hold him for a while. Now go sit on the floor with Freddy, until I call for you."

Alexander stepped closer. "I want you to listen to me, Roger. I am going to prove to you that the psychic world does exist. I will show you all manners of things; and I warn you not to attempt to close your eyes, or I will be forced to use a device that will keep them open. Do you understand?"

"I'm not going to be convinced by phony tricks."

"Quit showing your goddamned ego, Roger, and answer me. Do you understand what I'm telling you?"

"Yes!"

"Good." He stepped back and reached behind Melissa, who stood with her arms crossed as if she were waiting for something. "I want to show you, first of all, that we are serious." He picked an object from the table, then held it up for Roger to see. "This is Peter's hand."

Despite Alexander's warning, Roger closed his eyes when he saw the bloody end of the hand. Alexander slapped him across the face with the lifeless limb.

Roger forced his eyes open.

"I told you not to close your eyes. I show you this, so that you'll understand when I say something is to be done, it *is* done. Thomas or Freddy, either one, is capable of doing anything to anybody, without a hint of remorse or compunction. Indeed, I think Thomas rather enjoys some of his duties, and if he weren't mute, he'd probably say so. Of course, as you must have guessed by now, Thomas did disobey me once. I fit the punishment to the crime."

Roger glanced at Thomas and felt his scrotum tightening in response as he imagined how the man had been rendered mute.

"Now, Peter's hand is going into my collection of bizarre artifacts. I have a pair now. You saw the other one in the case, didn't you? That was Freddy's, of course."

Roger wondered what Freddy's crime had been—and what part of him might end up in the case.

"Now, the problem before us, as I see it, is how to convince a skeptic like the world-renown Roger Kant that he is truly a simpleton who knows nothing. It has bothered me for years, ever since I visited Tricia Mumford—on the night you 'exposed' her—in my other guise."

"Even then?" Roger asked, stunned.

"Yes. You see, I was there—not physically, of course. Later that night, I communicated to Tricia how enraged I was, and I vowed I would eventually take care of you. She even felt sorry for you, dear lady. I waited all these years because I wanted to give you enough rope to hang yourself with, if you will pardon the phrase, plus you were strong in your own way and difficult to get at. I suppose, I may even have thought you might change direction at some point—that you would be convinced—but hard-headed, stubborn Roger Kant persisted through the years, despite all the proofs put before him. It's most lamentable."

"Are you trying to tell me you've been planning this

since that night at Tricia's fake channelling session?"

"It wasn't fake."

"I proved it."

"You proved nothing. Saul, the entity she channels, is very real, and I've had many conversations with him myself. So has Melissa, and many others with trance medium powers. I only wish it were possible to conjure him up for you—he's a striking person and most imposing—but he prefers not to make himself visible, especially to a fool such as you."

"There's always an out, isn't there? That's very convenient." The Count Basie record clicked and replayed for the dozenth time. That was bothering him as much as any of his pain, but he refused to give Alexander the satisfaction of knowing it was getting through to him.

"But of little consequence. I can prove other things that are equally impressive, if not more so. I trust you're ready?"

"Nothing will convince me."

"We'll see. Thomas, take this hand and put it in a jar for me, will you? Then return here immediately."

Thomas happily grabbed the hand and rushed out of the room with the eagerness of a child asked to perform an important errand for his father.

"How shall I begin?" Alexander mused aloud. "Levitation? That's so damn simple. Show him, Melissa."

Melissa became very still, closed her eyes, and leaned backward. Then she floated in the air about four feet off the floor.

"Impressed?"

"It's an easy trick. I'm surprised you'd try something so obvious."

"Maybe we should make it more complicated, then." He waved his hand over the floating woman, and her robe whipped off, as if torn from her by a strong wind, leaving her nude.

Her red hair hung down from her head in beautiful strands, which Roger longed to touch. He was slightly aroused by the sight of her body, despite his newly found hatred for her, but he concentrated on Alexander's words to counteract his body's natural response.

"I want you to know, Roger, that I wouldn't do this for just anybody. But think of this—you'll have the satisfaction of knowing astral travel, all the psychic phenomena ever recorded, UFO's, pyramidology, communication with the dead—in short, the entire world of the occult and the supernatural you've always denied—exists and is a motive force in the universe, not the whimsy of little old ladies or other fools."

Roger said nothing. He *was* impressed by the fact that Melissa's levitation was a perfectly performed illusion. He could not determine how it was done, but that didn't mean it wasn't a trick.

Alexander tilted his head and gazed longingly at Melissa. "God, but she's lovely. She's in a trance right now. A deep trance. We could do anything we wanted to her without her knowing it. For example . . ." He ran his hands over her breasts. "I could even rape her, and she wouldn't know it. Well, she might suspect later."

"Make your point," Roger snapped. He couldn't endure watching this dirty old man fondle Melissa as if she were a plaything.

Alexander stopped touching her. "You do know how to spoil a man's fun." He held up his hands, and the sleeves of his robe slid down to his elbows. "You wrote a great deal about psychic surgery in your first book, *Optical Delusions*, didn't you? You even used it in your seminar in Columbus. But you screwed that up badly—that is to say *we* screwed it up badly for you. You will note there is nothing up my sleeves. Can you see clearly?"

"Yes."

"Then here goes." He extended the index finger of his right hand, then drew it along Melissa's stomach from her navel to her pubis, and a great gash opened up in her.

Roger gagged but fought the impulse to vomit.

Alexander used both hands to spread the gash apart, revealing the glistening insides of Melissa. Roger could see things rippling through her intestines, watched her stomach churning as it digested food, and observe blood pumping through arteries and veins. Alexander reached in and pulled out parts of Melissa and laid them on her chest. The resultant smell was making Roger's stomach suck in against itself.

"Quite a mess inside the mortal shell, isn't there?"

Roger could hold it no longer. He turned his head to one side and puked violently, spraying the contents of his stomach against the wall.

"I think that made my point. Freddy, clean him up."

Freddy came over with a big bucket of water and splashed it on Roger and the wall.

"Are you all right?" Alexander asked solicitously.

"Stop it," Roger pleaded. "Don't—do—that to her!"

"Oh, it's nothing. Keep your eyes open, or I'll make you watch the whole process again."

Roger nodded. He steeled himself to watch as Alexander put everything back inside Melissa where it belonged and pinched the gash shut. He took a rag from the table and wiped off her abdomen, and there was no evidence at all she had been cut open.

Again, Roger knew it had to be a trick. Yet he had no idea how it could possibly be done.

Alexander kissed Melissa's stomach. "Now it's all better," he said, smiling evilly. He waved his hands over her, and she drifted to the floor. "Sorry, Roger, but I can't help myself." He hiked his robe up to his belly and displayed a huge erection.

"You vile bastard."

Alexander ignored the remark and proceeded to rape Melissa with unbridled fervor. Her eyes remained shut and her body fairly rigid, quivering only slightly from Alexander's thrusts. When Alexander was finished, he let the hem of his robe fall to the floor again. Then he levitated Melissa from the floor, replaced her robe, and snapped his fingers. Melissa started to drop, but he caught her and steadied her to her feet.

"Are you all right?"

"Fine," Melissa said. "What did you do?"

"Maybe Roger would like to tell you."

"It was just a disgusting trick," Roger said.

Melissa seemed to be feeling herself from within, seeking the result of Alexander's "trick." Suddenly, an expression of extreme disgust wrinkled her features. "You took advantage of me, you dirty old son of a bitch."

Roger hung his head and blacked out.

Count Basie continued to play "One O'Clock Jump."

Roger was sailing, the wind blowing through his hair and cooling his naked body.

He was flying above San Francisco, fascinated by its many sparkles of light at night. On a whim, he circled the TransAmerica building and shot up high over the Golden Gate Bridge, then whipped under it, maneuvering through the air as easily as a bird.

Thank God, he thought, I'm dead. So this is what it's like.

Suddenly, he was aware of somebody sailing along beside him. He turned his head to look and saw the grotesque form of Alexander the demon laughing at him.

A blast of icy water jerked him back to reality. Thomas had returned.

Roger's arms and legs were bleeding from the shackles. He had been struggling in his unconscious state.

Count Basie began "One O'Clock Jump" again.

Alexander's face was right in front of him.

"You weren't dead, dear boy. You were traveling out of your body. That often happens during times of great duress, especially to prisoners who seek refuge from their punishment by taking their spirits out of their bodies."

"A dream," Roger muttered.

"Then how do I know about it? I can tell you everything you did. As an accomplished metaphysician, I can leave my body at will, so when I sensed you were gone, I came to watch you frolic. That maneuver under the bridge was expertly executed by the way."

"You weren't there. I imagined it."

"How do I know about it?" Alexander repeated.

"You read my mind, or—" Roger stopped himself. He couldn't believe what he had just said.

"Ah, ha! I see a glimmer of light in those dull orbs of yours. What do you think, Melissa? Is he coming around?"

"Perhaps," she said.

Roger frowned, more at himself than at them. How were they doing these things? Had they drugged him? Hypnotized him?

"Even if you were hypnotized, you wouldn't believe anything you wouldn't normally believe," Alexander said. "Am I correct?"

Roger's face went blank. He didn't understand how Alexander could apparently read his thoughts, either.

"I recall your offering anyone twenty thousand dollars if they proved a psychic phenomenon to you, Mr. Kant. Have I earned that check yet?"

Roger glowered at him.

"I guess not. I guess more demonstrations are in order, but I'll earn that money before our time is over. Close your eyes."

Roger did as he was told. In the darkness of his mind, a picture formed, blurry at first, then gradually became more detailed. It was a newspaper—the back page. There was a small story under a feature called, "People & Places." A subheadline under that said, "SEARCH FOR ROGER KANT CONTINUES."

Alexander said, "And I can read the story to you. 'A year after the mysterious disappearance of Roger Kant, known to his many readers as The Astounding One, FBI officials said today they were still hopeful of finding him.' Shall I continue? Should I read you the date on that newspaper?"

Roger saw the date in his mind—a year and a half in the future. He opened his eyes and shook his head. The picture had seemed crystal-clear, like a photograph.

"You have just experienced precognition."

"Another goddamn trick, that's all. I don't know how

you did it, but it *has* to be a trick!"

"Why are you so resistant?" Melissa asked, an expression of pained distress on her face. Was that because, Roger hoped, she did care for him, even a little? "Why do you wish to prolong this?"

"Roger, you distress me," Alexander added. "Melissa and I went to so much trouble getting you here. Look at the sacrifices Melissa herself had to make—having to sleep with you, for one—a paunchy, bald middle-aged man. . . ."

"You're no prize, yourself."

"Perhaps not, but I know how to satisfy a woman in ways you've never dreamt of. If you had read Aleister Crowley, you'd know your numb fumblings in the night are not much better than an adolescent's first pawing attempt at love. You should've learned something after having three wives. Why, Melissa herself told me you were a 'bad lay.' Didn't you, Melissa?"

Roger sought eye contact with Melissa. Had she really uttered this insult—or was it merely more mental torture?

Melissa averted her eyes and sulked.

"And then she had to say she loved you. How those words must have caught in her throat! But, being a consummate actress, I'm sure she said it well. We did all of this, just so that you could get this much-needed lesson. You'd think you would have the courtesy to admit we've impressed you if only a little."

Roger refused to answer.

"Gad, but you are a stubborn man. Maybe words and mere demonstrations haven't yet convinced you how serious we are. Freddy, come here."

Freddy's face lit up at his master's beckoning. He came over and stood by Alexander's side. There was a nasty-looking instrument fitted on the stump of his right hand; it resembled a scalpel.

"I was just thinking about that scar on the left side of your face, Roger—the one Nancy—you remember her—gave you the night you upset dear Tricia so much. That scar disrupts the general symmetry of your face. Freddy, carve a line in Mr. Kant's right cheek, so that Mr. Kant will have a scar to match the left one. Do a good job, and I'll send Suzanne to your room tonight."

Freddy licked his lips and grinned. He advanced toward Roger, lifting the deadly prosthesis toward his face.

"Be careful, Freddy. Don't hurt him too much. We wouldn't want André to have to dispose of his remains. Roger stew would be bitter and hard on the palate."

Roger twisted his face away from the scalpel.

"Don't move, damn it!" Alexander shouted.

Roger steadied himself; there was no escape from this. His mind screamed to shut down—to go out of his body—whatever was necessary to avoid the pain.

But Roger couldn't shut down this pain, bellowing so loud he couldn't hear the hundredth playing of "One O'Clock Jump."

Freddy carved his face with the care and delicacy he lavished on his flowers.

"Very good, Freddy. . . ."

Roger blacked out momentarily.

He awoke as a cold compress was applied to his cheek. Thomas was holding it there, dabbing at the fresh wound.

"That will stop the bleeding, Roger. We don't want you to succumb, when we have so much to show you."

Thomas took the compress away; the blood had coagulated. He gave Roger a drink, then went to sit by Freddy.

"Let's get on with it," Melissa said. "This is taking entirely too long."

"Hush, dear. I can't help it if Mr. Kant is such a stubborn case. He just refuses to admit he's been wrong all these years. It's a nasty business, I admit. Let's see, what is your most mortal fear? Perhaps that might stir something in you. Ah, yes, it's crippled people. I have shown them to you before in the visions I induced, and you resisted them admirably; but that's because you refuse to admit why you fear them. And I *know* why."

Roger became uneasy. Alexander couldn't know that.

"You were twenty years old, driving home from work on the snow-covered streets in the city of South Bend. The truck's brakes were bad, but you hadn't the money to repair them. . . ."

As Alexander spoke, vivid pictures of that day formed in Roger's mind.

"A child and her mother were walking along the sidewalk on their way from the supermarket to the parking lot next door. The child, a playful little girl, broke free from her mother's hand to run ahead to their car. The cold wind blew her cap off as she skipped along the sidewalk. The cap fluttered out into the street, and the girl—she was only four or five—ran foolishly into the street to retrieve it. You slammed on the brakes, but the street was too slick, and the brakes non-responsive."

Roger closed his eyes tight. He concentrated on the Count Basie tune. He made himself feel the pain in his cheek and the other sites of pain in his body. Yet the event persisted in replaying itself in his mind, regardless of what he did. As Alexander continued to tell the story, Roger saw the little girl bounce off the front of the truck and fly through the air, landing on the hood of a car parked by the curb.

"You panicked. You had no insurance. Instead of stopping to help, you accelerated, swerving crazily down the street. Frozen mud and slush covered your license plate, and the only witness was the little girl's mother, who was too distraught to notice anything but her little girl."

Roger opened his eyes.

"Later, you found out the girl was crippled for life. You never came forward. You weren't so strong and noble then. You never made any compensation to the girl or her mother—even years later, when you had plenty of money, but apparently not enough guilt to send them any of your ill-gotten cash. Am I correct—in all particulars?"

Roger bowed his head; he was crying. And confused. There was absolutely no way on earth Alexander could know about this incident. Roger had never told anyone—not even his mother. He had driven home and hidden the truck in the garage, then called in sick to work for the next three days—a time during which he kept expecting the South Bend Police to knock on the door any second, demanding to arrest him.

His cowardice had festered in him for months afterward. But with every passing day, the lie he was perpetuating became more comfortable to live with, and he rationalized that coming forth with the truth at such a late date would only make it worse on him. And he had to remain free to make a living for his family after his father had died.

Eventually, he learned to live with the guilt too. And Alexander was right; he had been too cowardly even years later to risk revealing himself by sending the girl or the mother money. He could have done it anonymously, but he was fearful it would be traced back to him.

The impact of the memory clouded his senses, and his head went limp. He thankfully accepted the darkness into which he was plunged.

Alexander slapped his face.

"Now, now, Roger. No sleeping on the job. You must quit leaving us like that, or I'll be forced to do something I wouldn't like."

Roger looked around warily. The myriad of pains in his body were approaching a crescendo. His wrists and ankles felt as if they were almost cut in two by the shackles. And his bladder was distressingly full. But he was alert.

At some point while he was in the darkness, his subconscious mind had been at work, and he had emerged with a plan. He would pretend to be persuaded to their way of thinking. Then the game would be over. His pride and stubbornness were getting him nowhere. It was buying time; but it was pain-provoking time, and he was wearying of it. He needed sleep. Or death. Whichever would make the end of this nightmare come. He was tired of being toyed with. Maybe if he agreed their mumbo jumbo was genuine, they'd let him down from the wall, and if he had any strength left, he'd have a chance to—

Alexander slapped him again. "Idiot!" He punched

him in the stomach. Involuntarily, Roger's bladder released itself, squirting urine all over Alexander's robe.

"Goddamn you!"

Roger smiled. "Piss on you!" He laughed hysterically at his own joke. He continued to laugh, even as Alexander kept hitting him in the face until Melissa pulled him away.

"That's doing no good," she said. "You're giving in to him—you're showing weakness."

Alexander calmed down immediately. "Of course, Melissa dear, you're right. I should show myself the stronger. A little urine never hurt anyone."

Roger's laughter had run its course, but he hung there on the wall with a stupid grin frozen on his face.

"Smirk all you want. But your little plan won't work. I won't settle for anything less than genuine belief, Roger. You can't fool me with pretenses."

"How the hell can I make myself believe something!"

"Because you must!"

Alexander paused and stroked his goatee. He seemed to be pondering his next move. Melissa had picked up a dagger from the table and was playing with it, idling the time away as she waited. She used it to scrape under her fingernails, then blew on the point and rubbed the blade on her robe to polish it. She didn't put the knife down, continuing to toy with it, probably to make Roger more apprehensive.

"The spirit world," Alexander said at last, "is a wondrous dimension, Roger. It holds tableaus of the past, the present, and the future. It is where the psychics get their information. I want you to see that. Then I will have earned that twenty thousand dollars, by God, though, of course, I'll never be able to cash the check."

"Do your worst," Roger replied, a hint of weary defiance in his tone.

"I intend to, dear Roger. Watch!"

The room was enveloped in a gray mist. As Alexander and Melissa faded away, vague outlines of other people formed in the mist. Gradually they became recognizable.

Roger's eyes remained open; he had suddenly lost the will to close them, even though he wanted to desperately.

He saw Wanda, his first wife, writhing passionately under a man. Then Sheila appeared; she had grown fat and repulsive, forced to commit repugnant sexual acts to attract a man—which she now did with an obese monstrosity whose penis barely protruded from his flab. That scene faded away, and Sandra, his last wife, was seen cavorting with her new husband.

Roger's face contorted with the pain of seeing this, but he was still convinced it was only an elaborate illusion.

"Still jealous and possessive of them, aren't you?" Alexander's voice broke in, sounding like it was coming from the bottom of a well. "I knew that would get your attention."

Then the mist became blue. The Count Basie tune, playing yet in the background, was muted now.

Roger's father emerged from the mist. He appeared exactly the way he had the last time Roger had seen him on the day before he left for college. His father gestured hopelessly at Roger as he approached him.

"It ain't right," his father's specter said.

"No!"

His father passed through his body, leaving behind a deep chill that almost numbed Roger's pain.

"Enough!" Roger shouted.

"Not yet," Alexander's voice answered. "You don't believe."

Roger saw a familiar room take shape within the mist. Edith was in it. It was very dark, but he sensed there was another being in there with her. Edith was determined to fight, if necessary, but she couldn't find her pistol.

An infrared light filled the scene, so Roger could make out all the details. He saw the hulking form of Alexander in his demon incarnation advance on Edith and slit her throat.

Roger gasped as the blood gushed from her neck.

The room disappeared, and the ghost of Edith, a ravaged, animated corpse acrawl with worms, walked toward him.

"Why?" she asked, and the ragged cut in her neck flapped obscenely as she spoke. "Why—were you so stubborn?"

She passed through him too. The cold this time was even worse, and the touch of her malodorous flesh lingered after her.

"She died for nothing, Roger," Alexander said. "Died just so we could get to you. You're to blame!"

"No. You did it!"

"Because of you."

Then the mist shifted again, becoming fluorescent green. Many figures formed, becoming a parade of deformed and crippled people; many of them he recognized as people he had seen during his recent travels. They all passed through Roger, each leaving behind a frigid residue.

The penultimate apparition was Peter, his face made even more repulsive in the eerie green mist. He held up the bleeding stump of his left wrist.

"You should trust no one," he rasped and passed through.

"Poor Peter, he bled to death. Too bad, isn't it, Roger? And it was because of you too. You made him disobey me."

"Please, God, it's enough!"

"You don't believe in God, Roger. He's not made in *your* image as you desire."

"I believe."

"Not yet, you don't."

A final small figure formed in the cloud: a little girl with one leg, hobbling erratically on crutches.

"Why did you run away, mister?" she asked.

The little girl walked unsteadily toward him, on the verge of falling over with each step.

Roger strained against the shackles. Blood streamed down his arms and feet. He twisted his body viciously, trying to break free, so that he would not have to endure the passage of the little girl.

Alexander said, "It was worse than you thought. She's

been dead for years!"

She stopped in front of him and looked up into his eyes, pleading silently.

"Why, mister?"

Roger thought his flesh would burst as the little girl seeped through him slowly, exacting every measure of psychic pain possible from the passage.

"I believe," he screamed at last, "I believe! Just let me be!"

And Roger really did believe.

Roger had collapsed again. He came to mumbling, "I believe," over and over, in a rhythm that almost matched the scratchy rendering of "One O'Clock Jump."

Alexander placed his hand on Roger's chin and looked deep into his eyes. "I think you really do believe," he said. "Do you see that, Melissa, The Astounding One believes. We finally penetrated that wall of ego and stubborn defiance in his closed mind."

"I believe."

"Ah, it would be so much easier if we had just burnt him at the stake as they did in the middle ages," Alexander said, letting go of Roger's chin.

"You've won, Alexander," Melissa said. "Don't get whimsical now."

Roger's watering eyes became brighter. Melissa had said Alexander had won. That meant the ordeal was over. He stopped mumbling and watched them hopefully.

"I believe," Roger affirmed again.

"Sometimes believing isn't enough, Mr. Kant," Alexander replied scornfully. "Sometimes total subjugation to an idea is what's needed."

"What . . . ?"

Alexander dropped his robe and transformed himself into the demon. He stretched out his claws.

"Now," the demon said.

"Finally!" Melissa said, and she also underwent a transformation as her garment dropped to the floor. Her hair became gray and stringy, her face withered and old. Her breasts drooped to her stomach, and her pubic hair turned white. Her skin changed too; it became yellowish and was covered with age spots, wens and moles. Roger was at last seeing her in her true form. She cackled as she advanced toward Roger, the dagger gripped in her hand. So that's why she had been so impatient—she was eager to participate in the final slaughter!

Alexander the demon gestured to the ever-present Thomas and Freddy, and they went to the table and picked out their own toys.

They all closed in on him.

Roger braced himself, hoping that he would die quickly.

Roger started to cry out, but the pain became so overwhelming so quickly, he was numbed by it and lost his voice. He felt things pinching and poking and peeling him, things ripping and tearing and digging at him, and things cutting and slicing, then finally the touch of fire . . . and his mind, trying to distance itself from the pain, reached outside of his body and watched with amusement as his mortal body was mutilated and maimed and gouged.

Ultimately, the body of Roger found its voice and screamed endlessly. But there was no one in the room who cared. Not even the detached spirit of Roger.

He was pulled back into his body but felt nothing. It was over; death would drain away the last vestiges of pain.

"And now you, Melissa . . ." were the last words he heard.

"One O'Clock Jump" played for the thousandth time.

20. A Quiet Evening at Home

It was February in California. The air was cool but comfortable outside.

Inside the mansion, Alexander Lewis was throwing a party with a few of his psychic friends in the huge banquet hall he seldom used. But the occasion demanded he entertain them here. He was having a coming-out party for one of his beloved servants who had been ill for some time.

Among his guests were Tricia Mumford, a psychic whose career was now recovering from the damage done to it so many years before; her friend and lover Nancy; a few other well-known celebrities who had gained notoriety in recent months; and Darrell J. Prince, a thin young man who constantly wore a turban and cassock. The party was also for Darrell's benefit as well; he had just returned from the dead.

Alexander, as usual, sat at the head of the long banquet table, basking in the friendship of his peers. Tricia sat on his right, and Nancy sat next to her. Darrell was sitting at Alexander's left.

"You know, the New Age is coming on stronger than ever," Darrell commented. "It's as if a major obstacle has been removed." He giggled. He and most of the others understood the reason for his mirth.

"You might be right about that," Alexander replied coyly. "I have noticed our movement gathering strength.

People are beginning to believe in the realms over which we hold sway, as the old gods and the old religions die. It's a wondrous age we live in."

"Where's Melissa tonight?" a heavyset black woman next to Darrell asked.

Alexander frowned. "Ah, poor Melissa. I had assumed everyone knew."

"Whatever is the matter?" Darrell asked.

"Melissa is unable to participate in parties. She suffered a terrible accident in which she lost all her limbs. She was always such a terrible driver, you know. I'm afraid she can function in only one way."

"What's that?"

"Never mind, Darrell. It wouldn't interest you. Let's talk of pleasanter matters. I want you each to tell me what you've been doing lately. It's so rare we all get together like this."

The guests all began talking. Alexander listened and smiled. He was having a great time.

Many servants hovered around the periphery of the room waiting on the guests, who were accustomed to their handicaps, deformities and disfigurements. They all knew how Alexander had a softness in his heart for the physically disabled.

But the conversation ended abruptly when Alexander's new servant entered, hobbling along, pushing a wine cart haltingly before him. He was the most disfigured wretch anyone had ever seen in Alexander's employ. His face was crisscrossed with numerous purplish scars. The end of his nose was missing, forcing one to peer into his porcine nostrils, and one ear was shriveled from having been badly burned. His head was a hairless mass of livid, half-healed tissue. A tiny stream of drool hung from his ragged lips which he could not close completely. He was also so badly crippled he could barely walk; both legs appeared to have been broken several times and had healed very badly.

He wheeled the cart to the head of the table and waited.

Nancy noticed he bore twin scars on his cheeks, one obviously older than the other. Recognizing that, she smiled to herself.

"Poor man," Alexander said. "This is my new servant, who just recently recovered from a long illness. It's difficult for a person with his appearance to get work; I feel so sorry for his kind that I feel compelled to hire them. But he is a very good servant, even though he's mute and somewhat dull-witted. He lost part of his brain in the war—the Crimean, I believe."

Tricia trembled at the proximity of the man. "He looks so familiar," she said. His ugliness was so profound she could barely endure looking at him.

"I used to have a servant named Peter who resembled him. That must be why he seems familiar to you."

"Oh," Tricia said uneasily.

"Now, let's get on with the party!" Alexander said. "Roger, please pour the wine."

Roger did as he was told.

Inside the head of the dull-witted servant, cloudy thoughts and murky feelings plodded through his mind. He knew he was an ugly person, and that he would never have this job if it weren't for the bountiful generosity of his master.

His master not only fed him and clothed him; but he also let him have sex with the lump-woman upstairs in the tower, and if he was especially good, he got to have his way with Suzanne.

Sometimes, too, the master would take him into a funny little room and show him a jar which he said had pieces of his brain in it. He always laughed silently at that, because he knew his brain was in his head, not in a jar. That was the way the master made jokes—showing him little novelties like that. The master always wanted everyone to have a good time.

He only wished he could speak, so that he could express his gratitude.

He was so glad to have a place to stay.

author's postscript

This novel is meant as an entertainment only. In the course of writing it, I have taken certain liberties with the actual meaning of the term "New Age." It was not my intention to imply there is anything evil about any of the philosophies generally grouped under that all-inclusive heading. Indeed, there is room in our society for any number of groups, the believers in the New Age among them.

I believe all things are possible. I believe many things are true that have not yet been proven. I have had what I believe were true psychic experiences myself, and I have seen demonstrations of psychic abilities for which I could find no rational explanation or any evidence of trickery.

I also believe that many of the anti-paranormal people who crusade against the possibility of astrology, psychic powers, psychic healing and other seeming wonders are often overzealous. Indeed, I think in their denial of the possibilities in this universe that they protest too much. They are deluding themselves by closing their minds to the infinite possibilities the cosmos presents.

There are literally thousands of documented cases of psychic powers, channelling, poltergeists, sightings of UFO's, and other phenomena. The anti-paranormal people generally cite a few examples—out of these thousands—as fakery. Perhaps so. But what about the rest of them?

And proving these isolated examples as fakery proves nothing. As Uri Geller said, "Anyone can imitate the Mona Lisa, but that doesn't make the Mona Lisa a fake."

I rest my case.

". . . he will carry his delusions with him to the grave . . ."

—The Amazing Randi, *Flim-Flam*!